# BIRTH OF A QUEEN

## SINS Series Book 2

# EMMA SLATE

This book is a work of fiction. Names, characters, places, and incidents are the product of the author's imagination or are used fictitiously. Any resemblance to actual events, locales, or persons, living or dead, is coincidental.

©2016 by Emma Slate. All rights reserved, including the right to reproduce, distribute or transmit in any form or by any means.

Six months later

## Prologue

*Mournful sounds of the viola caress my ears. I look up from the book in my lap and gaze around the music room. Opulence and beauty, old-world Russia, an era long forgotten is not forgotten here.*

*Igor Dolinsky stands in the corner with his eyes closed as he plucks the strings of the instrument. Somber, sweet notes glide toward me, and I sigh.*

*Dolinsky stops and opens his eyes. He smiles.*

*"My queen," he greets in Russian.*

*"My king," I reply in the same tongue.*

*He sets his viola aside and comes to me, kneeling before me. I run my hands through his hair, my thumbs stroking down his high Slavic cheekbones.*

*"Did I not promise you the world?" he asks, resting his head in my lap.*

*"You did."*

*"You have power, respect, and loyalty."*

*"It's easy to rule when I have a man like you at my side."*

*He lifts his head and grins. I lean over and place my mouth on his. I pull back so I can stare into his brown eyes.*

*"You have given me more than I ever thought possible," I say.*

*"You are beautiful," he murmurs.*

*He grasps my hands and brings me to my feet before taking a step back. His eyes suddenly widen in surprise and pain. He runs his palms down his chest, and they come away red, stained with blood.*

*He falls to his knees, begging me to save him.*

*But I don't. Because I'm the one who killed him.*

*As he lies still at my feet, I step over him and walk out of the music room and into the hallway. I catch a glimpse of my reflection in a long mirror. My cheeks are splattered with red blots. It reminds me of ink. I scrub at my face, but the blood remains.*

*My skin is stained by Dolinsky's death. Just like my conscience.*

## Chapter 1

I started, waking from the dream. Deeply unsettled, I took a breath, hoping to quell the nausea and fear coiling through me. I placed a hand on my chest. The rapid *thump, thump, thump,* of my heart hammered against my palm.

My husband reached over and touched my arm. "Barrett," he whispered, his voice thick with sleep and his natural husky timbre.

His Scottish brogue slid over my skin, cooling the tremors of anxiety that still pulsed through me.

I awkwardly shifted my bulk closer but didn't roll into him. My large belly wouldn't allow it. Intimacy was difficult to configure due to my late stage of pregnancy. Thankfully, Flynn was enthusiastic and imaginative. But at the moment, I wasn't looking for that kind of comfort.

He sat up, moonlight painting his bare chest. His blue eyes appeared black, but if there had been light, I'd see bright cobalt that was as unusual as the man I had married.

"You had another dream," he stated.

"Yes," I admitted.

Flynn and I had no secrets. We had once, but we quickly

learned it had been no way to live, no way to love. Secrets had the power to undo us.

"Dolinsky? Or Vlad?"

I dreamt frequently of the men I had killed. Most of the time, I found a way to live with their deaths. Dolinsky had kidnapped me. Vlad had tried to strangle me. Both of them had lusted for me. It had been their ultimate undoing.

Dolinsky had wanted my love. He'd done everything he could—seducing me with power, isolating me yet treating me like a queen. He'd almost succeeded, and that thought was more unsettling than any nightmare.

"I'm going to get a drink of water," I said, not replying to Flynn's question and attempting to maneuver my bulk to the edge of the bed. I hadn't seen my ankles in weeks, my back was in knots, and the baby was resting on my bladder and refusing to move.

"Want me to get it for you?" Flynn asked, throwing the covers off, ready to jump out of bed.

I smiled at him over my shoulder, enjoying the sight of Flynn's bare thighs in the moonlight. "No, love. Thank you."

Finally managing to get to my feet, I left the bedroom and walked into the hallway. The old wood floors squeaked as I made my way to the staircase. I held on to the ornate wood banister and carefully took the stairs. It was easy to lose my balance now that I resembled a hippo and weighed nearly as much.

Six months ago, Flynn and I had bought an apartment in Manhattan, only to come to the conclusion that we wanted to be in Scotland. Well, Flynn wanted to be in Scotland. Though he hadn't spent any great amount of time in the land of his birth since the death of his parents when he was a teen, he suddenly decided he wanted to raise our family in Dornoch, close to Malcolm Buchanan. Flynn's surrogate father was the leader of the SINS, an organization determined to free Scotland from English rule.

We'd bought a house—a small castle—on one thousand acres of land. There was an airstrip ten minutes from our home, a necessity since Flynn needed to be able to fly to New York at a moment's notice.

Though the castle had been restored and modernized years ago, we'd made a few of our own improvements. We'd gutted the kitchen and expanded it. If I was at the stove, I could glance out the large window, which took up the entire wall, and have an unencumbered view of Dornoch Firth and the rocky outcrop.

I stood in front of the large windows and watched a thunderstorm mercilessly unleash itself. It was still dark out, but that didn't mean much in Scotland. It was usually murky, dreary, and rainy. But it was a solemn, harsh beauty, and I loved it.

Before I'd met Flynn, I'd been a research assistant in the history department at Columbia—my specialty was Scottish history. Long before Flynn, Scotland had held a special place in my heart. Flynn solidified it.

I put a hand to my belly. My child would be Scottish—not just in birth but in culture, too.

Flynn's soft footsteps filled the kitchen. A moment later, he wrapped himself around me from behind. Brushing aside my auburn hair, he placed a kiss on my shoulder and pressed his face to my neck.

"You should sit, hen," he said, leading me to a chair.

I threw him a distracted smile as I took a seat. He sat across from me and tapped his lap. I lifted my leg. His large hands went to my ankle, and he began to massage my swollen, aching flesh.

I moaned in pleasure, knowing it sounded sensual.

Flynn's eyes darkened with desire as he stared at me. "You're beautiful," he murmured, head bent as he focused on his work.

I snorted. "No."

"Aye," he countered with a light squeeze. "You're carrying my son. Nothing more beautiful than that."

"Your son is sitting on my bladder," I complained. "Wants what he wants when he wants it. Just like someone else I know."

Flynn laughed. "Not much longer now. Just a few more weeks." He patted my ankle. I set my foot back on the ground and lifted the other one for him to rub.

"I'm ready for him to be here," I said. "I'm ready for the pregnant part to be over." I was uncomfortable and desperate for my body to be returned to me.

His face screwed up in a picture of worry. "Are you happy, hen?"

My lips softened, and I tried to lean forward so I could stroke his face. Unfortunately, my large belly got in the way. My flexibility wasn't what it used to be either.

"Of course I'm happy. You can't tell?"

"I just want to make sure—that you're living a life you want and not mine."

"Our lives are tied together, aren't they?" I asked.

"Aye."

"Flynn," I began. "I didn't think I wanted this, but I do. I want you. Your child. My place is with you."

"Is this going to be enough for you? You're intelligent and you loved your job. I—I took all that away from you."

I raised my eyebrows. "Did you? You didn't hold a gun to my head when you asked me to come work for you in your club. I did that because I wanted to help you."

"And to sever ties with your brother," he pointed out.

I hated talking about Andrew. I hated thinking about Andrew. We were related by blood, but I no longer considered him family.

"I could've gone back to work at Columbia," I said, moving past discussion of Andrew. "I even talked about it with you, remember? But things change. I changed."

Because of Dolinsky. Because of Vlad. Because of circumstances I never thought I'd have to live through, but I was here with Flynn because I wanted to be.

I looked down at my left ring finger; Dolinsky had broken it. It had healed, but sometimes it would twinge, reminding me that what I'd lived through was still with me—with us—even if it wasn't always obvious.

"Look at me," I said to Flynn. He lifted his blue gaze to mine, and the intensity of it stole the air from my lungs. "We're both here. Now. Let's live for now."

He nodded slowly, and all vulnerability he'd unveiled disappeared. Back was the persona I was familiar with—wealthy hotel mogul and high-ranking member of the SINS.

"Let's go back to bed," I suggested.

He stood up. Taking my hand, he led me back toward the stairs. "How about Angus?" he asked.

"No."

"Balfour?"

"Flynn, why do you hate our child?"

He let out a chuckle. "Cameron."

"Cameron Campbell? No alliteration."

"Flynn, Jr."

I groaned in dismay. "We're never going to agree on a name."

We entered the bedroom, and I went to my side of the bed, gazing longingly at my pillow, wondering if I'd be able to fall back asleep. Though the uneasiness of the dream had faded, I worried my sleep would still be restless.

Flynn got into bed next to me. "Glen, Hamish, Lachlan—"

"I like Lachlan."

"You do?" he asked eagerly.

I grinned. "No. Not really."

It was his turn to groan. "Go to sleep, woman. You're driving me insane."

"You like it," I said with a sigh as his lips kissed me goodnight. "Aye," he agreed. "I like it a lot."

The next evening, we went to dinner at Malcolm's house. He lived only ten minutes away from us but farther from the town of Dornoch. I lovingly called his old castle The Hermitage. It was drafty, the hearths were large enough for a grown man to stand in, and he had hounds. Three of them.

Zeus and Hera rushed to greet us the moment we walked through the door. Zeus pressed himself to my leg and then slumped down in a huff as if his belly was too big to hold up. Hera eagerly nudged Flynn for affection. Her brown ears twitched when he gave her a scratching.

"Give her a pat for me," I said with a grin. "I can't bend down."

Cronus, Zeus and Hera's father, ambled on arthritic legs toward us. He was old and blind, almost completely deaf, but he sniffed the air, and I swore a dog smile appeared on his saggy jowls.

Malcolm got up from his brown leather-backed chair by the fire, clutching a glass of scotch. "Hera's pregnant."

"Not with her brother's litter I hope," I said with a kiss to Malcolm's weathered, whiskered cheek.

Malcolm laughed. "No. But that would be just like the Greeks." Malcolm and Flynn embraced and when Malcolm pulled back, he slapped Flynn on the back. "I bred her with a neighbor's hound up the road."

"What neighbor might that be?" Flynn asked slyly.

"Mrs. MacDonald." A bright, energetic smile painted Malcolm's face, making him look ten years younger.

"You're kidding, right?" I asked.

"What? She's a widow," Flynn explained.

"Not that. Doesn't Mrs. MacDonald have a farm?"

Flynn and Malcolm exchanged a confused glance. "Aye, so?" Flynn asked.

I rolled my eyes. "'Old MacDonald had a farm'? Ring any bells?"

Malcolm frowned. "She's not old. Well, she's middle-aged, but she's a bonnie woman."

"My humor is lost on the Scots," I said with a rueful shake of my head.

Malcolm snapped into host mode. "Scotch?" he asked Flynn.

"Please," Flynn replied.

"And for you, Barrett?"

"Sparkling water."

"I tell you, lass," Malcolm said, moving toward the bar in the corner of the sitting room, "I can't wait for you to be able to drink scotch with me again."

I settled on the couch closer to the heat of the fire. Zeus had followed me and plopped down at my feet, and I was finally able to give him a good rubbing. "You and me both," I said.

Flynn sat next to me, and Malcolm brought us our drinks before retaking his seat in the high-backed leather chair. The flames of the fire flickered shadows across Malcolm's face, making him appear demonic. Though I knew better. He was gruff, but underneath he was a marshmallow. With me, anyway.

I took a moment to admire the splendor of the room. The first time I'd been to Malcolm's home, I'd gaped. Thick fur rugs covered the wood floors, paintings hung on the walls, and the rooms were elegantly furnished. I saw where Flynn had learned to enjoy the finer things in life. From a young age, he'd been surrounded by luxury.

"Do you want one?" Malcolm asked.

"One what?" I asked, realizing I hadn't heard a word of Flynn and Malcolm's conversation.

"One of Hera's puppies," Malcolm said with a smile.

"A new baby and a new puppy? At the same time?" I gaped. "Are you kidding?"

"Well, to be fair, Hera's puppy will be house trained a lot faster," Malcolm pointed out.

Cronus waddled over to the dog bed in front of the fire and promptly fell asleep. A rattling noise began to emanate from the aging hound. I looked at Flynn and teased, "He snores just like you do!"

Flynn shook his head. "I don't snore."

I rolled my eyes and smiled at Malcolm. "Yes, he does."

"Too bad about Ash and Duncan," Flynn interjected so we would have to discuss something else.

"They couldn't get out of it," I said.

"I know they had to have dinner with Ash's parents tonight, but they would've had more fun with us."

"Well, we are a laugh. I mean, if I'm awake past nine p.m., it's almost like I'm the life of the party," I quipped.

"Would *you* want to spend a night with Ash's parents?" he pressed.

"Yeah, okay. I get your point."

Ash's parents were cold bluebloods from old money. Any deep, lasting emotion they might've felt for each other at one point was gone. They'd stayed together but lived completely separate lives, except when their children were involved.

"Ash's brother is a decent fellow," Malcolm said.

Flynn glared. "He's in love with Barrett."

"No, he's not," I protested.

"Delusional."

"Oh, please. Jack looks out for me like he would a sister. And he's kept his distance."

"It's easy to keep his distance when there's an ocean between the two of you."

"You're exasperating," I said with a roll of my eyes.

"Thank you." He grinned boyishly.

Malcolm huffed out a laugh and rose from his seat. "Let's eat. Barrett, if you accidentally stab Flynn with a butter knife, I won't say anything." He came over and helped me up from the confines of his very plush, comfortable couch.

"I won't stab him with a butter knife," I assured.

"No?" Flynn asked in disbelief as he stood.

"No," I said with a wide smile. "I'll use a fork."

## Chapter 2

"Barrett, if you don't hurry up we're going to be late," Flynn called from downstairs.

"I'm growing a person!" I yelled back, knowing that would shut Flynn up and buy me five more minutes.

"We have an hour drive to Inverness. Your best friend will never forgive you if you're late!"

"Ash has forgiven me a lot. Now stop distracting me!"

With a sigh, I turned back to the full-length mirror. My auburn hair, glossier than ever due to the surge of pregnancy hormones, was pulled back into a messy, teased bun. My dress was black and long-sleeved, but it dipped low in the front, showing a good amount of cleavage. That, too, had gotten better with pregnancy. At my ears were the large diamond solitaires that Flynn had given me on our wedding day.

I thought back to that moment a little over a year ago. He'd married me to protect me from the FBI. They'd been determined to take him down and would've used me to testify against him. Flynn and I had married because I needed protection, but we'd stayed together because of love.

Life was bizarre.

"Three minutes, or I'm coming up there and carrying you

down the stairs!" Flynn impatiently shouted. "And you know I can."

"Might be worth it."

I swore I could hear him muttering under his breath. After smiling at my reflection, I grabbed my small black clutch and headed downstairs. Flynn was checking his pockets, making sure he had all his belongings.

"Don't forget your speech," I said, descending the staircase, my hand on the rail.

"I don't need—" He looked up and lost his train of thought, his eyes dipping to the swell of my breasts, the creaminess of my skin.

I hit the last step and then came toward him. I grabbed the lapels of his dress coat. "What don't you need?" I whispered.

His head dipped slowly. "My speech." His mouth covered mine as his hands stole across my back, trying to bring me closer. Our tongues dueled and tangled, and a coil of lust unfurled in my stomach.

Flynn tore his lips away and pressed his forehead to mine. "Damn, woman. Are you trying to make it so we'll miss Ash and Duncan's rehearsal dinner?"

I grinned wickedly. "We could be naked right now."

He groaned when my hand skated down his body, reaching for his fly. His hand locked around my wrist. "You don't play fair, do you?"

"You want to talk about playing fair? You own a kilt!"

"I'll be wearing it tomorrow at the wedding, so you better make use of it."

"Oh, I will," I promised. I grabbed my coat that hung on the stand, and with Flynn's help, somehow got into it.

"We can always leave early tonight—blame it on pregnancy exhaustion," Flynn said, holding the front door open for me. Thankfully the rain had abated, and we made it to the car without getting doused, but I never left the house without an umbrella.

Our driver opened the car door for us, and I climbed inside the Rolls. Flynn went around the other side, not bothering to ask if I could scoot over. When we were on our way, I said, "They'll know."

"What's that, hen?" Flynn asked distractedly.

"They'll know why we're leaving early," I explained. "I might have told Ash that I can barely control myself due to the influx of hormones."

"I'm not complaining," Flynn said. "I like that you can't keep your hands to yourself. It's like you're tipsy all the time."

I grinned and grasped his hand. "At least I haven't completely tired you out."

"Yet. You can try later tonight if you want."

"Oh, I plan on leaving you exhausted and wearing nothing but a smile."

He chuckled and then turned to look out the window of the car. The Highlands passed by in rolling hills and craggy mountains. I settled in for the hour drive to Inverness, resting my hands on the swell of my belly.

"I can't believe my best friend is marrying your surrogate brother," I said. "Then again I can't believe Ash is really getting married."

"Because the last time she was engaged ended badly?"

"Exactly." Not too long ago Ash had been engaged and then entered into a torrid love affair with her fiancé's father. It had all come crashing down around her, and I thought for sure she'd swear off marriage forever. "Is Duncan worried about it? That she was engaged before?"

"No, he's not worried."

I bit my lip. Flynn knew Ash had been engaged before, but he didn't know why it had ended. It wasn't my story to share. Duncan knew about Ash's past, and it was between them.

"Ash needed a strong-willed man because she's a strong-willed woman. From what I've heard of her other fiancé, he didn't challenge her or excite her."

"He was nice."

"Nice is not enough for women like you and Ash."

"Women like us?" I glanced at him and smirked in amusement.

"Aye." Flynn grinned. "You're both intelligent and you know your own minds. You don't respect men you can push around. Ash can't push Duncan around and you can't—"

"Careful," I warned with a teasing glint. "I don't push you around, but I do know how to gently coerce you."

"Maybe I let you coerce me," he shot back with a smug smile.

"Maybe we coerce each other," I said with a shake of my head. "I really can't believe it, though. I was sure when Duncan popped the question a few months ago, they'd be engaged at least a year so she'd have time to plan the wedding. But it all came together so fast and her parents are overjoyed."

"I can't believe she agreed to live in Scotland. She didn't even put up a fight about it," Flynn said.

"Ash always liked the idea of being an ex-patriot. And it's not as though Duncan could move to New York," I pointed out.

"His heart his here."

By heart he meant the SINS. As Malcolm's oldest son, Duncan was due to inherit the title of leader when Malcolm stepped down. "The cause comes first," I murmured.

Flynn squeezed my hand but said nothing. I hadn't really known what I was getting into when I'd learned about Flynn's affiliations. I had been able to reconcile it when I thought our life wouldn't have included children. But that had changed. I didn't walk away when I found out I was pregnant, but realizing my children would grow up in this world, weaned on the cause for a free Scotland, was something else entirely. Ash didn't care about her future husband's loyalties and had no problem compartmentalizing it. Duncan's cause wasn't her cause, but that wasn't how Flynn and I operated. We were a true team.

I'd die for Flynn.

The rest of the drive to Inverness passed in comfortable silence. The car stopped outside an old gray cobblestone building lit with antique gas lanterns that cast a welcoming glow. A slight drizzle-mist had begun to fall, and it coated everything it touched. It dusted our coats and hair, and made the uneven sidewalk slippery. Flynn held onto me as we walked toward the entrance, and I was grateful for his strong hold. Though my heels were barely heels, it would have been easy enough to lose my footing and tumble to the ground.

When we walked inside, a female hostess greeted us. She was thin, blond, and gorgeous and gave Flynn an obvious once-over before realizing I was standing right next to him. I bristled with annoyance, but Flynn put me at ease immediately when he helped me with my coat and kissed me softly on the lips. He stared into my eyes like I was the only person he saw.

"Let's get you some sparkling water," Flynn said, holding my hand. Without a backward glance, we left the hostess area of the tavern and walked down the hall. Our party was in the main dining room. Round tables with white tablecloths and expensive red orchid centerpieces were scattered around the room, but there wouldn't be a formal sit-down dinner. Guests had already begun to arrive. Duncan and Ash were holding court, and we strolled toward them despite the fact that they were surrounded by family and friends.

When Ash saw me, her face lit up. She embraced me, but I released her just as quickly, wanting to take in what she was wearing. Ash looked like a fairy ice queen. Her blond hair was up in an array of curls, and her strawberries and cream complexion was set off perfectly by the floor-length, pale blue gown. At her ears were diamond chandelier earrings that twinkled in the soft light.

"You look gorgeous," I told her.

She shook her head. "Me? Look at you."

"Please don't," I muttered. "I feel invisible and huge at the same time."

Ash frowned. "Well, that's ridiculous because you're stunning. Here, have some of my wine." She thrust her half-drank glass at me.

I stared at it for a moment. I'd read that once a woman was in her third trimester, a bit of wine was fine. Besides, this turkey was almost cooked. Taking a small sip, I sighed in relief.

"How beautiful is Barrett?" Ash asked Duncan who laughed at something Flynn said.

Duncan looked me up and down, and if I hadn't already been in love with Flynn, I definitely would've had a thing for Duncan. Sexy, broad, with a brogue thicker than clotted cream; he knew how to make a woman feel attractive. His smile was wide and genuine when he said, "Bonnie lass." He enfolded me in a bear hug before pulling back.

"Paw your own woman," Flynn said with a good-natured shove at Duncan's shoulder. Duncan's arm wrapped around Ash's side and hauled her close.

"That's a damn fine idea. Want to leave this party and go find a more private one?" he asked Ash, waggling his eyebrows at her.

"My son never could behave," Malcolm said as he joined our group.

Malcolm's whiskered jaw gently scraped my cheek when he kissed me.

"That's family loyalty for you," Duncan muttered. "How was I supposed to behave when Flynn was the one getting me into trouble? A year after he came to live with us, he swiped that bottle of hundred-year-old scotch and forced me to do shots."

"Like hell that's true," Flynn grumbled, but there was a teasing twinkle in his eye. "It was you, you bastard. Wanting to impress some local girls. If I recall you were the one who threw up all over both of them."

Ash couldn't contain her laughter. "Guess you weren't always a smooth criminal."

"He's still not smooth," another voice said.

I turned and saw Duncan's younger brother flashing Ash a megawatt grin. Ramsey Buchanan had inherited all the Buchanan charm. He had dark hair like Duncan, but it was a mop of curls that made a woman want to run her fingers through it. Instead of silver, Ramsey's eyes were a shocking green, the color of Highland hills. Deep, rich, and erotic.

"Please tell me you're running away with me tomorrow and not marrying this clown," Ramsey went on, hugging Ash.

Duncan growled and removed his brother's arms from around his fiancée. "Enough. Get yourself a drink and your own woman."

Immediately, Ramsey looked to me and turned on the flirt. "Hi, Barrett. You're looking ravishing. Or ravished—as it were." His gaze dropped pointedly to my belly before he plucked the near-empty glass of wine from my hand and downed it.

Malcolm shook his head in mock regret. "It seems I have two ill-behaved sons."

"Hey," Flynn protested.

Malcolm smiled. "I stand corrected. I meant three."

"Ramsey drank the rest of my wine," I complained to Flynn.

"I'll get you another," he said.

Ash looked at Duncan. "Barrett drank the rest of my wine."

Duncan chuckled. "I'll get you another. Come on, Flynn. We've got to keep our women happy otherwise they might leave us."

## Chapter 3

The willowy brunette that looked like she stepped out of the 1920s glided toward me on four-inch heels that put her taller than most men in the room. The manager of the Rex Hotel invented glamour. I suddenly hated the skinny bitch.

"Don't look at me that way," Lacey stated.

"What way is that?" I demanded.

"Like you want to kill me for being thin."

I grinned. "Am I that transparent?"

"No, you're just that—"

"Careful," I warned. "I'm a feral pregnant lady."

Lacey shook her head and smiled wide red lips. "How many people have you scared into submission?"

"Her husband, for sure," Brad Shapiro stated with a huge grin on his face. Brad resembled an aging linebacker; he was both broad and tall, and his hands looked more like paws than anything else. He was head of security for the hotel, and he was the perfect candidate for it.

"My husband is a saint," I joked with them.

"Flynn Campbell, bound for sainthood," Brad replied. "Now I've heard everything."

We all laughed.

Six months ago, I'd learned that Brad and Lacey were hooking up. I had no way of knowing if they were still secretly involved since I couldn't read their body language. They acted like nothing was out of the ordinary, just two old friends enjoying the evening.

Lacey put her hand on my arm. "I know we're here to celebrate Duncan and Ash getting married, but I brought you a gift."

"Oh yeah?" I asked with a raise of my eyebrows.

She nodded. "Come on. We'll leave Brad here."

Taking my hand, she led me away from Brad to one of the round tables. A few empty glasses rested on the top that the serving staff hadn't yet cleared away.

Lacey went behind the table and picked up a blue gift bag with white tissue paper sticking out of the top. "Here."

I put my hand in the bag and pulled out a white onesie. On the front, it had a "Made in Scotland" stamp.

"This is too cute," I said, awkwardly trying to hug Lacey. "Thank you!"

"And when he grows out of it, I'll buy him another."

I grinned as I folded the onesie and put it back in the bag. "So, are you going to tell me what's going on with you and Brad?"

She peered at me. "You sure you want to know?"

"Give me full disclosure."

"We're work and sex and that's it."

I frowned. "You're kidding? You've been able to keep it going this whole time?"

She sighed. "Well, we did try to date right after you and Flynn moved over here. But as it turned out, the only parts we're good at are the sex and work parts. And, by the way, Flynn totally knows about it."

"Really? But he never mentioned it to me."

"Probably because it's not a big deal."

"Wow, are you in denial."

"No. You are. Flynn doesn't care because work hasn't suffered and Brad and I can be adults."

"Work and sex, huh? I never could keep it that way."

Lacey smiled. "I know. I'm glad things worked out for you and Flynn, but that's not the way it is for everyone."

I nodded. "Fair enough."

"I really miss you guys," she admitted. "The hotel isn't the same without you both there."

"There's something you're not telling me."

"I'm thinking of making a change," she said, lowering her voice. "In the coming months."

"Yeah?"

She nodded. "I need to do something different. Helping to open the club in London was amazing, but ever since I got back to New York, I've felt a bit restless."

This past spring Flynn and I had lived in London while Flynn opened up the newest Rex Hotel. Lacey had stayed just long enough to train the staff who worked in the club. It had been nice having her so close by.

"I understand your feelings of restlessness. I can't imagine the club run by anyone else."

"Change is good for everyone. I was thinking of pitching Alia for the job. Start training her when I get back to New York."

Alia was a gorgeous, smart, talented Asian burlesque dancer who'd been at the club for years. We had become good friends when I'd been working undercover, and we still spoke frequently despite the ocean between us. "I think she'd be great at it," I said sincerely. "She'll have to know about Flynn's affiliations and that the Rex Hotels are just fronts for the SINS."

"She's got a cool head. I doubt it would throw her, but she'll want to tell Jake."

Jake was Alia's fiancé and head bartender at the club. "Maybe they should run the club together. You know, be a hot dynamic duo. Have you talked to Flynn yet about leaving?"

She shook her head. "I haven't even told Brad. I wanted to come to you first."

"Dip your toes in with me, eh?" I said with a smile.

Lacey chuckled. "Something like that."

A server with a tray of Scottish smoked salmon on toast points strolled by. Lacey wrinkled her nose, but I plucked three from the tray and took a napkin. I thanked him, and then he walked away to serve other guests.

"Yuck. I can't believe you like that stuff."

"It's amazing." I popped a toast point into my mouth, savoring the salty ocean taste of the fish. I let out a small moan of delight.

Lacey shook her head. "Your kid really is 'made in Scotland.'" She glanced away and sighed. I turned my head to see what had her sighing. Ash was leaning into Duncan's side as they continued to play the role of charming hosts.

"Damn, they look like a Ralph Lauren ad. It's nauseating."

"Hmm," I said noncommittally.

Lacey glanced back at me and rolled her eyes. "Never mind, I forgot who I was talking to."

"Sorry, I'll try to be less happy and in love," I joked.

"Don't. The world needs more of that."

I pulled out my phone from my clutch and sent Flynn a text. *Game of hide and seek?*

A moment later, I got a reply. *At your friend's rehearsal dinner?*

*It was a yes or no question.*

*Aye.*

I let out a laugh, feeling flirty and sexy. *I'll give you a clue. I'm in a place with a lot of hangers and a door that closes.*

I clocked it about three minutes until Flynn found me on the second floor, hiding in the coatroom. Hearing quick footsteps on the wood floor, I realized I was wrong. It had been only two minutes.

There was a slight rap on the door.

"What's the password," I called through it.

"She-devil," Flynn said, causing me to laugh.

I opened the door to see my husband looming in the doorway. Flynn wasn't standardly beautiful, but rough and wild like the Scottish Highlands. There was a magnetism that was uniquely him.

Sucking in a breath of air, I stepped back. He closed the door quietly. "There's no lock," he stated.

"Then we'll have to be fast," I said.

Flynn stalked toward me, a man ready to claim his woman. My body temperature spiked when his hands reached out to slide up and down my arms and then moved to cup my full breasts. His thumbs grazed my nipples over my dress before dragging his hands lower over my belly. He grasped my hips. Leaning down, he kissed me.

I grabbed the lapels of his jacket as I flicked my tongue against his. His mouth lifted from mine and skated across the apple of my cheek, to my ear, down my neck. He nipped at my breasts through my dress, the teasing torment making me want more.

He gently maneuvered me so I faced away from him. His hands ran down my sides, and then he hiked up the back of my dress. I felt a brush of air on my exposed skin and shivered when Flynn's fingers dipped into my underwear. He rubbed and pressed his fingers to my aching, sensitive body. The metallic zing of his zipper filled the small coatroom. A smile played on my lips as he moved closer and his heat enveloped me from behind. I leaned over and braced my hands on the wall to steady myself.

He pushed aside my underwear and the head of his shaft slipped into my welcoming entrance.

"Oh God," he gritted out.

I shuddered in pleasure as he continued to stroke me while sinking into me deeper and deeper. His other hand held me in place so I wouldn't fall.

"Faster," I commanded. Lust blazed in my veins as wave after wave consumed me.

Flynn let out an animalistic grunt, finding his own release. With a few final thrusts, he rode out his pleasure and then dropped his head to my back.

"You know how to liven up a party," he muttered.

I chuckled and he moaned. Feeling him twitch inside of me, I silently crowed with feminine power.

"So do you, Flynn. So do you."

After visiting the ladies' room to straighten my appearance, I let Flynn lead me back to the party. Lacey and Ash were talking, and both of them looked at me with knowing eyes when they saw me.

I shrugged as if to say *What of it?*

I never used to be the type of woman who would even consider doing something like that in public. Not that I'd ever been a prude, but I had been reserved. Time with Flynn, living in his world, exposed to all the things I had seen, had changed me.

If I wanted to have sex with my hot husband in a coat closet, then I was going to do it, damn it. Life was too short to care about what others thought of me. Flynn and I both had our brushes with death—so I was going to live every day loving and playing hard.

"Promise me something," Flynn said as we stood in the

corner of the party, the sounds of conversation and low music around us.

"Promise you what?" I asked.

"Promise me we'll still do things like this in twenty years."

"Have sex in 'inappropriate' places," I asked, using air quotes.

He grinned. "Yes."

"It might embarrass the hell out of our son—when he realizes his parents can't keep their hands off each other."

"It might embarrass him when he's a teenager because you're always embarrassed by your parents when you're a teenager. But when he's an adult, he'll be glad his parents are randy for each other."

I chuckled.

"My parents were like that," Flynn admitted. He hardly ever spoke of his parents, and I never asked about them. There were some things that even Flynn found too difficult to discuss.

"I never thought I'd have a marriage like them," he said.

"We don't have a marriage like them, Flynn. We have our own. And ours is just as unique and just as wonderful."

Flynn leaned down to kiss me. "You're so much more than sex in coat closets. You know that, right?"

"Oh, I know," I said, with an impish grin. "I'm also sex in bedrooms. Have a coffee. You'll need your energy later."

## Chapter 4

"How are you feeling?" Flynn asked me three hours later.

"I'm good," I said, not at all lying.

"You sure? We can go if you're tired."

I reached up and cupped his cheek. "I've spent most of the night sitting in a chair. I'm good."

He nodded and whispered in my ear. "Except for the time in the coat closet."

I shrugged. "Prenatal exercise."

Flynn laughed. "Do you mind if I go have a cigar with Duncan, Ramsey, and Malcolm?"

"Not at all."

He leaned down and kissed me on the lips. "Need anything?"

I shook my head and then watched as he walked out of the room with the men who were his family. Ash was stuck in conversation with Duncan's great-aunt Annis who was hard of hearing. At the moment she was giving Ash advice on how to conceive on her wedding night. I could hear her voice from across the room. Aunt Annis also had poor eyesight, so she didn't see Ash's horrified expression. Ash caught my eye and silently begged me to save her.

Before I could, Jack Rhodes plopped down in a chair next to me.

"Don't you dare," he stated.

"Don't I dare what?" I demanded.

He chuckled. "Don't rescue her. I like seeing her squirm. She's been on edge with me all week."

"She's a bride. Cut her some slack," I pleaded. "I haven't seen you all night. Where have you been?"

Jack shook his head. "I'm Ash's brother, which means I have to be a Rhodes."

"And that means what?"

"I'm an extension and I have to play a role."

"Don't we all?" I asked.

He shrugged and took a drink of his scotch. Jack and I had a falling out a few months after I had met Flynn. Though Jack and I had attempted to rebuild ten years of friendship in the last year, we still weren't back to where we used to be. We might never be—Jack didn't approve of Flynn or his affiliations. But it wasn't his choice whom I decided to share my life with. Just like he didn't have a say whom his sister married. Jack had said enough on the subject in the recent months; so much that Ash threatened to revoke his invitation to her wedding. He'd managed to hold his tongue after that. It was difficult since Jack liked to give his opinion freely.

"I need to find the restroom," I said, moving to stand up. Gentleman that he was, Jack helped me to stand and then hugged me.

"I'm glad she has you," Jack said into my ear. "Ash. I don't think she really knows what she's getting in to, and she's going to need you."

"You don't just mean marriage, huh?" I pulled back and stared at his face.

"My parents are overjoyed," he said slowly. "The Buchanans are one of Scotland's oldest and most powerful families; that's all my parents care about, Barrett."

I nodded. "I know, but Ash is really happy. Try not to worry about her."

"I worry about both of you," he admitted. "You're my family, too. You know that, right?"

His words were touching, and they tugged at the nostalgic part of my heart. The eighteen-year-old Barrett that had once been infatuated and in awe of Ash's older, handsome brother was no more. But I loved Jack, and he was right—we were family.

"And you're mine," I said, squeezing his hand. "Now, I really do need to use the bathroom. The bairn is sitting right on top of my bladder and refuses to move."

Jack snorted in amusement. "Bairn, huh? You're so Scottish."

I rolled my eyes. "Did you try the haggis yet? It's delicious. No? What about the blood pudding?"

Jack's face turned a bit green.

"What, you can eat *foie gras* and escargot but not haggis?" I demanded.

"Sheep intestines and oatmeal." He shuddered and took another sip of his scotch. "How can a country make the best drink in the world but also have the worst food?"

"Who needs food when you've got scotch. Am I right?"

"Cheers to that," Jack said, raising his glass.

I made my way out of the room and into the hallway. I knew the way to the bathroom since I'd had to use the facilities twice before. I passed the young hostess that had nearly salivated over Flynn when we walked in. She was currently flirting with a young waiter working the rehearsal dinner.

Guess she'd already moved on. I tried not to hold her reaction to Flynn against her. He was magnetic, and it was impossible not to look at him. But he was mine, and I was carrying his child. Jealousy was not an emotion I was accustomed to feeling, but with every pound, stretch mark, and varicose vein, I grew more insecure.

I was ready to have my child out of my body and into the world. I wanted to meet him. And I really wanted to be able to sleep on my stomach.

As I washed my hands after using the restroom, I thought about returning to the party but realized I was done for the evening. I'd had enough social interaction. Without Flynn by my side, my energy had quickly waned.

I wandered down the hallway toward the kitchen area and heard the clanking of washing dishes and the sounds of spraying water. Past the kitchen was the back exit. I opened the door and slipped outside. It was chilly, and goosebumps immediately dotted my skin, but I didn't want to go back inside just for my coat.

I found my husband standing with Malcolm and Duncan on a grassy spot. The gas lanterns made it easy to see the path as I made my way to them.

Duncan puffed on his cigar, his head bent toward Malcolm who was saying something in a low voice. Flynn nodded along.

Realizing I was intruding, I turned around, but Flynn's voice stopped me.

"Barrett!" he called. His dress shoes clopped toward me. After shrugging off his suit jacket, he wrapped it around my shoulders.

"Thank you. Sorry, I didn't mean to intrude," I said, addressing all three of them.

"You're not intruding, lass," Malcolm said. "Join us."

"Are you sure?"

He nodded. Needing no more words of encouragement, I joined their little entourage. I frowned. "Aren't you missing one?"

Duncan's grin was wide. "Ramsey found something far more pleasant than discussing politics with us."

"A woman," I stated.

Flynn cleared his throat. "Two."

"You're kidding!" I said with a laugh. The direction of the air changed, and I caught a whiff of smoke. It instantly made my stomach curl. I attempted to be discreet about moving my position, but Flynn noticed immediately and put out his cigar.

"It's making her sick," he explained to the other two.

When Malcolm and Duncan made a move to put their cigars out, I protested. "Don't stop on my account. I'll go back inside."

"We'd rather have you out here with us than smoke these things," Malcolm assured me with a pat on my shoulder.

I smiled and nodded. "So what are we talking about?"

"The London hotel and how well it's doing."

Malcolm hadn't originally wanted to open a hotel in London because he hated the English. Flynn pointed out that there was no better just dessert than using English money to free the Scots. It was genius, actually.

I loved Malcolm, but sometimes I wondered if he was really cut out to be leader. A leader needed to be able to see the whole picture and keep a calm head. Though Malcolm listened to those he trusted, he was still obstinate and stuck in his ways. The fact was, he was old and when a leader grew old, he became weak. It was simple biology.

Duncan was next in line to take over the leadership position, but he was known as The Tracker. He stalked enemies better than anyone else, and he seemed comfortable in the role and deferring to his father and Flynn to make the bulk of the decisions. It was Flynn who really had Malcolm's ear and had a hand in swaying him.

Lost in my own thoughts, I didn't realize Flynn was saying my name. "Sorry, what?" I asked distractedly.

"Are you tired, hen?"

I nodded. "I am. I'm ready to go whenever you are."

He gripped my hand and squeezed. "We'll go now."

I hugged Malcolm first and then Duncan and told them I'd see them tomorrow at the wedding. Flynn led me toward the tavern. "Are you really tired?" Flynn whispered so Malcolm and Duncan didn't overhear.

"Yes," I admitted. "But we have an hour drive in the car… Perfect excuse to nap and store up some energy."

Flynn chuckled and picked up his pace. Just as he was about to open the back door of the tavern, there was the sound of three loud pops. Before I could even register what was happening, Flynn pushed me down, his body covering mine.

My jaw rattled from hitting the ground, my heart rate accelerating. A wave of pain slid through my belly. There was a lot of shouting and yelling, but I couldn't see anything due to Flynn's large form obstructing my vision.

He looked around to assess the situation, and when he deemed it safe enough, Flynn slowly lifted himself off me and held out his hand to help me up from the ground. "Are you okay? Did I hurt you? How's the bairn?" His questions fired out of his mouth, one after the other.

"I think we're fine." I stole a hand across of my stomach. I felt a kick against my palm. "Yeah, he's kicking something fierce. He's okay. We both are."

"Stay here," he whispered.

I nodded and watched him sprint to the grassy area where Malcolm and Duncan had been standing. I didn't see them; anxiety and fear rolled through me.

"Barrett!" Flynn called from the darkness. "I need you!"

I tried to hurry toward his voice, but my body ached from landing on the solid stone walkway. Flynn was kneeling on the grassy patch by a still form, his hand pressed to Duncan's chest. I slipped on the dewy lawn and fell to my knees. Bracing my hands on the ground, I crawled the rest of the way. A shaft of moonlight peeked out from behind the gray storm clouds.

It wasn't rain that made the ground slippery—it was blood.

"Barrett," Flynn said, his voice sounding very far away. "Barrett!"

I looked up from my bloody hands into Flynn's intractable, harsh face.

"Come here," he commanded. "Take my phone. Call for an ambulance."

Adrenaline sank its claws into me, and I rushed to Flynn. I reached into his trouser pocket and pulled out his cell phone. While I dialed, I looked down at Duncan. His pallor was pale as Flynn tried to stem the flow of blood seeping out of his brother's chest wound.

"Malcolm?" I asked.

Flynn's eyes were grim. "Dead."

## Chapter 5

When we got to the hospital, Duncan was rushed into emergency surgery. After scrubbing my hands to remove the blood, I got checked out by the doctor. I'd hit the ground hard when Flynn protected me with his body. The baby was fine, and so was I, except for a few bruises.

Now, I sat in the waiting room, clutching Ash's hand. She looked completely shell-shocked; she hadn't said more than two words since we'd arrived.

Flynn was in the corner of the waiting room on his phone, snapping orders and jumping into the natural role of leader. Duncan's younger brother was nowhere to be found, and his phone kept rolling to voicemail. Flynn shoved his cell into his pocket and looked at me.

I nodded and squeezed Ash's hand before letting go. Flynn and I walked out of the waiting room, which was filled with Ash's nucleus family and Duncan's relatives. To say the mood was somber was generous. Malcolm was dead; he'd been shot in the head, and his son was fighting for his life.

Flynn and I trailed down the hallway past the nurses' station. I saw flashes of lightning through the large hospital windows of the lobby. Rumbling thunder outside had me running my hands up and down my arms.

Flynn pulled me to him, infusing me with some of his warmth. His lips brushed the top of my head. We were both still in shock over Malcolm's sudden death; I hadn't cried or reacted yet—there had been other things that needed immediate attention. Feelings could happen later.

"Do we have any idea who was behind the attack?" I asked gently.

Flynn shook his head. "Not at the moment."

"Still no word from Ramsey?"

"None. I think you should go home and rest. Security will be there to see to your safety. Duncan won't be out of surgery for hours and even then, he might—he might not—"

"I'm staying," I stated. "When we leave here, we'll leave together."

Flynn nodded absently as he rubbed a hand across his exhausted face. "I have to see to the funeral arrangements."

"Let me handle it," I said.

"Really?"

I nodded. "Ash isn't in a place to step up, and you have other things to worry about."

He leaned down to kiss me softly on the lips. "What would I do without you?"

"Don't even think about that."

Flynn glanced out the window, his blue eyes a bit dazed. "He's gone."

"Yes," I said, my throat thickening with emotion. I shoved my feelings down—they weren't important at the moment. Flynn had lost the man he considered a father. Malcolm had raised him, given him a home. And now he was gone.

Duncan, his brother in all ways but blood, was in surgery and might not make it.

I took Flynn's hand and tugged on it so that he was forced

to look at me. "You're going to find out who did this, and then you're going to make them pay."

"Aye," he said, nodding slowly.

"Revenge."

His jaw clenched. "Aye. Revenge."

∼

A few hours later, the doctor came to give us an update about Duncan. He survived surgery but was still in critical condition. The doctor had no way of knowing if Duncan would wake up and told us all to go home and get some rest. Ash looked like a shrunken, muted form of her usual self. Her hair was flat, coming down from its pins, and she had mascara streaks underneath her eyes. She wanted to stay at the hospital, but Jack and I finally managed to convince her to leave.

Flynn and I made it to the car, collapsing in exhaustion and dozing the entire ride home as weak sunlight leaked through the windows. Just as the car stopped outside our home, Flynn's cell phone rang.

Ramsey.

Flynn didn't want to tell him over the phone that his father had died from a bullet to the head and that his brother was in critical condition.

"He's coming over," Flynn said, hanging up.

"I'm surprised he hasn't heard the news yet. All he has to do is listen to one of his dozen voicemails."

"I can barely think straight," he muttered. He opened the front door, and the first thing I did when I got inside was kick off my heels. They weren't painful under normal circumstances, but my already swollen feet hadn't enjoyed them the past many hours.

"I'll make us some food," I said.

"I'm not hungry, hen, but thank you. I have some calls to

make before Ramsey gets here." He kissed me briefly and then disappeared into his study, leaving the door cracked.

I went into the kitchen to rustle up some food. As I whisked eggs, I mentally made a list of all the things I'd have to take care of for Malcolm's funeral. It would be at Dornoch Cathedral, which was in the center of town. Malcolm had been a pillar of the community, and people would want to pay their respects. Flynn needed to make a list of guests he wanted to invite. Aside from SINS members, and the people of Dornoch, I didn't know who else would want to pay their respects.

Maybe it was better if outsiders didn't know about Malcolm's death. The SINS were in a precarious situation. Their leader was dead and the heir apparent in critical condition. I knew Ramsey well enough to know he wasn't prepared to step into the leadership position if it should fall to him. Flynn continued to hold a substantial role in the SINS, and when he'd lived in New York, he'd operated autonomously, independently of Malcolm because Malcolm had trusted him.

I sat down to eat and fell asleep on my plate. Jarred awake by the doorbell, I groaned and reached for a napkin. I dabbed at my cheeks and went to answer the door, but Flynn had beaten me to it.

Ramsey looked disheveled and confused, but the moment he saw the grimness of Flynn's face, he realized something was wrong.

"Just tell me," he said before the front door had even closed.

"Let's have a drink," Flynn suggested.

"It's eight in the morning."

"When has that ever stopped you?" Flynn led Ramsey to the study and then shut the door.

I didn't wait around to overhear Ramsey's reaction. Too tired to function, I trudged up the stairs, knowing I needed at least a few hours of sleep before I could do anything else. I fell into bed and slept. I didn't even dream.

∽

The following morning, Flynn got a call that Duncan was awake. Flynn hopped in the shower and then left quickly. I stayed at home so I could prepare Malcolm's funeral. Flynn and I decided that it would be a small, family affair, but that still included some two hundred people. Coordinating could've been a real bitch, but when you had money, it took care of all indiscriminate details. And it took care of them fast.

A few hours later, I was finishing up the last of the funeral arrangements when Ash called.

"Hi, how are you, what can I do?" I asked immediately before she could say anything.

She let out a soft laugh. I could hear the relief in it. "Nothing. I just saw Flynn—he said you're taking care of Malcolm's funeral. I was calling to ask what *I* could do for *you*."

"It's almost done. So you don't have to do anything except focus on Duncan. How is he? Inane question, I know."

"He's okay, I guess. I mean, he woke up today, which—thank God—is a good sign. But on top of healing from a gunshot wound, he has to deal with burying his father. Do you know what happened? Who came after them?"

"I know nothing," I stated.

She sighed. "Yeah."

"I'm so sorry, Ash," I said quietly. "I'm sorry you have to go through this."

"This is the life, right?"

"Yes."

We fell silent, and I wondered if Ash was reevaluating everything. It was one thing to know your life was going to be in constant danger and that anything could happen. It was another to have your fiancé mowed down at your rehearsal dinner the night before your wedding.

"Oh, shit," I said. "I didn't even think about the wedding."

"Postponed until he's well enough to stand at an altar in a kilt."

I laughed. "So glad to hear that. Your parents? Jack?"

"They'll stick around until I get Duncan home. Hopefully that will only be for about a week, and then they'll leave." She sighed. "What's going to happen? With the SINS?"

"I don't know, Ash."

"I love Ramsey, but he's not—"

"Don't worry about it. Just focus on Duncan."

"Yeah, you're right."

We hung up and I paused, suddenly feeling like I was able to breathe a bit easier. I finished making the rest of the funeral arrangements before moving into the living room and curling up on the couch to wait for Flynn. As night descended, Flynn walked through the front door. Contentedly warm from the gas fireplace, I gave him a sleepy look. He lifted my legs and sat down on the couch before resettling me.

"You look tired, love," I commented.

"You're supposed to tell me I look handsome," he teased with a wan smile.

"You are handsome—but you also look tired."

"I'm exhausted," he admitted. "And sad."

"Yeah," I said, having no words of comfort, emotion constricting my throat. "I finished the funeral arrangements."

"Thank you." His hand stroked my ankle. "You always make everything better."

"I only wish I could do more," I told him truthfully.

He placed his palm to my belly, which I swore looked even bigger than it had a few hours ago. Maybe it was the angle.

"I have to talk to you about something," he said.

"All right."

Flynn looked at the fireplace, the reflection of the flames flickering in his eyes. "I've spoken to Duncan and Ramsey, and they both agree that I should be acting leader of the SINS. At least until Duncan is on the mend and able to take over the job." He glanced at me. "You don't seem surprised."

"I had a feeling it would come to this. You're a natural leader, Flynn."

He let out a sigh of relief. "It means more time away from home. Especially now that we have an unknown enemy."

"Is it really unknown?" I struggled to sit up and Flynn helped me. "Can't we narrow it down? Start with a short list or something?"

"I have some people on it."

That was Flynn code for *you don't really want to know what that means*. I let it go because it wasn't important. The only thing that was important was discovering who had wanted to shake up the SINS.

"So, in the meantime…" I asked.

"In the meantime we wait. We remain patient." His jaw clenched. "And we tighten security."

## Chapter 6

I sat in the front pew of Dornoch Cathedral and listened to Father Brooks drone on in an indecipherable Scottish brogue while he eulogized Malcolm. Duncan was, of course, absent, but Ash and Flynn flanked me.

Ramsey sat next to Flynn. He looked both solemn and angry, the lines around his mouth white with tension. I'd only seen Ramsey in good humor, but he belonged to the SINS, so I knew he had the courage, strength, and stomach for the cause.

When Father Brooks finished, Ramsey, Flynn, Brad, and three other men went to the front of the cathedral to Malcolm's coffin. As the processional began, the sounds of bagpipes filtered through the cathedral.

I saw Ash grimace and glared at her. Tradition was important, and if she was going to be the wife of the SINS leader, then she needed to get with the program.

We buried Malcolm under a gray sky. A light drizzle began to fall, and people opened their umbrellas. I stood next to Flynn, trying to hold in my discomfort. My back ached, and I wanted nothing more than to take a nap, but we were hosting the gathering at our house after the funeral. I would have to play hostess, make sure everyone was taken care of, and it would be several hours until we were alone.

The drizzle turned into a downpour. Father Brooks didn't appear like he'd even noticed; such was the weather in Scotland. The bagpipes stopped, and we all rushed to our cars with the promise of congregating in a warm, dry place.

"Careful, hen," Flynn warned as I nearly lost my footing on the slick stone walkway.

"What is it with you Scots?" I demanded. "Ever hear of cement?"

Flynn flashed me an amused smile. I stopped walking, forcing him to stop, too. My brow furrowed, and my hand went to my back.

"Love? What is it?" he asked.

I shook my head. "Nothing. Just a slight crick."

He didn't look convinced. "You sure?"

"Yeah. Come on, let's go."

I eased into the back seat of the Rolls, adjusting my body, but the pain had already eased. I was convinced it was nothing more than Braxton Hicks and not the real deal. As the car drove away from the cathedral, I felt a popping sensation, followed by a gush between my legs. An involuntary squeak escaped my mouth.

Flynn looked over at me, his face registering surprise and a bit of shock. "Hospital!" he shouted at the driver. "Now!"

∼

Our son was born eighteen hours later and weighed in at 7.5 pounds. I was beyond exhausted, but so completely happy despite everything going on around us. My body released a flood of hormones, and I alternated between wanting to sleep and wanting to cry. Watching Flynn cradle his newborn son in his arms filled a piece of my heart I didn't even know was empty.

"Well, hen," Flynn asked me quietly. "We've got to pick a name."

"So we do," I murmured.

"How do you feel about the name Gavin?"

"For your Da?" I asked.

He nodded. "And Malcolm? As a middle name."

"Gavin Malcolm Campbell," I said, trying out the sound of it.

"Gavin means 'white hawk' in Gaelic. We could call him Hawk. If you'd like." He smiled softly. "He looks like a Hawk."

"Yes," I said simply.

He gently placed Hawk in my arms and stared down at me before kissing me softly on the lips. "I love you."

"I love you," I said back.

Hawk and I slept for a little while before Flynn let Ash in to visit.

"I won't stay long," she said, pitching her voice low. "I want to get back to Duncan's side, but I just had to see him."

Ash stared down at Hawk and smiled. "He's perfect."

"I agree."

At the moment, nothing mattered except for the tiny bundle in my arms. We had started the day with a funeral, and we were ending it with a birth. Such was the cycle of life.

On the day we took Hawk home, we stopped by Duncan's hospital room to show him off. It revived Duncan's spirits and gave him a bit of excitement. He was already sick of being stuck in a hospital bed.

"Patience, brother," Flynn said, setting his hand on Duncan's shoulder.

"Patience?" Duncan growled. "My father is dead. We have enemies—"

"I'm aware, but you're no use to us and our cause if you kill yourself trying to get up and around before you're ready."

Duncan leaned back against the pillow, exhaustion and anger warring with each other. "I'm the best tracker we have."

"I'll keep you informed," Flynn promised. "I need to get Barrett and Hawk home. Rest."

I leaned over and kissed Duncan on the cheek. "I hate feeling useless, too."

"You're not useless," Duncan insisted. "You're a mother."

"But there was a time, not too long ago, that I was useful in other ways."

"You're still a mastermind," Flynn said.

"Thank you, love," I said with a tired grin.

I bundled up Hawk next to my body before leaving the hospital. It was cold, but surprisingly devoid of rain for the moment. Flynn helped me into the back of the Rolls. I strapped Hawk into his car seat, and Flynn ordered our driver to take it slow. A twenty-minute drive was going to take twice as long. Not that I cared; I was already learning that I could doze whenever wherever.

"I have to go to London in a few days," Flynn said.

"Issue with the hotel?" I asked.

"No. I have a meeting with Lord Henry Arlington."

I frowned. "You've never mentioned him, have you?"

Flynn shook his head. "No. He's in the House of Lords, and he keeps me informed."

"Ah," I said in understanding. "Lord Arlington is on the SINS payroll?"

"I'd rather not say."

"Uh huh. And are you meeting at the London Rex?"

"We are."

"And are you going to show him a good time?"

"Aye. Ply him with liquor and introduce him to gorgeous women."

"Hmmm."

"The man is married to the coldest woman I have ever met. I'm just trying to give him some joy."

"Right, by promoting infidelity."

"Divorce in his circle isn't really an option. Besides, most men of power keep mistresses."

I looked over at him, the car seat strapped between us. "Do you really want to be having this discussion after I just gave birth to your child?"

Flynn's lips quirked with amusement. "Valid point, love. However, I would like to say that most men don't have wives like you."

"That's true. I am in a class above the rest," I joked.

"You are," he said, sobering. "You would do anything to protect me. You've already proven that. I'd be an eejit to jeopardize that."

"Knowing and doing are two different things," I warned.

"Noted." He smiled softly. "I didn't think it was possible."

"What?"

"I didn't think it was possible to find you more beautiful, but I do."

I sighed, feeling strangely content at the moment. I was insulated in a bubble of new motherhood. "I trust you, Flynn. And I'll be here when you come home. We both will." My finger trailed down Hawk's cheek. There was nothing softer than baby skin, perfect and unsullied.

Flynn didn't need the added guilt of leaving his newborn son and me while he tended to SINS business. But that was the life. I was a warrior's wife, waiting for my husband to come home. One day, he might not walk through the front door—it was terrifying, and if I thought too much about it, I began to panic. So I didn't think about it often. When I did, I liked to be alone.

"Thank you," he said.

"For?"

"You want me to go down the list?"

I smiled. "Please."

He laughed. "It would take too long. Besides, we're finally home."

~

"Your son hates me," I said to Flynn over the phone.

Flynn chuckled. "Not possible."

"Ever since you've been gone, he's been fussy and refuses to sleep more than an hour at a time."

"You wouldn't be trying to make me feel guilty so I'll come home sooner, would you?"

"Is it working?"

"Aye."

I sighed. "Sorry. I just miss you."

"There are worse things in the world than having your wife miss you. How are you, really? Are you okay?"

"Yes."

"You're not overwhelmed? I left you alone and—"

"I'm terrified I'm going to cock up this parenting thing, and that wouldn't change even if you were here. We have a baby nurse and a housekeeper and SINS wives have reached out to make it clear they are here if I need any help. Some have stopped by because they're Scottish and nosy, but they've got the best hearts." My eyes burned with tears.

Taking a seat on the couch, I stared at the flames in the fireplace. "How are things in London?"

"Lord Arlington claims not to know anything."

"Do you believe him?"

"Well, I got him drunk and laid, and he still claimed not to know anything. I wish you were here. Two pairs of eyes are better than one."

"You need me for my eyes, huh? And here I just thought I was a hot piece of ass."

"You are still that—even if your arse is just a wee bit bigger. Just means there's more to grab onto."

"You're like a modern Robert Burns, you know that?"

"I try."

"Do you really think Lord Arlington is our way in? I mean, do you really think he knows who was behind the attack?"

"I think any man that can be bought has no belief in loyalty," Flynn said.

"So maybe someone else is greasing his palms to keep him quiet."

"That's what I think."

I paused. "Does Lord Arlington have any children?"

"Three girls."

I fell silent and let him come to the conclusion I was already thinking.

"I won't, Barrett—"

"I know you wouldn't ever do anything to hurt a child," I interrupted. "But he doesn't know that. I assume his wife already knows about his indiscretions, so we can't use that to hold over his head. You've got to hit him where it hurts."

"Sometimes I don't even know who you are," he said in amazement. "And I mean that in a good way."

I was glad he liked it. Sometimes I couldn't stand the ugly parts of myself. My mind never used to work this way, now it was just natural.

"If he knows who killed Malcolm, we have to use every tool we have," I said. I didn't need to tell him that whoever had killed Malcolm and had almost taken out Duncan might come back to finish the job.

But how did you fight an enemy you didn't know?

## Chapter 7

Three days later my best friend stood on my front porch. "My fiancé is driving me insane," Ash said the moment I opened the door.

"And you thought coming to hang out with me—your sleep deprived best friend—was a better option?"

Ash rolled her eyes and stepped across the threshold into the foyer. I shivered from the blast of cold air and quickly closed the door.

"Tea?" I asked her.

"I was hoping for something stronger," Ash admitted. She followed me into the kitchen and went immediately to the counter where Flynn and I kept a decent liquor collection.

I put on water for tea and asked, "So Duncan is driving you crazy?"

"Yes." Ash poured herself a glass of Balvenie Double-Wood and sat down at the kitchen table. "You look exhausted."

"Thank you. Perils of having a newborn. And being the only parent at home for the time being."

Ash groaned. "I'm an insensitive ass."

"'Arse,'" I corrected with a grin, but ruefully shook my

head. "You're not. Your fiancé was shot and almost died. We buried his father two weeks ago." I nearly choked trying to get the words out. "You've had to postpone your wedding."

"Okay, but I still feel really selfish."

"Don't."

The teakettle whistled, and I made myself a cup of chamomile before sinking into a kitchen chair. "So, why is Duncan driving you insane?"

"Instead of resting, he stays up wanting to discuss all the possible theories of who was behind the shooting. He hasn't grieved for his father—he's completely in denial about it."

"He's not in denial, he's in anger," I said. "He won't feel the loss of Malcolm until he knows who is responsible."

She shook her head. "I used to think you were crazy. For choosing to be with Flynn, knowing all of this, willingly putting yourself in danger."

"And then you met Duncan."

"And then I met Duncan. Still, I'm not like you. I freeze, Barrett. You have this—I don't know… I could almost believe you were cut out for this kind of life." She looked out the window and grimaced. "We basically live in Seattle. You know that, right?"

"Yeah, but at least here we get to listen to lilting brogues and our men wear kilts. And they make adorable babies."

Ash grinned. "Yeah, you're right. Hawk is adorable."

"He's perfect," I said with a sigh. "Let's go look in on him."

Ash finished her drink, and we headed upstairs to the nursery. Mrs. Keith, a grandmotherly woman, sat in the rocking chair, knitting.

"You're kidding, right?" Ash demanded in a whisper.

"The woman has knitted booties for every one of her ten grandchildren. She could do it in her sleep," I replied. It was one of the many reasons I was comfortable with her watching Hawk. Her experience with children—not the knitting. She was incredibly helpful, and when she imparted her many years of wisdom, she didn't make me feel at all stupid when I felt like I had no idea what I was doing. I was a new mother without any female members of my family to help me. If it hadn't been for Mrs. Keith, I would've been scared to give Hawk his first bath.

Mrs. Keith looked up from her knitting needles, the rims of her gold spectacles gleaming in the low light. She smiled. "Hello, dearie."

"Hi, Mrs. Keith," I greeted, tiptoeing toward the crib. "How's Hawk?"

"Sleeping soundly," she said. "Though probably time for another feeding soon."

"Why don't you go make yourself a cup of tea and stretch your legs," I suggested.

Mrs. Keith set aside her knitting before heaving her ample form out of the rocking chair. "He's such a sweet lad."

I smiled. "Thank you. I think so." I leaned over the crib and saw that he was stirring. I lifted my son into my arms and took him to the changing table.

"He's bigger," Ash said.

"Yes," I agreed.

"I'm going to go wash my hands, and then I'm holding him after you feed him." She looked at him. "Jeez, he really might be the most perfect baby I've ever seen."

I chuckled. "Wait until you have your own. You'll rethink that."

~

I felt a warm body slide into bed next to me. "You're home," I murmured.

"Did I wake you?" Flynn asked, reaching out for me.

"No, I was dozing." I snuggled against him, trying to find

his mouth in the dark. "I'm so glad you're home. What time is it?"

"Three a.m."

"You didn't want to stay another night in London?"

"I wanted to sleep next to my wife."

Flynn's hand ran down my back, and I shivered in delight. I reached for him under the covers, grasping his hard, firm length. He moaned.

"Don't torture me," he gasped.

"I thought you liked it when I tortured you," I teased, my lips trailing across his firm, sculpted chest.

"Usually. But you can't—we can't—"

"I want to take care of *you*," I said. I tugged off the covers so that I could see him. He was beautiful—sleek muscle, hard lines, warrior scars.

"Are you sure?" he asked.

"Positive."

I pressed my lips to the raised scar under his right clavicle. He was riddled with marks, at least two of them from bullets.

His breathing harshened when I nipped my way lower. I slid my lips over him, taking him into the wet heat of my mouth. Swirling my tongue around his shaft and gently skimming my fingertips along his thighs, I drew out his pleasure in the way I knew he liked. His hands wove their way into my hair.

"Barrett," he whispered.

I sucked and teased; I prolonged his sweet agony until I pushed him over the edge and felt his release in my mouth. He let out a satisfied sigh as I settled next to him.

"Thank you," he said. "How long before—"

"Another month."

"Damn it."

A vigorous cry sounded through the baby monitor, and I climbed out of bed, reaching for the robe on the chair in the corner.

"I'll come with you."

I smiled at him as he climbed out of bed and pulled on a pair of boxers. "Your turn to change him. You have two weeks to make up for."

Flynn chuckled as he wrapped his arm around my shoulder and led me out of our bedroom. Though we lived in a small castle, I'd put my foot down about Hawk having his own wing. He would grow up privileged, but he didn't need to be spoiled. His nursery was the room next to ours.

After I turned the light on low, I settled myself in the rocking chair as Flynn stood over the crib, lifting Hawk into his arms. Flynn took him to the changing table and put Hawk in a fresh diaper. My son continued to howl like a baying wolf and didn't quiet until I snuggled him to my breast.

"Is he sleeping more during the night?" Flynn asked, gazing down at us.

"Sure."

Flynn chuckled.

I stroked a finger down the curve of Hawk's cheek before leaning down to smell that perfect baby smell.

"You know you're a natural mother, right?" he said.

I smiled up at him. "Nah, Hawk makes it easy."

"For someone who didn't want bairns, you're settling into motherhood like you always wanted it."

"Strange, right? But let's not talk about that. Catch me up. Tell me about Lord Arlington." I switched Hawk to my other breast and then focused on Flynn.

"He genuinely doesn't know anything," Flynn said. "And men in fear tend to babble. There was no babbling. But he did promise to keep his ear to the ground."

I snorted. "How much is that going to cost?"

"Enough."

"Hmm. Well, I guess it's good that he has a monetary price. It means we'll get information. Eventually."

"I don't know what I'm going to tell Duncan and Ramsey," Flynn admitted. "I have no news for them."

I didn't give him placating words because they wouldn't have helped, and they would've been a lie. "Do we have any other information sources?"

"A few in the Highlands—allies of the SINS, but they're Scottish."

"Which means what?"

"It means they'll take their sweet time admitting anything. Scots do everything only when they're ready and not a moment sooner."

"So we're back to waiting."

"Have you noticed anything unusual?" Flynn asked. "While I was gone?"

I shook my head. "No. Then again, I've been inside with Hawk. You should check in with the security team you have stationed around the castle and grounds."

"I've been getting daily briefs."

Hawk finished nursing and put him to my shoulder to burp him. He let out a few good belches and fell right to sleep. I set him in his crib and then tiredly trudged back to bed. I'd be up in another few hours to do it all over again, but at least Mrs. Keith would arrive at ten in the morning to help me.

Flynn took me into his arms, and I pressed my cheek to his warm chest. His fingers rubbed circles on my neck, and I closed my eyes.

"There's not a trail," Flynn whispered. "What do I do if I can't find a trail?"

"There's always a trail," I murmured. "Who stands to lose the most if the SINS succeed and Scotland gains its independence?"

## Chapter 8

I woke up a few hours later to weak sunlight battling its way through gray clouds. Flynn wasn't in bed next to me, and the baby monitor wasn't on the bedside table. Taking advantage of a brief moment to attend to my needs first and Hawk's second, I took the world's fastest shower. After putting on clean clothes and twirling my wet hair up into a messy bun, I reached for my glasses. I hadn't worn contacts since Hawk had been born.

When I went into the nursery, I was surprised to find Hawk awake because he was quiet. I leaned over the crib to pick him up and kissed his nose. After a feeding and a change, I strapped him into the baby sling and carried him downstairs with the intention of finding Flynn. He was in his study, hair askew, eyes bloodshot. His nervous energy was palpable. I noticed the three mugs on his desk and realized the reason for his frenetic state. The missing baby monitor acted as a paperweight for a stack of papers.

"Morning," I said from the doorway.

"Come look at this."

I went into his sanctuary and immediately saw the far wall

covered in notecards, Post-its, and photographs. "A person of interest wall, huh?" I asked.

Flynn kissed me quickly and smiled down at Hawk. "How's our boy?"

"He's good," I said distractedly. I gestured with my chin to the wall. "Explain."

"These are all the groups who could've been behind the attack."

"There's not as many as I thought there would be," I admitted. "Are they all political?"

He nodded. "I don't believe the attack was a personal vendetta against Malcolm. These groups are domestic enemies. Other Scottish organizations that have had issues with us in the past."

"For or against an independent Scotland?" I asked.

Hawk made a noise, but I started to rock him. He quieted immediately.

"Both."

I sighed. "So, still a lot of different trails to follow. Why would another organization who also wants a free Scotland attack the SINS?"

"At this point, I don't know. Maybe people don't like the way we handle things? Maybe because we're the largest organization and the best equipped and someone doesn't want us to take all the credit for freeing Scotland? I still don't know. But this"—he pointed to the wall—"made me feel useful."

"Have you slept?" I asked.

"No. As soon as you fell asleep, I climbed out of bed, my mind working overtime." He ran a hand across his stubbly jaw.

"Okay. You need a break."

"I'm fine. I just need more coffee."

"Flynn—"

His gaze darkened. "I'm acting leader of the SINS. It falls to me to find out who's out to stop us."

"I know that, but you have to take care of yourself, too."

"You're my wife, not my mother."

I smiled, but it wasn't pretty. "I'm supposed to be the overtired, irrational one."

Flynn's jaw unclenched, and he gave a rueful shake of his head. "I'm sorry."

"You're under a lot of stress. I know that. I'm just trying to take care of you because I know you're trying to take care of everyone and everything. I'd never challenge your authority outwardly. I know how the SINS operates, and I've accepted the antiquated patriarchal edicts in public. But we're in our own home, and there's no one here but you and me. Let me take care of you."

Flynn touched my cheek and then leaned in to kiss me. "Aye. I'll let you take care of me."

I turned my face so I could kiss his palm. "Food. Then bed."

Flynn and I moved toward the door to leave the mess of his study, but then his cell phone rang. He plucked it off the desk and answered it. "Campbell," he said.

He listened for a moment, his eyes widening as he looked at me. "Aye," he said to the person on the other end. "I'll be in touch." He hung up, his mouth pulling into a grin.

"What just happened?"

"If you promise me one of your amazing omelets, I'll tell you."

～

I gaped at Flynn. "You've got to be kidding."

"I've never been more serious in my life," Flynn said calmly as he pushed away his empty plate.

Hawk was asleep upstairs, far enough away not to be disturbed when his parents got into a loud and heated argument, because it was about to get loud and very heated.

Sputtering in shock, I tried to speak but found I couldn't.

"I need you," Flynn said.

"I can't go," I said. "We have a two-week-old baby."

"I'm aware. But this is important, too."

"More important than our newborn son?"

"Don't do that to me, Barrett," Flynn said quietly.

I sighed and shook my head, a lump of guilt in my belly. "Sorry," I apologized. "That was unfair of me. Can't you take Ash with you? She's technically going to be the wife of the leader. She needs to learn how to do these sorts of things."

"There's no one I trust more than you, Barrett. Besides, you're a Scottish history buff—and you're a redhead."

I blinked. "I didn't know those two things went hand in hand."

"You're sexy, and you know how to get men to talk. That was my point."

Wrinkling my nose at him, I shook my head in disbelief. It was hard to feel sexy when you had to wear a nursing bra. "This conversation is not making any sort of sense to me. And maybe that's because I'm a new mother and I'm sleep deprived and my hormones are completely out of whack. I also have minimal brain function."

"Your minimal brain function is more than most people's full brain function."

"How would we even do this?" I demanded.

"Arlington would take you as his date."

"And you'd what? Sneak in past security?"

"Of course not. I'd pay them off."

"Why couldn't we go in together?"

"Because people recognize my face. People don't recognize you. Not yet. Elliot will have no idea who you really are. We can take the plane to London and then fly back that same evening. We'll only be leaving Hawk for a few hours."

Leave Hawk? How was I supposed to leave Hawk? When he was in a different room, I felt separation anxiety. I spent so much time staring at him, making sure I was there when he needed me. And now I had to leave him for hours at a time?

"I know Hawk needs you," Flynn said.

When I looked at him curiously, he explained, "You were talking out loud."

"See? I'm not operating on all cylinders."

"I need you," Flynn stated. "Mrs. Keith is a wonderful nanny. Hawk is in good hands."

I took a deep breath. Flynn was a father—it was different for him. Leaving his child with someone else didn't tug on his heart the same way it did mine. Because I was a mother. I'd carried another life inside of me. I wasn't the same, and I wouldn't be, ever again.

But Flynn needed me, too, and I couldn't walk away from him when he was asking, pleading with me to be his wife, his partner.

"Okay," I relented. "Okay, we'll do this. Together."

~

We held a meeting at Malcolm's house since Duncan and Ash lived there. Duncan was still bed bound, so we'd come to him. Ash sat quietly by his side. Ramsey was a bit more vocal and paced around Duncan's bedroom, anger and tension radiating off him. Ever since Malcolm had died, Ramsey's good charm had fled—he'd become a complete hot head, out of control of his own emotions, a pot ready to boil. He had no objectivity whatsoever, and I worried what would happen when we all learned who was behind Malcolm's murder. I was afraid Ramsey would go in, guns blazing, and get himself killed.

"I want to go to London with you," Ramsey said to Flynn.

"No," Flynn said.

Ramsey's face darkened. "That's not up to you."

"The hell it's not," Flynn argued. "I'm acting leader."

Ramsey looked away from Flynn and glanced at his brother. "What do you say, Duncan? Should I go to London?"

"And do what?" Flynn interjected before Duncan could speak. "You're not thinking clearly. What can you do? How can you help?"

Ramsey fell silent, but his eyes burned with an angry fervor. "And you really think you can do this?" Ramsey asked me.

"I do."

"She has a bit of experience in our world," Duncan interjected. "She stays calm and can think three steps ahead."

The old Barrett used to be able to do that—before my hormones and priorities changed. I shoved all those thoughts down, refusing to give them a voice. I would do this; I could do this. It might take everything in me to shelve motherhood for a few hours, but I'd do it.

"I don't like this," Ramsey stated. "I don't like this at all." In a supreme state of rage, he stalked out of the bedroom. A moment later, the front door slammed.

"We'll give you guys some time to talk," I said, looking at Ash. She rose from her chair and then followed me out of the bedroom, closing the door behind us.

"You're really going to do this?" Ash asked as we headed to the living room.

"I volunteered you for the job, but he—"

"No, you guys are like Bonnie and Scottish Clyde. Makes sense that he'd want you."

I put my head in my hands. "It's been a while since I've had to do this kind of thing."

"Yeah, well, being an incubator was a full-time job. And you couldn't really do the things you used to do while pregnant."

"And I can do them now since I've got my body back?" I muttered. "I have a baby."

"Nothing is going to happen when you're in London.

You're going to go into Lord Elliot's house, flirt with him, get him alone, and put the screws to him."

"Actually Flynn is going to put the screws to him. I just have to get Lord Elliot alone. I just hope he's not handsy."

"This guy is really supposed to know who wants to take down the SINS?"

"Lord Arlington, our informant, for lack of a better word, overheard Lord Elliot, discussing the financial ramifications if Scotland gained its independence."

"That doesn't mean anything."

"Lord Elliot discussed what it would mean for *him* if Scotland gained its independence."

"It's still a straw we're grasping at."

"They're men of action, Ash. It's killing them to do nothing."

"So Flynn is going to drag you to London on a whim?"

I stared at her. "Stand down, Ash."

## Chapter 9

"Did I tell you that you look gorgeous?" Flynn asked, taking my hand and bringing it to his lips.

I nodded and grinned. "You've already told me that."

"Well, I mean it. That dress is lethal."

My already curvy form was curvier. The emerald-colored gown highlighted my skin and hair, and I felt beautiful, despite the fact that I was wearing a thick bra and a stretchy device that held in my stomach. But my husband had given me emerald earrings the size of asteroids. It was a hell of a consolation prize. Even if I never got my body back, at least I'd have nice jewelry.

The car door opened, and I slid out of my seat, taking the offered hand from the chauffeur. Flynn put his palm to my hip and escorted me up the pathway to Lord Arlington's London townhouse.

"Here we go," Flynn said, ringing the doorbell.

The door opened, and a tall man in a tuxedo answered. His dark hair was salt and peppered, and there were only a few wrinkles at the corners of his eyes. I expected him to look more weasel-like, but I was surprised to find that he was decent looking.

Lord Arlington stood back so we could enter his home. Once we stepped across the threshold, Lord Arlington gave Flynn a clipped greeting, his eyes cold before turning to me.

"Mrs. Campbell, welcome," he said in a posh English accent. His tone had warmed considerably when he addressed me. I didn't know why considering I was Flynn's wife. How would Lord Arlington treat me if he knew I was the one that suggested using his children to get him to cooperate?

"Barrett, please," I insisted, shaking myself out of my thoughts. I looked around the foyer, noting the antique furnishings and paintings. "You have a lovely home."

"Thank you. Come into the library and we'll have a drink before we go."

We followed him down a long hallway and entered the library. "What will you have to drink, Barrett?" Lord Arlington asked. He stood by the liquor cart and waited for my answer. It was hard to find my tongue because I was too busy gaping at the gorgeous room. Leather-bound books rested on wooden shelves, and a huge fireplace was currently ablaze, giving off the most splendid heat.

"Barrett? Drink?" Flynn prodded.

I shook my head and smiled ruefully at Lord Arlington. "I'm sorry. I got lost in your library for a moment."

Lord Arlington smiled back at me. "A most excellent place to get lost in."

"I'll have a club soda please."

"Campbell?" Arlington asked Flynn. Though polite, Arlington's voice was cool.

"Same, thank you."

Arlington raised an eyebrow but said nothing. Flynn was usually a scotch drinker, but tonight, he had to be clear-headed. I didn't drink because I was nursing. A pang of guilt shot through my stomach when I thought of Hawk. But he was home, safely tucked away in his crib. If he cried, Mrs. Keith would pick him up and rock him in her dimpled arms.

She'd change him and give him a bottle of breast milk that I'd pumped before I left.

I had nothing to worry about.

We sat down with our drinks, and Flynn rested his hand on my thigh. I noticed Arlington's eyes dart to my bare legs, but he quickly lifted his gaze to my face.

"It seems congratulations are in order," Arlington said. "Your husband told me about your son."

I smiled. "Thank you."

"Must be difficult being away from him when he's so young."

"Very," I said.

After Lord Arlington asked a few more polite questions about Hawk, Flynn cleared his throat. "You two should get going."

Arlington nodded and set his glass down before rising. "Ten p.m. That should give Barrett two hours. Is that enough time?"

I nodded. It would have to be. I didn't want to draw this out any longer than necessary.

"Aye," Flynn said, squeezing my hand. "She can do it."

"I'll text when he's in place," I said.

Flynn nodded and then we kissed goodbye. Lord Arlington guided me to his waiting car and held the door open for me. I slid inside and he followed.

Driving through London traffic, I looked at the lights of the city, which reminded me of New York. I realized I didn't miss it. I'd come to consider Dornoch my home, and I couldn't wait to return.

"Anything you want to discuss before we arrive at Elliot's house?" Arlington asked.

"No, I think Flynn and I talked about everything."

Arlington smirked. "Perhaps you should call me Henry."

"Perhaps I should," I agreed. "Thank you for helping us."

"Your husband didn't give me much of a choice."

I stared at him for a long moment, trying to tamp down my feelings of dislike. It didn't matter if Arlington was charming or polite to me—he was weak, and he had no true loyalty.

"We all have a choice," I stated.

The car came to a stop, and Arlington adjusted his tuxedo jacket. "Are you ready?"

Grinning, I nodded. "Are you?"

∽

"That's him," Lord Arlington said, gesturing with his chin to point out Lord John Elliot.

I looked at our host for the evening. He was tall and still in decent shape for an older man.

Lord Elliot laughed at something a male friend of his said, looking affable and pleasant. "Where's his wife?" I asked, discreetly glancing around the ballroom.

"Attempting to keep their sixteen-year-old son away from the liquor," Lord Arlington murmured.

"Excellent," I said, squaring my shoulders.

"Should I introduce you?" Lord Arlington inquired, raising his eyebrows at me.

I shook my head. "No. When I toss my hair over my shoulder, interrupt us." Without waiting for Arlington's reply, I stalked toward my prey.

Lord Elliot glanced at me briefly and then whipped his eyes back for a longer look. He was an easy man to distract. Granted, my breasts did a lot of the work for me. Or maybe the birthday party he was giving his twenty-one-year-old daughter was just that dull. It was an aristocratic, black tie affair, and I wondered what kind of twenty-one-year-old wanted this sort of party. I quickly put together that this event was for her father.

I stopped when I had joined his group. There were four

men, all peering at me with interest and surprise. Keeping my eyes on Elliot, I smiled widely and said, "Lord Elliot. I'm so sorry for intruding on your conversation, but I just had to meet you."

My smile widened when Lord Elliot grasped my hand and brought it to his lips. "Not at all, Mrs.—"

I lifted my left hand so he could see my unadorned wedding ring finger. "It's Ms. And please, call me Barrett. Gentlemen," I said briefly, turning my attention from Lord Elliot to his friends, "Do you mind terribly if I steal his attention for a moment?"

Lord Elliot's companions gave their approval, and later, when they were all having a drink and smoke together in the library, they would no doubt talk about me in lewd and ribald terms.

When Lord Elliot and I were alone, I said, "You must be the greatest father ever, giving your daughter a party as lavish as this."

He chuckled. "I'm glad you think so. Though Jane's excitement doesn't match yours."

"Where is the lady of honor? I'd love to meet her."

"You don't know Jane? You're not a friend of hers?" He frowned in confusion.

I pretended to look abashed. "Ah, no. Look, I know this is going to sound really strange, but I really wanted to meet you."

"Me? Why?"

"Because I read about you," I blurted out, pretending to be a wide-eyed innocent. "You loaned your painting of Napoleon to the Frick last year, and I never got to see it. It's one of my biggest regrets in life. I'm a friend of Lord Arlington's daughter, Elizabeth, and I begged him to bring me tonight so I could meet you. I now demand that you show me the painting!"

Lord Elliot chuckled, his gaze appreciative as it skimmed over me. "My, my, you are a bold one."

"Forgive me for that. I'm a New Yorker. I come by it honestly."

His laugh was booming and nearly deafening. "You are intriguing, my dear. I'd love to learn more about you." His hand tightened ever so slightly on mine.

I flashed him a demure, yet just seductive enough smile. "I'd love to tell you more. Perhaps in a more private setting."

Lord Elliot's eyelids lowered in lust. I tossed my hair over my shoulder and before Lord Elliot could reply, Lord Arlington strolled toward us to rescue me. I had to tantalize Lord Elliot enough to leave him wanting more.

"Arlington, good to see you," Lord Elliot said, attempting to mask his displeasure at being thwarted.

Lord Arlington smiled. "Ah, I see you met my charming companion."

"She and I were just discussing her friendship with your lovely daughter," Elliot remarked. "How is Elizabeth?"

The two men exchanged pleasantries about their families. As they continued to speak, Lord Elliot's thin wife joined us. She looked as bitter as her husband looked approachable. They were as mismatched as any two people could be.

"This party is your creation," I said to Lady Elliot. "Isn't it?"

A reluctant smile flitted across Lady Elliot's stoic face. "Yes. I love event planning."

"Well, it shows," I said. "It's just beautiful."

Lord Arlington and I excused ourselves from the conversation since other guests were seeking Lord and Lady Elliot out. I made sure to lock eyes with Lord Elliot. He inclined his head ever so slightly. I dropped my gaze and bit my lip.

"Well?" Lord Arlington asked as we turned away.

"Hook, line, and sinker," I said with a triumphant grin.

## Chapter 10

My breasts ached, and I felt them straining against the confines of my bra. I instinctively thought of Hawk, at home, taking his meal from a bottle. I felt like a rotten mother.

Biology was a bitch.

Shoving away thoughts of my child, I focused. Lord Elliot and I had been exchanging stolen glances all evening across the room, and it was time to reel him in. It was almost ten o'clock, and I had to get him into his study.

I conversed with Lord Arlington while holding a glass of champagne I wasn't drinking. I lifted the glass to my lips and said behind the flute, "Okay, he's looking over at me. Excuse yourself to go find the restroom."

"It's too bad you're American," Lord Arlington said. "I think you would've had a great career as a British Secret Service agent."

I mockingly raised an eyebrow and took a small sip of champagne while I watched Lord Arlington depart. The champagne was crisp and tart, and I didn't like the taste at all. I handed the flute off to a passing waiter. My nerves twitched.

"Champagne isn't your drink of choice?" Lord Elliot asked as he came to my side.

"A little weak," I said with a grin.

"I know where you can get something stronger," he said.

"Oh?"

"My study. Where I keep the Napoleon painting." He lowered his eyes to my mouth.

"I'd like a real drink," I whispered huskily.

He gave me directions to find the study, but I already knew where it was. Flynn and I had memorized the layout of Elliot's house. Just in case.

"I'll join you in five minutes," Elliot said, his mouth close to my ear, his breath grazing my skin.

"Can't wait," I lied breathlessly.

Leaving the main room, I quickly found my way to the study. I had my clutch with me so Flynn and I could make a quick escape. Lord Elliot's study was steadfastly English with leather chesterfields, heavy furniture that could only be lifted by burly men. Dark drapes were currently pulled back to reveal the manicured lawns on the side of the townhouse. The Napoleon painting took up an entire wall from floor to ceiling. It truly was a work of art.

The door opened, but I didn't turn.

"Like it?" Lord Elliot asked.

"It's beautiful."

He trailed a finger down my arm. "Yes, it is. Can I get you a drink?" he asked, heading to the liquor cart.

"Scotch. Neat, please."

He peered at me with interest. "Should've known you were a scotch drinker."

"Why is that?" I asked.

"Just fits with your personality. You know what you want and you go after it."

"Do you, Lord Elliot? Go after what you want?"

His brown eyes dilated with lust. "Yes, I do." He poured two glasses of scotch and brought one to me. He clinked our glasses together.

"Cheers," he said.

My clutch vibrated. "Excuse me just a second," I said. "I need to check my phone."

It was a text from Flynn telling me he was delayed, and I needed to stall. *Fantastic*. Shoving the phone back inside my clutch, I gave Lord Elliot a sheepish smile. "Sorry."

"Everything all right?" Elliot inquired politely.

"Oh, fine. I hate that I am so tethered to this thing. I wish we didn't need them, you know?"

He nodded. "Technology comes with a certain set of problems."

"People expect you to be available at all hours. Your time isn't your own."

"So get rid of it."

"Can't do that. Wish I could, but I can't."

Elliot nodded thoughtfully. He set his glass down and peered at me. "Should we stop this feigned flirting?"

"Feigned?" I asked with sham innocence.

"Let's get right to the matter."

I frowned in genuine confusion. "Matter? What matter?"

He smiled, and for the first time it wasn't a jovial, absent pull of his lips. It was knowing and cunning. "Tell me, Mrs. Campbell, why you're really here."

~

Elliot knew my name. My married name. How?

What the hell could I say? Flynn and I had been operating under the assumption that Elliot had no idea about my true identity. That theory was shot to shit. Obviously.

I forced myself to stay calm and gave a sultry smile despite my racing heart. "I told you I wanted to see the Napoleon painting." I gestured to the work of art featuring one of history's most legendary leaders. How would Napoleon get out of this scrape? Probably blow Elliot's head off and call it a day.

But we needed information from Elliot—and I didn't have a weapon, anyway.

"Your flirtation is grating on me," he said. Leaning over, he lifted up his pant leg and pulled out a pistol strapped to his calf. He looked at me. "Should we try that question again?"

My heartbeat escalated, thumping loudly in my ears. I could only hope to brazen my way through this to stall for time. I just hoped Flynn was close.

"The Scottish Independence Referendum," I said.

"What about it?" Elliot asked, his hand still on his weapon.

"I want to know why you don't support it and how far you'd go to ensure it doesn't pass."

"I don't care about it one way or the other," Elliot admitted.

"No?" I asked, raising my eyebrows in disbelief. "But you were in your club talking about how much you stood to lose if Scotland gained its independence."

Elliot bared his teeth in nothing resembling a smile. "Have it all figured out, do you?"

I shrugged. "I know what I know."

"You know nothing."

"Jon Snow."

"What?"

"The line is 'You know nothing, Jon Snow.'"

He leaned back in his chair, appearing casual and unconcerned. "You have but a small piece of the puzzle, Mrs. Campbell. What I can't understand is why a woman like you would choose to marry a man like Flynn Campbell."

"You think you know me, Lord Elliot?"

"You think you know me," he pointed out. "I don't think you care one way or the other if Scotland gains its independence. This isn't your cause."

"Why? Because I'm American?"

"Because it's not your cause," he repeated. "This is your

husband's cause. You'll see a lot of violence if you stay with him. So will your children. Or child, as it were. How is Hawk?"

I swallowed. He knew about Hawk? What the hell else did he know? And why did I feel like I'd been the one to walk into a trap? The conversation was getting away from me. Lord Elliot wasn't what he appeared to be. But neither was I.

"Hawk," I said, not at all having to pretend to be worried. "His safety is my biggest concern."

"As it should be."

I shook my head and looked at him, feigning fear. "I don't want this to be my life. I don't want this to be my son's life."

Elliot lifted himself out of the chair and sauntered toward me, holding onto his gun. The only weapon I had was making Elliot think I needed help protecting my son. Men were strangely taken in by the damsel in distress.

Elliot stopped in front of me, the pistol still in his hand, but it was down by his side. Though he projected lazy intent, I didn't believe it. He was coiled, ready. I'd mistaken him. So had the others. And shit could get bad. Quick.

"You don't have to do this, you know," he said, reaching out a finger to slide it up and down the bare skin of my arm.

"Do what?" I asked, my flesh rising in goosebumps, feeling like insects were crawling beneath my skin.

"You don't have to worry about your son's future cut short because of your husband's cause."

"How do I not worry about that?"

"I can promise you protection. If you aid us."

"Who is 'us'?" I demanded.

Elliot smiled as he continued to glide his fingers across my skin. He grasped my arm and hauled me to him. I had to press my hands to his chest so my head wouldn't slam into his chin. Elliot enfolded me in an embrace to keep me from moving away. He was a lot stronger than I'd given him credit for.

My hands trailed up his suit-clad arms to lock around the back of his neck. I peered up at him through the sweep of my lashes and bit my lower lip. "You know," I began. "If you drop your weapon, you can wrap both of your arms around me."

With his arm caging me, he still managed to set the gun down on the end table by the couch, and then splayed his free hand across my lower back.

"Well?" Elliot asked, lowering his head ever so slightly.

"Well, what?" I asked.

"Are you willing to help us?"

"You haven't told me who the 'us' is," I reminded him.

I heard a pistol cock and turned my head. Flynn stood in the doorway, his blue eyes fierce and steady. He was staring at Lord Elliot, his jaw clenched.

"Mind letting go of my wife?"

## Chapter 11

Lord Elliot's arms dropped from around me, and I took a slow step back toward the end table. I picked up Lord Elliot's gun and removed the clip before setting it aside again. I'd learned how to handle pistols after what I'd been through with Dolinsky.

"Great timing, love," I stated. "He was just trying to recruit me."

Flynn raised an eyebrow. "Looked like he was doing a lot more than that."

"Yes, well, men are easily distracted by breasts," I said.

Amusement lurked in Flynn's eyes. "Recruitment, eh? For whom?"

"He hasn't said."

We kept our focus on Lord Elliot. There wasn't a lot of time, and there was a party going on with guests who would surely notice their host's absence. Not to mention an angry wife. If she came looking for him, she would just make all this worse.

Flynn gestured with the gun for Elliot to sit down. "Sit," Flynn commanded.

Elliot sat on the couch. His posture remained upright, and his face was alert, but there was no fear.

"Sorry I'm late," Flynn said to me. "Something came up."

"Usually does," I murmured.

"Can we get on with this?" Elliot asked.

Flynn raised his eyebrows at me. "He's in a hurry."

"He's got a party to get back to," I reminded him.

Flynn nodded. "Right." He strolled over to Elliot's liquor cart. "Nice collection."

"Want my scotch?" I asked conversationally. "I didn't finish it."

"I would," Flynn said.

I picked up the glass of scotch on the end table and brought it to him. He swallowed it in a few sips and then set the glass aside. "Scotch mellows him," I told Elliot. "Or does it make him in a fighting mood? I can never remember."

Flynn pulled up a chair in front of Elliot and took a seat. For a moment he just stared at the other man as he fingered his gun.

Elliot didn't squirm.

"Who do you work for?" Flynn asked.

Elliot remained silent.

"Did you have Malcolm Buchanan killed?"

Still, Elliot said nothing.

"He's got no incentive to talk," I remarked.

"You won't kill me," Elliot predicted. "Not in my house. Not when there's a party going on. Too many witnesses if things go wrong for you."

Flynn rose and took a step forward. He pressed the barrel of it to Elliot's forehead and grinned, but it wasn't friendly.

"Your daughter Jane is with one of my men. All I have to do is give him a call and—you know what? Hold on a second." With his free hand, he reached into his pocket and pulled out his cell phone. He pressed a button and held it to his ear.

"Put her on," Flynn said. "Jane? Someone wants to say hello." He pressed another button, and the phone went to speaker.

"Hello?" came a young woman's terrified voice.

"Jane? Jane, are you all right?" Elliot asked in a rush, his composure suddenly shaken.

"Dad, I'm—"

Flynn hung up on her mid-sentence and then looked back at Elliot. "Now you know I'm fucking serious about answers."

I swallowed a lump of bile in my throat. Using a man's child against him was low. But a good father would do anything to protect his daughter.

"All right," Elliot said, resigned. He looked exhausted. "I'll tell you whatever it is you want to know. Just don't hurt her. Please."

"Did you have Malcolm Buchanan killed?"

Elliot paused briefly. Flynn lifted the butt of the gun and bashed Elliot across the forehead. Elliot let out a moan, his hand flying to his bloody head.

"Fuck," Elliot muttered.

"Answer me."

"Yes, I had him killed."

Flynn's eyes went flat. "Three men were sent. Who are they?"

"Italian mercenaries. The White Company."

Flynn and I exchanged a glance, but I shook my head. I'd never heard of them. Then again, my educational background was Scottish history, not Italian.

"The White Company," Flynn repeated. "Why did you hire Italians?"

"Those were my orders."

"Orders?" Flynn asked. "Whom do you receive your orders from?"

"The Bureau."

"The Secret Service Bureau?" Flynn asked.

Elliot shook his head and looked at me when he said, "No. The FBI. I work for the Americans."

∼

The FBI? We were dealing with the FBI? We'd already *dealt* with the FBI last year.

We hadn't been prepared for Lord Elliot's statement. I had thought this was the British Government, Parliament, or other Scottish factions. Domestic, Flynn had said.

This was something else, and we still didn't know enough. What the hell was The White Company?

Flynn looked at me. I nodded. Flynn lowered the gun and put it away. Elliot's shoulders sagged, just a bit. Flynn took out his cell and made a call.

"Change of plans," Flynn said to the person on the end of the phone. "Meet us at the car. Bring Jane." He hung up.

"What? What are you doing?" Elliot demanded.

"Get up," Flynn commanded. When Elliot made no move to rise, Flynn went to him and yanked him up and shoved him toward the window. I was one step ahead of him and had already unlocked the window and pushed the two separate panes outward.

I turned quickly, one of my heels catching on the edge of the carpet. Stumbling, I gripped the edge of the large oak desk to keep myself from tumbling to the ground.

"Barrett? You okay?" Flynn asked.

"Yeah," I grumbled, straightening my spine. Women's dress clothes and heels did not aid in stealth. Flynn tossed me my clutch. I caught it and then threw it out the window before climbing down first. From my vantage point on the ground, I watched Flynn push Elliot toward the window.

Elliot put his hands on the windowsill, his face masked in resignation. Flynn turned his head toward the door of the library. "Hurry up," he stated, giving Elliot a shove.

The man fell through the window to the ground. He moaned.

Flynn nimbly hopped through the window like a Scottish James Bond. I looked at him in disgust.

He threw me a cocky grin before reaching down and hauling Elliot up by the collar of his shirt. Elliot's face was pale, and a bead of sweat dripped down his temple despite the chilly temperature. He cradled his left wrist to his chest, but kept his mouth shut. He knew better than to complain.

We quietly kept to the side of the townhouse, single file, Elliot sandwiched between us. I went first to keep an eye out, and Flynn was at Elliot's back so there was less chance of him attempting to flee, but that wouldn't have been a wise choice. We had the man's daughter, and Elliot was sporting an injury. It was no surprise that he was docile.

I didn't breathe an internal sigh of relief until we were a few blocks from Elliot's townhouse and turning down a side street where a black town car with tinted windows waited for us.

My lips parted in surprise when I saw who was leaning against the trunk, smoking a cigarette. "What are you doing here?" I demanded, shooting a look between Ramsey and Flynn.

"Boredom breeds trouble," Flynn explained.

Ramsey stomped out his cigarette and looked at Elliot who stood between us. "Zip ties are in the trunk." Flynn grasped Elliot by his neck and dragged him closer to Ramsey.

"Where's my daughter," Elliot demanded.

"Ballsy bastard," Ramsey claimed, opening the trunk.

Flynn shrugged.

"In the back seat," Ramsey answered with a feral grin. "Bound and gagged."

Elliot's face flushed.

Ramsey tied a piece of plaid over Elliot's mouth and then zip-tied his legs. When Ramsey took Elliot's injured wrist in his hands, the man screamed against the cloth in his mouth. His eyes rolled to the back of his head, and he passed out.

"Guess he broke his wrist when he fell out of his library window," Flynn said smoothly.

"Shame," Ramsey answered drolly. They managed to get an unconscious, bound Elliot into the trunk and shut it.

"It's a long drive to Dornoch. This should be fun," Ramsey said with another grin, heading to the door of the back seat.

"Aren't you going to drive?" I asked.

He shook his head. "Angus is driving. I get to sit next to our very gorgeous, very confused hostage."

Ramsey saluted and then opened the door. I saw a woman's zip-tied legs shoot out, trying to nail Ramsey in the groin with her high-heeled feet. Ramsey laughed and shook his head. "That's no way to greet me, darling." He climbed inside and shut the door.

"She's going to fall in love with him, isn't she?" I asked Flynn.

Flynn looked down at me and grinned. "It's a good possibility. They have a decent drive ahead of them and Ramsey is going to charm the hell out of her."

"I believe it."

Flynn shook his head, and he pulled out his cell phone. Pressing a button, he then put it to his ear. "Keep it in your pants," Flynn commanded before hanging up.

"Will that stop Ramsey?" I asked with a chuckle.

"Doubt it."

The town car's engine started, and Flynn and I moved out of the way. "He's not going to hurt her, is he?" I asked. "I know he's upset about Duncan and Malcolm, but—"

"No. He'll save his rage for Elliot," Flynn said, grasping my hand.

"What's going to happen now?" I asked. "We're carting

him and his daughter back to Scotland. That wasn't part of the plan."

"Plans change. We didn't know what we would find when he got a hold of him. We have to question him."

"Yeah, I don't want those details of how you question him," I stated.

Flynn inclined his head. "After we get what we need, Ramsey, Duncan, and I will figure out how to deal with him."

"And his daughter?"

"Don't know yet. That's still uncertain."

"We can't kill her," I said. "It's not her fault her father is working for the FBI, and we used her to get him to talk."

"Let's not have this conversation in an alley."

"Promise me, Flynn. Promise me we'll find a different way."

Flynn looked up at the sky when he said, "I can't make you that promise, Barrett. Believe me, I want to. But the SINS—"

"Yeah. They come first. I know."

Jane Elliot wasn't going to die. Not because of her paternity. I'd see to that. Flynn just didn't know it yet.

"We have bigger issues at the moment," Flynn said, taking my hand and tugging me out of the alley.

"Like finding a cab to take us to our private plane?" I asked.

"Not to mention the FBI."

"Hmmm. Do you have any idea what the hell The White Company is?"

"Add it to the list of shite we have to figure out," Flynn said, his eyes bleak.

## Chapter 12

"Stop staring," I said.

"I can't, they're huge."

"I'm aware. Drink your scotch," I commanded.

My hands gripped the seat rest while Flynn sat next to me, all but leering at my breasts.

"Distract me," I demanded. Usually I only had a problem during takeoff and landing, but tonight, we were flying through a rainstorm. Though our private plane was luxurious and comfortable, it wasn't a 747. It was easy to focus on every jerk and engine whirl.

"We'll be seeing our son in about an hour."

Closing my eyes, I smiled. "I'm not leaving him for the next three months and you can't make me."

"Barrett," Flynn said. "Will you open your eyes and look at me?"

Reluctantly, I did as he asked and turned my head to peer at him. His face was soft, his gaze earnest. "Thank you," he said. "Thank you so much for this."

"You're welcome."

The plane lurched, and I let out a shriek. Flynn wrapped an arm around me, and I snuggled into his embrace. "It's just a bit of rain," he said, trying to soothe me. "Nothing the plane can't handle. Unclench, love."

I relaxed just a little and said, "I didn't think I'd be able to do it. Leave Hawk."

"I know. You're incredible. Do you know that?"

Letting out a breath, I finally released my grip on my seat as we continued to soar home toward our son. We had the man responsible for Malcolm's death—we'd succeeded in what we set out to do. But now we had to unravel a bigger mystery. Why was the FBI still concerned about the SINS? How had they gotten a member of the House of Lords to aid them? What in the hell was The White Company? So many questions, not enough answers.

My breasts ached and I was exhausted. "I'm going to take a nap, okay?" Flynn's arm tightened around me, and I fell into a light doze.

I was jarred awake by the plane dropping a few feet. Shooting up in my seat, my seat belt kept me anchored. The overhead lights flickered and then went out. The plane dipped to one side as a flash of lightning lit the interior of the cabin.

"Flynn—"

"It's all right, hen."

"The emergency lights aren't coming on," I said in a near panic, my heart jumping into my throat.

"Look at me," Flynn commanded.

I could barely make his face out in the darkness. Another flash of lightning, a tilt of the plane, and I screamed.

Flynn's hands reached out to grasp my face. "Listen to me!" he barked.

I whimpered in fear but forced myself to take a breath. The plane continued to shake; the interior lights winked on for a second and then went off again.

"It's just a little storm," Flynn said. "Charles was in the air force, okay? He knows how to fly in weather like this. Did you hear me, Barrett?"

I managed to nod even as Flynn continued to cradle my head. The lights came on, and I let out a laugh of relief.

"See? Told you. Nothing to worry about."

And then the plane went into a nosedive.

∽

The pilot landed the plane in the middle of the Highlands on a stretch of land that was unusually flat. Rain continued to assault the windows, but the lightning seemed to have stopped. The emergency lights flashed on and off. I felt the pulsing of my rapid heartbeat in my neck as I tried to control my breathing.

The more I attempted to breathe deeply, the harder it became, and I grew lightheaded. Panic swelled inside me, surging up my throat. I scrambled to unlatch my seat belt, needing to get outside.

Hands reached out to stop my movements, and it only made me renew my struggle. "I'm going to vomit," I shouted. "Let me go!"

"No," came Flynn's voice. Calm. "You're not going to vomit."

Terror and bile clawed at my throat. I shook my head, one of my hands moving to cover my mouth.

"Barrett," Flynn said, his hands squeezing my arms. "You're okay. We're okay."

I fought him, but Flynn held on.

"We're okay," he repeated, hauling me toward him to force me against his chest. He crooned Gaelic words into my hair, stroking my back, soothing my terror.

"You're okay," he said one last time.

I pulled away, wiping the tears off of my face. The urge to vomit had passed. I heard the door to the cockpit open and the sound of Charles coming toward us.

"Radio's busted. I can't get a signal," Charles said.

The low lighting illuminated the pilot, painting him in yellow light. He looked unperturbed, like he hadn't just had to make an emergency landing in a rainstorm.

"Cell phone?" Flynn asked.

Charles shook his head. "No service out here. We're close to Ardross."

"So it could be a lot worse," Flynn said, squeezing my hand. "Good."

"I'm sorry. I have no idea where Ardross is," I said, still dazed.

"About thirty miles north of Inverness," Charles explained. "We'll be able to walk to Ardross from here. It's just a few miles."

I jumped out of my seat. "Let's go. Let's go *now*."

"Barrett," Flynn began. "We can't go now."

"Yes, we can. We have to—I have to get back to Hawk tonight!"

"Hen," Flynn said softly. "It's dark. There's a storm. And you're in heels. We'll just get hurt. We'll wait until tomorrow and then when it's light out, we'll head to Ardross."

"But, Mrs. Keith—"

"She's not going to leave Hawk, love. She's well familiar with the SINS. She won't worry if we don't call tonight. She'll stay with Hawk, and we'll see them tomorrow." Flynn looked away from me to glance at Charles.

"Charles will stay up here, and we'll sleep in the back."

I numbly let Flynn lead me to the rear of the plane to the private sleeping cabin. Exhausted now that the adrenaline had fled and we were safe, I kicked off my heels and perched on the bed. Flynn went to the dresser and pulled out pajamas for me.

I removed my tight dress and thick bra. I hissed when I tugged the T-shirt over my aching breasts, the fabric grazing my sensitive nipples.

"What is it?" Flynn asked.

"Biology."

~

*The hands around my neck tighten, squeezing the life out of me. Spots dance before my eyes.*

*"Please," I choke out. "Let me live."*

*"You have to die," Vlad states, his Russian accent brutal and thick.*

*"No," I whisper, struggling to breathe, struggling to live.*

*There's a moment, right before death, when you give up, when you want to embrace it. Pain drops away and there's only calm.*

*My hands fall from the wrists holding me down and crushing my windpipe. I smile into the darkness coming for me.*

*Suddenly the fingers around my neck are gone. I gulp a breath of air; it's never been richer. Blood rushes to my head, and so does anger.*

*A violent wave surges within me—swallowing me and anything good I used to be.*

*I want to be savage. I want to destroy. I want to take a life.*

*A gun appears in my hand. Lifting it, I aim for Vlad's chest.*

*He starts to laugh like a drunken, maniacal clown.*

*"You won't," he predicts. "You are too soft. You are not part of this life."*

*"I could be," I reply.*

*"If you pull that trigger, there's no going back. Are you going to become the thing you despise?"*

*I pull the trigger, feeling like I've been shot myself, but it's Vlad who bleeds out in front of me.*

*I walk toward him as the light drains from his eyes. Leaning down, I whisper, "I won't apologize for surviving."*

~

I awoke with a start, momentarily confused about where I was.

*Plane. Crash. Hawk.*

Rolling over, I nudged Flynn awake. He was asleep on his back, mouth just the tiniest big agape. He closed it as he came to.

My stomach rumbled, and I was in desperate need of a cup of coffee and a shower, but I had one mindless thought and that was to get back to my child. I scooted out of bed and reached for my dress, hating the idea of squeezing myself back into restrictive and tight clothing.

"Hen?" Flynn asked, running a hand across his face.

I pulled back the curtain of the window to reveal watery sunlight and gray clouds. "It's light out, Flynn. We have to go."

When Flynn made no move to rise, I snapped, "I love you, but if you don't get your ass up, I'm going to kill you."

Flynn's lips quirked into a smile of amusement, but damn if he didn't sit up. "Charles left for Ardross a few hours ago, hen. He's probably already there and making arrangements. He should be back soon."

"What? What are you—"

He looked at me in confusion. "Did you really think I was going to let you trek across the Highlands in high heels? It rained last night. You'd be slipping in mud, cold, and miserable. You would've broken an ankle out there."

I let out a sigh and flashed him a relieved smile. "You really do love me."

"I really do. Don't put that dress back on. Stay in your pajamas. It will be more comfortable for the drive ahead of us, anyway.

Nodding, I said, "I'll go find us some bottled water. Please tell me there's a box of granola bars around here."

"Should be." Flynn threw his legs over the side of the bed and reached for his suit trousers.

"I could really get used to this kind of luxury," I said as I opened the door to the private cabin.

"You still haven't gotten used to this, have you?" he said.

It was chilly in the plane, so I grabbed one of Flynn's sweaters and a pair of thick socks. I'd be in a heated car in no time at all, and I nearly sighed in pleasure when I thought about it.

"No, I haven't," I admitted.

"We live in a castle," he reminded me. "We have a private plane."

I looked at him and grinned. "A little over a year ago, I was living in a prewar studio on York and most of my clothes came from H & M. That doesn't just go away because we have a castle and a private plane."

Opening a cabinet, I pulled out two bottles of water and a box of granola bars. I tore one open and took a bite before handing it to Flynn. We ate in silence for a few minutes and sipped our water, each of us lost in our own thoughts.

"Do you miss New York?" he asked suddenly.

"It's complicated," I said.

"How so?"

I shrugged. "I don't miss the city per se. I miss takeout whenever I want it. I miss the culture, I guess. I miss the apartment we never got to live in. But I…"

"What?"

"I met you there," I said with a wavering smile. "And that's incredible, but it's also the place where I was kidnapped."

Flynn's steely gaze didn't leave my face. Jaw clenched, his nostrils flared in anger. He hated being reminded of the time he hadn't been able to protect me—and being reminded that his life had changed mine, making it dangerous to love him.

I reached out to touch his cheek. "I'm glad we live here. I love it."

"It's so dark and gloomy here," he muttered.

"Well, you Scots make good scotch. I think it gets you through the three hundred and twenty days of rain," I teased. "I love that Hawk is going to grow up here. I don't have any family, I don't have a village or a clan."

"You have me. You have the SINS."

I nodded. "I know. Even though I'm American, I feel Scottish. I feel it here, Flynn." My hand touched my chest over my heart.

He let out a breath and looked relieved. "Sometimes I just feel like I'm dragging you behind me, hoping you'll still be there when I look over my shoulder."

"I'm right where I want to be."

Flynn took my hand and brought it to his lips. "Let's go home."

## Chapter 13

An hour later Charles returned in a black SUV that easily navigated over rough, muddy terrain where most of the roads had been washed away. He didn't look worse for wear despite the fact that he'd walked to Ardross. I was starting to think he was more than just a pilot.

He was a Scottish Crocodile Dundee.

"Thank you!" I said, wrapping the man in my arms and kissing his cheek. "Whatever we're paying you, I'm doubling it."

Charles raised an eyebrow and glanced at Flynn. I looked back at Flynn who shrugged.

"It took me longer than I expected," Charles explained. "I had to make a few calls. Mechanics are on their way to see to the plane."

I scrambled toward the car. My heels sank into the mud, and when I tried to lift a foot, there was an audible suction noise, and my heel was gone—lost forever in the muck.

"Help!" I called to Flynn.

Flynn strode toward me and scooped me up into his arms. We managed to get the back door of the SUV open, and he stuck me inside. Charles climbed into the driver's seat, and

Flynn took his place in the passenger side. As we drove away, I saw the plane through the car window. Thank God for Charles.

I was silent while Flynn plugged in his dead cell phone. After a little juice, it beeped with the many missed messages and voicemails. Pressing a button, he turned in his seat to look at me. He smiled.

"Ramsey is back in Dornoch. Jane is giving him a hard time."

I chuckled. "I bet she is."

Flynn shook his head and then frowned as the next message played, but then his face smoothed out, and he smiled. He hung up.

"What was that about?" I asked.

"Mrs. Keith, wanting to let us know that Hawk went down easy and that she wouldn't leave the house until we got home. She also told me to tell you not to worry."

"Really? Or is that you telling me not to worry?"

He held out his phone. "You can listen to the message if you want."

I let out a sigh of relief but shook my head. "How long is the drive to Dornoch?"

"Forty-five minutes to two hours," Charles answered.

"How's that now?"

I caught sight of Flynn's smile before he turned back around to face the front.

"It means," Charles said, "that it will take forty-five minutes if we don't run into any road obstructions."

"He means Highland coos," Flynn said, his brogue thick.

"Coos?"

"Those hairy, shaggy brown beasts that don't budge no matter how much you yell at them."

I laughed. "Cows. You mean Highland cows."

"Aye," Flynn said. "We're going to stop in Inverness for a

minute. I need a to-go cup of coffee and a breakfast sandwich."

"I could go for that, too," I admitted. I was exhausted, having slept badly, waking every hour, feeling like something was missing. It was amazing how quickly I'd adjusted to having Hawk. I knew his habits, and I was beginning to know *him*. And yeah, he wasn't even a month old, so how could he already be turning into his own person? But he had a personality, and knowing his paternity, I wasn't surprised that Hawk was a greedy, demanding little bugger. Then again, weren't all newborns?

After we briefly stopped in Inverness for our food and coffee, we were back in the car. Flynn got on the phone and started making calls, dictating orders. I tuned it all out and closed my eyes as I continued to think about my son. He was as bald as a cue ball. It made me smile. When his hair grew in, would it be black like Flynn's? Auburn like mine? Or something else entirely? Was it cliché to hope he looked just like Flynn?

I tried not to think too far into the future or I would worry constantly. It wasn't enough that I'd chosen this life when I decided to stay with Flynn, but knowingly bringing a child into the world to grow up among the SINS? I had to be some kind of crazy. Parents were supposed to protect their children, not put them in harm's way.

Opening my eyes, I stared out the window, realizing we'd come to a stop. "We're not home," I stated.

"No," Flynn said with a sigh. "We're about twenty minutes out."

"Why have we stopped? Don't tell me? Coos?" I asked with a look around.

"No. Highland sheep," Charles said.

"For the love of God!" I muttered, sitting up straighter so I could see out the front windshield. A herd of Scottish Blackface sheep *baaed* as they ran across the road. An older man in a burgundy wool sweater, boots, and a green felt hat, trailed behind.

"A sheepherder," I murmured in stupid amazement. "A real honest to God sheepherder."

"My wife is from New York," Flynn explained to Charles who only nodded.

"Oh, be quiet," I said, unlatching my seat belt and opening the door.

The day was chilly, and my bare feet were cold as I walked across the pavement toward the older man. "Pardon me," I called out to him over the sound of the sheep hooves on the ground.

The man looked at me and raised his white eyebrows in question. "Aye?"

"I know this is going to sound really strange, but may I pet one?"

"They're not pets, lass," said the old man in a rough voice.

The car door opened and I turned to see Flynn get out. He moved to stand next to the hood.

"Sorry, Mr. Campbell," the man stuttered, "I didn't realize that you were with—that she—"

"My wife," Flynn said softly.

"Mrs. Campbell," the man said, his tone suddenly deferential. "I'd be honored if you'd—"

"What's your name?" I asked him.

"Barnabas Stuart."

"Barnabas, may I pet one of your sheep?"

He nodded quickly as I leaned down to pet the closest one to me. Out of the corner of my eye, I saw Barnabas trying to shoo his sheep off the road. It was totally ridiculous, and I couldn't believe I'd gotten out of the car. But if I learned anything while living in Scotland, it was that everything happened at a slower pace, and you just had to go with it.

While I was busy stroking the slightly dirty fleece of an

ewe, Barnabas managed to get the rest of his flock off the path.

"Barrett," Flynn called.

"Coming," I said. With a smile at Barnabas, I thanked him. The craggy old man managed to grin, and for a moment, I was reminded of Malcolm. The ache of grief caught me low in my stomach.

Just as I was about to close the door to the car, Barnabas ambled over. In his arms, he held a young lamb. He set it on my lap.

"I'd be honored if you'd have her," Barnabas said.

"Oh, but—"

"Thank you," Flynn interjected before I could give the lamb back.

Barnabas nodded and then closed the door for me. I looked down at my lap and stared into the brown eyes of the lamb.

"What the hell just happened?" I asked when Charles had started the car and we began our drive home again.

"He was worried that he'd offended me by initially refusing you when you wanted to pet his sheep," Flynn explained. "This was his way of making amends."

"That's all well and good," I said, stroking the fleece of the lamb on my lap. "But what the hell do I know about keeping livestock."

Charles and Flynn laughed. "We can find a use for him," Flynn said.

"It's a her," I reminded him.

"Whatever you do, don't name it," Charles warned.

"Why?" I asked.

He looked at me in the rearview mirror. "You'll get attached."

It took me a second to realize what he was implying. I covered the lamb's ears and said, "We're not eating her."

Flynn turned in his seat and shook his head. "Attached already, hmmm?"

I pointed to the lamb. "Have you seen this face? It's adorable!"

"You love lamb," Flynn pointed out, turning back around to face the front.

"Shut up," I pleaded, stroking the lamb's soft ears. She made a little noise and tried scooting closer. "We need to build a barn."

"For our one sheep?" Flynn asked.

"Her name is Betty."

"Oh lord," Flynn muttered.

"I heard that! And so did Betty!"

## Chapter 14

A hand touched my knee. I opened my eyes. Flynn had turned around in his seat, his cobalt gaze intense.

"Love, we're almost home."

I sat up from my slouched position; Betty curled up on my lap, and looked out the window. I'd somehow fallen asleep again, but it had been surprisingly easy. The warm body of Betty had felt like Hawk in my arms and lulled me into peace.

We drove through town. Some of the shops were open, but a lot remained closed. Store hours were subjective in the Highlands. We passed Dornoch Cathedral where we'd buried Malcolm. A welling of tears prickled my eyes. I felt like we hadn't had any real time to grieve for him. But knowing Malcolm, he wouldn't want us to waste energy on mourning —he'd want us to be strong, to fight back, fight for our cause, and destroy those that stood in our way.

I'd shoved thoughts of Elliot out of my head, but it all came screaming back. What were we going to do about him? How deep did this go? How long had Elliot been working with the FBI? And why? Did the FBI have something on Elliot, or did Elliot stand to lose a lot if the SINS succeeded?

Round and round the questions went, but I tried to cram

them into a box. I didn't have the answers, and I wasn't going to get them in the back of an SUV. I buried my face in Betty's neck, breathing in the smell of her fleece. I felt a tentative tongue on my cheek and smiled. Who needed a dog when you had a lamb?

We quickly left the town behind and drove deeper into beautiful green hills. The wild beauty of Dornoch still made me catch my breath. I wondered if I'd ever get tired of seeing it. As we got closer to home, the worry in my stomach eased. I would soon be reunited with my child, and my world would be right again. A surge of hormones flooded me, and my arms ached to hold Hawk. I settled for lavishing love on Betty, who hadn't moved since she'd been set onto my lap. I snorted.

"You all right, love?" Flynn asked.

"Fine. Where's Betty going to sleep?" I asked.

"We'll make her a pallet on the back porch."

"It's cold out there."

"Barrett—"

"Would *you* want to sleep out on the porch?" I demanded.

"I'm house trained," Flynn shot back.

"Is it always like this?" Charles asked.

"Ah—"

"Don't answer that, Flynn. I'd like to see either of you carry a baby in your body for nine months, squeeze it out of you, and then feel like you're back to normal."

"Fair enough," Charles relented. "I think Betty should sleep in the living room next to the fireplace."

"You're getting a really big Christmas bonus," I said to him. I watched Flynn shake his head, but at least he was silent.

I knew I sounded like a lunatic, but I couldn't help it. As Charles turned up the windy road to the castle, I bounced in my seat like a kid. Charles barely had the chance to park before I lifted Betty off my lap and set her on the seat. Unlatching my seat belt, I flung open the door. My bare feet hit the walkway as I dug through my clutch. Finding my keys,

I was inside the foyer before Flynn was even out of the car. Then again, I'd left him to deal with Betty.

"Mrs. Keith!" I called out, heading toward the kitchen so I could wash my hands. I hit the kitchen light and went to the sink. I lathered up.

I heard the front door open and Flynn's faraway footsteps until they drew closer. I turned my head as I rinsed my hands. Flynn stood holding the lamb under one arm like a football. He shook his head, but his face was resigned.

"Until she gets a bath, she sleeps on the porch," he said.

"That's fair."

Flynn moved through the kitchen to the back of the castle, muttering under his breath in Gaelic. I smiled to myself. After drying my hands on the dishtowel that hung on the refrigerator, I called out again for Mrs. Keith, but there still wasn't an answer.

Grabbing onto the staircase railing, I used it to help me run up the stairs. By the time I got to the top, I was out of breath, and my heart was pounding with anxiety. Something wasn't right. The house felt empty, stale. I rushed down the hallway toward the nursery, a sense of foreboding creeping down my spine, raising the hairs on the back of my neck.

I pushed open the door and screamed.

Mrs. Keith's still form sat up in the rocking chair. Her skin was a chalky white, her eyes open and unseeing. In the center of her forehead was a bullet hole. I began to shiver as I forced myself to walk toward her. A note rested in her lap. I picked it up and read the words that sent ice shooting through my veins.

*The sins of the father are to be laid upon the children.*

Clutching the note in my hand, I turned to the crib. Hawk's mobile had been wound and bumblebees flew around in a lazy circle. I crept closer even though I knew what I'd see.

The crib was empty.

Someone had taken Hawk.

## Chapter 15

I wasn't a religious person. I didn't believe in heaven or hell and frankly, I wasn't confident I believed in God. Though I liked the idea of a higher power, I wasn't sure one existed.

Good and evil were a sliding scale of gray.

But I did believe in karma. Retribution. Revenge.

*The sins of the father are to be laid upon the children.*

Sometimes things cut you so deep you didn't even feel the pain of them, just empty coldness.

There were noises around me, conversations, and sharp, angry words. I got up from the couch and left it all behind in the living room. I went into the kitchen and stopped, standing next to the granite island countertop, having forgotten why I was there.

The morning had started out bright. Well, bright for Scotland. Streaks of sunlight somehow managed to make their way through the puffy gray clouds. All traces of sunlight were now gone, and the gray clouds rolled closer, like a dark shadow covering the land.

"Barrett?"

I didn't turn at the sound of my best friend's voice. Didn't even register that she'd come.

"Barrett, what can I do for you?"

All the desperation and fear I wasn't feeling had been given to Ash. She sounded like a terrified mother whose child had been pulled from her arms.

"Do you know who took my baby?" I asked, far too calmly.

"No. Flynn and Duncan have some—"

"Do you know if my child is alive or dead?"

Can you hear a person flinch? Or did I just know Ash well enough to know she flinched?

*The sins of the father are to be laid upon the children.*

"I don't know anything about Hawk."

I paused for a time, finally speaking as the black shadow clouds opened up and released their anger. Fat raindrops splattered the windows. "No, Ash. There's nothing you can do for me."

My breasts ached. My empty arms ached. My body was screaming at the loss of my child.

She retreated, leaving me alone. Something inside of me finally broke. The numbness cracked, shattered, replaced by volcanic, violent rage. I broke dishes and expensive wine glasses. I threw Waterford crystal to the floor, the sounds of splintering glass a melody to my ears. When my wrath had run its course, I gripped the edges of the counter, panting for breath, trying to breathe through the pain that was swirling through my body.

Someone put their hands on my shoulders and gave them a squeeze. I turned so fast, I bumped my hip against the corner of the counter, pain radiating through me. I pressed myself to Flynn's chest and cried.

∽

"Drink this," Flynn commanded, pouring me a glass of scotch.

I sat down onto the couch and with a shaky hand, I brought the glass to my lips, the peaty, mossy smell of single malt scotch soothing. I took a small sip, savoring the flavor. A trail of warmth trickled down my throat. I swallowed a bigger drink.

I wanted to curl into myself, but that wouldn't help Hawk. I could barely think straight. Fear, pain, hope, all mixed together to make for a debilitating cocktail.

Duncan sat in a chair by the lit fireplace. He was supposed to be on bed rest due to the bullet he'd taken in the chest only a few weeks ago. But I knew why he was here. He was known as The Tracker. If anyone could find my son, it would be Duncan—if he was physically up to the task.

Ramsey sat in a chair across from him on the other side of the fireplace. Though usually charming and a big flirt, ever since the death of their father, Ramsey had been angry and wild, uncontrollable.

I was sandwiched between Flynn and Ash on the couch.

Flynn looked at Duncan and nodded. Duncan said to me, "Hawk is alive."

"How do you know?" I asked, feeling faint.

"Because he wasn't here in a certain state for you to come home to," Duncan said bluntly.

Something tight inside of me unfurled, just a little. It wouldn't go away completely until I saw that Hawk was alive and I could press him to my body.

"How did they get past our security? We had men patrolling the grounds…" I trailed off. I looked to Flynn for an answer, even though I already knew what had happened to the men who'd been tasked with guarding my son.

Flynn's hand reached over into my lap to grasp one of my hands. He clutched it tightly, and it kept me rooted in the present.

"This is a play to distract us, divide us," Duncan said.

"What do you mean?" I asked in confusion.

"If we're spending all of our resources and time looking for Hawk, we can't be focused on our cause, now can we?" Duncan said.

"But who wants us distracted? The FBI?" I wondered. "The same people who killed Malcolm?"

"That would be my guess," Duncan admitted. "But we can't rule out that there's another enemy involved."

"So where do we start?" I demanded, feeling the hysteria climbing up my throat.

"Elliot," Flynn said. "We start with Elliot. We haven't been able to question him yet."

I nodded, letting out a shaky breath and standing. "Let's go."

"Hen," Flynn began.

"I'm coming, Flynn. It's my right."

Flynn stood and grabbed my hand before tugging me out of the living room, out onto the back porch where we had a modicum of privacy. Betty, the lamb I'd been given, raised her head from her pallet of old blankets to look at me.

"You can't be there, Barrett. I'm not even going to be there."

I stopped, blinking in surprise. "No? Why not?"

"Because if I find out that bastard had anything to do with Hawk's disappearance, I'm going to kill him. And it won't be fast."

I saw Flynn tamp down a ripple of anger, but it lurked in his eyes, hardening him. He was barely in control of himself, and for some reason, that made me feel better. I thought I was feeling everything alone, because Flynn rarely let his deep emotions out, let alone control him. I wondered how he was keeping it all locked down. And then I realized he had to, because if Flynn let it all out, there was no putting a lid on it. It would burn and spread like fire in a prairie.

I moved into his arms, needing to breathe in the scent of him and feel connected.

I couldn't stay in our home or sleep in our bed, waiting to hear sounds through the baby monitor that wouldn't come. I couldn't go into the nursery where I'd found the corpse of Mrs. Keith.

I opened the bedroom dresser drawers and threw clothes onto the bed. Flynn was still downstairs talking to Duncan and Ramsey about things.

"Need some help?" Ash asked from the doorway.

"Can we stay with you?" I asked, looking at her.

"Of course. You can even bring the lamb," she said with a small smile.

I nodded but didn't return the gesture. Looking down at my dirty, bare feet, I realized I hadn't showered yet, and I was in desperate need of clean clothes. My breasts ached and I knew my milk had let down, leaking through my thick bra.

Her gaze strayed to my shirt, her gaze sympathetic. "We're going to find him, Barrett," she said.

I held up my hand. "Please. I can't. Not right now."

"Okay."

I turned away from her and headed toward the bathroom. I got the shower ready and stripped out of my clothes. Steam quickly rose, clouding the mirror and obstructing my vision. I climbed into the shower and stood for a moment, letting the hot water beat down on me. And then, with a sigh, I sank down into the tub, no longer having the strength to stand.

There was a knock on the door before it opened. "Barrett?" Flynn called. When I didn't answer, he ventured again, "Hen?"

I lifted my legs up to my chest and hugged them, resting my head on my knees. I shivered when Flynn entered the shower, letting out some of the heat. He crouched down behind me and wrapped his arms around me.

He didn't say anything, and I was grateful for the silence.

Empty platitudes were useless and wouldn't help or ease my sorrow and fear. Flynn's hands stroked up and down my arms, sliding across my wet skin. I hated that we couldn't be intimate. I wanted to lose myself in the comfort of intimacy and sex with my husband. Sometimes it felt like the only thing that made me feel sane in a world full of insanity. Whatever I was feeling, I could take it out on Flynn. He accepted it, embraced it, even asked for it.

His lips met the curve of my shoulder, and I closed my eyes, leaning back into him. Flynn's fingers painted whorls of desire on my skin. He caressed my heavy breasts, my aching nipples. He pinched them lightly, and then I felt sweet relief. His hand slid lower, resting between my legs. Teasing, light strokes had me shuddering in pleasure. Flynn's lips bathed my neck as he pressed his hand to the apex of my legs. My hand covered his and, together, we brought me to my peak. My legs went slack, and I slumped against him.

"Come on, love," Flynn whispered gruffly. "Let me wash your back."

## Chapter 16

Ash set a plate down in front of me. "Eat," she commanded.

The fireplace in Malcolm's sitting room blazed, throwing flame shadows on the walls. Hera was at my feet as was Betty. No one had made an objection when I demanded I keep Betty close despite the fact that lamb smell was different from dog smell.

"I'm not hungry," I said, finally supine across the couch, my hand reaching down to stroke one of the animals. Though they were no substitute for a child, pets needed to be taken care of. And at the moment, they needed me as much as I needed them.

Ash sighed, but held her tongue. It was just the two of us in the living room. Ramsey was with Elliot, interrogating the man while Duncan sat in a private room to watch it all unfold on camera. Though Duncan had wanted to be in the chamber with Ramsey, he was still healing and Elliot needed to know that we were strong. Ramsey had a lot of rage and that could be a new source of issues. He was in the room with the man who'd had his father murdered—I wouldn't be surprised if Elliot was left alive, but just barely.

Flynn was still at our home, seeing to the care of the dead

guards and Mrs. Keith's body. I closed my eyes as a wave of guilt struck me. The only crime the woman had committed was to believe we could protect her. She'd taken care of Hawk, held him in her arms, soothed his cries. And her repayment had been death.

Our choices, Flynn's and mine, were taking the innocent. No other way to slice it.

Hera *woofed* in her sleep, and Betty lifted her head.

"I just don't understand," Ash muttered as she took a seat near the fireplace. Though we were at home, she was dressed like a Park Avenue Princess, all done up for the day. I hadn't even bothered to blow dry my hair, and now it was frizzy and out of control.

"What don't you understand?" I asked.

"How someone was able to take out all the guards on your land and get into your home. Hawk and Mrs. Keith were well insulated and protected. So how the hell did this happen?"

The five security men we had stationed on a rotating basis since the death of Malcolm were members of the SINS, trained and well equipped to handle anyone that was a threat. They'd all been found dead.

I sat up suddenly, my heart beating frantically, turning over an idea in my mind. Like a key sliding into a lock, it snapped open.

"Oh my God," I whispered.

"What?" Ash asked, rushing to my side. "Are you okay?"

"Where's my cell?" I demanded. "I have to call Flynn. Now."

~

I waited for Flynn in the privacy of the guest room in the east wing of Malcolm's castle. Pacing back and forth, I went over it again and again, more convinced than ever my theory was correct.

The bedroom door flew open, crashing into the wall. Flynn stood in the doorway, breathing hard, like he'd run some great distance. He was still in his outerwear, and he dripped rainwater on the carpet. "What is it? Barrett?" He came toward me and put his hands on my arms, checking to see if I had any wounds.

"Take off your coat," I demanded. "Before anything else."

Flynn did as I told him and unzipped his jacket, taking it off and hanging it on the back of the bathroom hook.

"Seriously, you can't leave voicemails like that—not after—"

"I'm sorry," I said with genuine contrition. "But I didn't want to say anything over the phone, and I needed you here as soon as possible." I went to the bedroom door and closed it.

"What's going on with you? You're flushed." He came toward me, and his hand reached up to caress my cheek.

I didn't need comfort now—my brain was working overtime, and it was exactly what I needed. It made me feel useful, and it would help get Hawk back.

"What I'm about to say, just think about it. Don't react, okay?"

He frowned but nodded, his hand dropping to his side.

I took a deep breath. "I think whoever planned this—taking Hawk—I think it was a member of the SINS."

I waited for Flynn's reaction. There wasn't one. His breathing didn't change; he didn't even appear as if he'd heard me. So I went on with my theory.

"Think about it. The mobile was on when I entered the nursery, which means someone knew we were on our way home. How? The security guards."

"They were all found dead," Flynn said, his blue eyes shining bright with anger. I didn't know if it was because he hated my words—didn't even believe them—or that he did.

"Could it be possible that someone knew about their patrol? Times, changing of the guard, their route?"

"Have you told anyone else about this? Ash?"

I shook my head. "I wanted to tell you first. Flynn, do you believe me?"

"Where's the note," he asked instead of answering me.

"What note?"

"The note that you found on Mrs. Keith's lap."

I went to the bedside table and opened the drawer. I pulled out the folded piece of paper, not even wanting to look at it, knowing what it signified.

He took it. His brow furrowed as he perused it, clearly trying to work something out. "Where's Duncan?" he asked.

"I think he's still watching Ramsey interrogate Elliot." I used the term "interrogate" loosely.

He let out a curse in Gaelic. "I need to get down there before Ramsey renders Elliot unconscious. Do you want to come with me?"

I paused. "Will it be squeamish?"

"Probably."

I didn't even hesitate. "Yeah, let's go."

～

Because we were in a castle, and though it was restored and modernized, there was still a dungeon. Not *actually* a dungeon, but there was a stairwell that led to a basement of sorts. The dungeon area was equipped with a holding room, very much like a room in a police station, with two-way glass and cameras.

Duncan sat in a chair, peering into the interrogation room. I watched him shift position, and he wasn't able to conceal the grimace. When was the last time he'd taken a pain pill? Then again, they rendered him nearly comatose, and he was trying to remain alert.

"How's it going down here?" Flynn asked Duncan.

"Man won't talk. Damn soldiers. I thought we'd be able to break him, but…" he trailed off as he looked at me.

I shrugged. This was no place for nerves or disgust. I shut it all down so I could focus on what was ahead of us.

"He hasn't said anything? Nothing?" I wondered, finally looking toward the glass. Ramsey loomed over a bloody, bruised Elliot who was tied to a chair. His wrist was broken from falling out of his library window; I didn't know how he was still conscious. His eyes were nearly swollen shut.

"Nothing. As you can see Ramsey's been as persuasive as possible, but Elliot doesn't care, doesn't even engage."

"Did you threaten his daughter?" I asked coldly.

I saw Flynn and Duncan exchange a look out of the corner of my eye, but I kept my gaze on the two men in the room. The violence should've turned my stomach, but I'd lived through a lot. I'd killed men. I could handle unusual things.

"Aye," Duncan said. "But it didn't make him talk. He says we can't be trusted not to harm her even after we have the information we want."

"Let me talk to him," I said suddenly.

Flynn began, "Barrett—"

"Ramsey's obviously not getting anywhere. Let me try. What do we have to lose?"

"This is not how things are done," Duncan said softly, addressing Flynn, but it was me who answered.

"My son was stolen out of his crib from my home. Shit changes. Roll with it," I snapped.

My eyes met Flynn's. He was acting leader and my husband. Would he give me this? Did he trust me enough?

Finally, he nodded.

Duncan pressed a button and spoke into a microphone. "Ramsey. We need you."

Ramsey dropped his arm to his side. He'd been ready to

dole out another punch to Elliot's already beaten form. Ramsey exited the cell door and shut it.

"Why'd I have to stop?" Ramsey asked. He looked at me, his face registering surprise. "Barrett. Hello."

"Hello," I greeted back. I looked at Flynn. "Do you have a knife?"

He frowned. "Aye."

"May I have it?"

"Why?"

"Because I'm going to cut his hands loose."

"You can't—" Ramsey said.

"He's about to lose consciousness. I want him awake and alert. Well, alert as possible. Please?" I asked, once again deferring to Flynn.

With a sigh, Flynn reached into his pocket and pulled out a switchblade. He handed it to me.

"Thank you. Promise me something," I said. Flynn raised an eyebrow and waited. "Don't come in there unless my life is in danger. Unless he comes at me."

"What are you going to do?" Flynn demanded.

"Promise me," I commanded again.

He sighed, but then nodded once. "Aye. I promise."

I paused but a moment, holding the switchblade in my hand before heading toward the cell door.

## Chapter 17

The cell door was heavy, but I managed to open it. It slammed shut, a loud noise in the quiet. Elliot didn't even look to see who had come for him. I moved to stand in his sight line, waiting until he lifted his head to look at me.

I could detect a smattering of surprise lurking in his brown eyes, but he remained silent.

"I'm going to cut your hands free," I said, holding up the switchblade. "You promise you won't try anything? They'll be in here in a moment if you do."

He nodded and I noted the exhaustion, the tension he tried to keep in his body. He was losing steam, and he was dangerously close to that place where he'd say anything just to end his pain. We wouldn't be able to trust his words then.

I went to the back of his chair and crouched. One wrist was purple and bruised. I gently placed my hand on his good wrist and quickly managed to free his hands.

He couldn't stifle the moan of pain mixed with relief as he cradled his injured hand. He looked pale, despite the bruises on his face.

"If you think I'm going to tell you anything because you're being nice to me, think again."

"I don't think that at all," I said truthfully. There was another chair in the corner of the room; I dragged it in front of Elliot and took a seat.

We sat in silence for a long moment while we looked at each other, measuring.

"Do you remember Jane's first smile?" I asked, shattering the quiet.

Elliot appeared surprised for a moment before quickly hiding his emotions. "Yes."

I leaned forward. "What was it like?"

"It's one of those moments you remember forever," he said.

I nodded. "And one of those moments you never get back. Someone kidnapped Hawk."

Elliot didn't reply or react.

"I made my peace with it, you know."

"Peace with what?" he asked.

"Peace with missing out on his milestones. If I miss his first smile, I'll get over it. Just as long as I know he's safe and happy. Just as long as I know I'll get him back. Because, I can handle someone else seeing him smile for the first time, but I can't reconcile a life where I don't get to raise my son. See him become an exuberant toddler, a sullen and angry teenager, a man who finds the woman of his dreams. I can't let go of all the hopes I have for him."

Elliot's jaw had unclenched during my speech, but still he didn't say anything.

I stood up and pushed the chair away. My hands went to my jeans, and I undid the snap so I could shimmy out of them. And then I raised my shirt to show him my body.

"Look at me," I commanded.

Elliot's eyes trained on my stomach, to where I pointed.

"Do you see these marks? They tell a story. They remind me of the baby I carried inside me. You don't know what it's like, to feel your body being torn apart before getting the greatest gift the world has to offer. You're a father, and that's magic in its own right, but I'm a mother. I'm a *mother*, and my arms are empty because my baby has been stolen from me."

I let my shirt drop. "So I'm asking you, from one parent to another, for you to help me get my son back. And in return, I will see that your daughter comes to no harm."

Elliot didn't speak for a very long time; I continued to stand before him, waiting, hoping.

Praying. Something I hadn't done in a very long time, if ever.

Finally, he spoke. "I want one more thing."

"What?"

"Make sure my death is quick."

I dragged my eyes from Elliot's face to stare at the men I couldn't see behind the glass. "I promise you a quick death."

∽

Through the rest of the interrogation, I held my anger in as Elliot explained how deep this all went. Four hours later, Elliot was asleep in his cell, and the rest of us—Ash, Duncan, Ramsey, Flynn, and I—were in the sitting room, trying to wrap our heads around all that we now knew.

Ramsey shot up from his seat and began to pace, his face a mask of righteous fury when he looked at me. "You had no right to make those promises!"

Everyone began speaking over each other in an attempt to placate him and calm him down, but Ramsey was having none of it. He was like a tornado, and the angrier he became, the bigger the cyclone. He wouldn't listen to reason, and I was sick and tired of men dictating everything.

I stood up and without hesitation threw my glass of scotch at the stone hearth. Ramsey shut up mid-rant, and all eyes turned to me. Ash's mouth gaped, Duncan looked resigned, but Flynn didn't look at all shocked.

"Was your way working?" I asked calmly.

Ramsey glowered but stayed silent.

"Was it your son who was taken from you?"

"It was my father who was killed."

I nodded. "We have the same goal. Punish those that stole from us. Retribution, revenge. Elliot is a pawn. There's a bigger picture, here."

Some of Ramsey's anger drained away and reluctantly he nodded. "Aye, you're right." He came to me and wrapped me in his arms. He leaned in close to my ear and whispered so that no one else could hear, "You're incredible, Barrett. Flynn's a lucky man to have you."

He released me and took a step back.

"Another drink?" Ash asked, needing something to do.

I nodded.

We all took our seats again, and I asked, "Jane? How is she?"

"Alive," Ramsey said with a snarky tone.

"There's the Ramsey I know and love," I drawled. "I meant, how is she dealing with things?"

I knew what it was like to be kept in a gorgeous prison, unsure of my place, unsure of the game I was playing. Then again, I was seven years older than Jane and had been a little more prepared for what I'd been thrust into.

"Spitting mad," Ramsey said, though an appreciative smile slid across his face. "Every time I go to bring her a tray of food, she throws at least one thing at me."

If I had to venture a guess, when Jane was alone in the darkest part of the night, she finally let out the tears she held in during the day. We were her captors, and she had no way of knowing that her life wasn't in any danger. Not at the moment. Not because of us.

"What are we going to do with her?" Ash asked, finally speaking about the issue we needed to deal with.

"She can't go back to her life," Duncan said. "We can't kill her father and then send her back to London expecting her not to run her mouth."

"And the other option? She stays here? Locked away?" Ash asked.

"Well, she wasn't supposed to be involved at all," Flynn said. "She was an unexpected complication."

"One we're not killing," I reminded all of them. Even if I hadn't promised Elliot that we wouldn't kill his daughter, I never had plans to allow that to happen. She was an innocent bystander.

"We can't do anything about her at the moment," Flynn said. "So let's get to discussing what we learned from Elliot. Also, Barrett has brought to my attention something that needs to be addressed."

He looked at me and nodded. I told the rest of the occupants that I believed there was a member of the SINS who had turned against us and who had orchestrated Hawk's kidnapping.

"It makes sense," Flynn said, resigned.

"How do you figure?" Ramsey challenged.

"The note they left," Flynn went on. "'*The sins of the father are to be laid upon the children.*' Sins, in all caps."

"No," Ash said with a shake of her head. "Is it really that obvious? I thought it was a biblical reference. Sins of the father and all that."

"It is," Flynn said, "but this specific quote is from Shakespeare. Merchant of Venice. If it were quoting the actual bible, I would've assumed there was a religious tone behind Hawk's kidnapping. Some other faction upset because the SINS aren't affiliated with any religion."

Ramsey nodded. "Makes sense."

"I think I have a vague idea how this is all fitting together," Flynn said slowly.

We all stared at him, waiting while he gathered his

thoughts. "Let's assume a member of the SINS has turned on his own brothers and is working with the English."

"Elliot?" Ramsey asked.

Flynn shook his head. "No. As Barrett said, he's just a pawn. He took his orders from someone else."

"The FBI," Ash said. "But they're American."

"They're all working together," I said suddenly. "The FBI isn't behind Hawk's kidnapping and neither are the English. Not directly."

"You're losing me," Ash said.

"The FBI hired Italian mercenaries to have Malcolm and Duncan murdered. Italian mercenaries so they couldn't be traced back to the Americans," I explained. "The SINS member wants the leader—that's Flynn—occupied searching for his son."

"But Elliot told us about the mercenaries, right? And why would an Englishman in the House of Lords be working for the FBI?" Ash asked, looking like she was about to go cross-eyed.

"Because Elliot's working for both the English and the Americans," Duncan said in realization. "Without knowing it because they have the same agenda for different end goals."

"Exactly," Flynn said with a nod. "Let's think about this for a moment: the FBI is still pissed that we're bringing illegal guns into the U.S. The English don't want Scotland free because that would be a major loss of revenue and taxation. If the Americans and the English work together to get rid of the SINS, then poof, no more problems."

"But why would a SINS member give up his own leaders and cause for a free Scotland?" Ash asked in frustration. "That part doesn't fit."

"Not yet," Flynn agreed. "So until we find him, we won't know how or why he is involved."

"Another problem," Ramsey voiced. "We still don't know who has Hawk."

"You're right, we don't. But I've got a plan," Flynn said, taking my hand and bringing it to his lips. "I've got a plan to get our son back."

## Chapter 18

Flynn's head was between my legs. Moonlight caressed him as he caressed my skin. Heat, fire, and passion. There was nothing except this moment with this man. We could die tomorrow, and I still wouldn't have had my fill.

He lapped and laved, teased and sucked, careful not to penetrate. He made me beg, whimper, plead. He chained me to him, enslaving me in my own desire. I bucked against his mouth, coming hard, needing the release, knowing I'd need it again in a few hours.

Lifting his head, he grinned at me. I chuckled softly, raising my eyes to the ceiling.

"I think they heard you in the west wing," Flynn said.

"It's your fault," I teased, feeling somehow light and revived.

"I'll do it again. In fact, I promise to do it again. Later." He scooted up my body and rested his head on my naked stomach. My hands went to his hair while I watched him trace his fingers across my stretch marks.

"When you spoke with Elliot," he began quietly, "I…"

"What?" I asked when he trailed off.

He lifted his head to look at me. "I was so fucking proud of you. I knew what you were capable of. But I think Duncan and Ramsey needed to see it for themselves. You could've knocked them over with a feather when you began unbuttoning your pants."

I chuckled and Flynn put his cheek to my belly.

"You eclipse every other woman," he whispered against my skin. "You make men yearn for greatness, just so they feel like they deserve you."

"I don't need greatness," I said truthfully. "I just need my son. I won't sleep well until he's back with us. At least we know he's safe."

"So you believe Elliot?" Flynn asked. "He was so gone with pain he would've said anything."

"Maybe," I allowed. "But yes, I believe him. I believed him when he said he didn't know where Hawk was. But he gave us something, and he knew that if he lied about it—and we learned the truth—his death would no longer be quick. We would have no obligation to honor our promise to spare his daughter."

"Elliot's on a need to know basis," Flynn said. "He's not at the top, so he doesn't know everything. Only what his superiors choose to tell him."

"Are you surprised? That Elliot finally broke and told us about Hawk?"

"No. Ramsey couldn't get anything out of him. But you, you walked in there, freed his hands, showed him your body, and pleaded from your heart. No man can resist that."

"I'd like to assume that most of us, who live this kind of life, agree that children are off limits. But that's not really true, is it? We threatened Elliot's daughter. Someone stole Hawk. No real code of honor anymore, huh?"

"But we didn't really threaten Jane's life. Elliot just thinks we did," he said. "You're willing to protect that girl." He shook his head.

"What? What is it?"

"The SINS. We're changing. You're changing us. And I don't think that's a bad thing."

"Tradition is good," I said. "But I was never a fan of the archaic. If we want to succeed, we've got to evolve. The SINS must evolve if we have any hope of winning our freedom from England."

"Spoken like a true Scotsman," he said gruffly.

We fell silent and then he spoke. "He'd come. If you called him."

"Why can't you call him?" I demanded. "He'd come for you."

"Aye. Out of obligation. For you, he'd come for love."

"I can't ask him for that. Can I?"

"I trust him. And Duncan's still out of commission and Ramsey is—"

"A loose cannon," I finished.

"We don't know whom in the SINS we can trust."

"Was this your plan you refused to tell the others?" I asked.

"Aye. I wanted to talk about it with you first. But if he's here, it will bring up things for you."

"For us," I corrected.

"For us," he agreed. "But I can take it, if you can." His lips kissed my belly and then trailed lower. "No more talking."

∞

Flynn was up before me the next morning and gone from our guest room. My breasts ached, waiting for Hawk. Before anything else, I pumped. I'd been constantly pumping, not wanting to lose my milk. After, I went in search of Flynn.

I walked down the hallway of the east wing toward the stairwell, thinking Flynn was in the den, but I heard his voice coming from behind Duncan's cracked bedroom door.

"He's not one of us," I heard Duncan say.

I had plans to go downstairs to wait for Flynn, but I was instantly intrigued by the conversation I was overhearing.

"Times change, Duncan. You know that," Flynn replied.

"Aye, but you really trust him with this? And do you really trust him around your wife?"

Flynn paused and the tension-filled silence settled low in my belly.

"I trust Barrett," Flynn said finally.

"Not the answer to the question I asked."

Flynn made a noise that sounded like a growl. "What am I supposed to do? You're not well enough to see this through. No one I trust more to have my back than you, brother, but you've been shot. You're still recovering."

"So take Ramsey."

Flynn paused again.

"You don't trust Ramsey," Duncan surmised.

"I do. But not with this. He hasn't been able to control his rage."

"That's partly my fault. I let him interrogate Elliot. I let him unleash his anger without helping him channel it in a constructive manner," Duncan said.

"Stop," Flynn said. "We want to play the blame game? Someone kidnapped my son because of me. My wife has nightmares about it because of me. She cries out for him."

I frowned. I had nightmares about Hawk? I knew I dreamt about Vlad and Dolinsky, but I had no memory of my dreams of Hawk.

"You'll get him back," Duncan said.

"What if we don't? I don't think she'll ever forgive me."

Duncan sighed. "There's no hope for it then. You'll have to call him."

"I'll do anything if it means getting Hawk back," Flynn said fiercely.

I'd heard enough. Turning away from Duncan's door, I

went downstairs. I passed the sitting room and went into the kitchen. I opened the pantry door and went inside, flipping on the light. Closing the door, I leaned against it and sank to the floor.

Pulling out my phone, I stared at it for a moment before finding the courage to dial a number I knew by heart, a number I hadn't dialed in six months.

It rang.

He answered immediately.

"It's me," I said softly. "I need your help."

~

While Flynn and Duncan remained behind closed doors, no doubt discussing the potential culprit behind Hawk's kidnapping, I decided to pay a visit to our hostage. I hadn't met her yet, and I knew she was probably terrified out of her mind.

She was on the third floor. Though she had her own bathroom, being locked inside a bedroom for the last few days, it was of little consolation. For a brief moment I was shoved back in time to when I was living in Dolinsky's home. I still couldn't believe I managed to get out of that situation, and those I loved were left alive. It all could have ended so differently.

There were two guards stationed just outside her door, members of the SINS who would stop at nothing to keep Jane inside. If she fled, they'd pursue. They gave me a brief nod in greeting. I rapped on the door to announce my presence. I did it as a courtesy. I felt like I owed her that much.

The person I encountered was not at all what I expected. I assumed I'd see a cowering young girl, sitting on the queen-sized bed, shaking in fear.

What I got was an avenging, spitting-mad woman whose blue eyes were narrowed with hatred when they looked at me.

Jane Elliot was gorgeous. She was tall, taller than Ash.

Jane's long chestnut-colored hair had the tendency to curl. Her spine was straight, and there was a sensual regality to her. For a woman who had been kidnapped from her own birthday party and thrust into the midst of a political war, she looked as composed as anyone I had ever seen.

I had to hide my smile.

She had spirit and I let out a breath, eternally grateful that it hadn't been expunged from her being.

Though we'd brought her here in formal wear and heels, she was currently dressed in jeans and a forest green sweater that fell off of one shoulder, baring her fair English skin.

"You're not who I was expecting," she replied loftily.

"You're not what I was expecting," I said back to her.

She paused, no doubt confused about my honesty. She looked at me suspiciously. "What do you want?"

"I wanted to speak to you."

She laughed, a deep throaty sound. "About what?"

"Do you know why you're here?"

"Something to do with my father." Her tone was snide, angry. At us, definitely, but maybe angry with her father, too.

"I'm sorry," I said, hoping she heard the contrition in my tone. "You weren't supposed to be a part of this."

"Well too bloody late," she groused.

I couldn't help it; I laughed. The English curse coming out of her was a surprise. And in that posh accent! My amusement only enraged her further and her face flushed with emotion.

"Sit," I said. "And I'll tell you some things."

"Who are you?" she demanded.

"My name is Barrett."

She frowned. "Are you related to Ramsey?"

I shook my head. "He's my brother-in-law of sorts. I'll leave it at that." I took a seat in the chair in the corner of the room and crossed my legs. Jane reluctantly sat down on the bed. She looked at me and waited.

"We're in a bit of a predicament," I said, going straight for honesty. "You weren't meant to get tied up in this, but you are now. We can't return you to London because we can't be sure you won't turn us in, but we hardly trust you."

"What did my father do?" Jane wondered, her curiosity, her need for answers overriding her desire for anger.

"Can't tell you that, either," I said.

She huffed out a breath of air. "What *can* you tell me?"

"Nothing," I said. "The less you know, the better."

"So what's going to happen to me? Are you—are you going to kill me?" Her voice went thin and flat, but I saw a tremor go through her. Her courage was fierce, but it took an effort to maintain it.

I looked at her a long moment before answering. "No. We have no plans to kill you."

"How am I supposed to believe you?" she asked suspiciously.

I shrugged. "Your choice whether or not to believe me. But let me ask you this: have you been mistreated since you've been here? Roughly handled? I mean, if you can get past the fact that we kidnapped you, have you suffered?"

Jane looked around at the luxurious room where she'd been kept. Her shoulders relaxed ever so slightly. "I just want to go home," she said, her blue eyes widening. For the first time, I saw the vulnerable youth she actually was. She was twenty-one—and this hadn't been a choice for her.

"Your father is a bastard," I said. "He's the one that started this chain of events."

She nodded. "Yes. But he's still my father and I love him." She kept her gaze on me when she asked the next question even though I knew what it was going to be. "You're going to kill him. Aren't you?"

I refused to reply. She wasn't one of us. She didn't have our trust. What if we could never gain it? Keep her a prisoner the rest of her life? Death might be a blessing. But I couldn't have her innocent blood on my hands. There had to be a way for her to trust us and for us to trust her.

It wasn't just Scotland's freedom that was at stake.

## Chapter 19

The next afternoon we buried Mrs. Keith. Flynn had made sure the woman had a closed casket and only those that had to know the truth of her death were informed. To everyone else, they believed she'd had a heart attack.

The guards who lost their lives defending the innocent had been buried privately and no one knew the truth of what had happened to them.

It seemed all we were doing was losing people.

While I stood at the woman's graveside next to Flynn, I watched her children and grandchildren cry for their loss. Guilt for her death weighed heavily on me. She'd been a casualty in this war we were waging, the war for a free Scotland.

After the service, mourners came up to us, wanting to make small talk. They asked about Hawk. We smiled and lied. It took everything I had to pretend Hawk was at home in his crib, waiting for us to return.

Mrs. Keith's oldest daughter hosted the wake, and we gathered at her house to eat and drink and listen to stories about the woman. Scotch flowed freely, and many of the adults were well on their way to drunk. I wished I could've been one of them. I watched Flynn in the role of leader, marveling at how easily he filled the position. It was like he'd been born to it. Even when Duncan healed and was ready to take on the leadership, was it best for the SINS if Flynn relinquished the title?

Flynn murmured something to the elderly gentleman he was conversing with before looking up. His eyes met mine. Whatever he saw on my face made him excuse himself and come to me. He reached up to touch my face, and I placed my hand over his.

"Can we leave now?" I asked quietly, suddenly on the verge of tears.

He nodded, set his glass down, and took my hand. We excused ourselves from the wake, and I didn't breathe deeply until we were outside. I smelled rain on the air, and I rubbed my hands up and down my arms, the chill sinking into me.

"What is it, love?" Flynn asked, taking me into his arms.

"Not here," I said.

We walked away from the house, but I wouldn't let him steer me toward the car. Instead, I turned him in the direction of a grassy knoll, green from all the rain, with tall trees that would shield us and give us some privacy.

Flynn waited, his body tight. He always looked ready to spring into action. Though his face was fierce, his eyes were soft as they rested on me.

"It's been three days, Flynn," I said.

"I know."

"It's taking too long. The longer our son is missing, the greater the chance that Elliot's information isn't correct."

Flynn tugged me into his arms and said into my hair, "Do you trust me?"

"Yes."

"Do you trust that I know what I'm doing?"

"Of course."

"I'm getting our son back. There are some things in the works. Ears are to the ground."

"Do you think Hawk is still in Scotland?"

"I don't know."

"You couldn't lie to me and say yes he is," I demanded, pulling back so I could look at him. "Make me feel better that my child is—"

"Not with us. Doesn't matter, any way you slice it." He let me go, and I took a step back. "Besides, if I lie to you now, you won't trust me ever again."

I nodded, hating the logic of his statement, but knowing it was true.

"You are a strong woman, Barrett," he said softly. "Not everyone is cut out for this life—and you've chosen to stay by my side. I will not accept anything less than bringing our child home and destroying those that are responsible for taking him from us."

He came forward and reached up to hold my face in his large hands. "Don't lose faith in me."

I leaned into his touch, grateful for it. It anchored me to the moment, to the now. Closing my eyes, I nodded. His lips brushed across mine.

When Flynn made a vow, he kept it at all costs.

∾

The door to the private plane opened, and I watched Sasha Petrovich walk down the stairs, commanding the air around him. He was dressed appropriately for Scotland—trousers, a dark sweater, and a long black cashmere coat. The wind blew his blond hair, lifting it up off his forehead.

His blue eyes met mine, and I was momentarily thrown back to the last time we'd seen each other. I'd been in the hospital and Sasha had walked away from me because I had asked him to. He had needed time to get over his feelings for me, and I had wanted to give that to him.

Behind Sasha were two large, fierce-looking men who

were definitely packing. I didn't recognize them—then again as the new leader of the Russian mob of New York City, Sasha had probably gotten rid of all those loyal to Dolinsky and replaced them with men he trusted.

Sasha stopped in front of us. I watched Flynn and Sasha measure each other. Finally, Flynn reached out his hand. Sasha clasped it and they shook.

"Thank you for coming," Flynn said.

"*Da.* Of course."

It was strange to watch two equally powerful men interact. Their alliance solely existed because of me. In their natural habitat, these two predators would fight to death for control.

Sasha's Slavic bright blue eyes slid to me. When they looked at Flynn they were merely polite, calm. When he looked at me, they glittered with longing.

I accepted it but didn't dwell on it. I stepped forward and hugged him, squeezing him tight around the waist like I would embrace a brother. He hugged me just as fiercely as if knowing how close I was to losing it.

"I'm so glad you're here," I said truthfully, dropping my arms. He let me go, albeit reluctantly, and I took a step back and curled myself into Flynn's side.

Sasha's jaw clenched and he nodded. "Of course I'd come if you called."

Flynn gestured to our waiting limo. Sasha commanded something in Russian to his two men, and they picked up the luggage. We walked, exchanging pleasantries with Sasha about the flight and the mob dynamics of New York. In a roundabout sort of way, the Russians funneled money to our cause through their legitimate enterprises. It had been a way to forge an alliance as well as get the FBI off our trail. But somehow the FBI was still a thorn in our side.

We settled into the car and drove toward Duncan's estate. Sasha glanced out the window. "Beautiful country," he said.

"Aye," Flynn agreed.

Sasha finally returned his attention to the both of us. "Barrett was cryptic on the phone. She didn't mention why you needed me, only that you did."

Flynn looked at me in surprise. I shrugged and explained, "I didn't want to discuss Hawk over the phone."

Flynn took my hand and gave it a squeeze, letting me know I could fill in Sasha. I wasted no time.

Sasha wasn't able to conceal his shock and then his face registered fury. "Someone took a helpless child?"

I nodded. "It's not common knowledge. We buried the woman who was caring for Hawk, and everyone thinks Hawk is still with us. We thought it best not to alert people that we—well—things are out of our control."

Sasha nodded, clearly agreeing with our thought process.

"Hawk is just one part of it," Flynn said, taking up the story. I listened to him recount what had occurred with Malcolm and Duncan.

Sasha let out an impressive stream of Russian curses. I only recognized one word out of the bunch.

"Someone wants our attention divided," I said. "While we look for Hawk—who Flynn believes is safe—"

"But you don't?" Sasha interrupted.

"I don't know," I admitted. "I believe it because I can't even bear to think of the alternative."

"I understand."

"There's more," Flynn said.

"You're kidding?" Sasha asked.

"No," Flynn said, "but I think we should wait until we're with Duncan and Ramsey before unloading the rest."

## Chapter 20

Around midnight, Ash headed up to bed. She'd spent the last many hours, sitting and watching but contributing very little. I could tell it grated on her not to feel useful.

I made it until about two, but then my brain shut down, refusing to work. I left the men in the sitting room near a roaring fire. Flynn came to bed around dawn, and when I rolled over to greet him, my thoughts came to life.

After Flynn fell asleep, I climbed out of bed, knowing there were things I wanted to speak to Sasha about without everyone else around. I wasn't surprised to find him still awake in the sitting room. He sat on the edge of the couch, looking at all the spread-out files and papers on the coffee table, pieces of the puzzle to find out who had taken Hawk and why. Someone was pulling the strings, and we needed to find out who before it was too late.

Without a word, I took a seat in the chair by the fire. It had burned down to embers, but it was still warm. Sasha had taken off his coat when he arrived, but he was still in his thick sweater, looking much like he had hours earlier. Still alert, still focused.

"You look different," he said, finally breaking the silence, but he didn't glance at me. His eyes remained on the papers in front of him.

"I had a baby."

He grunted.

"What's that mean?" I demanded.

"It means you look different—and not just because you had a child."

"Good different?"

"Just different. Soft and fierce. I don't even know how to explain it." He finally lifted his eyes to mine. "You're beautiful."

"Sasha," I began.

He shook his head. "You didn't think it would work, did you?"

"What?"

"Time. To get over you."

I kept my eyes on him, refusing to be affected by his pronouncement. I knew there might have been a chance he still felt that way about me, but I'd hoped he found someone else. Found happiness.

"Be honest with me, and none of that false hope shit," I said. "Do you think there's a chance Hawk is still alive?"

He paused for a long moment and then drew a deep breath. "I think there's a good chance he's still alive. But," he said, his tone turning ominous, "the chances of us finding him are slim."

I nodded, feeling my heart lodge in my throat. It had been five days since Hawk disappeared. I barely slept at night, feeling the loss of him so acutely it was like he'd been cut from my body.

We were desperately grasping at straws. There were three men in the House of Lords who lived in London. Sasha and Flynn had plans to visit them and extract any information they could. Elliot had been the one to give up their names, so who knew if the man was actually speaking the truth. Lord Arlington couldn't corroborate it on his end. Not yet.

"I'm so glad you're here," I said.

"Why?" he asked curiously.

"Because," I said. "You think like us without being one of us. You can give us a different perspective. It's helpful. We're all so close to it. There was once a time that we wouldn't dream of asking for an outsider's help."

Sasha's jaw clenched, and his mouth clamped shut like he was trying to hold back words he didn't want to say. So of course I wanted to hear them.

"Out with it," I said quietly.

"Not my place."

"Always your place," I said. "You're more than my friend, Sasha. Remember? You were the one who stopped Vlad from strangling me. And you were there when Dolinsky..." I trailed off, not having to remind him of the video. Sasha had seen me raw and exposed while Dolinsky made me come against him and then broken my ring finger.

"I wanted to snap his neck," Sasha said, his voice low. "For treating you that way."

"He's gone now."

"Is he?" he wondered. "Or are you still haunted by him?"

I smiled, but it wasn't in amusement. It was in feral ferocity because Sasha knew me. He knew me, which was why I'd always let him speak his mind.

"Tell me what it is you really want to say, Sasha."

"You're an outsider, too. A foreigner. They'll never trust you the way they trust each other. It's a lesson you'll have to keep learning, because you're steadfastly loyal and full of heart. Their cause has become yours. Your son is Campbell's, and God willing, he'll grow up in the SINS. But you didn't. And there's nothing you can do to change that."

Rays of sunlight streaked through the window, and though the new day was unusually bright, I wanted nothing more than to crawl into bed next to Flynn, and block everything out.

I stood up and walked to Sasha. Leaning down, I brushed my lips against his cheek. "Get some sleep."

I left him in the sitting room with his own ghosts.

∾

The next time I awoke, it was close to noon. And I heard yelling. Mostly in Gaelic.

"What the fuck?" I muttered, feeling like I'd been drugged. My eyes had a hard time staying open, but I forced them.

The commotion continued even after I managed to throw on some jeans and a heavy sweater. I ran down the stairs, attempting to figure out what was going on. The front door was open, like someone had left in a hurry. Quickly slipping into boots, I followed the voices outside.

No one was on the front lawn, but then I heard a shout from the side of the castle. I jogged over and stopped. Ash, Flynn, and Sasha, along with a handful of men who patrolled the grounds, had congregated to watch the spectacle taking place.

Jane Elliot had tied her bed sheets together in the hopes of creating a rope and thrown it out the window. She was halfway between the window and the ground, looking both determined and terrified.

I didn't know if she was scared because she had a fear of heights or because Ramsey Buchanan waited for her. To be fair, Ramsey's glare was quite impressive, and I was looking at it from fifteen feet away.

"Crazy girl," Ash muttered with a wry look at me. "What did she think was going to happen?"

"I think she was desperate," I pointed out.

"Aye," Flynn agreed. "But let's say she'd made it to town

without us being aware of her escape. Someone would've called me."

"She's young," I said, defending her. "And clearly headstrong."

"You're headstrong, too," Sasha said quietly. "And you didn't attempt to run."

Flynn looked at Sasha and glared at him. Sasha shrugged, but he'd spoken the truth about how I handled myself when I was stuck in Dolinsky's home. Then again, I'd been in the middle of nowhere Vermont in winter. It would have been foolish to try to leave.

"We're not all built the same," I said. "And Jane is a sheltered young woman who was kidnapped from her twenty-first birthday party. We should cut her some slack."

"And find a better place to keep her," Flynn said with a shake of his head.

"Why not take her to one of those tiny islands off the Scottish coast," Sasha suggested. "Minimal security and if she tries to leave, she dies because of her own fallacy."

Ash looked at Sasha and grinned. "You're brilliant."

"Outsider," Sasha corrected with another look at me.

Jane had decided not to continue her descent. Instead, she hung steadfast to her bed sheet rope. Ramsey stood below her, hands on his waist, looking up.

"Might as well continue, lass," Ramsey called to her.

"I'm going to climb back up," Jane shouted, attempting to shove her chestnut hair out of her face with her elbows. The wind picked up, blowing her hair back into her face, and pushing the bed sheet rope ever so slightly so that it began to swing.

Jane adjusted her hands as if really attempting to climb back up, but one of her hands slipped, and so did her position. She cried out, attempting to grip the sheet tighter. Just as she was able to take a deep breath, there was an audible *rip* and the bed sheets split. She only had a few seconds before it ripped all the way, sending her to the ground.

"Jane," Ramsey bellowed. "Climb down now!"

She did as commanded, quickly lowering herself. When she was about five feet from the ground, the sheets gave way. She would've fallen and broken an ankle or leg, but Ramsey was there to catch her. Like a damsel in an historical romance novel, she fell into his arms. The look Ramsey gave her once he had her in his arms was one part rage, the other part lust.

Jane's fair skin went paler and then color stung her cheeks.

I looked at Flynn. "Ramsey should go with her to the island."

Flynn shook his head. "That's a bad idea."

"Do you trust me?" I demanded.

Flynn grinned. "Aye."

"Trust me. Ramsey should go with her."

We all looked back at Ramsey and Jane. He was still holding her in his arms, and she was outright staring at him.

Ash snorted. "Roughly nine months from now, I bet there will be a mini Ramsey Buchanan in the world. Anyone care to venture a bet?"

## Chapter 21

Ash and I watched the car depart with Ramsey and Jane in the backseat. They were Orkney Island bound, and I wondered how long it would be before Jane broke. Not because I believed Ramsey would ever lay an abusive hand on her, but when she caved of her own volition and demanded Ramsey touch her in desire. Alone, without the influence of outsiders, completely insulated, with just each other for company, the sparks between them had the chance to burst into flames. Though I'd never seen Ramsey look at a woman the way he looked at Jane, I worried her heart would get broken. Another casualty in our war for a free Scotland. But sending her away with Ramsey was the only hope we had of winning her loyalty; she was young and if she believed herself in love with him, we might be able to use that to our advantage.

"Let's go into town," Ash said when we could no longer see the car. "Let's get away from all the testosterone in the house."

Sasha, Flynn, and Duncan were locked away in the study, continuing to plan for Sasha and Flynn's time in London. I needed the distraction from thoughts of Hawk, so I readily agreed.

We took a car into Dornoch, but instead of having our driver drive us around, we got out to walk the town square.

"Let's go in here," I said as we stopped outside of a clothing store with Highland wool sweaters in the window.

Ash made a face. "Really?"

"You know you're going to freeze in winter, right?" I teased.

"I'm not buying long underwear," Ash said, putting her foot down.

Rolling my eyes, I opened the front door to the store. An older woman stood behind the counter, folding a batch of wool sweaters. She looked up and greeted us with a cheerful smile and introduced herself as Glenna, but otherwise didn't overwhelm us with retail help. It wasn't long before I found a handful of sweaters I wanted to buy. There were some adorable knit baby sweaters that had tears prickling at my eyes.

"You have a lovely selection," I said, bringing the sweaters to the counter, shaking off thoughts of my missing son.

"Thank you. They're made right here in Dornoch."

"Really?" I asked in surprise.

Glenna nodded. "Local sheep and many local women make a living knitting. As you can see we have hats, scarves—not just sweaters. We've made a thriving business here, and it keeps the town invested. We ship all over the world, you know." She preened with pride.

"That's incredible," I said with sincerity. I felt even better about buying handmade sweaters that came from the place I'd chosen to live. "That's missing from so many products these days. I'd rather spend more on something of quality, something unique, than something mass produced."

I handed over my credit card to her, and her eyes widened.

She attempted to hand it back to me. "I can't let you pay, Mrs. Campbell."

I frowned. "Why not?"

"Because you're the wife of—"

"Now stop just a moment," I said.

"What's wrong?" Ash asked, coming up to my side.

"Glenna refuses to take my money."

I'd received the same treatment from the old farmer Barnabas who'd given me a lamb in the form of an apology for not knowing my identity. It was ridiculous.

"I'm part of this town, too," I said to Glenna. "Please let me help support local businesses."

Before Glenna could respond, a young woman came out from the back room. "Grannie, I can't find the—" She stopped talking as soon as she saw me, her eyes widening. She clearly knew who I was, and I had to hold in an annoyed sigh.

"Katherine," Glenna said. "Come over here and meet the Campbell's wife."

"The Campbell?" Ash asked me quietly.

"I'll explain later," I whispered back.

Katherine was a mousy young woman with straight brown hair and brown eyes. At the moment her face was pale, and she looked terrified.

Glenna barked something in Gaelic and Katherine visibly jumped. She rushed to the counter and scooped up the sweaters I wanted to purchase and headed for the back room.

"She's going to wrap those up for you," Glenna explained. "Please consider them a gift."

I was apparently not going to win this war, because Glenna was adamant, so I decided to be gracious. "Thank you," I said.

Glenna looked relieved. "It's going to be a little while. There's a coffee shop just across the way. Why don't you have a cup and a scone, and I'll have Katherine run your bags over to you in a wee bit?"

I felt like I was being shooed out of the store, and Ash looked equally confused. We headed back outside and ambled toward the coffee shop that Glenna had mentioned.

"The Campbell?" Ash asked again.

"They're basically calling Flynn a laird. It's a sign of respect, and it means they know who's in charge."

"And as his wife, that means you don't pay for things?"

"They wouldn't charge Flynn, either," I said. "It's like in the old days when the peasants would give their lord their best animals."

"And you got a lamb," she pointed out. "That was weird. I thought it was weird."

"Barnabas lives by the old code."

"And you know all this because you studied Scottish history. Why do I feel like I'm never going to get the hang of this?"

I opened the door to the coffee shop, and before we even stepped up to the counter, we had cups of coffee and scones in our hands. Again, they wouldn't let us pay. Ash wanted to leave a huge tip, but I shook my head. Tipping wasn't customary in Scotland, and besides, they would've seen it as an insult. They took great pride and honor serving us.

"It wasn't like this seven months ago when you moved here, was it?" she asked as we took a secluded table near the back.

"No," I admitted. "But seven months ago, Malcolm was alive, and we didn't know Flynn was going to be acting leader. We shouldn't discuss this in public."

She nodded, looking down into her cup of coffee. There wasn't much we could discuss in public. I suddenly wanted to be home, so I didn't have to be on display or worry about what I could or couldn't say.

"I'm going to go use the loo," Ash said, rising.

I nodded and took my last sip of coffee. I glanced out the window and saw Glenna's granddaughter walking across the square. I went to meet her, wanting our business concluded as swiftly as possible. The air was cold and bit at my nose and ears. I pulled my coat closer to me as I braved the turning weather.

Katherine stopped in front of me, holding out the bag. I took it from her. "I'm sorry," she blurted out, her face devoid of color. Before I could ask her what had her apologizing, she turned and dashed away.

I heard the bell on the coffee shop door jingle and knew it was Ash. "Ready?" she asked.

"Yeah," I said absently, wondering why Katherine seemed afraid of me.

∼

Ash and I arrived home to a boisterous house. The men had vacated the study and were currently in the sitting room enjoying an early afternoon cocktail.

"Celebrating?" Ash asked as she perched her tight behind on the arm of Duncan's chair. She leaned down to kiss him, and even I could see that it was heated.

"You could say that," Duncan replied.

"What's going on?" I asked, setting my bag of sweaters down and coming over to sit next to Flynn on the couch. Sasha sat quietly in a chair, looking tired. Jet lag must have finally caught up with him.

"We've got a plan of attack," Flynn said. "Sasha and I are going to leave for London tomorrow."

"Tomorrow?" I asked in shock. "That's soon."

"Arlington called with a lead on Hawk's whereabouts," Flynn replied.

I felt like someone had punched me in the lungs. "Really?" I asked breathlessly.

He nodded and reached up to touch my cheek. The tears I'd been holding in suddenly spilled over, and Flynn wiped them away with his thumbs. Hawk had been missing for a week. A whole week of his short life gone, and I hadn't been there to witness it.

"Do we know who took him?" I asked.

"Not yet," Flynn said. "But right now, it's more important that we bring him home."

"And how are you going to do that?" I demanded.

"Those three names Elliot gave us are men against the Scottish Referendum. We got access to their phone records. All three of them call each other regularly as well as an unlisted number."

"A burner," I said.

Flynn nodded. "They're men involved in politics which means they don't ever do their own dirty work. They won't have the stomach for violence or blood. They'll cave and give us information."

I bit my lip in thought. "And Elliot?"

"He gave us these names. If he gave us false information, one of the promises you made to him won't be kept."

Flynn referred to Elliot's death being quick. I hoped for everyone's sake the information was correct.

"Do you think they know the SINS member who has caused all this?"

"We'll find out, won't we?" Flynn asked.

## Chapter 22

I should've been in bed next to my husband. He was leaving in the morning, and though we'd spent a few hours together, bringing each other to the height of pleasure without the benefit of sex, I hadn't been able to fall asleep.

Restless.

Sasha being here, being in Scotland, changed my orbit.

He was a trigger for old habits, and I wanted to be outside, under the white moon, breathing in the crisp air, and speaking of things that were easier to say in the dark.

Because he knew me, he waited for me by the front door, already bundled and dressed for the outdoors. I tied my boots and then slid into my thick, warm coat, wrapped a scarf around my neck and donned a wool hat. Our boots hardly made a sound as we trekked across fallen leaves. The earth was damp and spongy.

"You'll be careful," I said, my voice carrying on the air. It sounded ghostly as if a spirit had spoken. It was whimsical, maybe, to think that, but Scotland was full of ghosts and spirits from a violent and bloody history. Culloden came to mind.

"I'll be careful," he vowed. "I'll make sure your husband is careful, too."

"Thank you."

We stopped walking, and I closed my eyes to listen to the sounds of the night. I didn't know what was going to happen when Flynn and Sasha were in London. There was a good chance we wouldn't learn anything new, and we'd be going round and round in circles. But knowing Flynn, he wouldn't stop until he exhausted all avenues.

We found a clearing not too far from the house with a few smooth gray boulders. I sat on one and Sasha sat next to me, close enough that I could feel the heat of him. It was comforting.

"Do you have nightmares?" I asked him.

"Every now and again. You?"

I nodded. "Frequently. And there's been more of them ever since Hawk…"

Disappeared, I didn't say. I didn't have to.

"Campbell? Does he know about your nightmares?"

"Yes."

"In depth?" he wondered.

"No. He knows what I dream about, but I never describe in detail."

"Because you're shielding him—still. After all this time."

"My dreams remind him that he wasn't able to protect me," I admitted.

"So you carry the burden yourself."

"Maybe," I said with a shrug.

"What are your dreams about? Igor? Vlad?"

I nodded. "And blood. One or both of them dying in front of me."

"And?"

How did he know there was more? And how was I supposed to admit how depraved my subconscious could be? More often than not, I dreamt of both of them. Naked.

Together. Surrounding me. Their hands on me. In me. Painting my skin with their blood. I sometimes woke up with a scream of rapture lodged in my throat, my body racked with tremors of an orgasm I had in sleep.

Sasha looked at me and he knew. He knew the things I couldn't find a way to admit even to my husband. As much as I loved Flynn, as much as he loved me, I worried he wouldn't understand.

The wind picked up and I shivered, feeling an icy chill of foreboding skimming down my spine. Maybe it was the fingers of my ghosts, wanting to remind me that they'd always haunt me.

"Let's go back," Sasha suggested, reaching out a hand to me.

I took it, his palm warm against mine. And just like that, my ghosts were banished. For the moment.

˜

I crept back into the bedroom feeling like a teenager sneaking into the house past curfew. Quickly stripping out my clothes, I shivered. I scooted under the covers, seeking his warmth.

"Why?" he asked quietly.

I started, though I shouldn't have been surprised. I forced myself to calm, to melt against him, but Flynn remained unyielding, his body taut.

"I don't know," I said.

"That's no longer a good enough answer, Barrett." He rolled over onto his back, his face turned to the ceiling. "What can you tell him that you can't possibly say to me?"

"I can't hurt him with the truth," I said, trying to explain. "Because the biggest truth is I don't love him. Nothing I ever say to him is as bad as that."

"I hate that he gives you something I can't. You're my wife. I'm your husband."

The words I'd been holding in since Hawk disappeared came from deep within, escaping the confines of my throat, flapping their wings and soaring between us. "I blame you. For Hawk."

"I know," he said quietly. "I blame me for Hawk, too."

"I'm scared we won't find him. And if we don't find him, I don't know how I'm supposed to forgive you."

Flynn didn't reply or touch me. The distance between us we hadn't addressed until now yawned before us like a chasm. I felt it all the way in my heart.

"We've always been able to find our way back to each other," he said.

"Through intimacy. Through sex."

"Which we haven't been able to have because your body isn't healed. We have to find another way, Barrett. I can't lose you."

"What if I'm already lost?"

Flynn turned to look at me, his face harsh in the moonlight, like the wild beauty surrounding us. "If you're lost, then I'll find you."

"I'm not strong enough to survive losing him, Flynn."

"We haven't lost him yet. There's still hope."

I smiled at him, but it was sad.

He came to me, settling on top of me so we were skin to skin, heart to heart. "I'll be strong enough for both of us. Always."

My hands plowed through his hair and I brought his head close to my lips. "I love you."

I hoped it was enough.

∽

At dawn, Flynn kissed me goodbye. Though I was half asleep, I could still detect the meaning of the look in his eyes. Resolute, fierce, and full of promise. Promise that he'd find our son.

After Hawk was safe, Flynn and I could have a sensual reunion that recommitted who we were and what we meant to each other.

I loved that Flynn was strong when I couldn't be.

I fell back asleep with a smile on my face, knowing that Flynn would never let me go, no matter what happened.

My alarm went off at ten. I hadn't set my alarm in weeks, but today I had an appointment. I got dressed, grabbed my phone and purse, and was out the door. The drive to Inverness took a little under an hour, but like all doctor's offices, they were running behind.

I started to flip through a magazine, but my cell phone rang. Not wanting to be one of those people that disturbed others, I set down the magazine and exited the waiting room.

It was Flynn calling to tell me that he and Sasha were settling in at Lord Arlington's townhouse. Lord Arlington had given them use of it while he'd taken his family to visit the grandparents.

"I'll try to check in every night," Flynn said.

"But if I don't hear from you, you're underground," I finished for him. I smiled even though he couldn't see me. "I know the drill."

"Aye, you do," he said. I could hear his own smile. "I love you, hen."

"I love you."

We hung up, and then I went back into the waiting room just as a blonde, plump nurse called out, "Mrs. Campbell?" She looked around and then smiled when I nodded.

I followed her to one of the exam rooms, changed into a gown while she asked me some questions. I hopped up onto the exam table and waited for the doctor. Luckily, I didn't have to wait long, and we got right to the stirrups.

"I realize it's two weeks earlier than you'd normally see me," I said as she began her exam.

"Anywhere between four to six weeks is fine," she assured

me. "Some women heal faster than others. Some slower. Go with what your body tells you."

"My body is telling me I really want to have sex with my husband."

She let out a chuckle. "You can sit up now, I'm done."

"So?" I asked, reaching for my underwear.

"Everything looks good."

"Really? You're giving me the green light?"

"All systems are a go," she said with a laugh.

Boy, was she right.

She gave me some tips and some things to watch out for the first few times Flynn and I were intimate. "Your body has changed, so it might be a little different. Don't sweat it, okay?"

I nodded, already lost in thoughts of seducing Flynn the moment I saw him.

"Mrs. Campbell?" the doctor asked.

"Sorry, what?" I asked, realizing she had still been talking and that I'd tuned her out.

She smiled. "I asked about your son. How is he?"

I swallowed and forced a smile of my own. "He's perfect."

## Chapter 23

"Any word from Ramsey?" I asked Duncan that night at dinner.

The hounds were at my feet, begging for scraps which I refused to feed them. Betty was at my feet too, but she wasn't a beggar—she knew better.

"Radio silence," Duncan said, passing me the mashed potatoes.

"And Elliot?" Ash asked. "I'm still weirded out that we have a prisoner downstairs in our dungeon."

"That might be something you might have to get used to. It could become a regular occurrence," Duncan said.

Ash stopped her fork from going into her mouth. "Seriously?" She looked between us for confirmation.

"You know our lives aren't like others," Duncan said.

She glowered. "I'm aware."

"Are you?"

"You have no idea what it's been like for me," Ash hissed.

"Because you refuse to tell me!" Duncan bellowed back. "I ask you to talk to me, and you shut down completely!"

Apparently a fight had been brewing between them for a good long while, and now it was ready to explode. All over the dinner table. Standing up, I picked up my plate and quietly backed out of the room, leaving them to it. I could hear them yelling even as I went into the sitting room. Yelling turned into breaking plates, and then it was quiet.

I had a pretty good idea of what was occurring, and I didn't want to be in the house any longer. I quickly bundled up and escaped to the outdoors.

Tensions were high, the unknowns piling up. The more I thought about it, the more I realized that Ash wasn't cut out for this kind of life. She'd almost lost Duncan—and their fight was because she realized she could lose him at any time. Maybe she could've wrapped her mind around it except it all kept escalating. Malcolm was dead and Hawk had been kidnapped. No one was safe, and it was finally hitting Ash.

My heart wouldn't survive this. I missed Flynn, and I wanted to talk to him. As I walked around the grounds of Duncan's estate, I called my husband. I wasn't surprised when he didn't answer. Hanging up with a sigh, I knew there was nothing to do but wait. I refused to think about what would happen if we couldn't find Hawk. My brain wouldn't even go there. Maybe it was self-preservation.

I turned back toward the direction of the house, hating that I had to sleep in a big empty bed and that I had no idea where my son rested his head this night.

∼

*Hands skate down my body, eliciting chills of desire.*

*"Keep your eyes closed," a gritty voice whispers.*

*I'd do anything to keep feeling the pleasure shooting through me, so I keep my eyes firmly shut.*

*Warm lips brush against my mouth before moving downward. Strong arms hold me in place, rendering me helpless, making me a slave to my own desire. My lover licks and laves, teases and coerces, begging me to beg him.*

*His hands grip my hips as he slides into me.* "Open your eyes," *he commands.*

*I stare into the face of my husband. He moves over me, his face taut, our mutual pleasure binding us.*

*"I love you. You're mine," he states.*

*As soon as he says the words, Flynn's face changes, and it's Dolinsky moving inside of me. He reaches underneath my body and tugs me closer. My head snaps back in excitement, in shame.*

*"You're mine," Dolinsky states. "You'll never be free of me."*

*"No," I plead, wanting him to release me, wanting him to pull me closer.*

*"I'm so deep inside you, I'm in your skin, I'm in your heart. I'm exactly where you don't want me." His lips capture mine, and suddenly I'm tearing at his back, drawing blood.*

*The face above me changes again. Vlad's glittering dark eyes are as vast as the open universe. Hatred and lust war on his face; he wraps his hand around my throat.*

*"I have a part of you that no one else does," he grits, his deep voice thick with his Russian accent. "I took everything good from you, and I'll keep on taking it."*

*He pounds into me harder, faster. My brain is terrified at the loss of air, yet my body craves it. It knows what's happening. My psyche wants to shrivel up and die. My soul wants to fly from my body.*

*Vlad lets go of my throat and I come hard, clamping around him, wanting to bruise, wanting to break him, like he broke a part of me.*

*Suddenly the heat of him is gone and it's just me, desire slick on my skin. I hear a baby cry.*

*Hawk.*

*I search for him, but I don't find him.*

∼

I woke up, the echo of a baby's cry in my ears. I got out of bed, only to remember Hawk wasn't down the hall in Ash's home and he hadn't cried out for me. I shivered. I'd lit a fire before I went to bed, so I wasn't shivering because of the cold.

Without hesitation, I slid my hand down the front of my pajama bottoms. I was wet. And still aroused.

Climbing back into bed, I settled the covers on top of me. I glanced at the clock. It was a little past five in the morning; I knew I wouldn't be able to go back to sleep. If I were in New York, I would lace up my running shoes and hit the pavement of Central Park. Running always helped me clear my head.

"Fuck a duck," I said to myself. I threw off the blankets again. I couldn't go running yet—the doctor hadn't cleared me for it—but I could do some light exercise. I got dressed and looked out the window; it was snowing—light and dry, and hardly sticking, but I didn't want to be out in it.

I wished I still had a job, something to throw myself into. I'd loved my history research job at Columbia. But then Flynn had come into my life, and there simply hadn't been room for anything else. That sounded terrible, like I'd given up vital pieces of myself to be with him. Things were allowed to change because people did. I changed; I hadn't wanted children. Hawk had been an accident—a happy one in the end.

I crept downstairs, quiet, despite the fact that it was near impossible to disturb anyone since we were in a castle. I threw on my coat and boots, grabbed my keys and phone, and headed outside for the garage. There was always a driver on duty, and so I didn't worry about the early hour. We left Duncan's estate and headed in the direction of town. Nothing was open, not even the coffee shop, but I wasn't going into town. I had Callum take me to my home. If he was surprised by my request, he didn't show it.

When he parked outside the castle I shared with Flynn, I sat for a moment and stared at it. It had been the perfect place. I remembered the day Flynn had shown it to me nearly six months ago. I hadn't even made it across the threshold before knowing it was our home. We'd made love on the sitting room carpet in front of the fireplace, fallen asleep in each other's arms, and when dawn had come, we'd made love again.

Now it was just the place where my son had been stolen from me. But I had plans to reclaim it, exorcise the ghosts that had taken up residence, both in my home and in my soul.

"Ma'am?" Callum asked, looking at me in the rearview mirror.

He was solid and sturdy, a bear of a man. A true Scotsman.

"I need your help, Callum."

## Chapter 24

"Where have you been all day?" Ash asked when I came into the sitting room. She was alone, except for the hounds and Betty.

I collapsed into exhaustion onto the couch, envy pouring through me when I saw Ash with a glass of wine. True, I could drink. But I was trying to stay in a routine of pumping breast milk in anticipation for when Hawk came home.

"Out," I said evasively, not wanting to share what I was doing at the house.

Ash accepted my answer as she continued to flip through the design catalog on her lap. She leisurely took a sip of red wine.

I closed my eyes for a moment. "Where's Duncan?" I asked.

"Resting."

"Oh?"

"He didn't get much sleep last night," she said.

I opened my eyes to look at her. She smirked with feminine power and then reined it in, not wanting to rub it in my face, which I appreciated.

"We got some snow," I said, striving to change the conversation.

"Hmmm."

"Think they got snow in London?"

She set the magazine aside and shrugged. "Not sure. Haven't heard from him?"

"Not since yesterday morning."

"You're worried."

"Yes."

"You shouldn't be. They're just gathering information."

"You really don't get it, do you?" I asked.

She frowned. "I get it."

"No. You don't. After all this time, how can you say something like that? It doesn't make me feel better."

Her eyes widened in surprise. "Barrett—"

"You've got your head up your own ass," I said angrily, rising from the couch.

"Wait just a minute," Ash seethed, also standing. "You think because you've been in this world, what, a year, you know what the hell you're talking about?"

I laughed, but it was bitter and maniacal. I was exhausted, spent. "Should I remind you what's happened to me in the last year?"

My statement had Ash pausing. Her eyes dropped from mine, and her apology was quick. "I'm sorry."

Just like that, my anger drained from me. "Me too. I was picking a fight."

"I wish I knew what to say to you."

I thought for a moment. "Placating me doesn't help. Not right now. I'm also wicked tired. I was up early today."

"Yeah," she said. "I thought so. You weren't at breakfast. Go take a nap."

I shook my head. "If I sleep now, I won't sleep through the night. I had an idea I wanted to run by you."

"Me?" she asked in confusion.

"Yeah," I said. "Well, you and Lacey. I have to see if she'd even want to do it. But I wanted to pick your brain first."

We sat, and I stretched out on the couch, letting the ache in my back have a chance to ease. A bath in the large tub in the guest bathroom sounded like a good idea.

"Lacey wants to leave her job as club manager," I said.

"Get out."

"It's true."

"But she's so good."

"Yeah, she is, but she's ready for something new. I was thinking... You know she takes amazing photographs."

Ash fanned herself. "Uh, yeah. I've seen the one of you hanging in your bedroom."

I refused to be embarrassed. It was a photo of me on stage when I'd performed burlesque, and I looked like I was in the middle of an orgasm. It wasn't so surprising that Flynn wanted it framed and mounted on our wall.

"I think it's time she had an art show," I said.

"Ah, and you want me to call my contacts."

"I do."

"That's it?"

I shook my head. "No. You know those sweaters I bought in town? I want to sell those. In New York."

"Open up a little store?"

I smiled. "Yeah."

"And what about Glenna? Think she'd be on board with that?"

"I'm going to talk to her tomorrow."

∼

"*Ach, weel*, it's a very nice offer, dearie," Glenna said. "But, no, I don't think so."

"But why?" I asked in confusion.

We were sitting in the back of the storeroom having a cup

of coffee and scones that I'd brought. Apparently they did nothing to butter her up.

"The sweaters and scarves are fine Highland craftsmanship. What happens when there's too big an order and we can't fill it? We're doing fine, why tempt fate and reach for a new market?"

"Do you like running the store?" I asked her. "Or would you prefer to do something else? Spend more time with your grandchildren, perhaps?"

She smiled, her blue eyes twinkling. "You're a clever, lass, I'll give you that. But no. I've been running this store for twenty years. I knit some of the beautiful things in the store, but I work because I like to be useful. What would I do with retirement?"

How had I forgotten that the Scots were known for the stubbornness? Prideful, too. Somehow, I thought this would've been a slam dunk.

"Oh, cheer up, love," Glenna said with a knowing chuckle. "Some of the best things should be kept secret. Don't you think?"

"Thank you for your time." I stood to leave, finishing the last sip of my coffee. Glenna stayed behind, pulling out a clipboard to do inventory. Yep, the woman was old school.

I headed out to the front of the store and came face to face with Glenna's granddaughter, Katherine. The young woman's gaze darted from my face, completely skittish.

"Is something wrong?" I asked her as I passed the counter where she was standing.

"No," she answered. "Er, do you like your purchases?"

I thought it a strange inquiry. "Yes. Of course."

She nodded. "And the sweater for the wee one… did you look in that box?"

"What? What are you talking about? I didn't buy a sweater for—"

"It was a gift," she stressed. "Make sure you read the card."

In a total state of confusion, I left the Highland wool store, trying to piece together what the hell Katherine was talking about. I couldn't go home yet and figure it out because I still had a few more errands to run. I couldn't even do them in Dornoch, I had to go to Inverness.

I left another message for Flynn, just wanting to check in, but of course he didn't answer. I tried to believe that was a good sign, but I knew next to nothing. I also hoped Sasha kept Flynn from reacting with his emotions. Flynn was as close to breaking as I was. We were both like rubber bands, and when we snapped, we were going to inflict pain. I hoped it wasn't on each other.

I didn't for a second wonder what would happen when Flynn discovered who had taken Hawk. The bastard would pay, and not quickly. I wanted to look into the face of the man who had stolen Hawk from our home, right out of his crib, and deliver my own form of punishment. I never used to think I was bloodthirsty. I didn't believe in hurting the innocent, but this person wasn't innocent and had dared to take my child from me.

Aye, there would be a river of blood before all this was over.

∽

I loved Inverness. Considered the "Gateway to the Highlands," it was close to Loch Ness and the battlefield of Culloden. The streets were brick, and the large town was clean. There was also a university, and though it was newer and younger than Oxford or St. Andrews, it was close to Dornoch. I had a meeting with the head of the history department.

Though he was very kind, he couldn't offer me any sort of position at that time. I knew it had been a long shot, despite my own credentials. I never considered using the clout of the Campbell name to get my way. There were certain things that should be won on merit and character because it would mean more.

Before we left Inverness, I treated Callum to a quick bite in a pub before driving back to Dornoch.

"It's going to snow again," Callum said.

"Yeah?" I asked, looking out the window at the white sky. "It's not cold enough for it to snow."

"Temperature is going to drop. We'll get some snow that will stick."

"How do you know?" I asked.

Callum looked at me in the rearview mirror, and I could see that he was smiling due to the wrinkles at his eyes. "Because I've lived in Dornoch most of my life and I just know."

"Did you ever leave? For college or to travel?"

"Aye, I lived in Sydney for a bit when I was younger, but I came back because I missed the rain."

I chuckled. "And the scotch, right?"

"My family owns a distillery. Did you know that?"

"No, I didn't."

"It's not as well-known as Glenmorangie and what have you. We're a small but proud, family-operated distillery."

"Do you work there?"

"Not lately," he answered. "Driving for Flynn Campbell is a full-time duty."

"Do you miss working in the distillery?"

"Aye. I'm from a big family, you ken. It's hard not being there every day."

"Then why don't you quit? And go back to it?"

Callum turned down the road that would take us to Malcolm's estate. I still thought of it as Malcolm's home, and it was hard to reconcile the change that it now belonged to Duncan.

"Because there are some things that you have to fight for, that you believe in strongly."

"The SINS?" I asked.

He nodded. "My parents…they don't understand. Then again, they're set in their ways."

"I think that's the argument all children have been making against their parents since the beginning of time."

Callum laughed. "Aye, I suppose so. And I bet my own son will one day fight me on our differing ideas."

"I didn't realize you had a son," I said.

"Oh, I don't. I was speaking about in the future."

Did I really know so little about the men who were involved in this cause? Though I had met some of the wives and mothers of the SINS members, I didn't know them. Not really. As Flynn's wife, it was my job to stand by his side and unite our people in a different way. Because I did consider them my people even though I hadn't been born to them.

## Chapter 25

"Have you seen my shopping bag?" I asked Ash.

"Ah, no," Ash said.

"Do you even know which shopping bag I'm asking about?"

Ash dog-eared a page of her magazine and then looked up. "The one from the wool shop?"

I nodded.

"Jeanie took it—did something with it," Ash said, mentioning the housekeeper that cooked and did light chores.

"Maybe it's in the laundry room?" I asked.

"Maybe," she said absently.

I took the stairs that led down into the basement. It was in the opposite part of the castle from the dungeon and I was glad. I tried not to think about the prisoner we kept below. When I thought of Elliot, I became instantly enraged. Better to compartmentalize how I felt about him.

I flipped on the light of the laundry room, which clearly had once been an old cellar. It was chilly and I shivered. The washing machine and dryer were off, and there was a stack of folded sheets on the wood table.

My phone rang, and a feeling of relief ran through me. "Hi," I said.

"Hen," came Flynn's deep and gravelly voice. It never failed to turn me on.

"You've resurfaced."

"For the moment."

"Any news?"

"No."

"Damn."

"That's not why I called. I wanted to check in with you. How was the doctor's appointment?"

"Great. Better than great. We can get down and dirty."

"Best news I've heard in days," Flynn said, his voice becoming a husky growl. "All right, love, there isn't anything to report, and I better get off the phone before I start asking you what you're wearing."

"Hiking boots and nothing else."

"Sexy. Love you."

"Love you, be safe."

"Always," Flynn said before hanging up.

I went back to searching for the sweaters, but they were nowhere to be found. I saw the boxes sticking out of the garbage can. I retrieved them, setting them aside. I dug through the garbage, but I didn't find any note that Katherine mentioned. Completely frustrated, I thought for a moment. I took off the lid of the smallest box. There was an envelope taped to the underside. It had easily been overlooked because both were white. I pulled it off and ripped it open. My heart stopped beating for a moment.

*I have your son.*

There was a phone number.

I wasted no time debating; I called the number and held my breath. The person answered on the second ring.

"Barrett. Thank you so much for calling."

A gasp of surprise involuntarily escaped me. I recognized the voice.

"Still there?" he asked.

"Yes," I asked, but it came out in a breathy whisper. "I'm here."

"I'm guessing you want your son back. Obvious question I think."

"If you've harmed him—"

"You'll do what, exactly?"

I fell silent.

"Yeah, that's what I thought. Now pay attention, because I'm not going to repeat myself," Fred Winters said.

∼

I used to believe I could be rational under any and all circumstances. I thought of my time with Dolinsky. I'd somehow been able to compartmentalize all that I was feeling, shoved away my emotions for the greater cause of getting back to Flynn. I'd done whatever I'd had to, and I would've done more.

But nothing—nothing—resembling rationality existed when my child was involved. I'd gladly go through torture, literally walk through fire, to get Hawk back. My life was nothing if he wasn't safe.

During the phone call, I'd sunk down to the laundry room floor. Now, I pulled myself up and forced myself to stand.

Fred Winters.

The persona non grata ex-FBI agent had a personal vendetta against me. I hadn't just ruined his career—I'd made him look incompetent. I'd pretended to feed him classified SINS information, but it had all be a set up. He arrested me but hadn't had a warrant. Flynn and I had gone to the press as anonymous sources and ruined him.

And now he was back to ruin me. He'd taken my son. He wanted me crippled, malleable.

Sticking the card in the back pocket of my jeans, I headed for the stairs. Before I opened the door to the main floor, I pulled myself together because Ash could read me when something was wrong. No one could know about this. Not even Duncan. It had been one of Winters's stipulations.

I had to meet Winters alone—and he knew I would because the threat to my child was enough to get me to do his bidding.

"You're leaving again?" Ash asked, coming out of the sitting room into the foyer as I reached for my coat.

I nodded. "Yeah. I've been redoing Hawk's nursery. I started the project the other day. I'd like to finish it today."

"Want me to come along and hang out with you?"

I forced a smile. "Thanks, but I think I want to be alone. In fact, I think I'm going to drive over there myself."

She frowned. "Really? But you're supposed to take a bodyguard with you whenever you leave—"

"You ever just need to get out by yourself?" I asked her.

"Of course."

"I'm taking a car, and I'm driving myself the fifteen minutes to our house. I'll be fine."

"Okay," she said. "If you're sure."

"I am." I embraced her. "I'll be back soon."

The driver on duty, a younger man than Callum, didn't want to give me the keys to a car. But I was able to bully him into submission because I was Flynn Campbell's wife, and I used the power of my name and position to get my way.

I drove to the castle and parked. I didn't go to the nursery, which was a complete and utter mess. I hoped it would be put back together, and more than anything I hoped there was a baby to sleep in it.

Entering the master bedroom, I paused at the doorway. Memories of nights spent in this room came to me. I closed my eyes and thought about Flynn, his arms tight around me as he moved inside me. A cry escaped my mouth, and because I was alone, I allowed myself to break down. I cried for it all, wondering if I was ever going to see my son again, wondering if I'd be alive myself to watch him grow.

After I gave in to tears for a few minutes, I pulled it together. I went to the bedside drawer and got out my six-month wedding anniversary present from Flynn. I stuck the hairpin into my messy bun, and with a final look around, I went to meet Winters.

~

I drove an hour north west of Dornoch. I passed through Lairg, a town with the population of nine hundred people and who knew how many sheep. It was in the middle of the Highlands, and a unique town because it wasn't on a coast.

I turned off the main road onto a dirt one and bounced my way along the path. The road snaked through green and rolling hills, and if I was in a better frame of mind, I might have been able to appreciate the beauty of it. But I was heading into the unknown. Stupidly, foolishly, without backup, taking the word of a man who had no honor. It was for Hawk. I'd do anything for Hawk.

Fred Winters was resting against the hood of a black SUV. I parked and climbed out of the car. He looked different since the last time I'd seen him. His shorn brown hair had grown out a bit, and it fell across his forehead. The Scottish breeze teased the hair at his ears, and he pulled up the collar of his coat. After glancing at the sky, annoyance flitted across his face before he turned his gaze to me.

His irritation disappeared, and he smiled like he was seeing an old friend. "You came."

"Yes."

"Wasn't sure you would," he said.

I leaned against the closed door of my car, refusing to take a step toward him. "You have the most important thing in the world to me, but before we go any further, you show me proof."

Winters pondered my statement for a moment and then nodded. He pulled out his cell phone, tapped a button, and waited. He turned up the volume, and then I heard someone answering. Winters waved me over, and I came to his side and looked at the screen. Hawk was in a crib, sound asleep. In the two-and-a-half weeks since he'd been gone, I could already tell he was bigger, his cheeks plumper.

Something inside of me unfurled. Hawk was alive, and I would do anything to ensure he stayed that way.

Winters hung up, and the screen went black. He stuck the cell back inside his pocket and gestured with his chin to the black SUV. "Get in."

"No. I came here, we speak here."

He cocked his head to the side. "I'm not having a discussion out here. It's cold, it's about to rain, and I don't want to get soaked. This cashmere coat cost a lot."

"I didn't know ex-FBI agents could afford cashmere."

His jaw tensed. "Get in."

A small part of me was glad I could still get under his skin. The bigger part of me realized I needed to shut the hell up.

He didn't reply as he got into his car. With a reluctant sigh, I climbed into the passenger side and closed the door.

"Just so we're clear," he said, facing me. "If you kill me, you don't get your son back. Because if I die, your son is bound for America to be adopted by a nice barren couple. He'll grow up never knowing anything about you. You want that?"

I looked out the window and didn't answer.

"We have no reason to trust each other, you and me," he went on.

"Why?" I asked. "Why did you take Hawk? Was this a vendetta against me for destroying your career?"

"That would make me a psychopath," he pointed out. "Did you ever think I was a psychopath?"

"I'm starting to rethink everything I thought I knew about you."

"Don't waste your energy. In fact, you should rest."

I frowned in confusion. "Rest?"

Winters nodded. "I insist on it."

I felt the pinprick in the side of my neck.

*Not again.*

## Chapter 26

The sound of heavy rain battering glass caused me to crack my lids open. They were gritty, heavy with sleep.

"She's awake," came Winters's voice.

"About time," another man said. An Englishman with a posh accent. I knew that voice.

I lifted my head and looked toward the hushed tones. "I should've known," I said, my voice raspy.

Lord Henry Arlington stood next to Fred Winters, the angle of their heads making them appear as if they were conspiring.

Arlington looked at me. "Yes, you should've."

I tried to move, to sit up, but I was weak. "Where am I?"

"Not important," Winters said.

"Then why did you drug me?" I demanded.

"Because I knew you wouldn't have come willingly."

I glared at him. "You never asked."

"Let's not do this," Winters stated.

"You started it," I growled, finally managing to prop myself up in the chair. I felt like an old marionette, my arms and legs refusing to work unless someone controlled the strings.

I glanced around; I was in some sort of cabin. It was cozy and a fire was lit. I would've enjoyed it a hell of a lot more if there wasn't a dull ache at the base of my skull and my mouth wasn't dry and chalky.

Without having to ask, Lord Arlington came to me and offered me a bottle of water. I didn't thank him, but I chugged it down and let out a sigh when I'd finished all of it.

"So, you two are working together," I said, gripping the empty water bottle in my hands.

"We have the same end goal, if that's what you're getting at," Arlington stated.

It took me a moment to put it together. "You want Flynn."

Winters nodded. "Yes."

A ball of dread settled in my stomach. "And I'm here because—"

"You have a choice to make," Arlington interjected. "Your husband or your child."

"And if I don't help you take down Flynn, you'll ship Hawk off to America. Right?" I looked at Winters for confirmation. He nodded.

I wondered who was the mastermind behind this elaborate plot. It didn't make sense to me. Winters didn't work for the FBI anymore unless he thought bringing in Flynn would be his ticket back to an agent job. I knew Arlington didn't like Flynn, but I didn't realize it was full-blown hatred.

"You think she's putting the pieces together?" Arlington asked Winters.

"Yes. Barrett's always been smart."

I glowered, hating that they talked about me like I wasn't there. "Okay, let's go over this then. Let's say I'm on board and I hand Flynn over to you. How do I know you'll hold up your end of the bargain?"

"Do you really think we're the kind of men—" Winters began.

"Don't finish that sentence," I warned. "One of you, or

both of you hired The White Company to kidnap my child right from his crib."

They exchanged a look.

"Ah, didn't think I knew about that, did you?" I asked with a little smirk.

"They have Elliot," Arlington said to his partner in crime. "And he talked."

"Fuck. He's been out of London for weeks. I assumed he was running scared. Did you know they had him?" Winters demanded of Arlington.

Arlington shrugged. "I had my suspicions."

"You let one of your own fall, huh?" I asked, hoping to prod some more information out of them.

"There's a greater cause," Arlington said.

"So it won't bother you to know that your soldier is dead."

"He knew what he was signing up for," Winters said.

"Did he? Because Elliot told me he was working for the Americans. For the FBI. I'm thinking the FBI hasn't even heard of Lord Elliot. But he *has* heard of you, hasn't he?" I asked Winters.

Winters didn't reply and I knew I had my answer. Arlington and Winters had used Elliot as a pawn, given him just enough information so that if he failed, he'd hang himself. They were no better than the rest of us, shedding blood all in the name of their greater good. Fucking cowards. Kidnapping a child, threatening me to ensure that I got my own hands a little dirtier.

I turned thoughtful; this wasn't just about getting Flynn. They'd hired mercenaries to take out Malcolm and Duncan. Did they want the SINS in a tailspin? What was the connection? I felt like I was on the verge of putting it all together, but it was just out of my reach.

"She didn't give up Campbell when they were dating," Winters said to Arlington. "Can we really expect her to do it now that she married the guy?"

"A mother's love is different from a wifely love. And it trumps everything," Arlington stated. He looked at me. "Doesn't it?"

There was no point in denying it. "Yes."

"We have a problem, though," Winters said. "The last time I trusted her, she worked as a double agent. How do we know that she won't do it again this time? We don't trust her. She doesn't trust us. This isn't going to work."

"It'll work," Arlington said and then looked at me. "We'll know if you try to screw us."

How? I wondered. And then it hit me. They had a SINS member working with them. More of the puzzle pieces started to fit together. If Winters brought in Flynn to the FBI, the SINS would be without a leader. Unless Winters and the unknown SINS member struck a bargain. New leadership, new alliance.

*This was a fucking coup!*

A year ago, when Winters had approached me to help him take down Malcolm and Flynn, he'd mentioned wanting to stop the illegal guns coming into the country. That had always been his end game.

But Arlington… What did he gain by Flynn's fall? Did Arlington hate Flynn that much for threatening the man's children to get him to cooperate? Or was it something more? What did Arlington stand to lose?

At the moment, none of that mattered. All that mattered was getting my son back. I could compartmentalize many things—I had murdered two men, after all.

I'd find a way to get Hawk and protect Flynn. Once again, men were underestimating me, and I'd use their hubris to bring them both down.

∼

Winters drove me to my car. It took about an hour, and I was blindfolded with my wrists bound. He had taken steps to ensure the location where we'd met Arlington was kept secret.

When he parked, Winters cut me free, and I removed my blindfold. It had gotten dark, but thankfully the rain had stopped.

"Here." Winters tossed me a burner phone.

"How do you expect us to be able to communicate?" I demanded. "I'm watched, I'm monitored."

"You're protected," he corrected. "It's different. Besides, I'm sure you'll find a way. You were able to take a car and drive yourself here. Better get home. You've been gone all day, and I'm sure you have people concerned about you."

With a glare, I reached for the door handle and climbed out of his car. He waited for a few minutes while I warmed up the engine and then he tore off, muddy road spraying behind him. I pulled out my personal cell phone and saw the many texts and voicemails. Most were from Ash. One was from Flynn. I shot off a text to Ash telling her I was on my way, and then I put the car into reverse.

I drove on autopilot, my mind consumed. I couldn't trust anyone. If I went to Duncan, he'd no doubt want to use his "most faithful" men to help. What if one of them was trying to usurp the leadership position? Flynn was in London, and this was not a conversation to have with him over the phone.

Another hour later I was passing through Dornoch and saw the Highland wool store. The lights were on, so I knew the shop was still open. I pulled into a parking spot and hopped out of the car. Stomping up to the front door, I had every intention of barging inside. The doorknob wouldn't turn. I peered inside, but no one was on the floor. I pounded and knocked, waiting, hoping someone came out of the storeroom.

Just as I was about to give up, Glenna ambled her way from the back to the front counter. I knocked again. She lifted her gaze, looking startled and concerned. She rushed to the door and let me in.

"I was just finishing up some inventory in the back and I didn't hear you," she explained. "Come in, come in."

I stepped across the threshold of the store, feeling the numbness in my fingers dissipate. I'd been cold for hours, ever since I'd met with Winters. The irony wasn't lost on me.

"Sorry to bother you when you're closing up," I said. "But is Katherine here?"

Glenna frowned. "No, dear, she doesn't work today."

"Oh," I said, scrambling for a lie that would appease Glenna. "It's just that—the other day—she gave me a sweater for Hawk, and I never thanked her for her thoughtfulness."

Glenna smiled. "Och, she's a sweet lass."

"Do you have her number? I'd love to call her and thank her personally."

I left, armed with Katherine's phone number and a lot of rage.

## Chapter 27

My phone rang just as I drove the car into the garage at Duncan's estate. It was Flynn. "Hi," I said, injecting a note of false cheer into my voice.

"Hen," he greeted. "You sound different. Are you okay?"

"Fine," I lied. "How are you?"

"I called earlier and you didn't answer."

"Sorry. I was at our house."

"Doing what?"

"I've been changing the nursery for when Hawk gets back."

"Ah, love." He sighed. "We're coming home in a few days. Sasha and I."

"Why? Did you find out—"

"Dead ends so far. We've got one more lead to follow, but I'm not hopeful."

Shocking. Not. Especially if Elliot had gleaned his information by way of Lord Arlington. No doubt having Flynn out of Scotland for a little while had all been part of the plan to get me alone.

But I was glad Flynn would be away for a few more days. It would give me time to figure out stuff on my end.

"Well, I hope this last trail leads somewhere."

"Me too. Love you."

"Love you," I said and we hung up.

I walked into the castle and Ash immediately pounced on me. "Where the hell have you been?"

"Out," I said. "I went for a scenic drive."

"I don't believe you. You've been gone for hours, and you didn't answer your phone."

"Can we do this tomorrow? I'm kind of exhausted." I shrugged out of my coat and hung it on the rack.

I trudged toward the stairs, and Ash dogged my heels. I was in no mood to go round for round, and I was so worn down and beaten, I wanted to give in and tell her everything, which I knew I couldn't.

"Flynn and Sasha are coming home in a few days," she said.

"Yeah, I know. I just spoke to Flynn." I went into the guest room and collapsed onto the bed.

"Flynn called Duncan three times this afternoon when he couldn't get ahold of you."

Rolling over onto my back, I looked at her. She had her arms crossed over her chest, and she stared at me. There was a new strength to Ash that I'd never seen before. It was a quiet reserve. This entire time, I'd been so wrapped up in my own emotions, my own losses, I thought Ash wasn't strong enough to keep it together. But I was the weak one.

"Close the door," I said softly.

Frowning but listening, she shut it. She turned back to me.

"I'll tell you where I was today, but I need you to swear to me you won't tell anyone. Not Duncan, and not Flynn when he returns."

"You're keeping secrets from Flynn?" she asked in shock.

I nodded. "There are some things he can't know. Not right now."

"All right."

"Swear to me, Ash. Swear to me on eleven years of friendship. Swear to me on being my family, now and forever."

"I swear," she said, her voice soft but strong. She knew I wasn't fucking around.

I took a deep breath. "Remember Fred Winters?"

After recounting my day and everything I knew and my theories, I fell silent. To Ash's credit, she didn't seem as shocked as she would've been a year ago. That was the truth of this life. You evolved and changed until shocking things no longer had the power to shock.

"Glenna gave me Katherine's phone number, but I don't think she'll pick up if I call. She knows something. I just don't want her going underground before I talk to her."

"Well, Glenna's bound to mention it to Katherine the next time Katherine works, right? Katherine's the reason you found that note. We don't have a lot of time to find her."

"I know, but I don't trust anyone to—"

"Where's your laptop?" She looked around and saw it sitting on the bedside table. She grabbed it before flipping it open, typing the password automatically. Yeah, Ash and I were like that.

"What are you doing?" I asked.

"Looking her up on Facebook, obviously."

"Obviously."

"Katherine McConnell. Let's see where you're at. Ah, there you are."

"Really? That was fast."

"I'm a Facebook whiz."

"Let me see."

Ash clicked a few times and then turned the screen, showing me Katherine's face. She was actually quite pretty when she smiled; I'd only seen her when she was terrified and pale.

"Privacy settings, people," Ash said with a roll of her eyes.

"I can see everything. Jeez. And. Here. We. Go. Guess where she's going to be tonight?"

"Where?" I asked.

"Castle Whisky." She looked at me and grinned. "I think we should pay her a visit, don't you?"

∼

Castle Whisky was a local haunt and the perfect place for a pint after a long, hard day. Ash and I had told Duncan we wanted a girls' night out. He urged us to go, with his blessing, but he insisted we take a driver.

The pub had every local scotch in bottles across the many wood shelves along with a decent selection of beer. Ash and I ordered two beers, knowing we weren't going to drink them. We found a table that faced the door so we could watch for Katherine. The pub wasn't too full yet, but I knew that could change at any moment.

"You really think she's going to be here?" I asked.

"Her friend posted on her wall about looking forward to seeing her tonight, so yeah, I'm pretty confident."

"I'm glad you're here," I said.

She gave me a small smile. "Thanks for trusting me with this. We'll get him back. We'll get Hawk back—and then we'll find a way to screw it to those guys. Fuckers."

Ash with a potty mouth always made me laugh. Even though she looked like Manhattan Barbie, she had true grit.

A quarter of an hour later, Katherine walked in, her brown hair pulled back into a ponytail, wearing jeans, and cute boots. She looked low maintenance and a little nervous because she was alone. I turned my head so when Katherine glanced around for her friends, she wouldn't recognize me.

Katherine got comfortable at a table for four and pulled out her phone. A moment later, Ash and I were out of our booth, beers in hand. Katherine didn't even look up until Ash slid into the seat next to her, and I took the chair opposite her. I wanted to see her face.

"Hello, Katherine," I said pleasantly.

"Wha—what are you doing here?" she asked, her voice breathless, her face pale even in the dim bar lighting.

"Just wanted to thank you for the extra sweater you put into my bag," I said.

She looked at me warily before her gaze slid to Ash. Ash smiled and it was gorgeously sinister. Ash was embracing the dark side.

"You got the message?" Katherine wondered.

I wanted to smack the frightened doe-eyed look off her face. I wanted her to have some fire, have a fucking spine.

"How did you meet Fred Winters?" I asked.

She frowned. "Who?"

I leaned back in my chair and studied her. All her reactions were sincere and honest. "How old are you?" I asked suddenly.

"Um. Twenty-two."

"Were we like this at twenty-two?" Ash asked me.

I shook my head. "No."

"Thank God."

I shoved my beer toward Katherine. "Have some."

Without hesitation, Katherine took my beer and drank half of it before setting it aside.

"So, Fred Winters," I prompted.

"I don't know anyone by that name," Katherine said.

"Then who gave you the message to give to me?"

Her eyes dropped to the table. "He called himself Felix Summers."

"What a douche," Ash muttered.

"He came into the store a few times. He asked me out. We—he—"

"Yeah, I have an idea of what happened between you two," I said, cutting her off. "Is your family part of the SINS?"

She looked around and bit her lip. "Can we talk about this stuff somewhere less public?"

"Car," I stated.

We all stood and made our way to the front door. Unfortunately, Katherine's friends entered as we were leaving and we had to stop and chat for a moment. Katherine made an excuse that she wasn't feeling well and had to bail.

"Keys," Ash said, snapping her fingers at Katherine when we got to a small compact car.

Katherine dug around in her purse and tossed the keys to Ash.

"You drive a Mini? In Scotland?" I asked Katherine.

Katherine shrugged. I got into the back next to Katherine just to ensure she didn't put up a fight, not that I thought she would.

"Where are we going?" Ash asked as she pulled out of the parking space.

"The first private alleyway," I said.

"Right, chief."

Despite the intensity of the situation, I wanted to smile. If I needed a getaway car, I wanted Ash behind the wheel. The ride was short and silent while we found a narrow side road. Ash parked, angling the Mini so that at least other small cars could pass.

Katherine fiddled with her hands, which rested in her lap. She was an extremely nervous creature, but I wasn't about to assuage her fears.

"Start talking," Ash said, turning her body so that she faced us.

"He told me he was here on holiday—I took him to whisky distilleries and showed him the Highlands. I was never suspicious of him because he never asked pointed questions." Katherine's gaze dropped to her lap in shame.

Katherine was a naïve, young woman. She worked in her family business, and I assumed that meant she was protected and tethered. I wondered if she'd ever been far from her home. Fred Winters had exploited her innocence. He was a trained FBI agent; he knew how to find someone's weakness and use it against him. Or her, in this case.

"How did he know you'd be able to give me a note?" I asked. "I'd never been in your family's store before."

"It was coincidence. If you had never come into the store, I was supposed to send you the note anonymously."

I looked at Ash and then at Katherine. "You wanted me to know it was you who put the note in there, didn't you?"

Katherine nodded.

"But why?" Ash asked in confusion.

"Because she knows where Hawk is." I stared at Katherine. "Don't you?"

## Chapter 28

While Katherine sat in the backseat of her car, Ash and I stood in the alleyway in the chilly air discussing what we were going to do with the information; we'd learned Hawk's location. My first inclination was to arm myself and blast the shit out of anyone in the way when I went to get my son, but luckily rationality returned.

"How can we trust anything out of her mouth," Ash asked.

"When we came into the wool store, do you remember her reaction? She was terrified of me. Katherine can't lie to save her life."

"We're just supposed to take her word for it? That she overheard Winters on the phone discussing Hawk's location? You don't think she's setting a trap for you? We should tell Duncan. Let him handle this."

I rolled my eyes. "I know how that would go."

"He'll tell Flynn, you mean?"

"Yes."

"Well, he should tell him. And then we can wait until Flynn gets back—"

"No, we have to move on this information. Now. And

while I trust Duncan, we still have a potential coup on our hands, so we don't know who's loyal to whom."

"Duncan is called The Tracker for a reason, Barrett. You're too close to this."

I ran a hand across my tired face. I felt like I'd been awake for days. Maybe I wasn't thinking clearly.

"We'll take Katherine to the house. We'll check out her information and if it's solid, we can let her go—after we get Hawk back," I said.

And then I could spend time with Flynn plotting how to destroy Winters and Arlington. Rage simmered just below the surface of my skin, but I contained it, forced it back. Thinking with anger always resulted in reckless behavior. Closing my eyes, I took a deep breath.

"You're right," I said to Ash. "Let's take her to Duncan."

"What do we do with our driver waiting for us at the bar?" Ash asked.

"Leave him there for a few hours," I said. "Because we don't know if we can trust him."

We got back into the car and drove to Duncan's estate. Katherine was quiet, her gaze trained on her lap. She probably expected the worst considering she knew how ruthless the SINS could be.

I wondered what Katherine's childhood had been like, growing up in the shadows of the SINS but not really participating in it. It was a patriarchal group, very similar to a mafia family. The men were the soldiers, they doled out violence, and the women knew about it but weren't involved.

"Do you believe in the SINS?" I asked Katherine, shattering the silence.

She flinched. "Believe in them? Like believe in the cause?"

I nodded. "Yeah. I won't betray your confidence. I'm just curious."

"I would love a free Scotland," Katherine began hesitantly, "but I don't like how the SINS go about it."

"The violence?"

"Aye. I also don't like that—well—women aren't involved in any real way. We don't contribute. I have friends who…" she trailed off, looking nervous.

"Go on."

She took a deep breath. "I have friends—female friends—who would very much like to be"—she paused, searching for the correct word—"warriors, soldiers."

"But not you because of the violence."

"I don't have the stomach for it."

Ash snorted.

In a brief show of fire, Katherine pushed back. "I don't."

"But you clearly had no problem helping someone kidnap a child."

Katherine looked at me, wanting me to see her earnestness. "I know what your husband can do to me—and yet I still made sure you saw my face, so you'd know to come to me for information. I couldn't knowingly seek you out because Felix—Fred," she corrected, "keeps watch on me. He thinks I don't know, but I do."

"Fuck," I said.

"I second that," Ash said as she pulled the car into the garage on the estate.

"If you want to get your son back, you have to move fast," Katherine went on. "Because it's only a matter of time before Fred learns that I—"

"You'll be safe here," I said to her.

She nodded, but didn't look like she believed me. Maybe she wasn't so naïve after all.

∽

"You did what!" Duncan thundered.

I wasn't intimidated by his wrath. He was like a Scottish storm, blustery and angry, but it would blow over soon.

"Okay, you have the right to be worried," I said. "But if I hadn't gone, we never would've known that Arlington is working with Winters."

"For fuck's sake," Duncan grumbled, running his hand through his hair. He looked at Ash who was sitting quietly in a leather chair. The door to Duncan's study was closed, but I wouldn't be surprised if Elliot in the dungeon could hear Duncan's displeasure.

"Don't look at me," Ash stated fearlessly.

"You aided her in this preposterous idea to accost Katherine McConnell in a public place!"

"And now she's safely locked up in the room where we kept Jane," Ash went on, not afraid of Duncan's anger any more than me.

Duncan realized he was losing control of the situation. "Why didn't you come to me?" he asked me, his voice softening, his brogue thick.

"First, there wasn't time. Second, I didn't want anyone to know."

"You're reckless."

"Winters has my son!" I faced off with Duncan whose glare was back in full force. "Arlington stabbed us in the back! It was his word that sent Flynn and Sasha to London on a fucking wild goose chase. Why do you think he did that? Huh? He wanted me alone so Winters could talk to me."

Duncan inhaled a shaky breath and then nodded for me to go on. I'd filled him in on most of my day, but it was still patchy and full of holes. There was so much to discuss and time was against us.

"You think Katherine is telling the truth about Hawk's location?" Duncan asked.

"Yes."

"Why?"

"Intuition," I stated. And hope. Blind fucking hope because what else could I think?

Duncan cursed in Gaelic and then, "We have to call Flynn and tell him. We'll get him home and he and I, with a trusted few including Sasha can—"

"No," I stated. "There isn't time. Don't you get that? We have to go now. The three of us. I don't trust anyone else."

"Wait," Ash interjected. "What do you mean 'the three of us'? You might have some nerves of steel and can operate a gun no problem, but I'm not cut out for this."

"Getaway car," I said.

"Ah."

"You're both kidding, right? You both get this isn't a joke? We go in there, not having vetted the situation, we could die. Hawk could die."

I swallowed. "I know, but I—I don't know what else to do, Duncan. Winters wants Flynn. He said he'd give Hawk back if we gave him Flynn, but what if he's lying? In fact, I don't believe for a second that Winters is actually telling me the truth. It would be just like him to take Flynn and keep Hawk from me. I ruined his career. He wants to ruin me back."

"Flynn is going to kill me," he mumbled.

"Does that mean you'll do it?" I asked with hope.

"As you pointed out, we have a very small window. Give me half an hour."

~

Lord Elliot leaned against the wall of his dark cell with his eyes closed. I approached, but he didn't open his eyes. His chest didn't rise and fall like a man in sleep. He'd been held for days, the bruises from Ramsey's fists had faded. I hadn't seen him since I'd shown him my own scars and pleaded for him to help me save my son.

I watched Elliot for a moment. Resignation and weariness coated his body. His eyes finally opened, and we stared at each other, not exchanging words.

I gripped the bars of his prison cell, wanting to end the man's life, but it wasn't mine to take. Though I'd promised Elliot a quick death, it wouldn't be at my hand.

"Why did you come, then?" he asked. I hadn't spoken, but he recognized the look on my face, what I wouldn't do was reflected in my gaze.

"I don't know," I said truthfully. I didn't need to see Elliot in order to bring on my rage. Maybe I just wanted a final goodbye before I went to get Hawk.

"How's Jane?" he asked, showing some life, showing concern for his daughter.

"Fine." As far as I knew, she was. She was with Ramsey, and who knew what battles they were fighting. Lust, anger, love. Sometimes they all melded together.

"Any news about your son?" he asked.

I couldn't hide my surprise that he would care to ask.

He gave me a wan smile. "Why is it the innocent always pay in the war of the guilty?"

"The way of the world, I guess."

He nodded thoughtfully. "We all think we're right, you know? We all think we have life figured out, that our cause is the right one, our religion the superior, our lives worth more. But we're all just here, aren't we? Until we're not."

"I'm not in the mood for philosophy."

"Are you in the mood for advice?" he asked.

"Giving or taking?"

"Taking."

"Go on," I allowed.

"No mercy," he said softly. "Not when it comes to protecting your child. Anything goes."

I nodded, suddenly grateful for his guidance. Though he was technically my enemy, we'd reached an understanding.

"Will you be there? When they execute me?"

I'd done my own share of violence, but could I watch Duncan or Flynn kill a man? Was Elliot's death even about me? In the last moments of Elliot's life, would he look at me and go to his grave with peace, knowing that his daughter was safe because I had vowed to protect her?

Not all innocence had to be lost.

"Yes, Elliot," I said. "I'll be there."

## Chapter 29

The sliver of moon peeked out through the clouds and drowned the rolling hills in silver. When I was younger and had visited Scotland for the first time, I'd been fanciful. It had been easy to get caught up in the magic of Scotland. The earth was different here; the land pulsed with energy. A unique heartbeat. Now that I was older, I was still caught up in the magic of the land, but my love for the country had grown deeper. I'd planted my own roots here, binding together with Flynn and Hawk. Scotland was mine. This place was my home, and foreigner or not, this country owned a part of me, stole a part of me.

The SINS hadn't been my cause; I wasn't born to it, weaned on it. But I believed in it. Would I die for it? No. Would I die for my son? My husband? Yes. They came first. They would always come first. That was my true religion, my true reason for being.

It was nearly four a.m. when Duncan pulled the car to a stop on a modest neighborhood street in Edinburgh. He turned off the engine; the headlights dimmed and then went out. We sat in silence a moment, all of us unsure.

"Why Edinburgh?" Ash asked finally. I could hear the exhaustion in her voice. I was completely wired.

"Close to an airport," I said without thought. "A way to get Hawk out of the country quickly."

We fell into silence again. I stared out the back, side window of the car, gazing at the moderate white home about twenty feet away where Hawk was supposed to be. There were no lights on, but there was a small gas lantern porch that illuminated the red brick walkway up to the house.

"Are we clear on the rules?" Duncan asked.

"Yes," Ash and I chimed together.

"I'll go first. Check it out. When I've deemed it safe, I'll text."

Before Duncan got out of the car, he hauled Ash to him and kissed the breath right out of her. It was carnal, it was hot, and it wasn't a goodbye kiss. It was a promise to return. I averted my eyes and wished Flynn was with me.

Duncan leaned back and released Ash who sank into the passenger side, looking like all her bones had melted. Duncan got out of the car and closed the door softly. He walked toward the house and disappeared into the shadows.

Ash climbed over into the driver's seat, just to be prepared, just to make ready. In case.

"How long do you think we'll have to wait?" Ash asked.

"I don't know."

Time seemed like it was moving in reverse. I stared at my phone, willing it to buzz with a text from Duncan. That never worked. Ten minutes later, I was ready to sit on my hands to stop myself from texting Duncan.

"Any minute now," Ash whispered, no doubt trying to appease me and keep me calm.

My phone buzzed. Fumbling, I dropped my cell. "Damn it."

I found it on the floor, underneath the driver's side seat. I opened the text and choked on a sob. It was a photo of Hawk's sleeping face.

"He's in there," I said, showing it to Ash. There was another text, this time directions to the nursery by way of the back entrance.

I squeezed Ash's shoulder and then was out of the car, jogging toward the white house. I dashed around the side, tromping across manicured grass. My heart thudded in my ears, the sound of it obliterating anything else.

Grasping the knob of the back door, I hesitated only a moment before turning it. I entered the dark house. I rushed across the kitchen to the stairs and took them two at a time until I was in a long hallway. Passing room after room, I came to a halt, suddenly wondering why all the lights were still off. Trepidation skated along my spine, crawling up my neck.

A baby cried. I recognized the sound of Hawk immediately. I knew my child. I moved, wondering why Duncan wasn't tending to him. Unless of course he was busy dispatching those that had been entrusted to watch Hawk. I pushed open the nursery door. One lone lamp was on casting its warm glow. I went over to the crib and sighed in relief. Hawk was healthy and whole and completely angry. I scooped him up, immediately noticing how much more he weighed since the last time I'd held him.

Three bloody weeks.

I rocked him against me, breathing in his scent. He took a few moments to calm down, but I walked around the room with him. As soon as I had Hawk under control, I wondered where to find Duncan.

The light to the nursery flipped on and I turned, expecting to see Duncan. My arms around Hawk tightened ever so slightly and my son made a surprised squawk.

"You make my job so easy," Fred Winters said with a malevolent grin, a pistol in his right hand.

"Where's Duncan?" I asked, far more calmly than I felt.

"He's fine. Stabbed him with a syringe the moment he came through the door. He'll wake up in a few hours."

"That's your new MO, huh?" I said. "Why didn't you kill him?"

"Not for me to do. I just promised to deliver him. Anyone else come with you?"

I hesitated and then, "My friend Ash is waiting in the car."

"Toss me your cell phone," he demanded from the doorway of the nursery, the gun by his side, letting me know he was still armed.

I struggled to get the phone out of my back pocket while holding onto Hawk. "What are you going to do?" I asked.

"I'm going to text her. The last thing I need is her coming in here blowing this all to shit."

"Fine. But before you send it, let me read it."

"Why?"

"Because if you try to sound like me and you don't, she'll know something's up."

He nodded. I tossed him the phone, which he caught easily with one hand. He clicked a few times, and then he was texting with one hand. "Here's what I said, 'Hey, all is good. Gathering some stuff for Hawk and we'll be out in few minutes'." He looked at me for confirmation.

"Sounds like me, but add a smiley face or something."

He frowned. "Why?"

"It's what Ash and I do."

"Okay. Whatever. You kids and your dumb emoticons." He sent the text and then we waited for a confirmation. My phone buzzed. "She said, 'Great' and then gave you a thumbs up." He shoved my phone in his pocket before giving me his full attention.

"How did you know I'd find this place?" I asked.

"I knew Katherine overheard me on the phone. I knew she'd bait you into a trap and you'd be emotional enough to get caught."

I inhaled a shaky breath. "Not here, okay? Not in front of Hawk."

He nodded. I moved to the crib and gently set Hawk down on his back. I leaned over and pressed a kiss to his forehead, closing my eyes and committing him to memory. I pulled back and looked at Winters.

"I don't have any weapons on me."

"Pull up your pant legs," he said. "Good. Now your shirt and turn around."

I did as commanded.

"Okay. Let's go."

I walked to him, and he gestured for me to go out of the doorway first. He put the gun to my back, and I swore I could feel the cold metal through my clothes. Or was that the icy ball of fear in my stomach spreading through my body?

We went down the front stairs that opened up into a foyer. The living room was directly in front of me, and I could see Duncan's prostrate form on the ground. But I couldn't worry about him now. If I survived this, then I could worry about him.

The pistol jutted into my back with a little more force when Winters realized I had stopped walking. I immediately began moving again, past the living room and back toward the kitchen.

"Open that door," Winters commanded, motioning to the door in the hallway on the right.

He flipped on the light switch, and we traveled down another staircase until we were in a basement with a wood floor and stone walls. Cardboard boxes were stacked against the back wall, but otherwise, the cellar was empty.

"You've thought of everything," I murmured.

"Yes. Took long enough to plan, but it's all come together quite nicely."

"Oh?" I asked with curiosity.

He grabbed my arm and spun me around, getting close to

my face so I could see brown, soulless eyes staring into mine. "You're about to die. I'm not about to confess how fucking brilliant I am. I'm not a braggart."

"Noted."

"I have a question for you, though. How is it, even knowing you're about to die, you manage to have some courage? I've never understood that about you."

I shrugged, knowing that would infuriate him. He hated not having answers, and he never could figure me out. Even if I didn't have a plan, I lied and let him think I was one step ahead of him. And that got to him more than anything else.

"You're not going to break me," I said calmly. "You want to kill me? Get it done. Just promise me one thing."

"What?" he demanded impatiently.

"Make sure Hawk has loving parents, okay? That's all I care about."

He nodded, his jaw tight. "On your knees."

I dropped to the ground, seeing the world around me blur. Time slowed down. I licked my suddenly dry lips and made myself stare up at him. I would not bow my head like a soldier defeated in battle. If Winters wanted to kill me, he could look me in the eyes when he did it.

Winters raised the pistol and pointed it at me. The stench of fear permeated my nose. "Was it worth it?" I asked him.

"Was what worth it?"

"All this, just so you could be a celebrated American hero? Never mind that you were nothing but a disgrace to the FBI. They won't forgive you. They won't ever trust you again."

"Of course they will," Winters said, taking my baited hook like a kid taking candy.

"Why? What makes you so sure? Have you called your old superior? What was his name? Don Archer? Good guy. We talk, you know."

Winters's eyes widened. "Stop talking."

"Why?"

"Because I hate the lies coming out of your mouth."

"Really? Look at my phone. Scroll through my contacts and see if I'm lying."

I held in my smile of triumph when Winters was distracted by my ploy. He reached into his pocket and pulled out my phone, cursing when he saw his former superior's name.

"That's his cell number, direct line at the office, and his home phone number," I said.

"What the fuck!" Winters shouted. "How do you have this? *Why* do you have this?"

"Because he and I have a deal," I stated. "I give him just enough illegal activities to bust and he leaves the SINS alone. So you see, if you kill me, you won't be returning a hero—and Archer will take you out himself."

Winters howled like a man in a drunken rage. He threw my phone against the stone wall of the basement, and it fell to the floor, the screen cracked and useless. Making use of the distraction, I managed to get myself into a crouch and lunged at his legs. As he went down with me draped across him, a shot rang out. I felt a burning graze along my upper left arm, but it didn't slow me down; the pain only enraged me more. I was a mother with revenge on her mind.

"Barrett!" I heard Ash call. "Move!"

I rolled off Winters and hit the hard wood floor. Another shot rang out, but this time it came from the pistol in Ash's grip. Winters cried out, his hands going for his thigh. A hand came away bloody. He moaned and writhed like a pathetic animal I couldn't wait to slit from belly to nose.

While Winters was momentarily incapacitated, I sat up. Ash still had the gun aimed at Winters, but her hands shook. "You're good, Ash. Set it down."

She blew out a breath and dropped her arm to her side.

I crawled to Winters and swung my legs over his body to

straddle him. I pressed my hand to his injured thigh, and he groaned again.

"Duncan is in the living room," I said to Ash, not taking my eyes off Winters's pale face. His eyes were closed, but tears seeped from the corners. "And Hawk is on the second floor in a crib. Get everything ready."

"But, what about you—"

"I've got to take care of something first," I said. "You don't want to be here for this."

"You sure?"

I finally looked at her. Her face was drawn and tight, but she'd stick this out with me if I asked her to. "Yeah, I'm sure. See to Hawk and Duncan."

Ash picked up Winters's fallen weapon and with one last look at me, she headed for the stairs. I waited until I heard the door to the basement close before returning my attention to the struggling man underneath me. He attempted to buck me off, but he was rapidly losing blood from the wound in his thigh. Ash had nicked the femoral artery and if I waited long enough, he'd die. But I wasn't letting him off easy, nor would I let Ash become a murderer. She wasn't strong enough for that, which was why she hadn't blown his head off even though she'd had the opportunity.

Reaching up to my hair, I pulled out the hairpin Flynn had given me on our six-month wedding anniversary. My auburn hair tumbled loose. The hairpin was one long piece of metal, the handle intricate scrollwork. It was a dagger of beauty and craftsmanship.

I lowered the blade toward Winters's chest, and he let out a whimper. It only added fuel to my rage. Here was a man willing to kidnap a child and murder me; now that he was the one about to die, he cried like a sniveling coward.

I slit his shirt, baring his chest speckled with dark brown hair and tight nipples. I dragged the dagger lightly across his skin. "You mocked the emoticons," I said. "And yet, they're the reason you're in this position."

With a flick of my wrist, I slashed his skin and created a line right underneath his left nipple. Winters moaned in pain. I made a similar mark underneath his right nipple.

"And now for the smile," I said, my own lips pulling into a fierce and feral grin.

"No," Winters pleaded.

"Yes," I insisted, slowly trailing the point of the dagger across his belly into a half moon.

He yelled and screamed, but the sounds didn't penetrate my fog of rage. All I saw was a cloud of red. My vision narrowed at the pulse at his neck, throbbing quickly, attempting to pump blood through his body. But it was leaking out of him too fast. Much too fast.

"Please," Winters begged.

I leaned over him so that my hair brushed his bare chest. I stared into his eyes. "Please what?"

Winters's eyes were glazed with pain and I'd made my point. Three of them, actually.

*You can do this,* a voice in my head said. *This man took something from you. This is your revenge.*

"Aye," I whispered aloud to the voice of Igor Dolinsky's ghost.

Winters's brown eyes began to dim. I took the dagger and plunged it into the side of his neck, into the carotid artery. He jerked beneath me, spasming for a few seconds and then stilling.

I climbed off him and stood. I cleaned my dagger on Winters's torn shirt before twirling up my hair and sticking the hairpin through my bun. My hand that had been pressed against his bullet wound was bloody and damp. I wiped it on the back of my jeans.

With one last glance at Winters's dead form, I said calmly, "See you in hell."

## Chapter 30

I was covered in blood. Some of it my own. Some of it not. I was tired and cold. My vision was spotty, winking in and out. I leaned my head back against the wall that I'd slid down, unable to make it up the basement stairs.

"Barrett," a voice said.

I stared at my hands and started to giggle. "'*Out, damned spot.*'"

"Hen."

Looking up from my bloody hands, I stared into my husband's glittering blue gaze. "You almost look real," I said.

Flynn's jaw tensed, his hands moving over my body. "What have you done to yourself, love?"

His touch felt strong and sure. "You're here?"

"Aye."

"How?"

His fingers slid over my left bicep and I hissed. Cursing, Flynn ripped away my shirtsleeve to reveal the gunshot graze along my arm. He made a tourniquet to staunch the flow, pressing his hands to it.

"She's going to need stitches," Flynn said, turning his head to address the man in shadows.

Sasha nodded. "I'll tend to this."

He referred to Winters's corpse on the ground.

"Hawk," I whispered.

Flynn looked back at me, grabbing my hand to replace his. "Ash is with Hawk."

I closed my eyes and nodded. Relief swept through me. I felt myself being lifted, and I collapsed my head against the solid wall of Flynn's chest as he carted me up the basement stairs. He didn't stay on the first floor, but continued through the dark house to the second floor and into the bathroom of the master bedroom. Setting me down, he kept his arms around me which I appreciated since I was sure I would've fallen over.

Flynn turned on the light and set me on the closed toilet. Moving to the tub, he drew a bath before stripping me out of my bloody clothes, including the tourniquet on my arm.

"I'm going to have to stitch that, but it needs to be cleaned first," he said, holding out his hand to me and helping me into the water. It wasn't nearly hot enough, so I turned the hot water on full blast.

"Careful," he said. "You'll burn yourself."

"I'm cold."

I watched him explore the bathroom, looking under the sink and opening drawers. "What are you looking for?" I asked.

"First aid."

He came up empty and then looked at me. "I'm going to run downstairs and look around. You'll be okay?"

I nodded. "I need clean clothes."

"Aye."

He came back to the tub, leaned over, and placed his lips on mine. Connection and yearning zinged through me, finally making me feel something other than shock.

Flynn pulled back all too soon. "I'll be back."

The door to the bathroom shut softly and I was alone. I

turned off the water and reached for the soap. I washed my body and face, the water turning a murky pink. My left arm throbbed, and I examined the torn flesh of my arm. It didn't look deep, but it was flayed open.

Flynn still hadn't come back by the time I'd pulled the plug on the drain. I stood and reached for a bath towel to wrap around myself. As I dried off, Flynn returned with a small first aid kit. He set it on the sink and dug through it, pulling out a bottle of iodine, gauze, needle and thread.

And a bottle of scotch.

I shook my head. "No, I won't drink."

"Ash fed Hawk a bottle," he said. "Drink some. Trust me."

He unscrewed the lid and handed me the scotch. I took a drink straight from the bottle, enjoying the warming, burning sensation. "At least Winters had good taste in liquor," I muttered.

Flynn grunted, an excessively Scottish noise. It made me smile. "So how are you here? You and Sasha?"

As I sat in a towel, he cleansed my wound and studied it before threading the needle. I swallowed and kept my eyes trained on the bare bathroom wall.

"Duncan called before you left."

"I knew he couldn't be trusted," I said. "You and Sasha abandoned the plan in London."

"Arlington planted fake information." Though his touch was tender, when he pierced my skin with the needle, I let out an involuntary sound.

"What the fuck were you thinking?" he asked, head bent as he stitched up my wound. "Blazing in here? A lot of things could've gone wrong."

"But they didn't," I said. "We have our son back. That is the most important thing, isn't it?"

Flynn didn't reply, and I took another sip of whisky. He worked quickly stitching me up and then wrapped my arm in a layer of protective gauze.

"That'll hold until we get you to a doctor," Flynn said. His hand settled on my bare shoulder as he loomed over me.

I stared up at him, enjoying the feeling of heat running across my skin. Scotch, adrenaline, Flynn. I was feeling it all.

My arms ached with the need to hold my son.

"I need Hawk," I croaked.

"Aye," he said with a nod. "I found you a pair of sweats and a button-down. They're in the bedroom."

I reached up to pull back my hair. Flynn held out my hairpin that doubled as a weapon. I looked at it for a moment and then took it, jabbing it through my bun to keep it out of my face.

He grabbed my hand and led me out of the bathroom and into the bedroom. I quickly threw on clothes and then I was running for the door. Sounds came from downstairs, the shuffling of footsteps, voices in dulcet tones.

Flynn and I entered the living room. Duncan was awake. He sat on the couch, looking a bit woozy. Ash walked around, holding Hawk close and rubbing his back.

I held out my arms, and she set a sleeping Hawk into the crook of them. Flynn draped an arm around my shoulder, and for a moment, it was just the three of us having a reunion. Something inside of me clicked into place and I was finally able to take a deep breath for the first time in weeks.

"Glad to see you're awake," Flynn said to Duncan.

Duncan grimaced. "Bastard tranqed me the moment I stepped through the door. Where is he? I'd like to smash his face in."

"He's dead," Flynn answered flatly. "Sasha is in the basement cleaning up the evidence."

I didn't even want to know what that entailed, so I cradled Hawk closer and let my attention drift to the infant in my arms.

"Dead? How the—"

"Me," I said, interrupting Duncan. "I did it."

Duncan looked at Ash. "I'm missing something."

"I think we have a lot of puzzle pieces missing. Love, you should sit down," Flynn said to me.

I sank into a comfortable chair, feeling the adrenaline leave my body. It was nearly dawn, and I was suddenly exhausted; I'd been up for over twenty-four hours. I'd been reunited with my child. And I'd killed a man. Tortured him, actually.

Flynn knew. When he found me, I'd been covered in blood, not all of it mine. Sasha had no doubt learned the truth since he was dealing with Winters's body.

I looked around the room, noting the exhaustion, the faces lined with tiredness, the sluggishness of our mental faculties. None of us were operating on all cylinders.

"Where do we go from here?" Ash ventured to ask.

By default all of us turned to look at Flynn. "We wait until Sasha is finished in the basement. Let's all get comfortable. We aren't going anywhere for the time being."

## Chapter 31

I dozed as dawn turned into day. A baby cried, but I thought it was just a dream. It wasn't until I felt a hand on my shoulder and I woke that I realized it was Hawk.

Weariness tugged at my body, but I forced myself to stand and take Hawk out of the living room so he wouldn't disturb the other sleeping occupants. Ash and Duncan were spooning on the couch and Flynn was asleep, sitting up in a chair.

Sasha followed me upstairs to where I'd originally found Hawk. I took my son to the changing table and put him in a fresh diaper. I sat down in a chair and settled Hawk on my lap as I made a move to unbutton my shirt. Sasha turned his back to give me privacy.

Hawk had been drinking from a bottle for weeks, but I hoped he would go back to breastfeeding. I put him to my skin and waited.

"We have to burn down the house," Sasha said, his back still to me. "All of our prints are everywhere, there are a bullet holes in the walls, and a body."

"Hello, good morning to you, too."

Sasha didn't laugh at my jest.

"Is it weird that I'm not even surprised by what you just said? I'm either incredibly sleep deprived or a sociopath."

"Maybe both?" he said, finally showing me a hint of amusement.

"How are you still able to function?" I asked, sighing in relief when I felt Hawk nuzzling against me. Instinct would trump learned behavior. I hoped.

"Energy drinks," Sasha said, continuing the levity. He paused for a moment and then said, "Are we going to talk about the state of Winters's body?"

"I'd rather not," I said, switching Hawk to the other breast, but he seemed finished for now.

"Barrett," he said softly.

"Let's not do this, Sasha. You saw the body. Flynn saw the body. We don't need to rehash it." I closed my shirt. "You can turn around now. I'm decent."

He rubbed his jaw as he turned. His blond stubble made a raspy sound in the quiet, his blue eyes bright even though they were etched with fatigue. How was he still going?

"Because I'm the only one who can," he said, answering me.

I blinked. "Did I speak out loud?"

"Yes."

I sighed. "I'm more tired than I realized."

"We should wake the others. We all need to talk."

I stood with Hawk in my arms and followed Sasha back down to the living room. Duncan and Flynn were already awake, speaking in low tones while Ash continued to sleep. Duncan's hand stroked Ash's arm in a gesture of love and comfort.

"Any coffee in this place?" Duncan asked. "I can't plan without a cup of coffee."

"I'll see," Flynn said, pushing himself out of the chair. He strode to me and placed a chaste kiss on my lips and then ran a hand over Hawk's head, which had sprouted fine dark hair while he was away from us.

What else had we missed?

A bout of rage suddenly overtook me, making me want to kill Winters all over again, but make his death last longer. My kidnapped child combined with the wrath I felt toward Winters had taken me to a place inside myself that I hadn't known existed.

The bastard should've suffered more.

"Hen?" Flynn asked. "Why don't you come with me into the kitchen?"

I looked at him a moment. It was a subtle command in the guise of a suggestion. I nodded and stood. Carrying Hawk, I followed Flynn.

"Are you all right?" he asked me as he opened and closed cabinets, searching for coffee.

I adjusted Hawk and put him to my shoulder. My arms had quickly forgotten how it felt to hold my child; I remembered the weight of him, but he was bigger now. It was yet another reminder of what Winters had stolen from me.

"Am I all right?" I repeated quietly. "No, I'm not all right."

The smell of cheap coffee wafted through the air. It would get the job done, though, and at the moment, all we needed was enough caffeine so we could make the five-hour drive back to Dornoch.

"Talk to me, Barrett," Flynn said as he leaned against the counter.

"I can't. Not right now. I want to break things, I want Winters to still be alive so I can make him really suffer for what he did to me—to us."

Flynn's cobalt blue eyes glittered with his own anger, but he nodded because he understood.

He poured out the coffee into cups, but didn't have enough hands to carry it all back to the occupants waiting for us. It was slow moving, but finally everyone had mugs and seats. Hawk was asleep, but I wasn't ready to put him in his travel carrier. I needed him close to me, to remind myself that he was safe.

"Everyone lucid?" Flynn asked.

There were grunts and nods but we all looked as coherent as we were going to get without a good night's sleep.

"First of all, I want to address the situation of Winters," Flynn began. His eyes landed on Sasha.

Sasha nodded and answered, "I told Barrett that we need to burn the house down."

Ash pinched the bridge of her nose. "Oh, sure."

For some reason that made me laugh. It started as a giggle and then erupted into a full-on belly laugh. My body shook, and tears streamed out of the corners of my eyes.

Hawk made an adorable baby whimper and then quickly settled back down.

"I'm sorry," I said, gasping, trying to inhale a breath of air into my burning lungs. "It's just—"

"Completely ridiculous," Ash finished for me, her own face warring between mirth and disbelief. "This whole thing is fucking ridiculous."

I started laughing again and Ash finally joined in. The men looked at us like we were certifiable. They didn't understand.

I managed to get myself under control and so did Ash. Duncan ran a hand across her back. We were so close to snapping—I probably already had. I was at my limit and I was exhausted. I wasn't much use to anyone, and I certainly wasn't thinking clearly.

"Our prints are all over this place," Sasha continued as if nothing had happened.

"Not to mention Winters's body is in the basement," Duncan added.

Flynn nodded. "Aye. That's the best way to deal with this."

"And what about the rest?" I asked.

"Arlington," Flynn stated. "And the SINS member."

"We still don't know who that is," Duncan pointed out.

My arm started to ache and burn from the stitched-up bullet wound. I regretfully settled a sleeping Hawk into his carrier, tucking a baby blanket around him.

"We're not going to figure any of that out now, are we?" I asked. "Can we go home and deal with all of this?"

Flynn nodded. "I think that's the best idea. I'll stay and help Sasha with Winters—"

"You just found your son," Duncan interjected. "I'll stay."

"Thank you, brother," Flynn said softly.

"I guess that means I'm going with you," Ash said with a look at me.

I nodded. "Help me with Hawk's stuff?"

∽

An hour later, we were on the road homeward bound. The ride was silent. Flynn gripped the wheel, his face tense, eyes on the road. Ash dozed in the back next to Hawk, and even though he was close by, I felt myself turning around to look at him.

Flynn reached over and gripped my thigh. "You should sleep, love."

"I'm fine." I rested my hand on top of his. "You know what I want?"

"Tell me."

"I want a hot bath, my bed—with you in it—and our son sound asleep in a bassinet in our room."

"I think we can spare a day"—his eyes slid to me for one moment—"and a night."

I smiled in response as he turned his eyes back to the road.

"We're going to have to talk about it, you know. Really talk about it," he said.

"I know."

"Why won't you tell me? What are you afraid of? That I won't love you? That I wouldn't understand?"

I let out a laugh, but it sounded rusty. "You? You think this is about *you*?" I shook my head before leaning against the headrest and closing my eyes.

"You will not talk to Sasha about this," Flynn said, not letting the conversation go. "I want to be the one you turn to."

"You are the one I turn to." I opened my eyes and forced myself to stare at him.

"No, I'm the one who you use for sex whenever you need to work something out. You talk to Sasha."

"Not here," I said. "Ash is asleep in the back seat, and I don't want to her to wake up to witness our fight."

"Too late," came Ash's croaky, sleep-filled voice. "And I hate to be the one to break up the brewing fight, but your son needs changing."

## Chapter 32

Flynn was outside, hands shoved in his coat pockets, staring at the rolling hills. Ash and I had traded spots, and I was now in the back seat, trying to nurse a newly changed Hawk. He was having none of it.

"What's wrong with him?" Ash asked.

"Who? Flynn or Hawk?" I nearly groaned in frustration, wondering why Hawk was being so fussy.

"Both. But let's start with Hawk."

"I don't know." I altered Hawk's position, putting him to my shoulder and rubbing his back, hoping that would soothe him. His cry died out, and he whimpered against my neck. His tears broke my heart.

"How much did you hear?" I asked, finally lifting my eyes to Ash.

She bit her lip, but her blue eyes remained on me.

"Yeah," I sighed. "Thought so."

"Is he right? About what he said?"

"I don't have the brainpower for this right now. I'm exhausted and Hawk won't eat."

"Have you tried feeding him with a bottle?"

I shook my head. "I didn't even think that might be the issue." Unfortunately, I didn't have a breast pump on me.

"There's got to be a town between here and Dornoch that has a breast pump."

Breast pumps and murder. That had become my life.

I snorted with a bout of hysterical laughter. "I really need a nap," I said when Ash looked at me in confusion.

I set Hawk back into his car seat and strapped him in, keeping my hand on his baby belly. "We should go," I said.

Ash nodded. "I'll tell Flynn." She was about to get out the car, but she stopped.

"What?" I asked her.

"He's on the phone. And he doesn't look happy."

I took my eyes off Hawk long enough to glance out the window. The wind had picked up and teased the hair across Flynn's forehead. Even from a distance, I could see the tense ferocity coming from him. The phone was to his ear, and his jaw was clenched.

"You think something went wrong with burning down the house?" Ash asked. She ran a hand through her flat blond hair. "Yeah, I heard what I just said."

I shook my head. "I don't think so. Duncan and Sasha are capable. They've got that locked down. No, I think this is something else."

I watched Flynn hang up and then stride quickly to the car. He nearly ripped the door off its hinge. He sat for a moment gripping the steering wheel before finally turning on the ignition.

"Everyone buckled in?" he asked, his voice tight.

"Yes," Ash and I chimed together.

Flynn turned around to look at me and then at our sleeping son. He nodded and then faced front. We sped away in silence, but the tension was palpable. Ash and I waited for Flynn to speak.

"Someone tried to kill Ramsey," he clipped.

Ash gasped.

I shook my head. "How? Who knows he's on Orkney?"

"The million-dollar question," Flynn muttered, clenching his jaw.

"I'm guessing Ramsey is okay?" Ash asked.

"Well, it wasn't Jane Elliot calling, so aye. Ramsey's fine and he took care of the guy who came after him."

Ash glared at Flynn. "No need to get snippy. We're all tired. We should stop for coffee."

"No time," Flynn said. "Have to get home."

"Okay, then maybe you can stop for a breast pump," Ash said.

Flynn shook his head. "What are you talking about?"

"Hawk won't nurse," I said, finally speaking up. "A bottle might make it easier."

"Aye," he said, resigned. "All right. We'll stop, refuel, and get what we need. But then we have to get back to Dornoch."

We all agreed and kept driving.

"Did Ramsey call Duncan to tell him?" Ash asked, staring out the side window.

"No. I told him I'd tell Duncan. Duncan's got enough going on at the moment."

Ash nodded thoughtfully. "Wise."

"How's Jane doing?" I wondered. The poor girl had been kidnapped from her own birthday party, held prisoner in a remodeled castle, and was now on an isolated island with Ramsey Buchanan. There was an unmistakable chemistry between them, but I knew the power of Stockholm syndrome. More so when the captor wasn't a horrible monster.

"I think she's fine," Flynn said absently, eyes focused on the road. Storm clouds had rolled in, and raindrops had begun to fall, splattering the windshield.

"Fine?" I asked. I hoped he could hear the eye-roll in my tone. "Did you even ask about her?"

"No. Ramsey would've said something if she wasn't okay."

"You men," Ash huffed.

"I need to get out of this car," Flynn said. "I just keep putting my foot in my mouth, don't I?"

"We're all sleep deprived, and emotions are running high," I said in the way of explanation.

"Giving him a free pass, huh?" Ash asked with an amused chuckle.

"He *is* the father of my child. That gets him points," I said, shooting Flynn a grin in the rearview mirror. His gaze met mine, and I saw the lines around his eyes crinkle, so I knew he was smiling back at me.

I glanced at Hawk who was awake but quiet. I drew a finger down his smooth cheek, feeling content in the moment, knowing it wouldn't last because it never did.

∼

"That was Duncan. Everything went off without a hitch," Flynn said, hanging up the phone.

We all breathed a collective sigh of relief.

"Thank goodness," I said.

"They're on their way back to Dornoch. We'll see them in a few hours," he said, turning down the road that would take us to Duncan's estate. Though Flynn and I hadn't discussed it, we weren't yet ready to move back into our home. At the moment, there was safety in numbers—in those that we could trust. For the time being we'd stay in the east wing of Duncan's castle. There was certainly enough space.

"I'm so ready to be home," Ash said. "I need a shower and a nap."

"In what order?" I asked from the back seat. True to Flynn's words, after finding coffee and a breast pump, we hadn't stopped again. He'd taken some of the windy Highland roads a little fast, but the sky was now clear.

"I might fall asleep in the shower," Ash joked.

"Yeah, I think I've done that," I said.

"You have," Flynn said. "Right after Hawk was born. I walked into the bathroom, called your name, and got no response."

"Trying to prioritize your needs with a newborn's is damn near impossible," I reminded him even though I hadn't had to do it for very long. I thought of the weeks of Hawk's absence. The only way I was going to move forward was to compartmentalize it. He was back with us, safe, whole, and no worse for wear. Thank God. I'd still burn everything in the diaper bag from the Edinburgh house, not to mention any clothes that Hawk wore. I wanted no reminder of our time apart—it would be difficult enough to deal with it as it was.

Flynn pulled the car up into the driveway outside the garage and parked.

Ash was out of the vehicle and heading to the front door before I'd even managed to unlatch Hawk's travel carrier.

"Here, love, let me," Flynn said, taking Hawk from me. I gathered up the rest of Hawk's belongings and followed Flynn into the house.

The silence was eerie. No hounds came to greet us and neither did Betty, the lamb that had been given to me as a gift that I'd turned into a pet.

Flynn and I looked at each other, and he handed me the baby carrier. Flynn went ahead of me up the stairs, and I trailed behind him at a cautious distance. When we made it up to the second floor, I heard Ash scream. Flynn ran toward her bedroom at the end of the hallway. When I got to the bedroom doorway, I had to swallow the bile threatening to come up.

In the middle of the king-sized bed were the bloody remains of the three hounds that had once belonged to Malcolm.

Ash was turned away from the scene, shaking, and rubbing her hands up and down her arms.

"Take her downstairs," Flynn said to me.

I nodded, awkwardly trying to drag Ash out of the room. I clutched her hand tightly, struggling with Hawk's carrier in my other hand. "Come on," I said to her, leading her away. She had as much life in her as a limp rag doll. Tears streamed down her cheeks, and I wanted to wipe them away. But first I had to get us out of there.

"I'll check the rest of the house," Flynn said to my retreating back.

Betty, I didn't say. Because there was a good chance the lamb had found the same fate as the other animals, and I couldn't stomach the idea.

As I got Ash situated on the couch and grabbed her a glass of water, I thought about who had done this. The SINS member, obviously.

"Katherine," I said suddenly.

Ash looked at me with dull eyes. "What about her?"

"We left her here with guards. Where is she?" I demanded. "Watch Hawk." I dashed out of the living room and ran back up the stairs, continuing to the third floor. There were no signs of the guards that were supposed to be stationed outside of Katherine's room. I tried the door handle, discovering that it was locked.

I cursed. "Katherine?" I called out. "Katherine, it's Barrett."

There wasn't a reply. I didn't have a spare set of keys to unlock the door so I looked around, trying to figure out what I could use to get through the door. Who knew how long Katherine had been in there. Maybe she had pulled a Jane Elliot and made a rope from the bed sheets in an attempt to escape.

There was no way I could kick in the heavy, wood door of the room. I jogged back down to the second floor, calling for Flynn. He came out of a guest bedroom, eyes bright and bloodshot.

"What is it?" he asked.

"Katherine. Have you found the guards who were watching her?"

Flynn shook his head. "Is she still in her room?"

"I don't know. I need the key."

"Let's go," Flynn said. "I have a spare."

## Chapter 33

The room was empty. There was no sign of Katherine. Flynn checked the bathroom, came back into the bedroom, and shook his head.

It didn't make any sense.

"Where can she be? She was locked in," I asked.

Flynn's eyes were bleak. "I have no idea."

There was a noise, a shuffling of sorts, coming from the direction of the wood armoire resting against the far wall.

Flynn and I exchanged a quick look before he went to the armoire and opened the double doors. He pushed aside the hanging clothes to reveal Katherine sitting on the floor, her legs pulled up to her chest, her face resting on her knees.

"Katherine," Flynn said softly, crouching low to her level. She didn't raise her head. "Katherine," he said again, more forcefully. When she still didn't look up, Flynn waved me over.

Flynn moved out of the way so that I could speak to Katherine. "Katherine," I said. "It's Barrett." I touched the young woman's shoulder. She was so slight, fragile, and delicate.

A shudder worked its way through Katherine's body, and she finally lifted her head. Her eyes were listless and dazed.

"How long have you been in here?" I asked gently, purposefully keeping my voice low. She was like a frightened animal.

"I don't know," she said. She swallowed. "I heard shouting from the guards and then they left. I don't know where they went. I crawled into the armoire and haven't moved."

"Come on," I said, standing and reaching a hand down to help her up. "Let's get you something to eat."

Katherine looked at my hand before taking it. She swayed ever so slightly, and she wouldn't let go of me. I was suddenly feeling very protective of her, despite the fact that she'd abetted Winters. Though, to be fair, when she learned the truth behind Winters's deceit, she did attempt to do the right thing and help reunite me with my son. She'd fallen for Winters's charm, and he'd used her naïveté against her. She was only human.

Flynn followed as I took Katherine downstairs and into the living room. Ash held Hawk and was pacing back and forth in front of the unlit hearth. Hawk was screaming his head off.

"Here," Ash said, thrusting Hawk at me. I took him and put him to my shoulder, but he only cried harder.

"Hungry," I muttered. Hawk had terrible timing.

"Ash, will you take Katherine into the kitchen and get her something to eat?"

Ash nodded and Katherine trailed after her like a lost little duckling. When they were gone, I sat down on the couch, whipped open my shirt and prayed that Hawk wouldn't make it any more difficult. He nuzzled around for a moment and then latched on.

"I need to check out the dungeon," Flynn said, pitching his voice lower though there wasn't a chance Katherine and Ash could hear us from the kitchen.

"Do you think Elliot—"

"Probably."

"This mess just keeps getting bigger, doesn't it?" I asked, glancing down at Hawk.

"Aye." He came over to me and kissed me briefly on the lips before leaving.

I finished nursing Hawk and then changed him. Just as I was finishing up, the front door opened and Sasha and Duncan walked into the living room.

"We weren't expecting you for another few hours," I said, lifting Hawk and putting him to my shoulder again.

Duncan cleared his throat and looked away with an amused grin. "Barrett? You might want to re-button your shirt."

"Oops," I muttered. Exhaustion was finally getting the best of me. I set Hawk down in his carrier and quickly closed my shirt.

"Where is everyone?" Sasha asked, his voice strangely low.

I looked at him, noting the height of color on his Slavic cheekbones, the banked desire in his eyes. He wasn't even attempting to hide it. So I ignored it. I had bigger issues to contend with than Sasha's unrequited love for me.

"Katherine and Ash are in the kitchen. Flynn is in the dungeon."

"What's he doing down there?" Duncan inquired.

I briefly recounted what we'd discovered from the moment we walked through the front door—the dogs, Katherine hiding in the armoire, the absence of the guards.

Duncan let out an impressive stream of Gaelic curses. Sasha added his own in Russian. We were a regular melting pot, I thought, snorting with dry humor.

"I don't even know what to deal with first," Duncan said.

"Say hello to your wife," I suggested.

"Aye," Duncan nodded before heading out of the living room.

"I guess that means I'll go help your husband," Sasha suggested.

"He's been down there a long time. Which I guess means he found something."

Sasha nodded. "Those were my thoughts." He stared at me for a long moment, and then his gaze dipped to Hawk who had finally settled down enough to nap. "I'm glad we found him. I'm glad he's back where he belongs."

"Thank you for being here," I said sincerely. "It… Well, thank you."

"You're welcome."

I lifted Hawk in his carrier and said, "Tell Flynn I went up to our room. I'm about to pass out where I'm standing."

"I will."

As I walked past Sasha, his hand reached up to brush away a tendril of hair that had escaped the hairpin. "Don't," I whispered.

His hand dropped, and he let me walk out of the living room. I refused to look back at him. I refused to see the look of despair on his face, the look I'd put there.

∼

Our guest room had been untouched. There were no surprises when I entered it. I set Hawk down and immediately made my way to the bathroom. I shed my clothes and kicked them into a pile and took my hair down, setting the hairpin on the sink counter. I stared at my reflection, wondering if my eyes were a little harder, my resolve a little stronger, my soul a little blacker.

A decent person would feel remorse for the wrongs she'd done.

I wasn't a decent person.

Turning on the shower, I made sure it was scalding before I stepped in. I tried to keep my bandaged arm from getting wet as I scrubbed my skin, wanting to remove any and all traces of the last three days. I would never be clean enough, so I would learn to live with the dirty, ugly parts of me.

Hawk was still asleep by the time I finished my shower. I picked him up and cradled him against my naked chest. I needed him as much as he needed me. Crawling beneath the covers, I settled down and quickly fell asleep. I didn't wake up until a few hours later when the sky was dark. I briefly thought it might be nighttime, but then I heard the rumble of thunder.

"Did I wake you?" Flynn asked as he collapsed tiredly onto the bed.

"It's okay," I said, reaching a hand out to him.

"How's Hawk?" The words came out muffled because Flynn spoke into the pillow. His eyes drifted closed, and I knew he was having trouble keeping them open.

"Fine."

"Good. Found Elliot and the guards. Throats were slit."

I sent a silent apology to the man who I'd promised a quick death. A wave of guilt shot through me when I thought of the guards who had died because they had been loyal to Flynn.

"Found Betty."

"Please, don't tell me—"

"She's fine. She somehow got locked in the pantry."

"Thank God. I can't stomach more innocent blood being shed."

"I know." Flynn rolled over onto his back, looking more tired than I had ever seen him.

"So the last few hours were spent cleaning up?"

He nodded. "Aye. I'm so exhausted. Can we talk later?"

"Yes." I leaned over and pecked him on the lips. He scooted closer and then his breathing evened out. I felt Hawk stir against my skin and sat up, changing the angle of him to rest against my breast. I wondered if we'd ever have a routine again. After he nursed and I cleaned him up, I threw on some clothes and padded downstairs, leaving Flynn to sleep for a few hours uninterrupted.

The house was quiet, and I expected the kitchen to be unoccupied, but Sasha was sitting at the table and staring out the window. The storm was full throttle now, but I found it soothing because it was something I could count on. There had been so little of that lately.

Without a word, I set Hawk in his arms so I could have my hands free to cook. "You hungry?" I asked him.

Sasha didn't answer me right away because he was staring down at Hawk, a strange look on his face. Finally, he looked up at me.

"Sorry. What did you say?" he asked.

"You hungry?" I repeated.

He nodded.

I went to the refrigerator to survey the ingredients I had on hand. I wanted a tried-and-true omelet, and I had everything to make a really good one.

"Can I ask you something?" Sasha queried.

"Sure," I said, grabbing a sharp knife and a cutting board.

"What's your contingency plan? For Hawk?"

I frowned. "What do you mean?" I glanced up briefly from chopping chives. Sasha's eyes were a bright, ice blue.

"If you and Campbell die," he stated baldly.

"Can I ask *you* a question?" Without waiting for his nod, I went on, "Why do you call Flynn by his last name?"

"If I think of him as 'Flynn' he might just become a friend. And I don't know if I can be friends with him—not when I want his wife."

I pointed the blade at him. "This knife is sharp."

"You asked," he pointed out.

"Yeah," I sighed. "I did."

"Now you answer my question. About Hawk."

"I don't know," I said. "I used to think Ash and Duncan,

but their lives aren't very safe either. I don't have family. I suppose there is Ash's brother, Jack. I trust him."

"You still sound reluctant."

I shrugged and dumped the chives into the buttered skillet. "I don't like Ash's parents. And if Hawk lived with Jack, they'd be around."

"Hmm," he said.

"I never wanted kids," I voiced. "Never planned to have them."

"What changed?" Sasha wondered.

"Hawk was an accident," I said, not even feeling remorse over admitting it. It was the truth. "I felt differently—when I was forced to confront the actual situation, I made a choice I didn't expect. And now, I have to think about things like who will raise my son if Flynn and I die."

I whisked the eggs quickly and just long enough so they'd come out fluffy before dumping them into the skillet. "What about you?"

"What about me?"

"Kids?"

"I think I need to find a woman first," he said in a dry tone.

"Didn't answer my question." I shot him a look.

"We'll see. At the moment, I think I've got bigger problems to worry about."

## Chapter 34

Sasha closed the doors to the living room giving us an added measure of privacy. He took a seat on the couch, settling in for our meeting.

"She's asleep?" Flynn asked me.

I nodded. "The doctor gave her a mild sedative to help her. She was only too eager to take it. She's having nightmares."

Last night, Katherine had awakened the entire house by screaming in her sleep. Her erratic slumber, combined with the rest of us running on empty left us barely functioning. We'd sent for the doctor at dawn, not caring about the early hour. After the doctor had seen to Katherine, he looked at my arm, gave me a shot of antibiotics and left. My injury hadn't even fazed him, nor did he ask how I'd come by it. We'd all napped throughout the day, but it wasn't enough. Flynn and I had a melding of our bodies, nothing more than quick interlude, to solidify us. It was our version of a deep breath, of recommitting to one another.

Hawk was asleep in the bassinet in the corner. I looked over at him again before leaning down to pet the lamb at my feet. Betty had taken to following me around. I didn't blame her for feeling lost.

"I think Katherine should go back to her family," Ash said. "She's not a threat to us. And with Winters gone…"

Flynn nodded. "Aye. I agree."

I frowned at him. "That's not what I was expecting you to say."

Flynn stood by the lit fireplace, a glass of scotch in his hand. "The only people I trust are in this room—aside from Ramsey—and he's still on Orkney."

Flynn had told Duncan about the attack on Ramsey's life, but the younger Buchanan was resilient and safe. "Should we bring him home?" Duncan wondered.

"No. I have an idea," Flynn said.

Everyone glanced at me. "Don't look at me. He hasn't told me anything yet."

We all turned back to Flynn and gave him our undivided attention. He swirled his drink and stared at its contents before speaking. "We still don't know who's trying to take over the SINS, but we do know he tried to have the Buchanan line taken out. It's safe to say he wants me out of the way, too. They don't want any opposition. Arlington is playing every side, every angle, but I'm sure he's been tipped off that we're on to him. He's probably gone underground."

I nodded. Everything he said made sense.

Flynn took a deep breath. "The only way to bring out the traitor is to give him what he wants."

"The SINS?" Ash asked in confusion.

Flynn nodded. "Aye."

"But how do we do that?" she wondered.

Flynn's eyes met mine when he replied, "We have to die. The three of us. Ramsey, Duncan and myself."

"You want to stage your deaths," I said in complete understanding.

"Aye," Flynn said.

"Bloody brilliant," Duncan said.

"You can't be serious," Ash scoffed.

"Completely," Flynn said.

"But how?" Ash asked in exasperation. "How are you going to pull this off?"

"There was an attempt on Ramsey's life," Flynn said. "We just let people think he was assassinated. And before we take Katherine back to her family, we tell her. She'll help with word of mouth."

"And that will ensure that attention is focused on eliminating Flynn and me," Duncan said. "We'll stage our deaths together so it looks like they succeeded. I'm thinking a big explosion."

Flynn and Duncan chuckled. Ash had her own explosion. "How the hell can you find this funny?"

"Because we aren't really going to die," Duncan assured her.

"And what do you expect me to do? Wait around like a wife hoping her husband comes back from war?"

Duncan rose from his seat next to her and jerked Ash to her feet. He tugged her out of the living room even as she protested, loudly and vocally.

"We won't be seeing them again tonight," Sasha muttered.

"Probably not," I agreed.

"Why are you so calm?" Sasha asked.

"Because there's nothing to worry about," I said. I looked at Flynn. "Right?"

"Aye," Flynn said. He ran a hand down his stubbly jaw, black whiskers raspy against his fingers.

"What?" I demanded.

"I want you and Ash to take Hawk and go to New York."

My eyes widened so much I thought they'd pop out of my head. "You want—"

"That's my cue," Sasha said, rising and departing quickly.

The living room doors shut again, and Flynn and I were left in privacy.

"How can you suggest that?" I asked, standing up, ready to battle.

Flynn came to me, took my hand, and hauled me up toward his hard body. "You and Hawk aren't safe here, Barrett."

"And you think we'll be safer in New York?"

"Aye. You'll stay at The Rex. Brad will be close by. It will make me feel better."

I slid my hands up his arms to loop around his neck. "And I'm just supposed to go to New York while you and Duncan enact this plan to fake your deaths?"

"We've dealt with worse separations," he said, his mouth coming for my lips.

"Aye," I whispered, throwing that word back at him.

Flynn's lips covered mine, his tongue demanding entry. I gave in, sinking into his body. We struggled out of our clothes, and Flynn took me on the bearskin rug in front of the fireplace. Our coupling was fierce and passionate. We were saying goodbye, not knowing when we'd see each other again.

～

Flynn and I said goodbye to each other all night, but we ended up moving to our guest room and a bed. It was much more comfortable, but no less passionate. Hawk slept in our room in his bassinet.

Near dawn, Flynn took me into his arms; I pressed my head to his chest and fell asleep to the sound of his heartbeat in my ear. It felt like no time had passed when I was being shaken awake.

"Hmm?" I strived to open my eyes as I was tugged from unconsciousness. "Is it Hawk?"

"No, hen," Flynn said, his voice raspy. "It's time for you to get up."

When I registered that my son didn't need me, I rolled over and grasped Flynn's pillow and brought it to my chest. "Few more minutes."

Flynn was insistent. "A lot has to get done today, love."

I flipped onto my back and managed to crack my eyes open. "We're leaving today, aren't we?"

He nodded. "You're going to New York with Ash and Hawk."

"I know it's best for us—safer," I said. "But I hate being separated from you."

"I do too," he assured me. "But I have to know you both are safe. And Scotland isn't safe for you right now."

I threw my legs over the side of the bed, realizing I was still naked. A shiver worked its way down my spine as I got up and went to get some clothes. I checked on Hawk, but he was still sound asleep.

"We need to discuss something," he said.

"I'm listening."

"I want Sasha to go with you. Back to New York."

I paused. "You need him here. There are so few people you can trust at the moment, and he's one of them. You need him here with you and Duncan," I insisted. "I'll be in The Rex. Brad will be there, so will Lacey. I'll have people."

"Barrett," he began.

"Please, Flynn," I begged. "I'm leaving Scotland to protect our son. But I need you protected too."

"Sasha's done enough for me. I can't ask him this."

"Then I will."

"You don't fight fair," Flynn said.

"Do you?" I shot back.

"You fight to survive. At any cost."

He cradled my cheek in his large hand. I closed my eyes

briefly, wanting to soak up the last few moments together. Hawk began to cry, and Flynn leaned over to kiss my lips.

"We'll all be together soon," he promised. "This is just temporary."

I sighed and then stepped away to go to Hawk. I put him to my shoulder and began to rub his back, hoping to soothe him enough so Flynn and I could finish our conversation, but Flynn was heading for the door.

"Sasha stays with you," I said.

"Aye, Barrett. Sasha will stay with me."

～

I stood alone gazing out at Dornoch Firth. Dark, ominous clouds were far out on the horizon, and the waves crashed against craggy rocks. Rain was imminent, and it was cold enough that it might turn to snow.

Shivering, I hunched lower in my coat. I wasn't ready to go inside. Because the minute I went inside, I'd have to take Hawk and Ash and leave for New York. And I wasn't ready to say goodbye to Dornoch, the Highlands, my husband. For some reason, it didn't feel like an "until we meet again" kind of goodbye. It felt permanent.

Just as I was on the brink of exhausted tears, I heard footsteps behind me. I swiped at my cheeks, not wanting anyone to see how much leaving Flynn was killing me.

"Barrett?" I heard Sasha ask. "What's wrong?"

"Nothing," I said through a strained throat. "Why would you think something's wrong?"

"I can see you shaking. You're either cold or crying. Maybe both."

"I'm fine."

He came to stand next to me and shoved his hands deep into his pockets. The bitter wind teased the strands of bright blond hair at his temples. "Campbell said you wanted to speak with me?"

I inhaled a breath and nodded. "I can't thank you enough. For what you've done for me. For Flynn. For Hawk." I kept my eyes trained on his.

"Ask," he said softly.

"Will you stay with Flynn and help him with this? There aren't many people he can trust right now."

Sasha's gaze slid from mine as he peered out at the firth. "I can't, Barrett."

"Why?"

"Have you forgotten that I'm the head of the Russian mob?" he demanded.

I blinked. "Of course I haven't forgotten."

"I've been away long enough. I have to get back."

"Sasha," I pleaded.

"No, Barrett," he said harshly. "You do not get to do this. Not again."

"What am I doing?" I demanded. "Begging you to help my husband? You helped us once already. Why won't you do it now?"

"I came for you. I helped find Hawk because of you." He took a step closer to me, and before I could stop him, he placed his hands on my cheeks, crowding into my space so I couldn't breathe.

"You're killing me slowly, Barrett. And I don't have the strength to stop you. So please, don't ask me for anything more."

I hated the pain in his gaze; I hated that I put it there. Closing my eyes, I shut it out, so I didn't have to see it. I nodded.

Sasha held my face for a moment longer and then released me, but I was the one who took a step back.

"We leave for New York in an hour," I said, my voice clipped.

## Chapter 35

"It's cold in here," Ash said.

"I can have the temperature adjusted," I said as I held Hawk and fed him from a bottle.

"Oh, I'm not talking about the temperature of the plane," Ash said with a wry grin. "I'm talking about your treatment of Sasha."

The man Ash was discussing currently sat as far away from us as possible in the rear of the private plane. We were only forty-five minutes in to our eight-hour journey, and I'd been freezing out Sasha from the moment he told me he wouldn't stay in Scotland to help Flynn.

Rationally, I didn't blame him. Emotionally, on the other hand...

"I thought he was going to stay and help Flynn and Duncan," Ash said. "That's what Duncan told me."

"Change of plans," I said, not wanting to unload everything without even a modicum of privacy.

"How is Flynn taking the change of plans?" Ash asked, lowering her voice. "I can't imagine he's happy to have Sasha in the same city as you without him there."

I unhooked my seatbelt so I could move around in my

seat. Hawk finished his bottle, and I put him to my shoulder to burp him.

"What makes you say that?" I asked Ash.

She snorted. "Don't play dumb. Everyone knows Sasha is head over heels in love with you."

"Ash," I warned.

"It's painfully obvious, you know."

"Can we please talk about something else? Anything else."

"Fine. How long do you think it will take for all this to end?"

"Can you ask questions I have the answers to?" I grumbled.

"Tell me not to worry," she demanded. "Tell me I have nothing to worry about. Duncan survived a bullet to the chest. This next part of the plan will be a breeze. Right?"

Instead of replying, I looked away from her and glanced out the window. We soared through white puffy clouds. How did I tell my best friend that I was a "glass is half empty" person these days?

"Yeah, I was afraid of that," Ash said with a sigh. "I can see it all over your face. Do you have any idea what we're supposed to do while we wait around for all this to pan out?"

"Stay busy," I said.

"Obviously. Any ideas?" she pressed.

I sighed. "Can we just touch down and get situated first?"

Ash rolled her eyes and reached for her bag. "Fine. You relax. Take care of your son. I'll make a list."

Relax on an airplane? The last time I'd been on this airplane, we'd had to make an emergency landing due to weather. I remembered how Flynn had attempted to calm me down. A lump of emotion settled in my throat. I hated that we were separated, and that I couldn't be there for him. But it was only for a finite amount of time. I just wished I knew for how long.

It was around ten p.m. when I finally got Hawk to the private penthouse suite in The Rex Hotel. Flynn had already called ahead, and there was a bassinet and changing table in the bedroom.

Everything looked exactly the same. It was familiar and comforting—it had a special place in my heart. The night Flynn and I had met, he'd brought me here. Though we'd met due to my brother's callousness and selfishness, Flynn and I both had never imagined what was to occur between us. Kidnapping, the FBI, marriage, a baby. We'd lived a lot in our short time together. I just hoped there was more living to do.

I put Hawk down and then closed the bedroom door. My cell phone vibrated. I collapsed onto the couch and put the phone to my ear.

"How are you still awake?" I asked Flynn. It was a little after three a.m. in Scotland. "We didn't even sleep last night. Or was it this morning? I'm so jet-lagged."

"Running on scotch fumes," Flynn said. His raspy voice with his brogue sent tingles down my spine. I was exhausted and sad and yet I wanted him. Desire was a funny thing.

"I'm sitting in front of the fireplace, staring into the flames, and nursing a glass of scotch. If I weren't so damn exhausted, I'd be furious."

"I know how that goes," I agreed. "I'm worried that when I catch up on my sleep, all I'll feel is anger."

"I'm going to find the bastard that has caused us all so much heartache, and I'm going to kill him with my bare hands."

"Arlington, too," I reminded him, though I knew he needed no reminder.

"English weasel. No loyalty to anyone or anything."

"Easy, love," I said, wishing I was there next to him to tame the wild beast of his temper. "This royally sucks."

"Aye. It does." He sighed. "We buried Elliot today, and I took Betty to Barnabas and asked him to take care of her until you get back to Dornoch."

I fell silent, hating that I was even going to ask the question. To ask seemed to make it a possibility; it gave doubts a voice. I didn't need any more doubts.

"Will I come back to Dornoch?" I asked softly.

"Ah, hen," Flynn began. "I wish I was with you. I'd wrap my arms around you and promise to bring you home. For now, you'll just have to settle for my word. You and Hawk will be back in Scotland before you know it. In the meantime, keep busy. If you need anything, talk to Brad."

"I will."

"Good night, hen."

"Good night, love."

We hung up, and then I went to get ready for bed. I was so overtired I had trouble falling asleep, my mind spinning out of control. Though Hawk was nearby in the bassinet, he was still too far away for my liking. I got up to check on him, watching him sleep. I placed a gentle hand on his belly, the rise and fall of it the best form of comfort. With a deep breath of my own, I climbed back into bed and fell asleep.

∼

*Igor Dolinsky trails a finger up and down my bare arm, the white sheet from the king-sized bed pulled up under my breasts to shield my nudity. His bare chest is in my sight as his foot peeks out from tangled blankets.*

*"Why could you never admit your desire for me when I was alive?" Dolinsky asks.*

*"Why do I see you in my dreams?" I ask him back.*

*He smiles, his mouth twisting with humor. "Because I symbolize everything you detest about yourself. Every terrible gruesome thing you've ever done is mirrored through me. You see me because you're not sure you want absolution."*

"I still don't understand why I see you here. Like this." I gesture to our lack of clothing. I take in his rumpled hair. It looks like my fingers tore through it as I gripped him to me.

"Because only in your dreams can you admit to all the things you'd rather forget. You wanted me—you pretended to want me, in the beginning, but at some point, your wanting me became real."

"Stop," I command.

"No," he says, rolling over and taking me under him. "Admit it, Barrett. You wanted a killer. Desired him, wanted to feel his hands on your skin." He shifts and presses into me. I can feel his arousal hard against me.

"Admit it," he repeats. His head descends, brushing his lips against mine. My hand grasps the back of his head to bring him closer. We clash together, angry and violent, two killers, two people who will stop at nothing to have everything we want. We use people and toss them away.

I'm not sure I still know the meaning of love.

A baby cries.

Dolinsky kisses me harder. I bite his lips and draw blood.

"My son needs me," I pant against him.

"So go to him." Dolinsky climbs off me. "But just remember, I'll be here waiting for you. I'll always be here for you."

## Chapter 36

"You look like hell," Lacey said with a smirk as she embraced me.

I laughed. "I know."

Only a handful of people had an access key card to get into the penthouse suite without having to check in with the front desk. The manager of The Rex Burlesque club was one of them. I was glad to see her, but before I could wave her in, she was already at the refrigerator making herself at home.

"And where is your adorable child?" she asked, unscrewing the top of a bottle of sparkling water and taking a sip.

"Napping. Hawk suffers jet lag, just like the rest of us."

Lacey grinned. "So Flynn's son isn't infallible. Interesting."

I sat on the couch while Lacey took a seat in a chair, crossing her long legs encased in three-hundred-dollar jeans. She looked sleek and impeccable while I probably looked like a weathered hag.

"So far, Hawk is exactly like his father," I said. "Stubborn, unyielding, and very vocal when he wants something."

Lacey's smile softened. "Should we discuss the elephant in the room?"

"Which elephant? Because there are a few."

She didn't find me funny. Not that I blamed her. I was jet-lagged and exhausted on top of that. I doubted I'd be rational ever again.

"Hawk's kidnapping," she said. "Why didn't you let me come over there?"

"What could you have done?" I asked her.

"I could've been there for you."

I appreciated her sentiment. I did. But how did I explain it to her? Those weeks of terror, vacillating between hope and despair that I'd ever see my child again. Not to mention the strain it had put on my marriage. And just when Flynn and I were getting back on track, he had to fake his own death in hopes that the traitor might make a play for the leadership of the SINS.

"I needed what I needed," I said slowly. "And it wasn't about anyone else."

"Yeah," she sighed. "I know it wasn't about me."

"Can we please talk about something else?" I begged. "The last thing I want to do is rehash the last month. I think about it enough."

"That's fair," Lacey said.

"Are you still sleeping with Brad?" I asked her.

"Honey, if we're going to have man talk, I need a martini."

"Have at it," I said. "But count me out."

"Because it's too early in the day?"

"Because I'm breastfeeding."

"Oh. Right. Well, I won't drink alone."

I picked up the hotel phone and ordered every dessert on the menu. When I hung up, I looked at Lacey. "Will that do?"

"It's a valid substitute," Lacey allowed.

"Okay, so save the good stuff for when the dessert gets here. Tell me about the club."

"Alia is ready to take over as full-time manager," Lacey said. "And I'm ready to move on and do something else."

"I know you stayed at The Rex longer than you wanted to," I said. "I appreciate that and so does Flynn, but it's time you got what you wanted. Lacey, you're fired."

She grinned. "Really? You mean that?"

I mirrored her smile and laughed. "I mean it."

"Oh, wow." She leaned back in her chair and shook her head. "I might go on a vacation. A real one that lasts fifteen days and all I do is read trashy books on the beach while some sexy young man brings me piña coladas."

"That sounds amazing. Flynn still owes me a honeymoon."

"You'll have to bring Hawk."

I nodded. "I plan to. I'm never letting him out of my sight ever again."

∽

The next few days I spent close to The Rex, catching up on sleep and trying to get my life into some sort of orderly routine. Anger was the emotion I felt foremost. It was at the front of my mind. Every time I looked at Hawk, I was reminded of what I'd already lost, what I could've lost, and that Flynn and I weren't on the same continent.

Rage filled me up, strangled my throat, and made it impossible to focus on anything else. It made me snappish and volatile. I wanted to throw things just to see them break. I wanted to destroy.

"You need an outlet for your anger," Ash said to me one afternoon when she came over to visit. She was staying at her brother's apartment. Jack was away on business and Ash had the entire place to herself. Duncan wasn't happy that she'd chosen to stay outside of The Rex, but Ash now traveled with a bodyguard. And there was only so much Duncan could do with an ocean separating them.

"You should take up running again," she suggested. "You always liked to run in Central Park."

"It's winter," I reminded her and gestured to the living room window with the drapes pulled back. White flakes lazily floated out of the sky to land on the ground. It wasn't cold enough to stick, so the roads were clear, but it was just nasty enough that I refused to be out in it.

"The Rex has a gym."

"I can't leave Hawk."

"You've been cooped up here and refuse to leave his side. It's not healthy. For either of you."

"I can't leave him," I insisted again.

I'd left him once, and he'd been taken right out of his crib from our home. I didn't need a shrink to tell me why I was having issues leaving my son.

"I've been wanting to take a self-defense class," Ash stated, skating past my refusal to part from Hawk.

"Yeah?" I asked, getting up off the couch to put on another pot of water for tea.

"Yeah. I think it would make me feel better," she said. "I kind of freeze up in situations, and I want to do anything I can to change that."

I nodded. "That's a good idea."

"Will you take the class with me? I was going to hire a private instructor. He could come here. Then you wouldn't have to leave Hawk."

"You'd do that for me?"

"Of course," she said, her face frowning in confusion. "Why wouldn't I do that for you?"

I shook my head and then shrugged. While we waited for the teakettle to boil, I sat down on the carpeted floor of the living room. Hawk was on a blanket, flipped onto his back, his eyes slowly scanning the ceiling.

The teakettle began to whistle, and Ash hopped up from her chair. After adding a liberal amount of honey to my mug, she set it down on the coffee table for me. It was within my reach, but I left it to cool.

"This city sucks," Ash said suddenly, gripping her cup and settling back down into her chair.

I let out a startled laugh. "It's New York. The epicenter."

"Used to be," Ash began. "You know, when I first moved to Dornoch, I wondered what the hell I was going to do. The town is obnoxiously small and quiet—so quiet I could hear myself think. I didn't like that."

I smiled in understanding. "And now?"

"Now, I don't want to live in any other place. I miss Duncan."

"I miss Flynn."

"No, I mean I *really* miss Duncan," Ash stated.

I nodded. I knew what she was referring to. "Do you think all Scottish men are as amazing in bed as Flynn and Duncan?"

A beautiful blush stained Ash's fair cheeks. "I don't know. Maybe we should ask Jane Elliot the next time we see her. I'm dying to know what's happened between her and Ramsey."

I giggled like a schoolgirl.

"Don't deny that you want to know, too."

"No denying here," I assured her. "So have you made a list of the possible ways to keep us occupied while we're in New York?"

"I did."

"Do any of them include charity events?" I demanded.

"My mother might have mentioned a few she thought I should attend."

I rolled my eyes.

"My life was pretty shallow," she said softly. "How did we ever stay friends?"

"Your life wasn't shallow," I protested.

"Barrett," she warned.

"Fine. Maybe your life was a *tad* shallow—but you weren't. That's why we stayed friends."

"I've been thinking about something you mentioned way back when—about Lacey having an art show."

"Yeah."

"I think I want to open an art gallery in Dornoch."

"Really?" I asked in surprise.

She nodded. "I think it could be kind of great. It would give me a focus—something other than just becoming the wife of Duncan Buchanan and it would be a way for me to be in the community. Besides, it would absolutely help Lacey, and I love her work. I'd love to showcase it. What do you think?"

"I think it's a great idea," I said truthfully.

Now what the hell was I going to do?

## Chapter 37

I wiped the sweat out of my eyes and slapped my hand against the buttons on the treadmill. It began to slow to a cool-down pace. I'd only been able to run a few miles. I was out of shape. Really out of shape. Having a baby had taken its toll on my body—not surprising or shocking. I hoped it didn't take long to regain my strength and stamina.

Still on my kick not to leave Hawk alone, I'd called down to the front desk and had someone bring up one of the state-of-the-art treadmill machines from The Rex gym.

I climbed off the machine and grabbed the towel hanging on one of the arms. I dragged it across my forehead as I waited for my breathing to return to normal. Running seemed to take the edge off my lingering anger. For the moment anyway.

The hotel phone rang, and I went to answer it. Simone at the front desk informed me that I had a visitor by the name of Sasha Petrovich. I told her to send him up.

I hadn't seen or spoken to him since the night we landed in New York. I wasn't sure I wanted to see him now, but it seemed petty to refuse.

As my head was in the refrigerator to grab a bottle of

water, the elevator doors chimed open. I stood up and watched Sasha stroll into the living room, our eyes meeting. His gaze slowly swept down my body. I was in a sports bra and spandex shorts.

He'd seen me in less.

Clearing his throat, his gaze came back up to my face. "Sorry, I didn't call."

"It's okay." I took a long swallow from the bottle of water.

"How's Hawk?" he asked.

"Fine."

He nodded.

"Why are you here?" I asked.

"I wanted to check in on you," he admitted. "I don't like how we left things between us."

I sighed. "Do you want something to drink?"

He shoved his hands into his trouser pockets and shook his head. "I'm good."

We stood, neither one of us saying anything, the awkwardness between us growing. We'd never had awkwardness—not even after Sasha had videotaped me with Dolinsky. Why were we awkward now? We were at an impasse, I realized. Our relationship thus far had been me taking from him. It wasn't fair and he didn't deserve it.

"I'm an awful person," I said.

"No," he insisted. "You're not."

"I hate how I treat you."

"I let you."

"You were right, though. That I use your feelings for me against you. I never would've dreamed of asking you to stay in Scotland with Flynn and Duncan if—"

"Stop," he begged. "I can't take this. Not from you. It's all gotten so fucked up, Barrett. Six months! I don't hear from you for six months, and then the moment you called, asking me for something, I came. I know I'm not your husband, and I know you don't love me, but I can't keep being a masochist."

I nodded, my throat tight. Hawk cried, the sound of it filtering through the cracked door of the bedroom. Before I knew it, my feet were carrying me to him. Pure instinct. I changed him quickly and brought him out to the living room. Sasha had finally taken a seat on the couch, stretching out his legs in front of him.

Hawk needed to be fed and I wanted to make him a bottle. Unfortunately, I couldn't hold him while doing it.

"I'll take him for you," Sasha said when he saw my struggle.

"You sure?"

He nodded. I gently set Hawk into his arms. It made me pause for a moment, like when I saw Flynn or Duncan holding Hawk. Powerful men cradling a fragile baby always made my brain scramble.

When I had Hawk's bottle ready, I moved to take him back in my arms and feed him, but Sasha offered to do it so I could take a shower. I made sure it was fast, not wanting to take advantage of Sasha any more than I already had.

"Thanks," I said, coming out into the living room, dressed in comfortable sweats. I reached for Hawk, and Sasha gave him to me.

"Oh, no," I said with a chuckle, gesturing with my chin to Sasha's shirt. "Looks like you've been Hawked."

Sasha frowned in confusion before his gaze found the wet splotch on his shirt. He chuckled. I went into the kitchen and grabbed a dishrag. I dampened it and then tossed it at him. Dabbing at the spot, he smeared it around, making it worse.

"Give me your shirt," I said. "I'll have it laundered."

"That's not necessary."

"Please?" I asked quietly.

Sasha sighed and then began to unbutton his shirt. He wore a black T-shirt underneath that strained over his chest. My eyes were riveted to Sasha's sculpted muscles. Somehow, I'd never noticed. Had he always looked that way?

Sasha gave me a wry grin as he set his shirt aside. He noticed me checking him out. Well, I was married, not dead. Suddenly, I ached for Flynn. I ached with need, wanting to feel him against me, moving inside of me.

I dragged my eyes away from Sasha's strong form and went to put Hawk in his bassinet in the living room.

"So you've been working out?" Sasha asked lamely, gesturing to the treadmill.

"Starting too," I said. "But I don't think it's working."

"I think it's working," he replied.

I let out a laugh. "Thanks. I think. No, I mean, the exercise helps, but I'm still angry."

He frowned. "Angry?"

"Yeah."

"About…"

"Everything," I finally admitted. "Hawk's kidnapping. Arlington's betrayal. Winters. Myself." I didn't mention Flynn even though he was part of the list.

"Have you told Campbell how you've been feeling?" he prodded.

"No. He's got enough to worry about. I don't want to add to it."

"I kickbox," he said, changing the subject. "It helps when I'm in a mood."

"Kickboxing," I repeated. Maybe that would help me and my homicidal rage. I snorted with laughter. It wasn't funny. Not even a little.

"You want to train with me? I'd be glad to help."

And just like that, I knew where Sasha and I stood.

~

I put Hawk into his sling, his weight comfortable against my body. After calling down to my bodyguard who was stationed in the lobby, I headed for the elevator. Taking a deep breath, I realized how much I needed to get out of the penthouse.

My bodyguard, Nathan, was a jacked guy with a crew cut and he greeted me when the elevator doors opened.

The lobby, decorated in old world tones and furniture, wasn't overly crowded with guests. I breathed a sigh of relief. Living in Dornoch this past many months had changed me.

"Where to?" Nathan asked.

"Just to the club," I said, pointing in the direction of Rex Burlesque.

He nodded and then proceeded to stick to me like glue. I wasn't usually a fan of bodyguards, but I was glad for Nathan's looming, muscly presence. The man was downright gallant as he opened the club door for me.

The club wasn't yet set up for the evening show. Chairs were stacked on tables and a bunch of boxes littered the top of the bar.

"You bitch."

I turned at the sound of the voice and grinned. A woman of Asian descent, tall, and gorgeous strolled toward me on clackety heels.

"You've been in New York a week, and I have yet to see you," she said.

"Yeah, well, I've been busy."

She raised a perfectly sculpted eyebrow, and then her gaze dropped to the bundle resting against me. "Busy," she agreed, her smiled wide.

I pulled back the sling to reveal Hawk's sleeping face.

"God, he's adorable!" Alia said. "I want to scoop him up and eat him." She looked at Nathan who stood on guard by the doors. "Who's that?" she whispered.

"My protection," I said. "You know Flynn…"

"Hmm. Sexy protective Mr. Campbell. He didn't come to New York with you?"

"He had some things to take care of in Dornoch," I said

evasively. Though Alia had been brought into the fold about the casino and the brothel, she didn't know the true reason they existed. We thought it safer for her not to know about Flynn's political affiliations.

She and I made our way to Flynn's booth, the one he used to sit in to survey his club and watch the dancers. I shivered, remembering a time when Flynn and I had fought our attraction to each other.

The result of that attraction was sleeping in my arms.

"You know, photos just don't do him justice," Alia said when she was seated across from me. Even though I'd moved to Scotland, I'd kept up with Alia, sending her photos and emails. We chatted as much as we could, but due to the time change and our schedules, it had been difficult. Still, our friendship picked up right where it left off. Good friends were like that, and it was important to keep them close.

"I know. I'm also terrible with the camera. I want Lacey to take some photos of him."

"That's a good idea. She's so freakin' talented. I'm bummed she no longer works here, but good for her for moving in another direction."

"And good for you," I teased. "Ms. Manager. How are you liking it?"

"Love it."

"You don't miss dancing?" I asked her.

She shrugged. "Kind of. But change is good, right?"

"Is that who I think it is?" a male voice called.

I turned my head and grinned. Alia's handsome fiancé set down a box of liquor and rushed over to us. He leaned down to give me a hug, but it was awkward due to Hawk in his sling.

"Is this the little monster?" Jake asked, a devilish grin on his lips.

"The one and only."

Jake took a seat next to Alia and wrapped his arm around her. "Did you tell Barrett yet?" he asked.

"No, not yet."

My gaze darted between them. "Well, tell me!"

"We set a wedding date," Alia said.

"Finally," Jake added.

Alia rolled her eyes at me. "Men. They have no idea what goes in to planning a wedding."

"You pick a date and then I show up," Jake said. "How hard is that?"

I shrugged. "I let Flynn handle all the details of our wedding. Granted, it was an elopement, so it was easier. I was grateful for that. So, when is your wedding?"

"Two weeks from now," Alia said.

"Two weeks from now?" I looked at her in shock. "But how—"

"We're keeping it simple," Alia interjected. "A friend of ours is officiating. Jake's good friend, Annie, is a chef, and she's taking care of the food. She's amazing. We're keeping the wedding small. It's an early evening ceremony, and then we have cocktail hour."

"We just want to be married," Jake said. "And celebrate with our close friends and family."

"So, will you come?" Alia asked.

## Chapter 38

"You're sure you're okay doing this?" I asked Lacey.

She grinned. "Are you kidding?"

"No, I'm serious." My eyes scanned her face, my worry evident. Tremors began to shake through me when I thought of leaving Hawk.

"We'll be fine. I promise. Ash is coming over to help me. Your bodyguard is down in the lobby and Sasha himself is coming to get you."

I let out a breath and nodded. I'd hardly slept the night before. The dreams were back full throttle. They seemed to abate when Flynn was next to me though they never disappeared completely.

"It will be good for you," Lacey said softly. She fiddled with her high-tech camera before holding it up to look at me through the lens. She snapped a few test shots and then peered at them.

"Honey, I don't mean to be a bitch, but you've got to start sleeping."

"The bags are bad, huh?" I asked knowingly.

"Yeah, they are."

Well, at least I had a friend who valued the truth. She'd never lie to me.

My cell phone buzzed, and it was a text from Sasha letting me know he was in the lobby. I grabbed my keys and workout bag and with one last look-in on Hawk, I left.

The private elevator doors chimed open, and I stepped out into the lobby. With a wave at Nathan, I hurried over to Sasha who sat on a cream-colored chair while waiting for me.

"No spandex today?" Sasha asked with a glance at my more concealing workout clothing.

"Nope. Let's go."

He attempted to take my workout bag from me, but I clutched it in my hand. It wasn't heavy, so it wasn't necessary for Sasha to carry it. I appreciated his old-world manners, but at the moment they were unwarranted.

We stepped outside into the cold weather but before the low temperature registered, Sasha had the back-passenger door open to the black car. I climbed into the warmth and set my bag on the floor. Sasha got in next to me and shut the door. A moment later, we pulled away from the curb and headed for Sasha's home.

"I never told you where I lived, did I?" he asked.

I shook my head. "No."

"I bought an old meatpacking warehouse on Gansevoort and had it converted."

For some reason, his announcement surprised me. It was a trendy neighborhood, and I wouldn't have guessed the large open floor plans of warehouse architecture would appeal to Sasha.

Traffic was surprisingly light, and we made it to the west side quickly. The driver pulled into an underground garage and parked. I hopped out of the car and followed Sasha to an elevator. He pressed the button, and the elevator doors opened immediately. We got inside, and he fished out his keys and stuck one into the PH hole. We zoomed to the top floor, and the doors opened into a hallway.

"Why only one door?" I asked while Sasha stuck his key into the lock.

"Safety," he said.

"But what about the rest of the building? How do you get access to it?"

He glanced at me and smiled. "You'll see." He pushed the front door open, and I followed him inside his abode.

Large windows along the far wall let in a massive amount of light, but they had nothing—nothing—on the skylight that took up half the ceiling.

I craned my neck and gawked. "How do you keep it cool in here in summer?" I asked.

Sasha closed the front door and went to a keypad on the wall next to it. He pressed a few buttons, and there was the sound of gears and whirls. A canvas stretched over the skylight, and instantly the lighting of the room changed.

"Nifty," I admitted.

"I'm pretty proud of it. Come on, I'll take you on a tour."

The floor was one open room connecting the kitchen and living room. The wall opposite of the large windows was exposed brick. It was a lot homier than I expected.

"Ready to see the rest of it?" he asked.

I nodded.

"Grab your gym bag."

I trailed after him as we made our way to a spiral iron staircase. It reminded me of a fireman's pole.

"If you take these stairs up, it goes to the master bedroom. Take them down, you'll get to the gym."

I held onto the rail as we descended. Automatic lights illuminated the way until we got into the gym. Sasha flipped a switch, and overhead lights came on.

Mats graced the floor, and a sandbag hung in the corner. There were weights and exercise machines that I'd never seen before. A few windows made it less tomb-like, but it didn't have the open, airy quality of the main living floor.

"You have everything you need a few steps away, huh?" I teased.

He grinned back. "You live in a hotel," he reminded me. "You can call the front desk, and they'll do anything you want."

"Yeah, it's pretty good," I admitted. I tossed my gym bag into the corner and looked at Sasha. "Okay. You going to teach me to channel this rage, or what?"

∼

An hour later, I collapsed onto the mats in a sweaty, heaving mess. I groaned in tiredness, but I finally felt the release of some of my anger.

"You're not sleeping," Sasha commented.

I tilted my head so I could see him. Part of me registered his ripped arms and chiseled legs as he lifted a water bottle and took a drink. The other part of me, the reasonable part of me, shut it down. Quickly.

"No," I admitted. "I'm not sleeping. I was, right when I first got back to New York, but not anymore."

"Why not? Your anger issues?"

"Nightmares," I said quietly. "I have nightmares."

"You talk to anyone about them?"

"You."

He gave a small smile. I sat up and held out a hand. He tossed me the water bottle, and I guzzled half of it.

"Seriously, Barrett."

He meant did I tell Flynn about my nightmares. How the hell could I? My dreams were violent, angry, and filled with lust. And Flynn wasn't the star of them.

"No. I mean, he knows I have them. He's woken me up a

time or two, but they've gotten worse. More frequent, more…intense."

I dropped my gaze and attempted to get up off the mat, but my legs felt like noodles, and I sat back down again. The stitches in my arm itched, and I was dying to get them out. The sweaty gauze protecting them didn't help.

"Remember when you told me not to apologize for what I had to do to survive?" I asked him.

He nodded and waited for me to go on.

I took a deep breath. "I didn't have to torture Winters. I could've just shot him and been done with it, but I wanted him to suffer. I wanted to watch the light snuff out in his eyes. What the fuck does that say about me?"

"It says you have demons. Like the rest of us."

I huffed on a laugh.

"Why don't you talk to Ash about it?" he wondered.

"She wouldn't understand. She'd comfort me, but Ash hasn't killed a man. I've killed three. I'm a fucking murderer."

"But she's still your best friend, and she's stuck by you. And she knows what you've done. Maybe not all the details, but she knows enough. Does she treat you any differently because of it?"

"No." I shot him an amused look. "God, I'd kill for some vodka."

"I have a good Russian brand upstairs," he said. "We could sit on the couch in front of the fireplace and have a few shots. Demons don't stand a chance against vodka."

## Chapter 39

I checked in with Lacey and Ash—who assured me all was well, and that Hawk took to the camera like a perfect little baby GQ model. When I knew he was fine without me, I took Sasha up on his offer of vodka, but only after I showered in his guest bathroom and changed into clean clothes.

I curled up on the couch while Sasha, recently showered, poured me a glass of expensive Russian vodka. We clinked glasses, and I took a tiny sip, letting it coat my tongue before swallowing. It burned on the way down.

"I was surprised when you asked for vodka and not scotch," Sasha said as he went to the gas fireplace and flipped a switch. It was chilly in the loft, and I grabbed the blanket that rested on the back of the couch and covered myself with it.

"When in Rome," I stated. "Or, when in Russia, I guess."

Sasha laughed and it sounded lighthearted. We'd had so little of that lately. I felt myself relaxing, sinking into the cushions.

"Thank you for today," I said sincerely. "Thank you for everything, actually."

He raised his glass and then took a sip. "I hope I helped."

"You did. So did the kickboxing."

"I do that every day."

Not surprising, I didn't say. From the state of his body, it was obvious.

My phone buzzed from somewhere behind me. I realized I'd left it on the kitchen counter. Somehow, I managed to haul myself up from a very comfortable position. I set my glass of vodka down on the glass coffee table and went to answer my phone.

It was Flynn.

"Hi," I said, instantly glad to know he was on the other end of the call.

"Love," he greeted. "How are you?"

"I'm good." I glanced at Sasha, but he wasn't paying any attention to me. He was staring into the fireplace, holding his glass of vodka.

"And Hawk?" he prodded.

"Hawk's good." Last time I checked which wasn't even an hour ago. I cleared my throat. "What's new with you?"

He paused. "Are you all right? You sound different."

For some reason I didn't want to tell him where I was or who I was with. It would open up a new stream of conversation—about my newfound anger, about my nightmares. Flynn had enough to worry about.

"Just tired," I said which was a half-truth.

He made a Scottish noise in the back of his throat. "I won't keep you long. I just wanted to tell you that Ramsey's death will be written about in tomorrow's paper."

"Getting the ball rolling, huh?" I asked.

"Aye. Everything in its time. But Duncan and I are ready to get moving. I want you and Hawk home with me. I miss you." His voice lowered, his sexy brogue raspy, and I knew we were moments away from inappropriate words. A delicious shiver worked its way down my spine.

"I miss you," I whispered.

"Ah, love, I miss your sweet—"

"I have to go. Hawk needs me," I interjected, hating that I lied, but knowing I wasn't in a place for this kind of conversation.

He sighed. "All right."

I glanced at Sasha whose bright blue eyes were trained on me. I gulped and then looked away. I asked softly into the phone, "Will you be up later?"

There was a pause followed by a husky laugh. "I'm sure of it."

I let out a laugh, knowing he was referring to a certain part of his anatomy. "I'll call you back in a few hours."

"Promise?" he demanded.

"Promise."

We hung up, and I set my phone down on the counter. I took a moment to compose myself before heading back over to the couch. Looking out the large windows, I realized it was already dark. I hadn't even noticed.

I could feel Sasha's eyes on me, wanting to ask questions but holding back. He wanted to know why I hadn't told Flynn that I was with him.

Picking up my glass of vodka, I took a hefty swallow. Savoring be damned. My arm itched and I sighed. "How are you at removing stitches?"

∼

The next morning while I fed Hawk a bottle, I read the newspaper. The fake death of Ramsey Buchanan was on the front page of *The New York Times*. The details were vague, of course, as were his affiliations, but it made him sound like he was a ringleader in the Scottish mob.

Close enough.

The article also mentioned the death of Malcolm. A lump of emotion formed in my throat when I read his name in print. His death was still fresh. I kept promising myself I'd grieve for him, but so many other facets of life kept getting in the way. It sounded ruthless and terrible, and it was another thing that I hated about myself—about who I was becoming.

And then I glanced down at my hungry child and every bit of self-loathing slipped away. Anything for Hawk. Always and forever. Anything for Flynn, too, I realized, but it was different. Love for my child was pure, unadulterated.

After Hawk finished his bottle, I gave him a bath. Though my body was sore from yesterday's workout with Sasha, it had done the trick. I'd slept soundly, only waking when Hawk cried.

While Hawk had his late morning nap, I called Brad Shapiro, head of security. I had barely seen him in the week and half I'd been in New York, but that was to be expected. He was busy and rarely had a minute to himself.

I invited him up to the suite for lunch, which he graciously accepted. We ate and chatted, and I asked him about adding a kickboxing gym to The Rex. He looked pleasantly surprised by my request, but agreed to it, especially when he realized I'd be using it.

"So, what, you're a resident badass now?" he asked.

I laughed. "Hardly."

"Not from what I've heard."

I raised my eyebrows. "Flynn kept you in the loop?"

"He might have clued me in." His hand held a glass of mineral water, but he didn't drink from it.

"You're not reporting back to him, are you? Keeping a close eye on me for him?"

"No, it's not like that," he insisted. "But he's there, and you're here, and the last few months have been rough. He's just concerned."

I nodded. "It just feels like I've been running from one disaster to the next, and I can barely catch my breath." In between those moments, Flynn and I held each other, and it got us through.

We'd survived our son's kidnapping. We'd found Hawk and our family unit was back—together, cohesive, strong. I just wished Flynn and I didn't have to spend so much time apart.

Brad and I finished up our lunch and then he left. On his way out, Lacey was on her way in. Though they weren't a couple anymore, they'd worked together for years, and their exchange was warm and genuine. There was no awkwardness between them.

Lacey set down her leather brown camera bag, but not before she took out her iPad. "Sorry, I would've been here sooner, but I'm still adjusting. I don't have to work nights anymore. That's weird for me."

I smiled in sympathy. "How late were you up last night?"

She grimaced. "Four a.m."

"Hey, you should've called me. I was awake."

Lacey chuckled. "Late night dirty chat with your husband?"

"Fussy baby."

"That doesn't sound as fun."

"It wasn't." I watched her unlock her iPad and then press a few buttons. She handed it to me, and I began to scroll through black and white photos of Hawk.

"These are very different from the photos you usually take," I said, my finger lingering on a photo of a sleeping Hawk.

"Hey, I got some good naked shots of your kid. But yeah, it's not the same as snapping photos of scantily-clad burlesque dancers." She threw me a wry grin. "I got to experiment with my camera, though, so that was also fun. I set it up on automatic, and it took like a thousand photos in twenty seconds. Or something like that."

"Still learning all the nuances of your camera?"

"Definitely. So, I wanted to run an idea past you."

I handed her iPad back to her. "Shoot."

"I want to photograph you and Hawk together, and I want it to be for the gallery show."

I blinked. "You're kidding."

"Why would I be kidding? I've photographed you before," she pointed out.

"Yeah, but that was for—and that photo is in the privacy of my bedroom in Scotland." Lacey had more than a knack for photography—she captured intimate moments.

"You'd get veto power," she said. "Come on, what do you say? You need something to keep you busy."

"I have things keeping me busy. I've started kickboxing, and I'm back to running, and Ash and I are going to take a self-defense class—"

"Wow, so exciting. And to think, we used to drink martinis before cocktail hour. Please, Barrett? You know, if it hadn't been for you, I never would've gotten back into photography. So, this—me asking you—is your fault."

I let out a laugh. "Okay, fine. I'm in."

## Chapter 40

"You really nailed that guy in the crotch," Ash said, her blond ponytail somehow still perky after our lesson with the self-defense instructor.

"Yeah, well, rage helps," I said in a teasing voice. "Besides, he was wearing a cup. I didn't even faze him."

Ash collapsed onto my couch and chugged her bottle of water. "Thanks for doing this with me."

"I'm here at the service of my friends," I quipped. "Lacey wants to photograph Hawk and me for her show."

"Yeah, I know. It was my idea."

"Ah, so you both have been conspiring against me, huh?" I asked with a smile.

"You're photogenic, your son is photogenic, and Lacey enjoys photographing both of you. Plus, she'll get some good shots for the family photo album. I'm sure Flynn will love them."

"Have you talked to Duncan? Since the 'news' hit about Ramsey?" I asked, using air quotes.

"Briefly. They're about to go underground. Spinning a web, laying a trap and all that."

"How are you handling all of this?" I demanded.

"How are you?" she shot back.

I sighed. "Fair enough. I have to go shopping for this wedding I'm going to. Want to come with me? Shopping, I mean. Not the wedding."

Ash's blue eyes lit up. "Shopping? You? Really?"

I nodded.

"Who's getting married?" Ash asked.

"Alia and Jake. Alia is Lacey's replacement at the club."

Conversation focused on the impending nuptials though I knew very little about the event except the time and the place.

"Can I ask a favor? Will you babysit Hawk?" I asked her. "Though he'd look adorable in a baby suit, he's not ready for such a formal occasion."

"Sure," Ash said easily. "I'll get to spend the night with a cute guy, and Duncan can't get jealous." She winked at me. "Speaking of which, have you told Flynn about your kickboxing training sessions with a certain Russian?"

I shook my head.

"Why not?"

"Really? You're really asking me that?" I demanded.

"Spell it out."

"Flynn knows how Sasha feels about me. If he knew I was spending a lot of time with him, it might give him something to be jealous about."

"Does he have the right to be jealous?"

"No. I don't have feelings for Sasha."

Ash stared at me for a long moment. "Okay."

"I don't," I protested. "It's just that… How do I explain this? I can say anything to him and not have to worry about how it will be perceived."

She frowned. "You can't do that with Flynn?"

I took a deep breath, finally ready to let Ash all the way in to the darkness that was becoming part of me. "I have nightmares. Ever since Vlad and Dolinsky, I have nightmares. And now I have them about Winters too."

"About you killing them?" she asked gently.

"Sometimes. But there's more."

"Hey, you can tell me," she said when I stopped speaking.

"This doesn't go beyond these walls," I stated. "And after today, we don't speak of it ever again."

She nodded. "I understand."

I told her one of my more graphic nightmares, watching her eyes widen in shock. When I went silent, she didn't speak for a while, digesting what I'd shared with her.

"And that's why I can't tell Flynn."

"But you can tell Sasha?" she asked in confusion.

I shook my head. "No, I haven't told him anything explicit, but when he was in Scotland, we'd go for late night walks, just the two of us and just—I don't know, he understands my demons without me having to explain them. If I told Flynn, it would just hurt him."

"You think if you told Flynn that you have sexual dreams about Dolinsky that will hurt him. Yeah, that makes a lot of sense."

"It will just remind him of my time with Dolinsky and that Flynn didn't protect me. It will bring up a lot of guilt."

We were quiet again, and I listened for any sound from Hawk, but he wasn't stirring. Ash got up and began to pace. She looked at me.

"Dreams aren't always literal," she said.

"The one thing that's always the same is Dolinsky. He tells me that he's all my dark parts that I keep mashing down and he's just a mirror of my gruesome, ugly—"

"Hey," Ash cuts me off. "There's nothing ugly about you. You've lived through some things. Terrible things."

"And done some things no one should ever have to do. But I've done them and now I have nightmares."

She bit her lip as she contemplated what she wanted to say next, and then finally, "Did you have feelings for Dolinsky? Do you still have unresolved feelings for him?"

I closed my eyes when I nodded.

"Oh, man…"

Maybe I did need to tell Flynn everything. But how would that help? I loved Flynn. I'd done everything in my power to get back to him, but maybe along the journey, I'd gotten lost in the part I'd been playing. Dolinsky had been charming and courteous, gentlemanly, but upfront about what he wanted from me. He'd been an expert in seduction, demanding when necessary. I had very little doubt that if I'd stayed locked up as his prisoner, I would've succumbed to his charms.

He'd made me feel powerful in my sexuality. He'd unleashed a part of me I hadn't been aware existed—and he never let me apologize for it. He had wanted everything from me, and he hadn't accepted anything less.

But I still felt like I was treating Flynn with a pair of kid gloves, and I knew that wasn't fair.

"I think it's time I stopped feeling guilty," I said slowly. "I don't think I ever really let go of that."

"Listen, I'm the last person to judge you for having feelings for a man who isn't your husband. I had an affair with my ex-fiancé's father, if you remember."

Hawk began to cry, and thankfully our conversation was put on hold while I went to tend to him. I still didn't believe unloading everything onto Flynn would help assuage my guilt, but telling Ash had alleviated some of my burden.

And in the meantime, there was always kickboxing.

∼

"Oh, no, dear, not that strapless one," Celine, the boutique assistant said when I came out of the dressing room in a strapless black dress.

Ash frowned from her seat in a comfortable chair. "I think it's lovely."

"I like it, too. It's the only one that shows off my amazing cleavage but it's still loose enough around the waist that I don't have to wear something to hold in my stomach," I protested. "I know it's winter, but I'll be inside. So what's wrong with the dress?"

The gown hit a few inches above my knee, so it was a good length and didn't chop me in half. What was the problem?

Celine looked at me with shrewd brown eyes and gently touched my left arm where the stitches had been recently removed. It was still red and clearly obvious to any observer. I didn't want to have to wear a shawl the entire evening.

I looked at Ash for her opinion.

"Fuck it," she said with a shrug. "The dress looks great on you."

Celine blanched, but I looked at her and smiled. "Thank you for your help. I'll take this dress."

Knowing it was more important to make a sale than it was to try to talk a customer out of something, she nodded. "Do you need shoes to go with it?"

"Yes, please. But nothing too high."

"I have just the thing."

I disappeared back into the changing room. Looking at myself in the full-length mirror, I noticed that my auburn hair was in need of a cut, but overall, I was happy with my appearance. The bags under my eyes weren't as pronounced. The last few nights I'd slept soundly due to the exhaustion from kickboxing. The gym in The Rex was finally set up so that I didn't have to go far to pound on a sandbag.

I hung up the dress on its hanger before slipping back into my jeans and green cashmere sweater. I pulled back my hair, and then I was out of the dressing room, handing off the dress to the newly returned Celine. She held up a pair of black pumps with a pointy toe and just enough of a heel not to be frumpy. I tried them on and deemed them worthy.

Celine gathered up my items and then carted them to the

register to ring me up. I handed her my credit card and turned to Ash.

"I need a haircut," I said. "I wouldn't mind a mani-pedi either. Can we go to your salon?"

"Why not get all of that done at The Rex Spa?" Ash inquired.

Because the last time I'd been in The Rex Spa I'd been kidnapped from a massage table. I didn't say that to Ash though, I just looked at her until she understood.

"Got it. I'll see if Marco can squeeze us in."

"Thanks."

Ash stepped a few feet away from the counter to make the call. Celine handed me back my credit card. "Thank you for shopping with us."

"Thank you for all your help, Celine," I said kindly, taking the bag from her.

Nathan, my ever-present bodyguard, rose from his chair by the door. Daniel, Ash's bodyguard who sat next to Nathan, also stood.

"Your husbands are very patient men," Celine said, trying to make idle talk. Ash and I had been at the boutique for two hours; Nathan and Daniel hadn't rolled their eyes once.

I didn't want to correct Celine and tell her that Nathan and Daniel were our bodyguards. Instead I said, "Yes, super patient."

Ash clicked off her phone and smiled at me. "Marco can squeeze us in now."

"Let's go," I said.

With a final wave at Celine, we were out the door. The New York day was cold but clear as we navigated the busy sidewalk to our waiting town car. Nathan held the passenger door open, and Daniel took my shopping bag.

I climbed inside, and Ash scooted in next to me. She gave our driver the address to Marco's salon, which wasn't far from our current location. We hadn't ventured outside the Upper East Side.

"What are you doing?" Ash asked as I pulled out my cell phone.

"Calling Lacey," I said.

"Hawk is fine."

"I know he's fine."

"If you know he's fine then why are you calling?" Ash demanded.

"You'll understand when you have children."

"Which won't be for a very, very long time."

I chuckled.

"What? You don't believe me?"

"Take it from someone who didn't even want them to begin with. Life has a funny way of giving you exactly what you need when you least expect it."

She glowered at me. "Shut up, Barrett."

## Chapter 41

I lifted Hawk into my arms, cooing in delight as I pressed his body against my chest. "I missed you. How was he?"

Lacey tossed down a magazine. "Your son threw up on me."

"Oh no," I said with a light laugh. "Is that why you're wearing one of my T-shirts?"

She nodded. "I sent my shirt out to be dry-cleaned. I thought I'd hang out for a little while longer until it's done."

"Be my guest."

"Can I see the dress you bought for the wedding?" Lacey asked.

"Sure. It's in the shopping bag."

Lacey was on her feet and picked up the shopping bag Nathan had insisted on carrying up for me. He was back down in the lobby, keeping guard until Cole, the nighttime bodyguard relieved him.

"I bet this looks fantastic on you," Lacey said as she pulled the dress from its box.

"I clean up good," I said, rubbing Hawk's back.

Lacey folded the dress and put it back in its box and then dug around in the shopping bag. She looked at the heels, nodded, and then set them aside. "I don't see any lingerie in here."

"That's because I didn't buy any. It's not like Flynn's here to see it." I set Hawk in his bassinet.

"I wouldn't be too sure of that," a masculine voice said.

I looked up sharply into the handsome, smiling face of my husband. I gawked at him.

"That's my cue," Lacey said with a grin. "I just wanted to see your reaction." Even as she made her way to the elevator, I was running toward Flynn. He lifted me into his arms, and I wrapped my legs around him.

The elevator doors chimed shut, and my lips were on his. "I can't believe you're here," I whispered in between the clashing of our mouths. "*How* are you here?"

He released me so that I slid down the length of his hard body. He reached for his sweater and pulled it over his head before he answered.

"Ash called me. Said you weren't doing well—that you needed me for a few days."

Warmth curled in my belly. "You came? Even at the cost of the plan?"

He shrugged and then removed his undershirt, showing me his taut stomach. "You're more important than anything else. I think you needed a reminder. Now are you going to stand there gaping at me or are you going to take off your clothes?"

I stripped in record time and so did Flynn. I placed a hand on his warm chest and pushed him so that he walked backwards into the bedroom.

He took me into his arms, kissed the breath out of me, and then hoisted me up to lay me on the bed. He climbed on top of me, his hands and mouth driving me wild, making me spin out of control.

I tugged on his hair impatiently, wanting him to fill me. But he wouldn't give in. Not yet. His thumbs grazed my pebbled nipples, and then he took a tightened bud into his mouth. He sucked and laved until I writhed beneath him.

"Easy, hen," he said, his voice hoarse.

His hands grasped my hips as he guided his length into my body. He slid home, grew larger. My eyes rolled back into my head. He put an arm beneath me, lifting me up as he began to move inside me. I clasped him, squeezing him, wanting it harder and faster. Gentle could happen later.

"Oh God," I moaned, the tide of my release close.

"That's it."

I jerked as ripples of pleasure washed through me. With a groan, Flynn came, triggering another orgasm. I gasped and sighed and then bit his shoulder.

Flynn looked down at me, a smile on his lips. "I don't do well without you, either, love. Just thought you should know."

~

"How long are you in town?" I asked Flynn as I sat in nothing but his undershirt and my underwear.

Flynn looked down at his son who was drinking from a bottle. Though he was finally re-accustomed to breast milk, he preferred to take it from the bottle instead of its natural source.

Hawk let out a milky burp, causing Flynn to smile.

"Few days," Flynn said, setting the near-empty bottle aside and placing Hawk to his shoulder. "I'm not interrupting any of your plans, am I?"

"Alia's bachelorette party is tomorrow night," I said. "I promised her I'd go, but I can get out of it."

"No, you should go," Flynn insisted. "I can spend some quality alone time with my son."

I arched an eyebrow. "You sure you're cut out for that?"

"Sure, why not?" Flynn asked. "I am his father."

I tried to hide the smile at Flynn's affronted tone. "Yes, love, I'm very much aware of that fact."

"You don't think I can do it," Flynn said as he continued to tap Hawk's back.

"Of course I think you can do it. It's just that…"

"Yes?"

"Nope. You know what? I have complete faith in you."

Flynn grinned. "I'm going to prove you wrong, you know."

I grinned back. "Can't wait."

I cleaned up the remains of our room service dinner while Flynn changed Hawk and put him down. We climbed into our own bed, and I snuggled into Flynn's embrace.

"How did Duncan react when you told him you were coming to New York?" I asked.

Flynn worked his way under my shirt and trailed his fingers up and down my spine. "He was in favor of it. It meant he got to come and see Ash."

I laughed.

"What?" he asked.

"The two most feared and strongest member of the SINS couldn't stand to be away from their women. It's just funny."

Flynn chuckled, but then he sobered. "I once told you it was easy to give everything to the cause because there was nothing to come home to. But you and Hawk… If something happened to either of you, I—"

I put my fingers to his lips to stop him from speaking. "I know. Any news about Arlington?"

"Silence."

"Really? Even after blasting Ramsey's fake demise to the press?"

"Aye. No traitorous SINS member has surfaced. When Duncan and I get back, we're moving forward with our plan immediately. We can't wait anymore, and I want this finished."

"Shhhh," I whispered, pressing my lips to his chest. "No more talking about it. Not right now."

∼

The next morning, Flynn and I pulled ourselves out of bed long enough to meet Ash and Duncan for brunch. There were smiles all around, even when Hawk cried in his carrier.

Luckily, we were in the corner of The Rex Bar and Restaurant, so Hawk didn't disturb the other patrons. He settled down quickly.

Duncan leaned over and whispered something in Ash's ear that made her blush and beam, but shake her head. Duncan wrapped an arm around her and pulled her close.

"Ash and I followed in your footsteps," Duncan announced.

Flynn and I exchanged a look. "What footsteps?" I asked.

"Eloping," Ash clarified, a grin spreading across her face. "Duncan and I got married this morning."

My mouth dropped. "What? But how? You're only in town for a few days, and New York has a waiting period," I said to Duncan.

"Your husband's arrival was a surprise to you," Duncan said. "But I let Ash know we were coming."

"I'd already gotten the marriage license," Ash stated proudly.

"We didn't want to make a big fuss," Duncan said.

"Please don't be mad," Ash said to me. "I just couldn't go through with a huge wedding."

I raised my eyebrows. "You mean, I get to celebrate your marriage with you, but not have to wear a bridesmaid's dress? I think we both win."

We all laughed.

"I'm so happy for you both," I said, tears in my eyes. After Ash's last disastrous engagement, to hear that she'd gone through with a low-key, legal ceremony, I knew it meant she truly loved Duncan.

Flynn rose from his seat and lifted his coffee mug. He said a short few sentences in Gaelic and then sat down.

"What did that mean?" Ash asked.

"It was an old Scottish wedding blessing," Duncan explained, looking at his new bride. "He said, 'A thousand welcomes to you with your marriage kerchief. May you be healthy all your days. May you be blessed with long life and peace. May you grow old with goodness, and with riches.'"

"Cheers to that," I said, raising my own glass of water.

## Chapter 42

I looked at Flynn one last time as I grabbed my black clutch. My husband was on the couch, the TV on mute, Hawk asleep in his bassinet.

"Go on, love," Flynn said with a knowing grin. "We'll be fine. You don't want to be late."

Though I loved Alia, I wasn't feeling up to her bachelorette party. I was tired and Flynn was only in town another two days before he and Duncan had to return to Scotland.

"I'll be here when you get back," Flynn promised, reading the thoughts on my face. "Go be with your friends."

When I got to the lobby, Nathan slid next to my side and escorted me to the waiting town car. Alia's bachelorette party wasn't going to be anything out of a movie—no strippers, no penis straws, no tiaras. She'd sworn to me. All we were doing was going to a wine bar in the NYU area where she and Jake had their first date.

I could do a wine bar.

When the car stopped across the street from the wine bar, I looked at Nathan. "Do you promise not to be obvious that you're my bodyguard?"

"Promise," Nathan said with wry amusement. "The

bartender is not going to like me hanging out on a stool and not drinking."

"Give him a few bucks."

"Like a twenty?"

"Wow, are you this generous with the women you date?" I demanded. I opened my clutch and gave him a one-hundred-dollar bill, but he refused to take it.

"Have you ever heard of a joke?" Nathan asked, the smile still in place.

I stared at him a long moment and then nodded. "You'll do, Nathan. You'll do. Come on. Trail me at a discreet distance."

I ducked my head to hide it from the slight wind, but I was glad I'd decided on a thicker coat. I still looked surprisingly trendy despite the fact that my usual attire geared toward comfortable stretchy yoga pants. I made a vow then and there to try more with my appearance.

The warmth of the intimate space hit me, and I pulled off my coat immediately. I moved deeper into the room and spotted Alia and her group of friends. When Alia saw me, she jumped up. After embracing me, she took my hand and led me back to the table.

"Ladies. The queen has arrived," Alia said in a teasing tone.

I recognized three of the four faces immediately. Lacey sat with a martini in front of her while everyone else had wine. I hugged Renee and Shawna, two women who worked in The Rex burlesque club.

"I'm not the queen tonight," I said with a wink as I sat down next to Lacey who moved her skinny tush over so I could share the booth.

"Alia refuses to be queen," Shawna said. "She wouldn't let us get her a fuzzy crown."

"Maybe when we do this again for my second marriage," Alia quipped and we all laughed. Alia and Jake had been together for years already and were still in the honeymoon phase.

I looked at the woman sitting next to Alia and immediately noticed the family resemblance. Alia had a younger brother, so I assumed this woman was a cousin.

"Hi, I'm Barrett," I said, holding out my hand.

The woman smiled. "I'm Jenna, Alia's cousin."

Before I could tell her I wasn't drinking, Alia picked up the wine bottle and poured me a glass.

"Thanks," I said, taking a tiny sip before setting it aside.

"Okay, toast time," Shawna said, raising her glass. We all followed suit. "To Alia's last hours of freedom."

We clinked glasses and giggled, and I took another tiny sip. Lacey glanced at me as she set her martini down. "You not drinking?" she asked lowering her voice.

"Not, not drinking," I said. "I'm just kind of tired. If I have any chance of making it to eleven o'clock tonight, I'll have to really pace myself."

"Got it," she said in complete non-judgmental understanding.

Conversation drifted away from wedding talk. Renee and I were coerced into pulling out our phones to show pictures of our children. Renee's daughter had lost her two front teeth and in most of the photos, she was grinning broadly to show the gaps.

"How much did you pay her for her teeth?" Alia asked.

"A buck a tooth. And you know what she said? She said the Tooth Fairy hadn't accounted for inflation and she should've given more."

We all had a good laugh.

"We have a young economist on our hands," Shawna said.

"It just goes to show you that kids listen," Renee said. "My husband and I talk about finances, and I guess Sophia pays attention. Until she's a teenager. I'm worried she's going to be too smart for her own good, and she's going to realize we have no power over her."

"Just remind her who pays the cell phone bill," Jenna said, piping up.

Renee looked at her with widened eyes. "I hadn't even thought of that. Brilliant!"

The ladies drank on while I continued to nurse my first glass. As time marched forward, they grew rowdier and more forthright if that was even possible. Shawna was the worst. Already brazen and outspoken, she had very little filter. Combined with alcohol, it upped the ante.

But I was having fun and even though my phone was close by, I managed to stop myself numerous times from checking in with Flynn.

"How are you liking being awake during the days?" Renee asked Lacey.

"Still getting used to it," Lacey admitted, swirling around the rest of her martini.

"Even though I've been working nights for years, my managing hours are even later," Alia said. "I'm still having a hard time with that. But at least Jake and I are on the same schedule."

"It's impossible to date," Shawna complained. "Unless I go out with other people in the industry, but they're all so crazy!"

We all looked at her for a long moment.

"What?" she demanded. "I might be crazy, but I don't do drugs and stuff. I know people who do coke to make it through their shift and then smoke weed to be able to sleep. That's nuts."

"Then why do people do it?" Jenna asked. She was a graphic designer, and I guessed she'd never been in the service industry.

"Do you know how much money you can make?" Shawna asked her.

"A lot, I guess," Jenna answered. "But if all your money is going to drugs, doesn't that tell you something?"

"Not everyone is like that," Renee insisted. "Which is why I love working at The Rex. I get health benefits without having to work sixty hours a week."

Alia lifted her drink again. "To The Rex. A good place that brought most of us together."

"I'll toast to that," I said.

∼

"The hottest guy I've ever seen is sitting at the bar," Shawna said, not at all discreet about looking.

"You always say that," Renee said.

"Yeah, but this time I mean it. Look at him." Shawna gestured with her chin, and we all swiveled our heads to see whom she was talking about. There were three men at the bar. Two of them were middle-aged; one was bald. The third man was Nathan, leaning over the bar, his muscles straining against his sweater.

"Stop salivating, he's not a steak," Alia teased Shawna. "But damn. He is hot. And he looks familiar."

I wondered if Alia would remember that she'd seen Nathan that day in the club when we'd met to catch up. "I could go for a steak," I said, suddenly ravenous. "And maybe a baked potato."

Lacey shot me an amused look and shook her head.

"Would you guys hate me if I just hit on him for like five minutes, gave him my number, and came back?" Shawna asked us.

"Five minutes?" Renee repeated. "Really?"

"Five minutes," Shawna assured us as she got up from her chair. She adjusted her shirt, pulling it down ever so slightly before sauntering toward the bar. Shawna went right to

Nathan, and I was intrigued to see how my bodyguard was going to handle it.

A moment later, we all heard Nathan's robust laugh. True to her word, Shawna returned, a smug smile on her face.

"Someone mentioned something about a steak?" she asked.

## Chapter 43

I made it until midnight.

The ladies wanted to move from a wine bar to a club, and that's when I made my graceful, sober exit.

Nathan and I stopped for falafels on the way back to The Rex, which gave me a chance to grill him about his exchange with Shawna.

"A gentleman never tells," he quipped with a roguish grin, earning him a smile from me.

The penthouse was quiet when I got home. All the lights were off except for a lamp in the living room. I struggled out of my boots and unbuttoned the top button of my jeans as I made my way to the bedroom.

My men were asleep. I briefly checked on Hawk and then quickly undressed, threw on pajamas, and then wormed my way under the covers next to Flynn.

His arm snaked around me and brought me close. "You're back," he said sleepily, his lips brushing my forehead.

"Hmm," I mumbled closing my eyes.

"How was it?"

"Tell you tomorrow."

The next morning, Flynn woke me with a cup of coffee and an already fed Hawk.

I sat up in bed, the covers around me, and reached for the coffee. "So, you both survived last night without me."

Flynn grinned. "It was touch and go there for a moment, but yes, we survived."

I nodded thoughtfully. "So, calling Ash every five minutes last night…"

"Damn it. I begged her not to tell you," Flynn grumbled. "It was fine. At first. He likes you better than me."

"Of course, I'm his mother," I teased, reaching out to touch Flynn's cheek. "He'll like you better when he needs your advice on how to get girls to notice him. But by that time, all your moves will be considered old-school."

"You're a cruel lass," Flynn said, leaning over and brushing his lips against mine. "You seem surprisingly clear-headed this morning. Didn't you drink last night?"

I shook my head. "Just a glass of wine. Didn't feel like drinking."

Flynn squeezed my leg through the comforter. "I have a few calls to make."

I nodded and watched him leave the bedroom. After coffee, I ambled my way into the shower. Flynn was finishing up on the phone when I came into the living room, pulling my wet hair into a ponytail.

"Everything okay?" I asked.

He nodded. "That was Duncan. Arlington was spotted outside his London club."

"Who's giving you the information?" I demanded. "Are you paying for it? Because you know—"

"The Russians," Flynn interrupted.

"The Russians? You mean Sasha?"

"Aye. He sent some of his most trusted men to help." He looked at me in confusion. "You didn't know?"

I shook my head. "You didn't tell me. Neither did he."

"He apologized for not being able to do it himself, so he sent men in his stead," Flynn explained.

I'd been spending most of my mornings the last couple of weeks kickboxing with Sasha, and he never mentioned anything to me. Why?

"Let me guess. This means you're leaving sooner?"

Flynn got up off the couch and came to me. He wrapped me in his arms and pressed his chin to my head. "I hate it too."

I helped Flynn pack which didn't take long since he hadn't brought much. Before I knew it, he was carting his suitcase to the elevator. I was tired of saying goodbye, and I vowed this would be the last time I'd have to do it.

"I'm a pretty understanding wife, wouldn't you say?" I asked him.

Flynn smiled. "The most understanding."

"And you would do anything to make me happy?"

"Anything," he agreed.

I hauled him to me and pressed my lips to his. "Then come home to me in one piece. And when you do, we're taking Hawk and going on a month-long vacation."

He tucked strands of hair behind my ears and then cradled my face. "That sounds pretty good to me. You pick the place." With one final kiss, he left.

Ash came over and we commiserated, spending the day watching movies and eating takeout.

"Have you and Duncan talked about where you're going to go on your honeymoon—when all this is over?" I asked.

"I really want to go to Portugal. Duncan doesn't care as long as I'm naked most of the time."

We both laughed.

"He wants kids. Like right away," Ash said.

"And you?"

"Eh, I think I could be talked into it, but I'm happy to wait and babysit yours in the meantime."

I shook my head. "It's kind of insane. If you'd have told me two years ago that I'd be married with a baby I would've laughed in your face."

"Guess you really got over not wanting kids, huh?" she teased.

"I'm just glad it's with Flynn. I wouldn't want anyone else's babies."

~

"You're getting really good," Sasha said as he released the sandbag.

I removed my gloves, tossed them aside, and reached for a towel. "Thanks."

"Is it helping?"

"Yeah, I think so." It was hard to tell what helped me sleep at night. It could be the kickboxing. Or it might be that I'd had a talk with my conscience about feeling guilty over things I couldn't change.

I had to live in the present—it was the only way to survive.

"I didn't expect a place as classy as The Rex to have a kickboxing section of the gym."

"It was my doing," I explained. Though we'd been practicing at Sasha's place, this morning I finally asked him to The Rex.

"Are you going to have a kickboxing gym put into your home in Dornoch?" he asked.

I took a drink of water before answering. "Haven't thought about it, actually."

"No? Why not?"

"Trying not to think too far in advance," I admitted. "By the way, there's something we should talk about. Why didn't you tell me you sent men to help Flynn?"

Sasha drank from his water bottle and looked away. "I guess I didn't want you to know because I didn't want you to feel guilty or feel that you were manipulating me again without trying to."

I groaned. "Why? Why is this all so fucked up? Why can't we have a normal friendship?"

In two strides, Sasha was in front of me, pulling me into his arms.

"What are you doing?" I demanded, panic in my voice.

"What I should've done months ago."

"And what's that?"

"Proving there's something more between us than just friendship."

His mouth covered mine. There was passion and unrequited love behind his kiss. I felt something; an ember of desire and given enough fanning, it would blaze into an inferno.

"Is that what you want?" I growled against his mouth. "Proof?"

I yanked him closer, tearing at him, becoming the aggressor. His hands were everywhere, stroking my curves, taunting and teasing.

When I deemed it enough, I bit down on his lip, tasting blood. His breath hitched, startled out of his desirous trance. He took a step back from me, breathing hard, like he'd run a marathon. I felt like I was looking at him from far away, my vision narrow.

"Whatever debt I've incurred, it's been repaid. You touch me again, I'll kill you."

∼

I entered the penthouse to find Lacey and Ash on the floor with Hawk. Lacey was fiddling with her camera, snapping pictures. We were supposed to have our first "photo shoot," but I was in no mood. I wanted a soak in the tub and time to myself.

I'd blown my friendship with Sasha to smithereens. I'd kissed a man who wasn't my husband.

But I'd learned recently that there was no room for guilt. And my heart belonged to Flynn.

"Hi," Ash greeted, her voice bright and chipper.

"Hi," I mumbled, heading to the fridge, so I had an excuse to hide my face.

"How was your workout?" Lacey asked.

"Good. Thanks."

"Great. So do you want to take a quick shower and then we can start—"

"I'm really not up for this today," I said, speaking nothing but the truth.

Lacey peered at me. "You okay? You look really pale."

I nodded. "I'm fine. I just don't have the energy."

"Okay," Lacey said with a nod. I could tell she was disappointed, but I didn't have the reserves to take care of anyone else's feelings at the moment.

I wanted to climb into the tub and then call Flynn on the burner phone. I needed to hear his voice and for him to tell me the choices I'd been making weren't all selfish and deplorable—that I wasn't turning into a sociopath. I wasn't sure anymore. I killed to protect those I loved. But if I really felt that way why couldn't I reconcile it?

Could I really reconcile anything? Maybe I just buried my feelings deep in my psyche, and they were rotting me from the inside out.

"Barrett?" Ash asked.

"Yeah?" I turned my head to glance at her.

She looked at me in confusion. "Are you sure you're okay? I was talking to you and you didn't even hear me."

"Didn't sleep well," I said.

She nodded like that made sense. "Flynn left and now you're back to not sleeping. I get it."

I rubbed my third eye. I could use a massage, but I didn't

get them anymore due to the trauma surrounding them. First kidnapped and then almost choked to death.

Sasha had saved me. Our friendship had begun in debt.

God, what I wouldn't give to be able to drink it all away, drown myself in scotch and Flynn.

Lacey set her camera aside and got up off the floor. She came over to me, her brow furrowed. "Do you want us to go?"

I nodded.

Ash picked up Hawk and brought him to me. "I just fed him so he should be good for a little while."

"Thanks," I said as I took my son into my arms. I breathed in the scent of him and closed my eyes to savor it.

I heard my friends leave and knew they were talking about me all the way down to the lobby.

## Chapter 44

Snow began to fall, and I found the white flakes soothing. A blanket of silence.

My cell phone rang again. With a look of disgust, I silenced it. It had been three days since my encounter with Sasha, and he'd been calling nonstop since then. I'd already talked to the front desk and removed him from the approved visitor's list just in case he had the audacity to try to come up to the penthouse.

I felt like a prisoner in my own home, and my cell phone was holding me hostage. The only reason it was still on was because I didn't know if or when Flynn was going to call. Our communication had been sparse since he'd left New York. I knew he and Duncan had gone to London to follow the Arlington lead.

My cell rang, but it was Lacey's name that flashed across the screen. I picked up. "Hello?"

"Hello. You've been avoiding my calls," she said.

"I've been avoiding everyone's calls, so don't take it personally."

"You're home, right?"

"Yes," I said.

"Good. Ash and I are in the lobby. We're holding bags of Thai takeout, and we want a girls' night."

I groaned. They knew I loved Thai.

"But Hawk is here," I said, suddenly feeling lighter than I had in days.

"He's the one man I'll allow at our girls' night," Lacey said with a chuckle. "So is it okay if we come up?"

"Yes. I'd love to see you guys." I sprang up from the couch to get out plates and silverware. The elevator doors chimed and then opened. Lacey and Ash stepped out. Both looked gorgeous and fresh—and not at all weighed down by life. I envied them.

I hugged both of them and said, "You're not allowed to comment on the fact that I've been MIA."

"Wasn't planning on it," Ash obviously lied.

Lacey took the bags of takeout to the kitchen table and began to unload enough food to feed five people. Challenge accepted! I'd eat my weight in curry and that would definitely improve my mood, though the company was doing a fair job of that.

"Why do you guys always look like you're dressed to go out?" I asked them.

"What do you mean?" Lacey asked.

"Like, both of you have done your hair, put on makeup, picked out a cute outfit—but if you were coming here, why the need to impress?"

"Awww, you're feeling frumpy, aren't you?" Ash asked in understanding.

"Not *frumpy* but definitely not on your level. I should try more."

Lacey and Ash exchanged a confused look. "Okay," Lacey said. "What's really going on?"

"What do you mean?" I asked.

"I mean, you've been underground for a few days, and now you're all worried about your appearance?" Lacey said.

"Yeah, Barrett. That was never like you," Ash added.

"I don't know," I admitted. "I had a fight with Sasha a few days ago, and I've been out of sorts since."

"A fight? You guys have been as thick as thieves," Ash said.

I shrugged, not willing to go into details about what had occurred. I took a bite of the curry and wrinkled my nose. It tasted foul. I chewed it quickly and then washed it down with some water.

"Pass the Pad Thai, please," I said.

Ash handed me the container, and I lifted it to my nose and sniffed. It smelled good, so I dumped some of it onto my plate.

"Uh, Barrett?" Lacey asked.

"Hmm?"

"Why did you just sniff the Pad Thai?"

"Because the curry tasted funny, and I wanted to be sure the Pad Thai wasn't rancid," I explained.

Ash reached over to my plate and scooped up a bite of curry and stuck it into her mouth. She frowned. "The curry tastes fine."

"It tastes like garbage," I said.

"Let me taste," Lacey said. She chewed for a moment and then swallowed before saying, "Yeah, it's fine. Really good actually."

"Huh, maybe I got a bad forkful," I said, taking another sample. It was halfway to my mouth when an unpleasant aroma wafted up my nose. I shook my head. "Nope, it stinks!"

Lacey and Ash dropped the line of conversation, and we ate for a few minutes in silence. Ash finally broke it.

"So, you've been really tired lately."

I shrugged. "Yeah. I wasn't sleeping well."

"Are you sleeping well now?" Lacey prodded.

"Really well."

"Are you napping?" Ash asked.

I frowned. "I guess. Sometimes when Hawk goes down for his afternoon nap, I take one too."

Lacey and Ash exchanged a look.

"What?" I demanded. "What's that look for?"

"And you've been kind of…" Lacey trailed off.

"Moody," Ash supplied. "Totally moody."

"Well, I guess," I allowed. "Because I hate being separated from Flynn."

Lacey let out a sigh. "Barrett, is there any chance you might be pregnant?"

I laughed. "Pregnant! Are you kidding? Have you guys been drinking?"

They both stared at me with serious expressions. My laughter fizzled out. "I can't be," I protested weakly. "I mean, it's totally ridiculous. We've been using protection. Plus, I read that it's really hard to get pregnant when you're breastfeeding."

"But you weren't always breastfeeding," Ash said slowly. "What about when Hawk was gone?"

"I was still pumping. Not a lot, but enough—I wanted to make sure I could still breastfeed when we found Hawk."

I thought back to the few days after we'd come back from Edinburgh with Hawk. So much had happened, and I'd been running on no sleep. Things were hazy, but…

I dropped my fork and it clattered on the plate. "Oh God."

Lacey reached over and grabbed my hand. Ash jumped up from her chair and headed to the master bedroom.

"What are you doing?" I called out, feeling like all the blood was rushing from my head.

"Remember when I brought you pregnancy tests?" Ash yelled back. "I'm seeing if you still have them."

"Medicine cabinet," I squeaked, somehow managing to

stand. Lacey followed me and just as we reached the bathroom, Ash popped her head out, holding an EPT box.

She handed it over. "We'll wait out here."

"Fuck all that," I said. "Get in here."

"You want us to watch you pee on a stick?" Lacey demanded, striving for levity.

"You can look at the wall," I said. "But I can't be in there alone."

"This is very Ya-Ya Sisterhood," Ash joked.

"There were four in the sisterhood," I said, pulling out a test and unwrapping it.

"If Ramsey gets together with Jane, she can be our fourth," Ash suggested.

"Who's Jane?" Lacey asked.

"I got this," Ash said. "I can tell this story in three minutes. Barrett, get peeing!"

~

"You're going to have Irish twins!" Ash said, injecting a note of enthusiasm into her voice.

I glared at her from my position on the couch. I was sprawled out with Hawk lying on top of me, sound asleep.

"They're Scottish," I reminded her.

She shrugged. "Fine, so you'll have Scottish twins."

"That's not a thing," I hissed, feeling the hysteria rise from my stomach into my throat.

"We can make it a thing," Lacey said, sipping on a martini.

As soon as the pregnancy test turned positive, Ash and Lacey opened up the liquor and began to celebrate. I hated them. And I loved them. Mostly, I just wanted to cry.

"At this rate, I'm going to have my own football team," I said miserably, still in shock.

"American football or European football?" Ash asked. She hiccoughed and then giggled.

"Are you unhappy about it?" Lacey asked.

"No," I admitted. "But Hawk is only a few months old! I was supposed to have a few years with him before I decided on a second one. And for fuck's sake, I just got done being pregnant. I don't want to do it again that soon."

"Don't think you have much of a choice," Ash said drunkenly.

"You both suck. A lot."

"This is not the worst thing in the world," Lacey interjected. "Sure the timing isn't the best, but you love Flynn and he loves you. And if you think about it, Hawk and his new sibling will be close in age, which means they'll probably be good friends."

I snorted. "Or they'll be in constant competition with each other."

"Oh, we're in a 'glass is half empty' kind of mood. Got it," Ash said with a grin.

"I'm never going to sleep ever again. I'll nurse one and as soon as he's done, I'll have to nurse the other. Diapers. So many diapers."

"Okay, so it might be harder in the beginning, but when they're older, it'll pay off," Lacey said.

"How?" I demanded.

"Um, Ash? A little help?" Lacey said.

"Hire a nanny," Ash suggested.

I sat up on the couch and adjusted Hawk and put him to my shoulder. "Bite me."

"Hey!" Ash interjected. "We were there with you when you peed on a stick. Have you forgotten already?"

"I'm going to bed," I stated.

"But the night's just getting started," Lacey said.

I rolled my eyes. "Not for me it isn't." My gaze softened. "I do love you guys. Thanks for trying to cheer me up."

"It will be okay," Ash called out. "You make beautiful babies! You got this!"

"Oh, I just had a great idea," Lacey said. "I can photograph you during your pregnancy. Month to month, ya know? This is great! I'm so glad you got knocked up. Again!"

## Chapter 45

The morning of Alia's wedding I went to the doctor who confirmed I was six weeks pregnant and completely healthy. Some of my worry evaporated at her words, but some still remained.

How the hell was I going to do this? It had been hard enough to protect one baby from the SINS and all the blowback—and I hadn't even been able to do that. And now there was going to be another? Even when Flynn and Duncan found the traitor, the danger wouldn't be over. Something new would pop up because it always did. My children were going to grow up surrounded by bodyguards. They wouldn't have normal childhoods. They'd learn about the cause early; they'd be thrust into the violence, and they'd witness it firsthand. They might even be a part of it.

I got dressed and left the exam room. Nathan sat in the waiting room, reading *People* magazine. It made me snicker, seeing my ripped bodyguard hastily close the magazine and set it aside. The doctor spoke to the receptionist about my next appointment and then her gaze wandered over to Nathan.

"Oh, is this your husband?" the doctor asked. Before I could answer she said, "Congratulations."

Nathan looked perplexed for a moment and then he stood, a goofy grin spreading across his face. "Thank you!" He wrapped an arm around my shoulder. "We're really happy about the news."

"Shut up," I said, digging my elbow into his ribs. He released me with a wince. To the confused doctor, I said, "Nathan is just a friend."

The young, attractive doctor's eyes lit up appreciatively as she obviously checked him out.

"Let's go," I muttered, attempting to shove him toward the exit.

Nathan wouldn't budge. He spent a few minutes flirting it up with the doctor and then as if realizing I was still standing next to him, finally said his goodbye and we left.

As we climbed into the waiting town car, I said to Nathan, "We need to get a few things straight."

"I've never read *People* before in my life."

I rolled my eyes. "I'm serious."

"Okay, go ahead."

"First of all, you can't tell Flynn I'm pregnant. I know you report back to him, but I need you to keep this to yourself. I want to tell him when the time is right."

He nodded. "Not my news to share. Congratulations, though."

I waved away his words. "What was that up there?"

"What was what?"

"You flirting with the doctor."

He frowned. "It was just a little harmless flirting."

I pointed a finger at him. "What about Shawna?"

"What about her?"

"She's my friend and you hit on her."

"Actually, she hit on me. Which I'm glad she did because she's cute. Did you finally tell her that I'm your bodyguard?"

"Yeah. I did."

"Are you going to forbid me from seeing her?"

"Forbid?" I asked with a laugh.

"Bad choice of words. I meant outlaw. Are you going to outlaw me from seeing her?"

"Well, I am the sheriff," I quipped. "Just don't hurt her, okay? The last thing I need is a broken-hearted friend."

∽

A waiter with a tray of bacon-wrapped dates passed by, and I grabbed a toothpick along with a napkin. Alia and Jake's small, intimate wedding ceremony had been short and sweet, and now the guests were enjoying hors d'oeuvres and champagne.

I was enjoying a club soda.

"Have you talked to Flynn?" Lacey asked, taking a sip of her champagne.

"No," I said. "He called while I was at the doctor this morning. I tried to call him back, but it went to voicemail."

"I'm guessing you didn't tell him you were pregnant over voicemail."

"Nope. I want to see his face slacken in shock."

"Yeah, some things are just better live," she teased. "But try to set up a camera and record it. I'd like to see that."

I laughed.

"How are you feeling about it?" she went on.

I tucked my toothpick into a cocktail napkin and shrugged. "Still in shock. That seems to be my general MO. But I'll be happy about it."

"Good." Lacey let her eyes wander around the room. "I've got to say, I'm impressed that Alia pulled all of this off with only a few weeks' notice."

"Sometimes you just have to hit the ground running and

hope it all comes together. Besides, Ash spent a year planning her first wedding and that all went to shit. Time is not always a good thing."

"Yeah, what happened there? Why did she split up with her first fiancé?"

"Ah, look, more dates," I said. I smiled at the passing waiter for his impeccable timing.

"Okay, so I'll ask her what happened," Lacey said with wry amusement.

"I'm really glad you guys became fast friends. It's been nice having the both of you to turn to."

Lacey took my hand and gave it a squeeze.

"Look at that picture," I said, gesturing with my chin to Alia and Jake. They were moving toward the dance floor as the band began to play. They looked happy and in love, and it would've been nauseating except I felt the exact same way about Flynn.

"They're too cute," Lacey said with complete sincerity.

"Does it bother you? Not being in a relationship when you're surrounded by your friends who are? Sorry, that's blunt and harsh. I've been back in New York a little over a month, and it's already rubbed off on me."

She chuckled and shook her head. "No, it doesn't bother me. I ran Rex Burlesque for years, and now I get to follow my passion. Would it be nice to have someone to share my successes with? Sure, but I'm not going to settle for anything less than what I want. Plus, I like my independence."

"You would be an awesome second wife to a successful silver fox," I teased.

"Second wife? Honey, please. I'm third wife material."

We shared a laugh and then Lacey said, "I'm going to go find the restroom. I'll be right back. Unless you want to tag along? Seems to be our thing now."

I laughed again. "Nah, I'm good."

While Lacey was gone, I had three more dates and an invitation to dance with Alia's eighty-year-old grandfather. I happily accepted and made polite chit-chat with the adorable, white-haired man.

A hand politely tapped Grandpa's shoulder. "May I cut in?"

Grandpa's hands dropped from me, and he took a step back, a wide smile on his face. "Sure. Thank you for the dance," he said to me.

"Thank you," I said back, but my eyes were trained on the blond-haired, blue-eyed uninvited guest.

I thought briefly about refusing to dance with Sasha, but then I realized it was childish to make a scene at Alia's wedding.

Sasha's hand went to my waist, and he pulled me toward him as he took my other hand and began to move us toward the edge of the dance floor.

"What are you doing here?" I demanded. I addressed his suit lapel since I refused to look him in the face.

"You wouldn't answer my calls," he said.

"Yeah, I've been avoiding them."

"No, I don't mean the last few days, I mean this afternoon. I've been trying to get a hold of you for the last hour. It's Flynn," Sasha said.

The use of my husband's first name wasn't lost on me. A cold snake of fear wrapped itself around my spine.

"What? What is it?" I asked.

Sasha's hand tightened on my waist. "Not here." He released me and then took my hand, dragging me out of the room and into the hallway. Away from the reception, Sasha stopped and turned to me.

"Now will you tell me what had you tracking me down at a party?" I snapped waspishly. With no audience, I was finally able to let my displeasure out.

Sasha dropped my hand and then placed his hands on my

shoulders. He looked me in the eyes and said, "Duncan and Flynn were ambushed in London, Barrett."

"Ambushed?"

"They walked into a trap," he said slowly. "And I don't know if they're alive."

## Chapter 46

I sat in the SoHo restaurant, sipping on a glass of sparkling water. My stomach was in knots, my nerves were frayed, and I'd barely slept in the last three days. Ever since Sasha had told me that Flynn and Duncan had been ambushed in London, my mind spun like it had been put into a cotton candy machine. There was still no news if they were dead or alive.

"Another glass of water, ma'am?" the cute, young waitress asked. She was pleasant and attentive.

I shook my head. "No, thank you. I'm waiting on someone. When he arrives, will you please bring him a cup of coffee?"

"Sure," she said before walking away.

I faced the entrance, my back to a wall. It was an old mafia trick—always know your escape routes, always plan for an exit should the need ever arise. Not that I expected any sort of trouble even though my bodyguard was only yards away to ensure my safety.

A quarter of an hour later, my companion strode into the restaurant. He was a tall, distinguished man in his early fifties with salt and pepper hair. His forehead was lined from years of stress. My FBI contact slid into the seat across from me. The waitress brought over his cup of coffee; he thanked her before she left again.

"Thanks for meeting me," I said.

Don Archer nodded as he added cream to his coffee. "You were vague on the phone."

I smiled slightly. "You never know who's listening."

Don raised an eyebrow. "A not-so-subtle dig at my division?"

"Perhaps. How are things?"

"Things are things," he stated. "You lock up one criminal, three more take his place. It's a damn pest control problem. But I know you didn't call me to discuss my job. What's up?"

Don and I had a backdoor alliance. I'd promised to give him information about certain illegal activities going down in the States and in return, he didn't bother with the SINS. Even though the SINS had a foothold in New York through The Rex's casino and brothel, Don had realized early on that there were bigger fish to fry and left us alone.

"You saw the front page of *The New York Times*, I take it? A few weeks ago?" I prodded.

He nodded. "Ramsey Buchanan's death. Sorry for your loss." The way he said it let me know he knew it was a sham. Good. I liked Don. I liked that he was intelligent, could connect the dots on his own, and focused on the bigger picture.

"Thank you," I murmured. "It seems the SINS are dealing with a coup though we aren't sure who it is."

"Ah, and you want a list of all the active members, right?"

I grinned. "How did you know?"

He shrugged.

I wasn't going to explain all the minute details and thankfully he didn't ask. Don was FBI and at the end of the day, I didn't trust the FBI. Not after the shit Winters had pulled. Once I knew more about how Lord Arlington, Winters, and this SINS traitor were all connected, then I might consider letting Don in on it. Until then…

"Anything else you want to tell me?" Don asked. "You did make me come out all this way."

"Out all this way? We're in SoHo." I chuckled. "There's an illegal shipment coming into Boston at the end of the month."

"The Irish?" he asked.

"Possibly," I said. "Might be the Sicilians."

Don cursed and then drank the rest of his lukewarm coffee. "I'll send you an email with all the information."

I nodded. "Thanks."

Don stood up and reached for his wallet, but I quickly waved him to put it away. He smiled ruefully. "You're a decent sort, Barrett. It's a damn shame you're married to a criminal."

∼

*Decent sort.*

I snorted at the thought. Maybe I had been, before all of this, before Flynn. Maybe I used to have a clear picture of right and wrong, good and evil. But I refused to waste time thinking about it anymore. I had to be cold, efficient; I had to think clearly so I could figure out what had happened to Flynn and Duncan.

Since the ambush, I waited for news that the English authorities had found their bodies, but there had been nothing. I didn't believe they were dead.

I entered the penthouse suite of The Rex to find it filled with people. Ash paced back and forth across the carpet, looking harried and out of sorts. Lacey sat in a chair with Hawk in her arms. Brad and Sasha stood by the window, their heads bent toward one another and speaking in low tones.

Everyone turned when they saw me.

"How'd it go?" Brad asked.

"Fine. Archer is going to send over the names."

He nodded. "Good. Our guy in London hasn't found anything yet."

Brad referred to a connection that had access to security footage in the city. I wasn't quite clear on how we knew this guy or how he had access to private information, but I wasn't going to question it.

Sasha didn't speak—his men that he'd sent to help Flynn were dead, taken out by Arlington's trap.

"So basically, we have nothing to go on, and we just have to sit on our asses," Ash snapped. Her color was high and so was her temper. Our reactions to the situation had been completely different. I'd gone ice queen survival mode, my brain clear and calm. Ash had turned into a hothead.

"Pretty much," I said. "Waiting is all we can do at this point."

"I called Ramsey," she stated.

"You what?" My eyes widened at Ash's announcement. "We agreed to wait until we had more information before calling him."

"No, *you* agreed."

"It wasn't your call to make!"

Hawk began to cry, and Lacey got up from the chair and headed to the bedroom to soothe him while I had a fight with my best friend. Sasha and Brad wisely decided to stay out of it.

"I am Duncan's wife and Ramsey is his brother. He had a right to know," Ash said.

"I'm not negating that," I said, my own voice still calm. I was as composed as Ash was irate. "But from here on out, we have to make decisions together."

Ash crossed her arms and looked away from me, but finally she nodded.

I sighed. "How did Ramsey take it?"

Her gaze dropped to the floor. "He and Jane left Orkney. They're back in Dornoch."

I closed my eyes. "This is what I *didn't* want."

"What were you hoping to do?" Ash demanded. "Carry out Flynn and Duncan's plan—tell the media that the Buchanans are dead? That your husband is also dead and the SINS are without a leader? News flash, Barrett, that plan is shot to shit. I didn't like it, anyway."

Of course we needed a new plan. Arlington was still out there, along with the faceless traitor that had tried to stage a coup. But we still didn't know enough. I needed to stop thinking about how Flynn or Duncan would've handled this because that hadn't gotten us far. I had to think like me.

I looked at Brad. "I need a whiteboard and markers. While I'm waiting on Archer to get me the information, I want to put up some stuff on the board."

Brad nodded. "I'll call down and have one of my guys send it up."

Lacey came out of the bedroom without Hawk. She fixed Ash and me with a glare. "Hawk is asleep. You two done yelling at each other?"

I looked at Ash and she looked at me. "For now," we both said.

"Does anyone have anywhere they have to be?" I asked. "No? Good, get comfortable. We're going to be here a while."

## Chapter 47

Darkness surrounded me. Outside the safety of the penthouse, the city was cold and snowy. Everyone had left hours ago. We'd spent the night brainstorming, planning, talking. Unfortunately, I didn't feel one step closer to discovering anything.

I listened for a moment, wondering what had awoken me. It wasn't Hawk; he hadn't cried. I listened again, hearing the faintest sound of a spoon clinking in glass.

I got up out of bed and went into the living room. Ash sat on the couch, bundled up in her robe, cradling a mug of tea in her hands. She'd been staying at her brother's apartment while he'd been out of town, but when we'd gotten the news about Flynn and Duncan, she moved into the penthouse. I'd had a bed put in Flynn's study—Ash shared her room with books and a desk, but at least she had a door to close.

"Sorry, did I wake you?" she asked with a glance at me.

"It's okay." I took a seat next to her.

She shook her head. "I'm so used to having my own wing. Weird, right?"

"Very."

I stared at the whiteboard that was covered in different color markers. It looked like a jumbled mess. The clutter bugged me. I got up and flipped the whiteboard over to its clean side. I picked up a blue marker and at the top, I wrote *Arlington, Winters, and Pretender.*

"You can think at two a.m.?" Ash asked. "Impressive."

"Something has been nagging at me, like itching at the back of my brain. I'm close to figuring something out, I just know it. Will you be a sounding board?"

"Sure. I can do that."

I nodded. "Thanks. Okay. So here's what I know. Winters wanted back in the FBI, right? Flynn and the Buchanans were in his way because they brought guns into the States. That's why Winters tried to get me to make a deal and bring down Flynn and Malcolm."

"Right," Ash said nodding.

I wrote *guns* under Winters's name and then gestured the pen to *Pretender.* "The Pretender wants the SINS, which means he has no qualms about taking out Flynn and the Buchanans."

"But didn't Lord Elliot tell you Arlington and Winters hired The White Company?"

"Yes. Hired Italian mercenaries that couldn't be traced back to the English or the Americans. Arlington is English. Winters is American."

I wrote *The White Company* in the middle of the board.

"Okay," Ash said. "So I understand why Winters wanted a new SINS leader—someone who would promise not to bring in guns into the States. Winters would've made a deal with The Pretender. No guns in the country, and then Winters would keep the FBI off the SINS's backs."

"Winters would've returned a celebrated hero instead of a rogue ex-agent. Yeah. Okay."

"But that still leaves Arlington. What's his role in all of this?" Ash asked. "Why would a member of the House of Lords make a deal with a Scottish rebel group that wants a free Scotland?"

"Duh. I'm so stupid!" I said, smacking my head. "Arlington is financing The Pretender."

Ash frowned. "Connect the dots for me."

"If Scotland gained its independence, it's a huge financial loss for England. Arlington, along with the House of Lords, would still make laws, but they'd lose their grip on Scotland's economy."

"So this is about control?" Ash asked, tapping her chin.

"Yes—and money."

"But I still don't understand. Wouldn't Arlington do anything possible to ensure that Scotland *doesn't* gain its independence?"

"Unless Arlington stands to make a lot of money if Scotland wins. Think about it. He puts The Pretender in charge of the SINS, the largest rebel faction in Scotland, and Arlington is the financial backer which means—"

"He controls the SINS," Ash finished. "Bloody brilliant."

"Arlington and Winters united for a common goal but for different reasons," I said.

Ash's brow furrowed as she nodded. "Yeah, that makes sense. But if Scotland wins their independence, the need for the SINS is over. Right?"

"I guess, technically," I admitted. "Still, the SINS wouldn't just disperse."

"Wouldn't they?"

I shook my head slowly. "Not unless there's another enemy to fight."

"You think Arlington and The Pretender have another enemy lined up?"

"I think they want Scotland for themselves, and they'll take out anyone in their way."

"Holy shit," Ash breathed. "What if your theory is correct?"

My gaze was bleak. "Then we have a big fucking problem."

The next morning, I fed Hawk a bottle while I waited for the printer to finish its epic job. Don Archer had been as good as his word and sent me an email to a private account that couldn't be accessed by anyone except the two of us.

Ash looked at the pile of papers in the paper tray and groaned. "Fuck. This is going to suck."

We were going to pin up every scrap of paper with a face, cover the walls, and figure out this shit, and I was going to use any means necessary to find out the name of the man I called The Pretender—the traitor who had turned on his own clan and was in league with an Englishman.

My cell phone rang but my hands were full. "Will you see who that is?"

Ash got up from her seat and went to the kitchen counter where my phone was charging. She picked it up and said, "It's Ramsey."

"Answer it."

She nodded. "Hey, it's Ash. Barrett's got her hands full of baby." She listened for a moment, nodding at whatever Ramsey was saying. "Okay. I'll let her know."

"What's up?" I asked when she hung up my phone.

"You're not going to like it."

"Probably not. Tell me anyway," I said with a sigh.

"Ramsey and Jane are in London, and they're on a mission to find Duncan and Flynn."

I blinked. "That's a bad idea all around. The media knows Ramsey's face now that he's been in the newspaper. And Jane was kidnapped from her party months ago. What happens when all of a sudden she resurfaces? And for that matter, did we successfully recruit her?"

Hawk finished his bottle, and I put him to my shoulder to burp him while I waited for Ash to explain.

"Okay, first of all, this was all Ramsey's idea. Right now,

he's fearless and angry, and he still thinks dangling himself as bait is a way to bring Arlington and The Pretender out of their holes."

"Fearless? Or foolish?" I demanded.

"Take it up with him," Ash snapped. She was instantly contrite. "I'm sorry, but I want Duncan back. Ramsey is a Buchanan, and he isn't as foolhardy and young as he's led us to believe. He's paid attention over the years and picked up some of Duncan's tricks, but Ramsey has never had to step up. He wants—needs—to step up now."

"Okay, I'll agree to that. But Jane?"

"Ramsey told her about what her father was involved in. She wants Arlington dead as much as we do. She blames him for her father's death."

"She doesn't believe we're responsible? We did kidnap and torture him with the full intent to kill him."

"Ramsey told her that Flynn found Elliot's throat slit and it wasn't done by us."

"A woman with a vendetta." I nodded. "Revenge on her mind. Got it. How is she going to help Ramsey in London?"

"She's the daughter of a Lord, isn't she? She knows the right people, knows the right clubs."

"Can't really argue with that logic. I just hate the idea that they're going to run around London and play spies."

"You suck at delegating, you know that?" Ash stated. "That's your problem."

"What? What are you talking about?"

"I know your husband was acting leader of the SINS while Duncan was healing, so you took on a lot of the roles that go along with being a queen, or whatever. But you can't do everything yourself." She pointed to Hawk. "You have a son. You're also pregnant. You want to tell me you'd feel better running around London trying to piece together where and how Duncan and Flynn were ambushed?"

"Valid point, yet again."

"Duncan and Flynn are alive. I know it," Ash said.

"I agree. If they were dead, The Pretender would've made a play for the SINS, but he hasn't yet."

Ash smirked in wry humor. "Plus, our men are *really* hard to kill."

I let out a laugh. "Thank God for that."

## Chapter 48

I ran a washcloth underneath cool water and then put it to my head. The woozy feeling was leaving, but the back of my neck and palms were clammy. I'd already thrown up.

Morning sickness. I'd survived it once. I'd survive it again. I looked down at my stomach. "You better be really cute."

There was a knock on the door. "Barrett?"

"Be right out," I said to Ash.

With one last glance in the mirror, I made sure I didn't have anything gross on my face and headed back into the living room. Ash was writing something on one of the printed faces that had been taped to the wall. The living room was covered with papers of faces, most of whom I didn't recognize.

"I'm almost finished," Ash said. "With the first-tier members, anyway."

By first-tier, Ash meant men who weren't just considered soldiers, but leaders in their own right. The Buchanans and Flynn were at the top and oversaw the entire SINS operation. They were kept informed by other SINS leaders who led smaller pockets of rebels all over Scotland.

"I've made Xs across the members that are deceased, and

I've written down what I deem are important facts about each member."

It was overwhelming to look at, and there was still a stack of papers to go through when we managed to field our way through the pictures on the walls. There were at least five hundred pages in total.

"You know," I said. "Our plan is genius except for one major flaw."

Ash didn't look at me when she answered. "What's that?"

"We didn't grow up with the SINS. We married into it. We have no insider knowledge."

Ash stopped writing mid-scrawl and looked over her shoulder at me. "Fuck."

"Yeah."

"And Ramsey's in London so we can't use him," Ash went on. "Damn it! Who else is there? Who can we trust?"

I was in the middle of shaking my head when an idea came to me. I couldn't believe it had taken me this long to figure it out. My smile was slow.

"What?" Ash demanded. "Why are you smiling like the Joker?"

"Because I've figured out the solution to our problem."

~

"It will never work," Brad said.

I frowned. "Why not?"

"Because they aren't warriors," Sasha said, like it was obvious.

"Save me from bullheaded men," I muttered.

Ash let out a laugh. She was finally looking relaxed. Even though our husbands were MIA, we at least had a solid plan that we believed in. Or maybe it was the glass of scotch in the early afternoon that had lulled her into good humor.

"Barrett," Brad began.

I held up a hand. "Let me lay it out for you. Right now, everything is in a tailspin. Flynn and Duncan aren't around to call the shots, so for right now, you might as well call us"—I gestured to Ash—"the Princess Regents. Okay?"

Brad shook his head. "I don't like this. What's Flynn going to do—"

"When he finds out that we used women to help save his antiquated, patriarchal rebel faction?" I snapped. "He'll be glad. If he were here right now, well, we wouldn't be in this bloody mess, would we?"

I pointed to the walls of the penthouse. "Do you know who these men are?"

Brad sighed. "No."

I looked at Sasha. "Do you?"

Sasha shook his head.

"And neither do we," I said.

None of us wanted to discuss what would happen to the SINS if Duncan and Flynn were found dead. Until then, I was operating on the assumption that they were alive, in hiding, and coming back. Hopefully Ramsey would check in soon with some information.

"Besides, it's too late," Ash interjected. She threw back the rest of her glass of scotch and stood. "Barrett already called Katherine. She and her friends will be here tomorrow night."

"You called Katherine!" Sasha fumed. "She can't be trusted!"

"This isn't your call," I stated calmly. "You're not one of us."

"You're not one of them!" Sasha yelled, color rising to flame his high cheekbones. "When will you learn?"

"Lower your voice. Hawk's asleep."

Sasha shook his head and dropped his gaze. "You're asking for trouble."

I shrugged. "No more than usual."

"So you basically called this meeting to lay down a new law?" Brad asked.

"Pretty much," I said. "And to ask you to have three rooms readied."

Brad rose from his seat and moved toward the elevator doors. "I'll see to it." He looked at Sasha. "You want a beer?"

"More than anything," Sasha grumbled.

The men left and Ash and I were alone.

"Why is it that men claim to love strong, fierce women, but when put into practice, it's not the case?" Ash wondered.

"Our men love us the way we are," I said. "Brad and Sasha aren't our men. They have no obligation to love us."

"Except that Sasha *does* love you. Will you finally tell me what happened between you two?" Ash asked, getting up and heading to the bar.

"When and what time," I quipped. "We're always fighting."

Ash poured herself three fingers of scotch. "I'm talking about the day you came back to the penthouse suite and told Lacey you didn't have the energy for her to take photos of you and Hawk."

"What makes you think something happened?"

"Ah, you're avoiding, so I *know* something happened. Come on. Aren't you and I done with all the secrets?"

Could I really tell Ash what had occurred between Sasha and me? I had finally told her about Dolinsky and my mishmash of feelings. This wasn't any worse.

"See, okay," I began. "It's you and me. And Flynn and me. And you and Duncan. Now, if you and I have a secret, I don't want you to feel like you have to keep a secret from your husband who would feel obligated to tell *my* husband."

"You're keeping secrets from your husband? Now I *have* to know."

Just as I was about to blurt it all out, my phone buzzed. It was Ramsey.

"Hey," I said, my heart thumping. "Do you have news?"

"Turn on your TV," he said.

I could barely hear him. In the background, I heard the wailing of sirens and yelling.

"What's going on?" I demanded even as I went to find the remote.

"Turn it to BBC."

Ash looked at me in curiosity. I flipped on the television and clicked over to the news station. On screen was a building engulfed in flames, an attractive reporter at the scene.

"Behind me is the Palace of Westminster where the House of Lords were congregating to discuss the Scottish Referendum. A bomb exploded not too long ago. We already have a well-known Scottish rebel group known as the Sons of Independent Nationalists for Scotland taking credit for the explosion," the reporter said to the camera.

"What the hell!" Ash yelled at the TV.

"Ramsey," I breathed into the phone.

"Aye, Barrett," he said. "Flynn and Duncan didn't do this. They would never have taken public credit for it. This was The Pretender making a play for the leadership role. He's getting desperate. He's hoping to drive them out of hiding."

"Because Flynn and Duncan's bodies weren't found at the scene of the ambush," I realized. "Which can only mean…"

"They're alive, lass. My brothers are alive."

~

Ash and I tromped through the snow of Central Park. Late last night, a winter storm had hit, dumping at least six inches of snow on the ground. The park was full of people: parents with their children building snowmen, exuberant teens having snowball fights.

"Want to go sledding on Pilgrim Hill?" Ash asked, her cheeks pink with cold. She pulled down her black wool hat with a pompom over her ears, the action awkward because she wore mittens.

Pilgrim Hill was at the 72nd Street and 5th Avenue entrance of the park, and unfortunately, we didn't have time for that. Katherine and her friends would be arriving soon.

"Hawk's a little young, don't you think?" The three-month-old in question rested warmly and comfortably against me. My coat and arms insulated him from the cold. He hadn't made a peep since we'd left the hotel forty-five minutes ago.

"I wasn't asking about him, I was asking for you and me." She said with a rueful shake of her head.

"I wish."

"Another time then."

Nathan and Daniel, our faithful bodyguards, trailed behind us, giving us the illusion of privacy. They were far enough away that they couldn't overhear our conversation but close enough should we need them.

I breathed in a deep breath. Ever since Ramsey's call a few hours earlier, I hadn't been able to stop smiling, and my fear for Flynn and Duncan had eased. It wouldn't disappear completely, not until I spoke to Flynn and heard his voice, and knew he was safe.

"I don't want to go back inside," Ash complained even as we turned to head back. "I felt like this was the first time I could leave the penthouse without feeling guilty."

I nodded. "I know what you mean. Every waking moment has been spent in limbo."

Ash let out a breathy sigh. "I feel hopeful, ya know?"

"Yes," I said with a grin. "I do know."

We got back to the hotel, and on our way through the lobby, I talked to Simone at the front desk, requesting that hot chocolate and pastries be sent up. Simone smiled and said it would be done. She also informed me that three hotel suites had been prepared for Katherine and her friends.

Back in the penthouse, I shucked off my outer layers and

removed Hawk from the body sling. I changed him and then put him in his bassinet in the bedroom for his nap. By the time I got back to the living room, the hot chocolate and pastries had arrived.

"I love pastries in the afternoon," Ash said, a glob of cherry jam on her lip.

I laughed. "There's just something so decadent about it." I picked up a buttery croissant and pulled off a flaky corner. I put it into my mouth and moaned. "This is the best thing I've ever tasted. It might also be the only thing I can seem to keep down lately."

"Morning sickness is bad?" Ash asked.

I nodded. "More than bad. Worse than with Hawk."

Ash made a face. "That sucks."

"It does," I agreed. "But hopefully it will be over soon, and then I can enjoy the beautiful aspects of my pregnancy. And when Flynn gets back, so can he."

## Chapter 49

Katherine and her two friends, Mary and Elizabeth, arrived early that evening. When I met them in the lobby, their eyes were as wide as saucers as they took in the opulence and wealth of The Rex. I wondered if they had ever been far from Dornoch.

A handsome young bellman with a cart loaded up their bags. He doffed his hat and smiled. The girls tittered and blushed. I'd forgotten how young they were.

Surprising me with a hug, Katherine wrapped me in her spindly arms. She pulled back to meet my eyes. "Thank you for giving me this chance to make things right. I won't let you down."

I smiled at her. "I appreciate the sentiment, and I have complete faith in you and your friends." The trio of girls chattered in their thick Scottish brogues as I led them to the elevator.

"You have your own elevator?" Mary asked. She was a cute, petite brunette with a bright smile. Her hand slid down the paneled wall of the elevator car.

Sometimes I forgot the wealth I'd grown accustomed to.

The power. It was dangerous; it lured and seduced and before you even realized it, you were in its clutches.

"I didn't know New York got so much snow," Elizabeth said, her blue eyes curious.

"We're close to the park," I said. "I'll take you guys out there. It's beautiful."

"I'm surprised by all the people," Katherine said. "Dornoch is so quiet."

The elevator doors opened, and the girls stepped out into the penthouse, gawking like tourists. Their excitement grew when they saw Ash holding Hawk. They crowded around my son, cooing their delight.

My best friend handed Hawk over to me. "I'll get everyone drinks," Ash said.

When everyone was settled, Katherine opened her shoulder bag and pulled out a tin and handed it to me. She smiled. "From my grannie. Her chocolate covered shortbread."

"Thank you. I'll call and thank her myself." I set the tin aside and got down to the matter at hand. "I want to thank you all for coming. I know I'm putting you in a difficult situation. I'm asking you to defy your families, to keep secrets from them, to help me discover who's behind the coup."

They were silent, waiting, riveted.

"I'm putting your lives at risk, but I can't do this alone. Ash and I can't do this alone. We need your help."

"Why us?" Mary ventured to ask.

"Because Katherine mentioned to me that she had friends who believed in a free Scotland and hated that they were left out of the SINS merely because they're women."

Elizabeth glanced at Katherine. Katherine nodded. "It's okay. Barrett trusts us, so we should trust her."

"I didn't think it was fair to ask this of you unless we were face to face," I said.

"Why are we in New York?" Mary frowned. "Why aren't we in Dornoch?"

"Ah, this is where it gets tricky," I said. I gave them the abridged version of the last few weeks and then went on to explain what had happened to Flynn and Duncan in London and the faceless, nameless man actually behind the bombing at the Palace of Westminster.

"Listen, you all grew up in Dornoch and have years of gatherings under you." I looked at Mary and Elizabeth. "Your fathers were two of Malcolm Buchanan's trusted few."

Mary nodded. "Aye. We had tons of people to our house over the years. I'm sure to remember some faces."

"Me too," Elizabeth added.

"Then why am I here?" Katherine asked. "My family is low in the SINS hierarchy."

"You're here because you proved your loyalty to me by reuniting me with my son—you're here because of your courage."

∼

After the girls ate a light supper in the penthouse, I had Brad show them to their suites. The wall of printed faces could wait until tomorrow.

"Ten bucks says they're jumping up and down on their beds like five-year-olds," Ash said as she sprawled on the couch.

"Nah, I bet they've succumbed to exhaustion," I said from my spot in the chair.

We were quiet a moment, each plagued by our own thoughts. "Why haven't they called yet?" Ash asked, shattering the silence.

"Because they're not safe."

"Alive, but not safe." Ash closed her eyes. "Hunted. What

happens when we discover who The Pretender is? Are we going to let Flynn and Duncan handle it?"

I frowned.

"What are you thinking about?" Ash asked, sitting up.

"I'm thinking Sasha was right."

"About what?"

"I'm an outsider," I said slowly. "I'll always be an outsider. Even though my children are Scottish and will be part of the SINS, I can't change the fact that I wasn't born into the life."

"Where are you going with this?" Ash demanded.

I grinned. "I used to lament the fact that I was an outsider, but you know what? Not anymore. And do you know why?"

"No, but I'm sure you're about to tell me."

"As an outsider, I have a different perspective. And so do you. It was our idea to bring Katherine and her friends into the fold—entrusting them with secrets. The SINS are a dominant, patriarchal rebel group, but this is the twenty-first century."

Ash grinned. "Change is gonna come."

"Oh, I think it's already come. So answering you in a roundabout way: will Flynn and Duncan handle The Pretender? That will be up to the SINS. The men as well as the women."

Ash laughed. "I can't wait to be there when you tell Flynn how it's going to be."

I smiled. "I can't wait to fight with him again."

"Come on, let's go to bed." Ash stood and stretched her arms over her head. "We have a busy day tomorrow."

Late the next morning, the girls stumbled into the penthouse bleary-eyed and hardly awake. I sent for breakfast and coffee, not at all surprised that they were listless. We were fighting an unknown enemy and jet lag. I made sure the coffee was strong. An hour later, the girls were lucid enough to begin looking at the walls.

A yawning Ash finally emerged from her bedroom. She

poured herself a cup of coffee and settled into a chair to watch the show. The girls spoke quickly and in thick Scottish brogues, and it was almost impossible to understand them. But they were excited, and I could tell they were happy to feel useful. How long had they been overlooked simply because they were young and women?

"Can I ask you guys a question?" I asked.

"Sure," Mary said, not taking her eyes off the wall, her brow furrowed.

"Are there more of you—women that is—that would like to have a say in the SINS?"

"Aye," Elizabeth voiced. "My Mam, for sure." Katherine and Mary added their two cents on the subject as well, admitting they had older cousins and aunts who wanted to be involved too.

"What are you thinking, Barrett?" Ash asked, covering her mouth as another yawn escaped.

I looked at her curiously, but she just shrugged. I turned my attention back to the girls. "Has the topic ever been brought up? About women joining the SINS?"

The three of them exchanged a look, and then finally Katherine shook her head. "I don't think so."

"Why not?" Ash demanded.

The girls swapped another look, but it was Elizabeth who answered. "We don't know."

I raised my eyebrows. "What do you mean 'you don't know'?"

A flush spread across Katherine's cheeks, and she dropped her gaze. "Sometimes things go on a certain way for so long that people don't ever challenge them."

"I understand," Ash said, nodding.

I supposed I did too, but I found it strange how easy we were lulled into accepting the status quo.

Mary pulled off a printed face from the wall and held it up to her friends. A large black X was marked across the face; the sign that he was deceased. The other two nodded, and then Mary set the paper aside.

"What was that?" Ash asked.

"We're just making sure your information is correct," Katherine said. "John Hamish is, indeed, dead."

Ash groaned. "Fuck. You're telling me Barrett's FBI contact might have wrong information?"

"Ash," I hissed. I hadn't wanted the girls to know about Don Archer and my relationship to him.

"I heard nothing," Mary chirped.

"Me neither," Elizabeth added.

Katherine giggled, and then three of them pretended to be the three monkeys that see no evil, hear no evil, speak no evil.

To my consternation, I laughed. There was something about being around the three of them. Their youth and giddiness reminded me of a time not so long ago—before my life had changed, before I'd met Flynn. I wouldn't wish to go back and change anything. Because after everything I'd lived through, was still living through, I'd found a family, a clan. I'd found my place, and I'd found love.

## Chapter 50

It had been two days of non-stop staring at walls of faces and waiting for either Ramsey to call or for Flynn and Duncan to make contact. I had a headache, and the morning sickness had lasted the entire day.

"You sure you don't want to come down with us?" Ash asked. "You could use a night off from all this SINS stuff."

"No, I just want some time and space to myself."

Ash nodded, biting a bright red lip. She was ready to go out even though "out" was only the burlesque club in the lobby. She'd decided to take three Scottish chicks under her large, mother hen wing.

"If you change your mind..."

I smiled. "I'll know where you'll be."

"Should I move into my own suite?" she asked, blue eyes meeting mine.

"Only if you want to."

"You sure? You're overrun with people all the time. I can move out and—"

"Stay," I interrupted. "I mean that. I like having you here."

"Okay, if you're sure." She hugged me and then left.

I breathed a sigh of relief and settled down onto the couch for a night of terrible TV and an early bedtime. Just as I began to doze, the elevator doors opened. I groaned. I remembered why I'd wanted to move into a house with more privacy.

Sasha strode into the penthouse, dressed in a dark suit, white shirt, and black tie. His blond hair was combed off his forehead, his ice blue eyes bright and intelligent.

"Hi," I murmured. "You don't call anymore?"

"I did," he said. "You didn't answer."

I looked around for my phone, realizing it was on the nightstand in the bedroom. "Sorry," I said, not bothering to move to sit up. "What's up? Haven't seen you for a few days."

"I was in Boston," he said, going to the bar area and pouring himself a drink.

"What's in Boston?" I asked.

He looked at me and raised an eyebrow. "I was helping clean up a certain mess."

"Fuck," I muttered, realizing I'd thrown one of Sasha's friends under the bus. "Was it the Irish or the Sicilians?"

"The Irish."

"I didn't think you had an alliance with the Irish. And not in Boston."

He smiled. "I don't tell you everything."

"No?" I closed my eyes and rubbed my head.

"You feeling okay?"

"Just a slight headache," I admitted.

"Did you take something?"

"I don't like meds."

"You're in pain. Take something," he insisted.

I sighed. "I'm pregnant." I ventured a glance at Sasha. His eyes were wide with shock. Yeah, I knew that feeling.

"What? How?"

I laughed. "The usual way. Do you want me to get you a pop-up book?"

"Holy hell," Sasha breathed. "Does Campbell know?"

"No. Not yet."

He opened and closed his mouth like a fish. "Still no word on his and Duncan's whereabouts?"

A lump formed in my throat. "None."

"But he's safe?"

"Don't know that either."

He was silent a moment. "I'm an ass."

"How do you figure?"

"What happened between us—in the gym—"

"Oh, you mean when you kissed me?"

He shot me a look. "You kissed me back."

"Yes."

He looked shocked again. "You're admitting it."

"Sasha, it was a good kiss. A great kiss—and if I wasn't in love with Flynn, there could be something between us, but this—"

"Needs to end." He nodded. "I know. There's only so long that a man can act like a pathetic dog hoping to win the woman he loves."

I smiled sadly. "I was never yours. Not in the way you deserved. I do love you, though."

"And I love you," he said softly. "But it's time I let you go." He stood up. "You'll keep me posted? About Flynn and Duncan?"

"You called him Flynn."

"That's his name, isn't it?" With one last look, he left. But I didn't feel bereft or upset. Just lighter.

I headed to bed and fell asleep almost instantly. I was jarred awake when my cell phone buzzed. In my haste to answer it, I knocked it to the floor. Thank goodness for carpet or Hawk might've woken up. I reached for the phone on the ground, nearly tumbling out of bed.

"Hello?" I croaked, glancing at the clock. It was three a.m.
"Barrett?" asked a raspy, deep voice.
"Duncan?" I was instantly awake.
"Aye, it's me."
"Oh God. Are you okay? Are you safe?"
"Aye," he repeated. "We're safe."
"Good, let me speak to Flynn."
"He can't come to the phone right now."
"What?" I nearly shrieked. "Why?"
"That's why I've called, Barrett. It's Flynn. He's dying."

∼

The town car zoomed toward the airstrip, the late-night lights of the city bright against the sky. Ash sat next to me, still dressed in her "going out" clothes.

"I have to come with you to Belfast," she said.

I shook my head. "We've been over and over this, Ash."

"It's bullshit," she hissed.

"Ash," I pled. "I need you to stay here. Take care of Hawk, so I can take care of Flynn."

We fell silent, and Ash reached over to take my hand. She squeezed it, and I wished it made me feel better. She didn't give me platitudes or empty words that Flynn was a fighter. I knew he was a fighter.

I hated leaving Hawk, especially since I'd just found him, but I was not about to jeopardize his safety. Flynn wouldn't want me to.

"How bad is it?" Ash asked.

"He took a bullet to the stomach. He has sepsis." I closed my eyes, fear swirling inside of me. I tried to have hope. I tried to believe that Flynn could come back from this, but I didn't know if he could.

"Why are they in Belfast?" Ash asked.

"I don't know. I didn't think to ask."

We arrived at the airstrip, and I climbed out of the car. I had a tiny suitcase with me—it had been packed and ready to go for just this sort of situation. Ash hugged me goodbye, and then I was running toward the private plane.

Eight terrified hours later, I landed in Belfast. Duncan was there to greet me. He embraced me quickly and then ushered me toward the idling town car.

"Tell me everything," I said when the car began to drive toward Flynn.

Duncan sighed and rubbed a hand down his exhausted face. He'd lost weight in the last few months—after he'd survived his own gunshot wound.

"We were in London," he began. "And we were just outside Arlington's gentleman's club."

"Because Sasha's men tipped you off."

Duncan nodded. "Only when we got there, Sasha's men weren't. By the time we realized Arlington had lured us into a trap, it was too late. One of Arlington's men got off a few shots, and Flynn took the hit. Brandon took another, but it was in the leg."

I frowned. "Brandon? Who's Brandon?"

"Flynn's cousin on his mother's side," Duncan said.

"Cousin? I thought Flynn didn't have any living blood relatives."

"His mother was Irish," Duncan began. "She was survived by a brother and his three children."

"But why didn't he tell me?"

"Because when Caitlin Kilmartin married Gavin Campbell, a high-ranking member of the SINS, Caitlin's very Irish family shunned her."

"But Brandon—how did he—"

"I'm getting to it," Duncan said. "Caitlin's brother lives just outside of Belfast—that's where we're going. Flynn reached out to his uncle months ago. Flynn and James had plans to sit down, attempt to build a relationship. That all got put on hold, obviously."

"I wish he'd told me," I said quietly, my heart aching for my husband. I knew what it was like to have family that didn't want you. My own brother had been that kind of sort.

"Man has his pride. If James had rebuffed him…"

I nodded. "I get it. So, Brandon."

"Aye, Brandon. Flynn called his uncle explaining what was happening to the SINS. James took pity on Flynn's plight and sent his son, Brandon, to help."

"I still don't understand."

For the first time that morning, Duncan smiled. "James and Brandon belong to the IRA, lass."

My eyes widened. "So it *was* you and Flynn who set the bomb?"

"No. The SINS took credit for it because it was The Pretender. This was his play for leader."

"The news didn't release any names."

"Doesn't matter—everyone in the know about the SINS is aware who leads. The Pretender wanted the authorities to do his job for him and take us out."

"How did you wind up in Belfast?" I demanded. "How did you get out of London?"

"Brandon and I managed to get Flynn to a hospital." Duncan shook his head. "We didn't want to do it, because we'd have to register him, but what could we do? Brandon was injured, too, and if Flynn had any hope of living, he needed a doctor. Immediately. The doctor didn't want us to move Flynn because he's intubated, but he wasn't safe in London. We booked a private ferry to Belfast and here we are."

"And the doctor?"

Duncan rubbed the back of his neck. "We kidnapped him."

I closed my eyes. "We have to stop kidnapping people."

"It's better than killing them," Duncan pointed out.

"Yeah, you're right." The car hit a pothole on the windy road. A wave of nausea coursed through my belly. I didn't know if it was carsickness or morning sickness.

"Duncan, we have to pull over," I said.

"Can't. We're almost to James's house, anyway."

"Duncan, either you have the driver pull over, or I'm going to be sick in the car."

## Chapter 51

"You're pregnant?" Duncan's eyes were wide as his gaze dropped to my still relatively flat belly.

"Listen, no one was more shocked than me to find out," I said, wishing I had a toothbrush. "If you make a joke about the power of Scottish sperm, I'm gonna slug you."

Duncan laughed. "Oh, lass, I'm so glad you're here. You're just what Flynn needs to come out of this."

I nodded resolutely. "If he dies, I'll fucking kill him."

"That's the spirit."

James Kilmartin's home looked like it belonged on a postcard for Ireland. It was winter, and the hills were brushed with white. Nestled in the rolling hills, the yellow house looked welcoming and warm. Light gray smoke from the stone chimney curled in the air before disappearing into the murky sky.

We got out of the car, and the front door opened. An older couple, gray at the temples, came out to greet us.

James Kilmartin was tall and wiry with gorgeous mossy green eyes. His wife's smile was genuine and as welcoming as the home behind her.

"James, Moira," Duncan introduced, "Flynn's wife, Barrett."

"Welcome, Barrett," Moira said with a faint Irish lilt.

"Thank you," I said, my gaze straying to James. He watched me carefully, not as friendly as his wife. "Can I see Flynn?"

As we were ushered into the house, I briefly noticed the simplistic beauty of the stone washed walls and decor. I followed a silent James up the steps to the second-floor hallway. He took me to the last room on the right and opened the door.

Flynn was in bed, ashen and gray-faced, a layer of sweat at his temples, a tube down his throat breathing for him. He was hooked up to an IV and I had no idea how Flynn was even alive. He'd needed medical care, and moving him while he was unconscious and plugged into wires couldn't have been easy. He didn't look like my strong, robust husband. He looked small. Mortal.

Clenching my fists at my sides, I slowly approached him. A man sat in a chair by his side and stood when I came closer.

"Dr. Gerard," James said to the man. "This is Flynn's wife."

Dr. Gerard was young and looked hardly out of his residency. I just hoped he was competent enough to save Flynn.

"Mrs. Campbell," Dr. Gerard said, shaking my hand. "I don't know how much you know about your husband's condition, but let me assure you, I'm doing everything I can. The fact that he didn't die immediately at the scene is a miracle."

"You were the one who operated on him?"

Dr. Gerard nodded. "He wasn't shot at close range, thank goodness, so he has a fighting chance. Now, it's just a waiting game. He shouldn't have been moved from the hospital." He glared at Duncan. "My advice clearly wasn't taken."

I had a pretty good guess how Duncan had managed to "coerce" the doctor into moving Flynn.

I glanced back at the still form of my husband. "How long has he been like this?"

James's face was grim. "Since Duncan brought him here three days ago."

"His fever has been hovering at one hundred and two," Dr. Gerard added. "I've got his IV bag pumping antibiotics into his system."

"Can I have a moment?" I asked. "Alone with him?"

The two men nodded and then left, closing the door behind them. I stared at Flynn, watching the rise and fall of his chest. It was so strange to see a machine breathing for him. Finally, I moved closer and crouched down next to the bed. Searching for his hand, I found it under the covers. It was cold, clammy. Lifeless.

"You have to stop doing this," I said softly. "It's not fair, you know. Hawk needs you. I need you. The new bairn needs you."

I waited, hoping the news that he was going to be a father again was powerful enough to wake him. It wasn't.

"I'm a little over six weeks along," I said, going on. "The morning sickness is worse this time around. The only thing I can stomach are croissants."

With my free hand, I pushed back the damp hair across Flynn's face. "I'll be here when you wake up. I promise."

∽

An hour later, Flynn's temperature skyrocketed. I bathed his forehead with cool water, my own brow beading with perspiration. My back ached, and my limbs were sluggish.

Dr. Gerard offered to relieve me of my nursing duties, but I resolutely shook my head. Duncan tried to get me to rest, but I refused to listen. Finally, it was Moira who managed to get through the tiredness and fear.

"You need to tend to yourself," she said from the doorway of Flynn's bedroom.

"I can't leave him."

"He won't be alone," she stated, her own voice firm. "If you won't think of yourself, think of your child."

"I am thinking of my child," I said, unwilling to take my gaze off Flynn.

"Not the one you left in New York. I'm referring to the one you're carrying now."

I looked at her. "How did you—"

"Duncan shared the news with me." She smiled softly. "Come have some broth. It will do you some good."

I dropped the damp rag onto the bedside table and left Flynn to Dr. Gerard. Moira took my arm in a strong grip and helped me downstairs. I was grateful for her taking charge.

The kitchen was filled with a delicious aroma, and I closed my eyes, thinking I could fall asleep where I was standing. Moira gently urged me into a kitchen chair, and then she went to the stove to ladle out a bowl of chicken soup.

The other occupants around the table included Duncan and James. They didn't have empty bowls in front of them, so I assumed they'd already eaten.

"Something to drink?" Moira asked me. "Some tea, maybe?"

"Tea would be great," I said with a smile. I spooned chicken soup into my mouth and nearly moaned.

"Duncan, will you take a bowl of chicken soup up to Dr. Gerard?" Moira asked as she set a tray.

Duncan rose from his chair and dutifully carried the tray out of the kitchen and up the stairs. Moira finished fixing my tea and then said, "I'm going to go check in on Brandon."

I blinked. I had completely forgotten about Brandon. "How's his leg?"

"He'll heal. You can meet him later." On her way out, she

gave her husband's shoulder a squeeze. He reached up to catch her hand and brought it to his lips before letting her go.

James watched me eat and drink in silence. When I finished and gently set the spoon down, he finally spoke. "You look tired."

I nodded. "Very."

"We have a bed made up for you. Don't even think about refusing," he said. "Duncan told us you're expecting; you need to rest."

Without thought, I grumbled, "You're just like your nephew."

"Stubborn?" James asked, a slight twinkle in his green eyes.

I nodded. "And a tyrant."

James finally cracked a smile, and it softened the countenance of his lined face. "You've got spirit."

"I'd have more if I wasn't so damn tired," I admitted.

James got up and went to the counter. He pulled out a loaf of bread from the breadbox and sliced up half of it. He put the pieces on a plate and grabbed the butter. Setting both in front of me, he said, "You're also looking thin. It's Moira's family recipe for Irish soda bread and homemade honey butter."

He sat back down and watched me. I wasn't going to argue. The tangy scent of the bread called to me. I slathered a slice with a hefty amount of honey butter and took a bite.

"How is it," I asked when I had finished chewing, "that you and Moira aren't five hundred pounds. This is the best bread I've ever had."

James smiled and then it dimmed. "Flynn didn't tell you about me, did he?"

I shook my head, feeling emotion constrict my throat. I continued to eat as James talked. He seemed to need to unburden himself.

"I was a fool," James began. "My parents—they didn't

accept Caitlin's choice. They took it as a slight to them. And I, well, I was stupid, too. I loved my sister and I never should've shut her out, shut Flynn out. It was wrong. I was wrong."

"He's an amazing man," I said.

James nodded. "He's loyal, he has honor."

"If he loves you, he loves you with his whole heart," I said. "I hope—" My voice broke. "I hope you have a chance to get to know him."

"Me too. Your son, you named him for Flynn's father?"

"Yes. We call him Hawk."

James smiled. "Do you have photos?"

I nodded and pulled out my phone. I had a few missed calls from Ash, probably to check in. I'd call her later. Unlocking the screen, I found my way to the photos. I slid my phone across the kitchen table. James scooped it up and began swiping through them, his smile soft.

There were footsteps on wood and then Duncan appeared. "Barrett—"

"Please don't make me go to bed yet. I've got a few hours left in me before I crash."

Duncan shook his head, his smile broad. "It's Flynn. He's awake. And he's asking for you."

I shot up from the chair, overturning it. I ran past Duncan and headed for the stairs, dashing down the hallway and coming to a stop in the doorway of the sickroom. Flynn's eyes were dull and tired, but they were open. And the tube was out of his throat, which meant he was breathing on his own.

"Hen," Flynn croaked.

It was the sweetest sound I'd ever heard.

I rushed to his side, my smile so wide it was in danger of splitting my face. "I knew it."

"Knew what?" he asked.

My hand trailed gently down his cheek. "Some men are too stubborn to die."

## Chapter 52

"It was my idea to send for Barrett. So really, you waking up is because of my good thinking," Duncan said from the doorway of Flynn's bedroom.

Flynn chuckled and then winced. "Don't make me laugh. It hurts."

Duncan's face sobered.

"Can I have some water?" Flynn asked.

I went to the bedside table and poured him a glass from the pitcher. I brought it to him and helped him take a few sips. It exhausted him to do it, and when he was finished, he leaned back against the pillows, breathing hard.

"Moira made some chicken soup. Think you're up for some?"

He flashed me a weak smile. "If you spoon-feed it to me."

"You're bedridden and yet you're still managing to flirt with me." I shook my head.

"Glad?"

I beamed. "Ecstatic. I'm going to get a bowl for you. Be right back."

I went downstairs and Moira already had a tray ready for

Flynn. I thanked her and took it upstairs. As I came into the room, I saw Duncan pull his hand back from Flynn's shoulder.

"Glad to have you back, brother," he said.

"Glad to be back."

The door shut behind Duncan, giving Flynn and me privacy. I set the tray on the bedside table.

"You're going to hit me, aren't you?" Flynn asked before taking a spoonful of broth.

"When you're well, it's a definite possibility."

"I'm sorry I ever gave you something to worry about."

I nodded, my eyes brimming with tears. The silver spoon blurred. "I'm just glad you're awake." I began to feed him again, and I was content with the silence.

"I had the weirdest dream," Flynn said, a look of remembrance passing over his face.

"Oh?" I asked. "Fever dreams can be weird."

He nodded. "I dreamt that you told me you were pregnant."

I blew out a puff of air. "Not a dream."

Flynn's eyes widened. "You're pregnant?"

"Yeah. I kind of wanted to wait until you were better, but—"

"No," he whispered. "This is good news and when I'm better, we're going to celebrate."

I smiled and leaned over to kiss his lips. Flynn tired, and I only got a few more spoonfuls into him before his eyes were shutting. I climbed off the bed and leaned over to brush my lips against his forehead. He still felt warm but not like he had been.

He was asleep by the time I left. As I returned to the kitchen, I noted the lowering of the sun. It was nearly twilight. The beauty of the dying light hitting the hills had me yearning for Scotland.

A bottle of Jameson was cracked open and James and

Duncan were already a few shots in. Moira sipped from hers and Dr. Gerard had water.

"Patient is asleep again," I announced.

Moira smiled, setting her glass of Irish whiskey down. "And now you have no more reason to stay awake." Like the motherly woman she was, she helped me upstairs and showed me the guest bedroom with the already turned down bed. My suitcase had been brought up, but I was too tired to sift through it for anything.

"Sleep," Moira commanded. "I'll wake you if there's need. But rest."

As soon as I was alone, I kicked off my shoes, fell face first onto the bed, too tired to even shimmy out of my jeans. I awoke a few hours later and thought about getting up, but the softness of the bed and the dark sky outside lulled me back to sleep. I slept soundly until morning.

I brushed my teeth, checking my phone. There were texts from Ash. Some were photos of Hawk and updates about him. And then there were a few that told me to call her immediately, no matter the time.

With a frown, I dialed her back. I rinsed my mouth, feeling a bit restored, but I wanted a shower. Ash was a deep sleeper, and I doubted she'd wake up the first time I called her. I was wrong.

"Barrett?" she asked, sleep in her voice.

"It's me."

She yawned. "I turned my phone on the loudest setting."

"Your texts sounded urgent. Everything okay?"

"Hawk's fine," she said automatically.

"Good. Flynn woke up."

"Duncan called and told me. I'm so glad," she said. She was slowly sounding lucid.

"So what's up?" I asked. I unbuttoned my jeans and got them off me.

"The girls found something unusual."

"What do you mean?"

"They were going through all the deceased members of the SINS, sort of as a double check, you know?"

"Yeah."

"Well, they came across a picture they all recognized and thought that we might be wrong—that this person might not be dead. His name is Edward Roehenstart."

I frowned. "The name sounds familiar, but I don't know why."

"Well, I did a little Googling," Ash said. "And something weird came up. Have you heard of Charles Edward Stuart, the Count of Roehenstart?"

"My Scottish history background is more Mary, Queen of Scots. I've heard of Charles Edward Stuart—Bonnie Prince Charlie. But who is this count?"

"He's the grandson of Bonnie Prince Charlie."

I shook my head even though she couldn't see me. "Okay. Help me out, Ash. I haven't had coffee yet."

"Bonnie Prince Charlie didn't have any legitimate children with his wife. His mistress gave him a daughter named Charlotte. Charlotte, in turn, also had a few illegitimate children. One of whom she named Charles Edward Stuart. He was the Count of Roehenstart. The history books claim that the Count had no children, but what if he did? You know the records in the seventeen and eighteen hundreds were shit. What if this count guy actually had a child?"

"Why would it matter?"

Ash sighed. "Because Edward Roehenstart, member of the SINS, who's not deceased, might be the person we're looking for. Roehenstart is not a common last name—it stands out. And if Edward Roehenstart believes he's a descendant of Bonnie Prince Charlie, maybe he thinks he has the right to lead Scotland to its freedom. Maybe he believes he has the right to lead the SINS."

My heartbeat quickened. "You mean we might be dealing with a Jacobite rebellion in the twenty-first century?"

"We *have* been calling him The Pretender," Ash pointed out.

"Fuck," I said.

"You should learn how to curse in Gaelic. I think it would be appropriate in situations like these. Besides, this is just a theory. And a huge stretch."

"It's the best theory we've got. I'm going to call someone who knows or has the resources to flesh this theory out."

"Who?"

"My old boss. The head of the history department at Columbia."

"Brilliant. There's more, though."

"Tell me," I said quickly, my mind waking up.

"Edward Roehenstart, member of the SINS, is related to someone you know."

~

I took a fast shower and then dressed in clean, warm clothes. Before heading downstairs, I checked on Flynn. He was sleeping, but Dr. Gerard informed me that Flynn had had a comfortable night. His fever had broken. I felt a weight lift off my shoulders when I realized he was out of the woods. It would take him time to heal, but he would. That was the important thing.

I sat down at the kitchen table but before I could make polite conversation, I was back out of the chair and running for a bathroom. After breakfast, I went upstairs to meet Brandon. He looked just like Moira with a thick head of brown curls and her hazel eyes. He was charming and affable and didn't seem at all put out having to be laid up in bed and having his mother tend to him. He told me about his other siblings, Colleen and Molly, who lived nearby with their families.

A snap of cold weather moved through Belfast, and the usual rain turned to sleet. I asked Moira if there was a place to make some phone calls, and she showed me to the den. It was a cozy room filled with books, comfortable sofas, and a wood-burning fireplace that James lit for me.

I sat down in a chair near the fire and turned on the iPad. I opened up a blank email and quickly typed a letter to my old boss who had a PhD in Scottish History. He was the only person I knew who could recite the Scottish monarchy line of succession. He had liked to bring that skill out at faculty parties. If he didn't know about Charles Edward Stuart, the Count of Roehenstart, then he knew people who did.

Hitting send, I let out a breath. My phone rang, and I had a brief but efficient conversation with Ash. We hung up, and I felt strangely hopeful. Ash had everything under control both with Katherine and her friends and with Hawk. Lacey checked in with text and so did Sasha. I sent them back responses and updates about Flynn's condition.

At the moment, there was nothing else to do but wait. I left the den and went up to Flynn's room, passing Dr. Gerard on the way. Flynn's color was already looking better, and his smile wasn't marred with pain. His eyes were glassy.

"Hi, love," I greeted, kissing his mouth, expecting to smell liquor fumes.

"Hen," he said.

"You haven't been drinking for the pain, have you?"

"No. But Doc gave me the good stuff."

"Morphine," I guessed.

"Morphine," he repeated.

I held in a giggle.

"How are you feeling, love?" he asked as he pat his side of the bed. "You and the bairn?"

I smiled and took a seat, taking his hand and placing it on my flat belly. "We're fine. Don't worry about us. Just get well."

"Aye." His eyes drooped closed, and I took that as a sign to let him rest. I kissed him quickly, yearning for the night I could crawl into bed and sleep next to him.

## Chapter 53

Duncan paced back and forth across the den floor, his face blustery and angry. "So you're telling me," he began, "that my hotheaded younger brother is in London looking for Arlington —and he took Jane Elliot with him—all because my *wife* decided to keep him in the loop?"

"She made an executive decision. I wasn't happy about it to begin with, but what else was she supposed to do? You and Flynn were AWOL, and she and I were stuck in the penthouse in New York, wringing our hands like simpering, useless wives!" I snapped.

"Fine," he groused. "I'll make my peace with the fact that she interfered in SINS business—"

"Oh, for fuck's sake!" I snapped. "You men and your damn dirty pride! Ash might have figured out the name of The Pretender, you giant arsehole!"

Duncan took a step back, his face slackened in shock.

"Get with the times, Duncan. Things are changing. There are women who want a free Scotland as much as men. And they should have the right to be a part of the SINS. What kind of leader are you going to be if you can't listen to reason?"

"I'm not the leader," Duncan said, his voice losing all traces of anger. "Flynn is."

I shook my head. "No, he's always been acting leader. The leadership should fall to you. It's your right—by birth."

Duncan ran a hand across his stubbly jaw as he thought. "If you're telling me to change with the times, it might do us good to really change things."

"How so?"

"The SINS members, the men and the women, should be able to cast a vote for who they want as leader. It shouldn't be handed to me just because my father and his father before him held the title."

He glared at me in sudden understanding. "That was your idea all along, wasn't it? To get me to think that was my idea."

I smiled slowly. "Maybe. Do you want to be leader of the SINS?"

"I never thought of not being leader," he mused. "Not the question you asked, I know. Flynn really has a knack for it, though. I'd just assume let him lead, and I'll be his close second."

Would Hawk one day be leader? Would he want that? He'd grow up with a target on his back no matter what—unless Flynn gave up the SINS, and I wasn't ever going to ask that of him. We chose this life, we would see it through, whatever that entailed.

"There's more, isn't there?" he asked with a sigh. "More things you're going to tell me that I'm not going to like?"

"My face gave it away, huh?"

"No. You just usually like to dump a bunch of shite at my feet. It's your way."

"Thanks," I muttered. "Edward Roehenstart. Does that name ring any bells?"

Duncan frowned. "No. Should it?"

"You know Barnabas? The old man who gave me a lamb?"

"Aye, I know old Barney."

I nodded. "Barnabas's grandson is Edward Roehenstart." I went on to explain about the Count of Roehenstart being Bonnie Prince Charlie's grandson. "Even though it's documented that the count was married twice but had no children, I wondered if that could really be substantiated. I emailed my old boss—the head of the history department at Columbia and Scottish history scholar—to see what he can tell me."

"And while we're waiting on him, what do you suppose we do?"

I grinned. "How do you feel about a trip to Dornoch?"

∼

Duncan and I sat in the kitchen glaring at one another. "No," he stated.

"Come on," I taunted. "Afraid you're going to lose?"

"Aye. And I'm man enough to admit it."

I grinned. "Rock, paper, scissors. It's the only fair way. Two out of three."

Brandon entered the kitchen, using a cane to favor his injured leg. "What's going on in here?" he demanded when he saw what was about to occur.

"Should you be up and moving?" I asked.

He shrugged.

Duncan sighed. "We're playing rock, paper, scissors. Loser has to tell Flynn we're leaving him here to recover while we go to Dornoch."

"Dornoch isn't safe," Brandon said.

"And we're expecting a major, vocal disagreement. I still think Duncan should be the one to tell him. I'm pregnant. I can't have excitement in my delicate condition."

"You're pregnant?" Brandon asked in surprise. "Don't you have a young—"

"Yes," I snapped. "I'm fertile. Everyone should get the hell over it!"

"I guess we've entered the rational stage of pregnancy," Duncan teased.

"Just you wait," I warned.

Duncan blinked. "Is Ash—"

"No, you goon," I interrupted. "I'm saying this for when she is."

Brandon glanced at Duncan. "What are you doing wrong?"

"It's not lack for trying, believe me."

"Yeah, if that's all it took," I muttered. "Come on, let's do this. Two out of three."

Duncan lost three out of three. I grinned broadly, good mood suddenly restored. It didn't matter that I'd already thrown up twice that day. I moonwalked across the kitchen floor, rubbing it in Duncan's face, being a completely terrible sport about it and loving it.

"I don't know everything well enough," he voiced. "I can't keep up with your big brain."

"Flattery won't get you out of this. Good luck telling my husband we have plans to enter the lion's den."

Duncan cursed. His phone rang, and he was only too glad to answer it. "Ramsey! I should murder you the next time I see you." He paused to listen, his eyes widening. "You're not."

"He's 'not' what?" Brandon whispered to me. I shrugged, just as lost.

"Aye, I'll come." He hung up and looked at me. "Guess who just landed in Belfast?"

"Ramsey? Really?" I asked.

"Aye, and one Miss Jane Elliot."

"Hot damn," I breathed.

"Who's Jane Elliot?" Brandon asked, attempting to move a heavy wood chair with one hand so he could take a seat.

Duncan helped him with the chair, but otherwise let Brandon sink into it himself.

"Who is Jane Elliot?" Duncan repeated. "A damn fine question."

"One with many answers," I added with a grin. I liked Jane. The young woman had spunk, and despite her initial introduction into our lives, she hadn't shown fear. I admired and respected her. I couldn't wait to see her—and find out how she felt about Ramsey. Ash would kill me if I didn't discover something good and worth passing along.

"Just another thing to tell Flynn, I guess," Duncan said.

I nodded. "It also means we should postpone our trip to Dornoch. At least for a few days. Then we can take Ramsey with us."

"The Buchanan hothead. Aye. Good plan."

I rolled my eyes at Duncan's droll tone. "Or maybe I should just leave you Buchanans here."

"Go alone?" he asked, jaw agape. "Think again. If anyone's going to Dornoch alone, it's me."

"First of all," I stated. "Barnabas gave *me* the lamb. I think if anyone has a chance of getting information out of him, it will be me."

"Fair point. Go on," Duncan allowed. Brandon choked on his laughter. "But I want to go with you."

"You're a wanted man at the moment," I said. "What happens when you step foot on Scottish soil? Hmm? You're basically an outlaw."

"There's no way you can go to Dornoch without backup. And what about Hawk? I won't let you endanger your life and potentially leave him motherless. Not to mention, Flynn would murder me."

"You are a dramatic bunch," Brandon said.

I looked at Brandon. "Where are your parents?"

"Taking their daily walk together," Brandon answered.

"Do you think it would bother them if we had a few more guests?"

"Barrett," Duncan warned. "What are you thinking?"

"I'm thinking you miss your wife and I miss my baby. Lacey can keep an eye on Katherine and her friends. Daniel and Nathan can fly over with Ash and Hawk. Then I can take Nathan with me to Dornoch. Back up problem solved."

"Good Lord, is it always like this?" Brandon muttered. "I'm exhausted just listening to you coordinate!"

"Darlin'," I teased, "You ain't seen nothin' yet."

## Chapter 54

Later that evening, I checked my email to see if Dr. Albright, my old boss, had gotten back to me. All I had was an automated *Out of office* response.

"Damn," I muttered.

"Bad news?" Moira asked. It was just the two of us sitting in the den, the house quiet. Flynn and Brandon were asleep, and Duncan and James had gone to Belfast to fetch Jane and Ramsey.

"Not bad news, not good either," I said. "I was hoping to hear back from Dr. Albright, but he's not readily available. I might have to call and harass him via phone."

"Guess you will," Moira said.

"He's almost impossible to get on the phone. He turns his cell on silent and then loses it."

Moira laughed. "You're painting the classic picture of an absent-minded professor."

"He is that. Brilliant but forgetful in everyday life."

"A lot of highly intelligent people are like that."

"Dr. Albright never wears matching socks—and he never notices." I sighed. "You and James really don't mind about having more house guests?"

"Of course not. I'm just glad I get to meet your son."

I smiled. In a few days, I'd get to hold Hawk. Then we would have our family back together. Our expanding family, I mused.

"You look dreamy," Moira teased.

My hand went to my belly.

"Ah. Thought so."

"Can I ask you something? Personal?" She nodded and I went on, "How do you cope with James and Brandon being part of…what they're a part of?"

"It's not easy. That's for sure. But James isn't as active anymore. He sort of mellowed with age. And after his treatment of Caitlin, the whole thing kind of soured him."

"Was Caitlin political?"

"Not really. She accepted that Gavin was a part of the SINS, but she never had the drive to join his cause. She loved Gavin fiercely and that came first. Always. And then of course Flynn came along, and that only made her love stronger. No. She didn't care about politics."

"You speak as though you knew her well."

"I did. She was my best friend. I even spoke to her after her family shunned her. That surprises you," Moira said.

"I guess I just assumed—"

"I never agreed with how the family treated Caitlin. James knew, of course, that I kept in contact with her. I sometimes volunteered information about her and her life, but he never asked. Not until recently."

I smiled sadly. "In his older years when people start thinking about all their great regrets?"

She chuckled. "Something like that."

"It's tragic," I said. "How much time we all waste."

"Don't waste yours," she warned. "It's easy to forget how fast time goes by."

I stood and went to hug her. "I'm so glad to have met you, Moira."

She smiled. "Sleep well, *a leanbh mo chroí.*"

~

The next morning, I was awake before most of the house. I'd been asleep by the time Duncan had gotten back with Ramsey and Jane, so I hadn't seen them yet.

Tiptoeing down the stairs, I made sure I was quiet. I was startled to see James already in the kitchen, awake with a cup of coffee in his hands.

"Morning," he greeted.

"Hi," I said.

"Sleep okay?"

I nodded. "Is there going to be enough room—for all of us?"

James grinned. "We have a barn. Perhaps we can make the Buchanan boys sleep there."

I let out a soft chuckle and poured myself half a cup of coffee before sitting down. "I can move into Flynn's room. Hawk will bunk with us. Ash will sleep with Duncan but where does that leave Jane and Ramsey?"

"There are two double beds in Brandon's room. Ramsey slept there. Jane is asleep on the couch." He smiled. "This isn't crowded. When Brandon's sisters come to visit and they bring their husbands and children, we make do. We'll make do when Ash and Hawk arrive. We'll just have to do some shuffling."

"I guess now is the time I should mention Ash is bringing Daniel and Nathan—our bodyguards."

"Okay, will have to do *a lot* of shuffling." He grinned and took a sip of his coffee.

"What have you got there," I asked, gesturing to what looked like a leather-bound photo album.

"Family photos," James said slowly. "Mostly of Caitlin when she was younger. Before she…"

I nodded in understanding. It was a shame that Flynn had lost so many years with his uncle. Then again, it hadn't been the first time in history that pride had come between families.

"May I?" I asked, gesturing to the photo album.

James pushed it toward me. I began to sift through the pictures of the Kilmartin family. Caitlin's smile was radiant in every photo, her cobalt blue eyes sparkling with a devilish secret. I saw where Flynn had gotten that unique trait. She had dark hair and fair skin, Black Irish, people called it. As I watched her grow older on film, I noticed her transformation from slender, cute girl to striking, beautiful woman.

"How did they meet?" I asked. "Gavin and Caitlin?"

"A pub in Dublin. Caitlin and Moira were best friends back then, and they were off on one of their adventures."

"Weren't supposed to be in Dublin, I take it?" I asked with a smile.

James shrugged, nostalgia painting his smile. "They were eighteen. Fearless. Lad-crazy. They went to Dublin and from the moment Caitlin walked into the pub, Gavin couldn't take his eyes off her. She ran away with him that night."

I blinked. "You're kidding?"

"No. She went with him to Scotland, married him, brought him home to meet us, and my parents lost their minds."

"Well, sure. Eighteen, married to a man she hardly knew who wasn't Irish. I can see that being a source of struggle."

James shook his head. "The thing is, Caitlin did know him. She was an extremely good judge of character, even when she was a young lass. But did my parents remember that? Did I remember that? No. All I saw was a twenty-two-year-old quiet Scotsman who'd taken my baby sister away from us. Never mind that it had been Caitlin's choice."

"They were so young," I murmured.

"And Flynn came along pretty soon after. My parents always expected Caitlin to realize she'd made a mistake, and we'd find her one day on our porch step, holding Flynn and telling us she was ready to come home."

"But she never did."

"Even if things with Gavin had been terrible—and I knew they weren't because Moira told me—Caitlin's own pride would've kept her away. She never would've admitted she had made a mistake."

I shook my head. "Does Flynn know any of this?"

"I don't know. He was a teen when they died. If they did tell him anything, I doubt he would've heard through the hard-headedness and hormones of being a teenage boy."

I chuckled. "Something to look forward to with Hawk."

James grinned. "Well, if he's anything like Flynn's father, you're in danger."

"Campbell men. They got charisma—and obstinacy."

We laughed together and then I shook my head.

"What is it?" James asked.

"I just think it's miraculous, you know? Flynn is upstairs recovering and yet, his injury has somehow brought us all together."

James nodded thoughtfully. "Can I ask you a question? About Malcolm Buchanan?"

I started, unprepared for the change in conversation. "Sure."

"He raised Flynn as his own?"

"Yes. Flynn calls Duncan and Ramsey brothers."

James looked relieved. "Moira and I…when we heard about the accident…we had plans to take in Flynn."

"Really?"

"Aye. It would've been difficult, taking him away from his home and his friends. We would've done it—and been glad to do it—my way of making amends, I guess. But it worked out the way it was supposed to. I'm happy the both of you are here now."

I smiled and closed the photo album. "I think you should be the one to give him this."

∼

The house finally began to wake up and before I knew it, the kitchen was overrun with people. I helped Moira feed the masses, but she seemed to have a good handle on things. She and James had a large family, and she definitely had learned a few tricks along the way.

Jane Elliot looked different since the last time I'd seen her. She still looked regal and elegant, but something had changed in her. Her chestnut hair was pulled back into a haphazard ponytail, and her face was scrubbed clean of makeup. I watched her interaction with Ramsey with laser focus, wondering if I could detect what had occurred between them when they'd been alone together on Orkney.

Ramsey stood at the counter, eating a piece a toast. Jane reached out to swipe away a trickle of butter at the corner of his mouth. He shot her a crooked smile.

Yep. They were *together*, together.

"So, who convinced who to go to London to search for Arlington?" Duncan asked. He sat in a chair at the kitchen table, his long legs stretched out. His hand gripped a mug of coffee as he pinned Ramsey with a stare before transferring it to Jane.

"We should get out of here," Moira said, shooing James and Brandon from the room.

"I just got here," Brandon complained, but dutifully followed his mother out of the kitchen.

"I take full responsibility," Ramsey stated when it was just the four of us.

"Liar," Jane huffed.

"Should we wait to discuss all of this until Ash arrives? I mean, we have a lot of information to exchange, and wouldn't it be better if we just waited? Besides, Flynn's not even in this meeting," I said.

"Flynn is bedbound," Duncan said. As if I needed a reminder. "And he's not up for a meeting."

I crossed my arms over my chest. "If I recall, we didn't spare you from a meeting when you had a bullet taken out of your chest."

"Oh, zing," Ramsey said.

"None of this is going to get solved right now," I said, ignoring Ramsey. "We wait."

Ramsey looked at Jane and grinned. "See. Told you Barrett was going to put Duncan in his place."

"You were right," Jane said with a nod. She looked at me. "Can we speak? Alone?"

## Chapter 55

Jane and I bundled up and went outside for a walk. I breathed in the fresh, crisp air, glad to see the sun.

"It's sunnier here than in Scotland, isn't it?" Jane asked, breaking the quiet.

"Yes, I was just noticing that."

We walked for a few more feet in silence. A light dusting of snow had fallen the night before. Every so often, sunlight glinted off snowflakes, flashing winks of gold in the whiteness.

"I want to apologize," Jane began.

"Apologize," I repeated in shock. "Why?"

"For how I treated you."

I frowned. "When?"

"When you came to meet me that first time. Back in Dornoch. When I was locked up in Duncan's home."

A smile spread across my face. "You have nothing to apologize for, Jane. We kidnapped you from your birthday party. I expected more vitriol, actually." I shook my head. That all seemed so long ago.

"No," she insisted. "You were nothing but honest and genuine with me."

"But you couldn't have known that," I insisted. I cocked my head to one side. "What brought all of this on?"

Jane looked away, choosing to focus on the landscape. "Ramsey didn't treat me badly when we were on Orkney. It made me realize that even though I was being held hostage, you weren't bad people. I'd just gotten caught up in something because of my father."

She sighed and went on. "Listen. I don't care about the SINS one way or the other. I don't care if Scotland is free. I helped Ramsey in London because, well, I felt like I owed a debt. My father—"

I interrupted her immediately. "Let me say something about your father. I don't know how you feel about him after finding out what he's done, what he was a part of, but let me tell you something about Lord Elliot." I took a deep breath. "At the end of the day, the only thing he cared about more than himself was you. He bartered for your safety."

"He was in league with the men who kidnapped your son," she interjected, her voice cold. "I don't care who you are or what you believe in, but taking a child from its mother…" She shook her head.

"You've got your own mind, Jane, and I really admire that about you. But before I went to find my son, I spoke with your father." It had been the last time I'd seen him alive, but I didn't think it was necessary to tell that to Jane.

"Do you know what he said to me?" I asked. "He said, 'Whatever it takes to get your son back. No mercy.' He knew. He knew the wrong he'd done. Forgive him."

"I can't," she stated resolutely. The late winter Irish wind blew the hair around her face. She hastily pushed it back. "Finding out about my father has made me reevaluate my life."

"What about Ramsey?" I asked.

She frowned. "What about Ramsey?"

"How much do you love him?" I demanded.

"I don't love him," she lied obviously.

"Oh, honey," I said in sympathy. "Take it from a woman who knows. If you can, get out now. Otherwise you'll always be looking over your shoulder for danger, waiting for it to jump out at you. Waiting for it to come for your children. If you can live without Ramsey, you should."

She blinked in surprise. "You're not going to tell me love conquers all and it's worth it?"

I put a hand to her arm. "My husband is upstairs in bed, recovering from a gunshot wound that almost killed him. This life will make or break you. But once you're in, you're in. There's no going back. You can't be prepared for everything, so you better prepare for that."

∼

I swept Hawk into my arms, holding him close and breathing him in. He was heavier, bigger, and it had only been two weeks.

"Thank you," I said to my best friend. "Thank you for taking care of him."

"He was not well behaved on the plane. I didn't get to sleep at all," Ash groused as she followed me into Moira and James's home.

Daniel and Nathan trailed us. We never could be too careful.

"How's Flynn?" she asked.

"Asleep."

She smiled. "I could use a nap."

"Me too," Duncan piped up from her side. She shot him an amused glance.

Once in the foyer, I introduced Ash to the Kilmartins and Moira went about fixing her a plate of something to eat. Ash accepted it gratefully.

"How are Katherine and the girls?" I asked.

"They love living in a hotel," Ash said after she swallowed a bite. "They might also be obsessed with burlesque, and they might also be attending the beginners dance class."

"We should open a burlesque club in Dornoch," I stated.

"I'll stick to the art gallery."

"Art gallery? What art gallery?" Duncan asked.

They hadn't been able to communicate much in the past few weeks, and all the minute details of their lives were suddenly part of the discussion. Hawk began to cry, and I soothed him against my shoulder.

And like all the natural evolution of conversations, when there was a baby in the room, everything gravitated toward him. Hawk was the center of attention.

"You'd think he'd be a pro at flying by now," I said, shushing a cranky Hawk. "Guess it's nap time."

"I'll second that," Ash said, rising with her plate. "Thanks, Moira. It was great."

"Wait until you try her soda bread and honey butter." I winked at James and he chuckled.

Duncan led Ash to their room, and I just hoped their *rendezvous* was quiet. It was long overdue, so I doubted it.

Hawk had settled down, and I decided to take him to see Flynn. He was awake, flipping through the family photo album, a pained look on his face. When he glanced up and saw me standing over the bed, his face softened, and he smiled.

"He's had a long day," I said, gently placing Hawk onto Flynn's chest. I watched my husband steal a hand across his son's back. Flynn pressed his cheek to Hawk's head and closed his eyes.

"I've missed so much," he muttered. "He's nearly a damn teenager."

I would've chuckled, but it wasn't funny.

"Close the door," Flynn said. "We have something to talk about."

I did as he asked and then gently settled myself at the foot of the bed. "What's on your mind?"

Flynn looked thoughtful before answering, "I want to leave the SINS."

I blinked. "Excuse me?"

"I want to leave the SINS," he repeated.

"But, why?" I sputtered. "This cause means the world to you."

He shook his head. "No. It *used* to mean the world to me. Then I found you, and Hawk came along. Now we're having another bairn. I can't take this, Barrett. I can't keep putting my family in danger. For what?"

I tried to speak but found I couldn't.

"This isn't on you," he continued when he saw the look on my face. "You never once made me choose between the SINS and our family. Which is why it's so easy to choose you."

"You can't," I protested. "You're a natural leader. The cause needs you."

His gaze dipped to our son. Hawk had fallen into a peaceful sleep. Perhaps all he'd needed was the warmth and strength of his father's chest to feel secure.

"The leadership role is meant for Duncan."

"He doesn't want it," I said.

"Doesn't matter. It's his to take."

"Not if we change how the SINS operates."

Flynn raised his eyebrows. "Change?"

"Yes, change. Why does it have to be all or nothing? Duncan and I shared some ideas, and he seemed open to them."

"What kind of ideas?"

I briefly told him about how there were women who believed in the cause and wanted to be a part of it and then explained that Duncan believed the members should vote on the leader.

Flynn's mouth slackened in shock. "Duncan believes in change?"

"I might've yelled him into submission," I said. I reached out to stroke his face. "Let's first deal with Arlington."

"And The Pretender. Bastard still hasn't showed his face, has he?"

I sighed. It looked like Duncan would get a reprieve. "I need to catch you up on a few things."

## Chapter 56

Dr. Gerard deemed Flynn well enough that he no longer required round-the-clock care. The doctor also made sure to inform us that he had no plans to return to London any time soon. He was taking a much-needed vacation, heading for the sunny climate of an island paradise.

We took his word on faith, knowing there was little we could do unless we wanted to do something drastic in order to keep his silence. We had one of our guys hack the London hospital where Flynn had been taken and erased his record—so we let Dr. Gerard go. I would miss him—he was kind, had a good bedside manner, and had saved my husband. I owed more than a debt of gratitude.

The house was crammed full of people, and I momentarily felt bad that Moira and James's home had been overrun with guests. They both informed me we were family, and it wasn't an inconvenience. I hoped they felt the same way when Hawk screamed his head off in the middle of the night. But Flynn wasn't well enough to travel, and we were still moving pieces on a near-invisible chessboard.

When Ash awoke from her nap, restored and looking more human, we decided there was no time like the present to have a meeting. Ash, Duncan, Ramsey, and I crammed into Flynn's bedroom.

The room's windows were cracked to let in fresh air, and it eased the scent of antiseptic. I'd already helped Flynn bathe earlier that day, so at least the odor of stale sweat was absent.

"Where do we start?" Ash asked.

I looked at Duncan, automatically deferring to him as the leader. He nodded for me to speak. "I don't know who knows what, so let me recap it for everyone. Okay? With the help of Katherine and her friends, and Ash's Googling, we believe Edward Roehenstart is the man staging the coup."

"Fucking coward," Ramsey groused.

"Ash and I think Arlington is backing Roehenstart," I said. "I want to talk to Barnabas. Maybe he has some insight on Roehenstart's whereabouts or what he's up to."

Flynn shook his head. "Why would you need to talk to Barnabas?"

"Because Barnabas is Roehenstart's grandfather," I explained.

"Wow, I didn't see that coming. Barnabas would've told us if he knew anything, though, aye?"

"Not necessarily," Duncan argued. "And besides, he might be in the dark about it."

"We don't even know if Roehenstart is our man," Ramsey went on. "This is all a big stretch."

"Either way, if I speak to Barnabas, it means I can learn the truth about Roehenstart. Why was he declared dead by the FBI? You don't think that's sketchy?"

"I think it was an oversight—a miscommunication," Ramsey said. "Nothing more than that."

We all fell silent, trying to think our way out of this mess. There had to be something I wasn't seeing. I was usually good at connecting dots, at finding the common thread, but I was feeling useless and too close in on it.

"We've been going about this the wrong way," Flynn said

finally. "We've been searching for needles in haystacks, attempting to lay traps. What we need to do is challenge him."

We all looked at him blankly.

"Duncan and I summon every member of the SINS to Dornoch, and in front of everyone, we demand The Pretender come forward and compete for the leadership of the SINS the old-fashioned way."

Duncan slowly smiled in understanding. Ramsey began to laugh, and he nodded eagerly. Ash and I were still lost.

"Care to clue in the Americans?" Ash demanded.

Flynn grinned. "We're going to hold the Highland Games. Let the bastard prove to everyone he's strong enough to lead. If he wants the SINS, then he has to be man enough to show his face. Subterfuge is his way. Not ours. We'll call him out, list his transgressions, and finally make everyone aware of the coup that's been happening under their noses. They'll either be incensed or agree with him. Either way, it's better to know if the SINS we've all vowed and sworn to uphold is no more."

"I say we just kill him when he steps forward," Ramsey said drolly.

"I'm with Ramsey," Ash stated.

I looked at her. "When did you become so bloodthirsty?"

She shrugged.

"I'm surprised we haven't dealt with anything like this sooner," Duncan said. "There's only so long the status quo works."

"Aye," Flynn agreed. "Change is change. But frankly, I don't want to be part of a group that would support a man going behind his own, planning murders and kidnapping. Whatever way the chips fall, we'll know."

"The SINS will never be the same," Duncan said thoughtfully.

"When are the Highland Games supposed to happen?" Ash asked.

"Anytime from spring to early summer," Duncan answered.

"And who's going to compete?" she demanded, looking at the three of them.

"We'll figure that out later," Flynn said.

"We can't figure that out later," I insisted. "You are bedbound, and even by the beginning of spring, you won't be back to yourself. That leaves Duncan." I looked at him. "But you don't want the role of leader."

"I'll do it," Ramsey volunteered. "I'm healthy and I have a lot of rage."

I snorted. "Do you want to lead?"

"Not really."

"Then you're out, too." I gripped my hair in frustration.

Flynn leaned back against the pillows in obvious exhaustion. I played the role of an overprotective wife and called the meeting to an end so Flynn could get some rest. Everyone filed out, and I made a move to leave too.

"Where are you going?" he asked me.

"I need to relieve Moira who has been watching Hawk."

"Wait," he said. "You forgot something."

I frowned, walking over to him. "What?"

"Come here," he said, crooking his finger.

"Flynn," I began, leaning over so I was closer to him.

The sparkle in his cobalt blue eyes was all devil. His hand grasped the back of my head, and he pulled me down toward him. His lips met mine in a fervent, passionate kiss. His tongue entered my mouth, eliciting shivers up and down my spine. Flynn pulled back and grinned.

"You must be feeling better," I said breathlessly.

"I'll be back to my old self in no time," he promised. "And then you better watch out."

My phone buzzed, startling me out of a sound sleep. I reached for it, hoping it wasn't an emergency. A number I didn't recognize appeared across the screen. I answered it.

"Hello?"

"Barrett?" a voice asked. "Is this Barrett Schaefer?"

"Yes," I said.

"Barrett! It's Dr. Albright! How are you?"

I glanced at the alarm clock on the nightstand. It read two a.m. "I'm fine, Dr. Albright. How are you?"

"Oh, good, good. Listen, I'm sorry it took me so long to get back to you. I was on vacation when I got your email. Fascinating question about the Count of Roehenstart."

I yawned but quickly stifled it.

Dr. Albright went on, "It's assumed that the man died without children even though he was married twice. Still, he was reported to have had a mistress, and there is no official documentation on whether or not she gave him children. There's a book written by…oh, darn, I've forgotten the title. It was repudiated by the scholars."

"Sir, you're rambling," I said.

"Right. Sorry. If only I could remember the title. Anyway, it was written in the eighteen-twenties, I believe."

I put a hand to my third eye. "Do you remember the name of the author?"

"I can't remember the first name, but the last name was Stuart."

"Like the House of Stuart?" I asked.

"Yes, exactly. I really wish I could remember—Oh! Augustus Stuart. Give that a try."

Dr. Albright was only in his sixties, much too young to be senile. Then again, maybe not.

"Thank you, sir. I'll see what I can dig up."

"I do like a good puzzle," he went on. "I'll look on my end, now that I've remembered the name. I sure do miss you at Columbia. You always had a way of helping me clear away

361

the clutter in my brain. I wonder what knowledge I'd find if I swept up there." He chuckled at his own attempt at humor. Despite myself, I grinned.

"Thank you for your help, Dr. Albright. I appreciate it." Not wanting to feel like I was rushing him off, I asked him about his vacation. And then I got a thirty-minute monologue about the shellfish buffet at an all-inclusive resort in the Bahamas.

When we finally hung up, Hawk was awake. I fed and changed him and then settled back into bed with him, my brain somehow on. I fired up the iPad and began Googling Augustus Stuart.

I sifted through pages and pages of esoteric dead ends until I found a glimmer of something useful. Augustus Stuart had written a journal about being the ignored son of the Count of Roehenstart, and it had been published in 1823.

If Edward Roehenstart was descended from Bonnie Prince Charlie, would that give him delusions of grandeur? Would that give him enough of a reason to want a free Scotland and be the one to lead the cause?

I needed to speak to someone who would know for sure. It was time to see Barnabas.

## Chapter 57

"No," Flynn stated the next morning. "You can't go."

I raised my eyebrow but forced myself not to raise my voice. "*Can't?*"

"I won't let you put yourself in danger."

"Are you going to physically stop me?" I demanded.

Flynn attempted to get up out of bed, like he actually had the fortitude to prevent me from going. I rushed over to him and put a hand to his shoulder. He was sweating and breathing hard, clutching his belly in pain.

"You damn fool," I said softly, helping him get back into bed. "Please, Flynn. I have a hunch and I want to follow it. I wanted to go weeks ago, to confirm that Roehenstart was our man, but Duncan thought it was best to wait until we had more information."

"What good will talking to Barnabas do?" he demanded. "Except alert Roehenstart that you're back in Dornoch and unprotected."

"I'm not unprotected," I said. "I'll be taking Nathan. Have you seen that guy? He's a tank."

"I'm aware. I was the one who hired him." He grumbled. "He better do a better job than your last bodyguard."

"Does that mean you'll give your blessing and let me go? I don't really need your permission, love. Please don't force the issue."

"I have no control over the SINS, and now I have no control over my wife. I'm a laughingstock."

"Oh, Flynn," I said with a wry grin. "You never had control over me."

Flynn laughed. "True."

"Besides, nothing better than word of mouth."

He frowned. "What do you mean?"

"Give me the date you want to call all the SINS members together. I'll tell Barnabas."

"And Barnabas will tell everyone else," he said with a smile. "He'll make sure Roehenstart knows about the meeting. Genius."

"Do you notice that we're always leaving each other?" I blurted out. My eyes began to fill with tears. "Either you leave me, or I leave you? We've both left Hawk. I'm a terrible person."

"Oh, love, come here," he said, gesturing for me to sit next to him. "How can you even think that after all we've been through?"

"Exactly because of what we've been through," I said. I took a seat on the bed.

"Rest with me a minute."

"I don't want to hurt you."

"You won't."

I scooted in, careful not to jostle him. He wasn't having any of it and attempted to drag me closer so I could place my head on his chest. His arm wrapped around me, soothing me like I soothed Hawk.

We held one another until my breathing calmed and my tears abated. I didn't remember falling asleep, comforted in the embrace of my husband.

# Birth of a Queen

Nathan held the umbrella and helped me out of the car. I tucked my hand in the crook of his arm as he led me up the pathway of the castle Flynn and I had restored.

It felt like forever since I'd been here, slept here, dreamt here.

"You really love Scotland?" Nathan asked, clearly appalled by the dark sky. We'd taken a commercial flight from Belfast to Edinburgh and driven to Dornoch. It had been raining since we touched down in Scotland, and it wasn't going to stop any time soon.

I grinned at him. "Wait until you see the house. It might change your mind about this place." Unlocking the door, I pushed it open and stepped into the foyer. I took off my outerwear and struggled out of my boots.

Nathan stood stock-still, his mouth agape.

"I know," I said with a laugh. "Close the door, you're letting the heat out."

I'd called Katherine's grandmother, Glenna, and asked her if she could discreetly come to the house, turn on the heat, and do a minimal amount of grocery shopping. She didn't ask questions, knowing her granddaughter was in New York. I liked that about the SINS women; they could keep a secret.

After Nathan took off his raincoat and shoes, I asked if he wanted a tour of the house. He nodded enthusiastically. As we walked through the castle, he ran his hand across the walls and the stair banister. I briefly showed him Hawk's newly redesigned nursery, realizing I'd need another crib. There was more than enough space for Hawk and his new brother or sister to share a room. It would make things easier in the beginning.

"You could rent out all the extra rooms," Nathan said when we were in the kitchen. I opened a beer and handed it to him, glad that he was here. The house was big, and I didn't want to be alone.

"There's an idea," I said. "You hungry?"

"I could eat. So, what's the plan? When are you meeting with this Barney guy?"

I smirked. "Barnabas. I plan on dropping in on him tomorrow."

"Should I be worried?"

"He's seventy-years-old, so I doubt it. He is a sheep farmer though, so he might be tougher than he looks."

Nathan pretended to look menacing. He ruined it by smiling. Despite his bulk and the fact that he carried a gun, he was strangely good-humored. I hadn't seen him in action, though, and I hoped I never had to.

We ate a light dinner and then I left Nathan to enjoy the entertainment center while I soaked in the bath. Depending on what I gleaned from Barnabas, my plan could go a number of different ways.

The Pretender hid behind hired soldiers and preyed on children. Arlington was no better. I would find a way to destroy both of them, ensuring that the SINS remained intact, led by either a Buchanan or a Campbell.

∽

The next morning was cool with a clear sky. I wasn't sure how long it would last, knowing Scotland's penchant for rain and dark skies. Nathan took the wheel of the car and I gratefully sat in the passenger side. Though my morning sickness seemed to have disappeared, it now manifested itself in motion sickness. I stared out the window while we drove to Barnabas Stuart's farm, but the passing landscape did nothing to keep my attention away from my rolling stomach.

"Are you and Shawna dating?" I blurted out.

"That's a personal question. Are you even allowed to ask me that or is that against the rules?"

"Nathan," I said through a slow breath, "I feel like I'm about to vomit. Talking about your love life is a worthy distraction. Humor me. Please?"

He shot me a grin. "All right. I'll oblige. Shawna and I went on a few dates when we were in New York. Nothing serious, though."

"She not good enough for you?" I asked, pretending to sound like an overbearing parent.

He laughed, showing white teeth. "No, she is. Definitely. She's funny and smart but self-deprecating. She knows what she wants, and I admire that."

"I'm sensing a 'but.'"

"*However*," he said with a wry grin. "I'm not in a place where I can get serious with someone."

"Do you want to? Be serious, I mean?"

"Not really. Besides, my employer is a regular jetsetter. She's demanding and—"

I laughed. "Ah, so it's my fault you don't have time for a girlfriend."

"Yes, exactly."

Nathan turned down the road that led to Barnabas's home. It was an old stone structure, which had probably been around since the 1800s. We parked and I got out of the car.

I glanced at Nathan. "Try not to look too menacing. We don't want to give him a heart attack."

"You think I'm that scary? I'm flattered."

"Save me from sarcastic men," I muttered, approaching the stone pathway. I knocked on the front door and waited.

The door opened and Barnabas's robust frame filled the doorway. At first, he appeared confused, and then it morphed into pleasure.

"Mrs. Campbell!" he greeted enthusiastically. "Are you back in Dornoch? Are you here for Betty?"

I smiled. "Not today."

Barnabas's gaze drifted from me to Nathan. Barnabas frowned. "Who are you?"

"Nathan is a friend of mine," I interjected.

"Friend," Barnabas huffed.

"Bodyguard," I clarified.

"Bodyguard," Barnabas repeated and then nodded. "Aye. Well, come on in, I just put on water for tea."

He waved us inside to the cozy interior and shut the door. He ambled toward the kitchen and we followed.

"Sorry to drop by unannounced," I said. The kitchen was surprisingly modern despite the architecture of the house. Gray granite and steel made up the decor.

Barnabas moved around the kitchen, grabbing three mugs for tea. "Not a worry. It's been a while since I've had visitors. It's a nice change to talk to people instead of sheep, ye ken."

My heart contracted. I never realized Barnabas lived alone or that he could be lonely.

Barnabas finished making our tea and handed us mugs. "I have some biscuits if you'd like."

"Oh, no, that's—"

Before I could finish, Barnabas put a plate of fluffy biscuits on the counter. Nathan had no qualms about filching one. He made an appreciative noise and then devoured the thing in two bites.

Barnabas seemed pleased, his blue eyes warm. "Now lass, I know you're not just here for a visit. What can I do for you?"

I thought about how to phrase my question, but then I realized the Scots were blunt and preferred that method of communication.

So I let it rip.

"I wanted to talk to you about your grandson."

"Bobby?"

"No."

"Lachlan."

"No."

"Ang—"

"Edward," I interrupted, wondering how many grandsons he had.

Barnabas's eyes narrowed. "Why would you want to be talking about Edward?"

Well, here went nothing. I took a deep breath. "Because I think he's trying to take over the SINS."

## Chapter 58

Tension filled the room. Barnabas's welcoming gaze closed off, and I worried that he would refuse to speak about his grandson. But he surprised me.

"That good-for-nothing lout," Barnabas declared vehemently. "We don't speak of him."

"We?" I asked softly.

"The family. We've disowned him."

"Why?"

"Why?" he blustered. "Because he's caused us nothing but trouble. Always in and out of scrapes with the law. Arrogant, prideful beast—all because we're descendants of Charles Edward Stuart. Bonnie Prince Charlie as he's called." He shook his head in disgust. I didn't know if it was over his grandson, or Prince Charles's derogatory nickname.

"Calls himself Edward Roehenstart. Pompous ass," Barnabas muttered.

"There are no records that Charles Edward Stuart—Count Roehenstart—had any children," I said.

"No records? I'll show you records." Barnabas jumped up from his chair and left the kitchen. Nathan and I eagerly followed, exchanging a look.

Barnabas went into the den and headed to the far wall bookshelf. He plucked a leather-bound book from the middle shelf and brought it to me. "This bible once belonged to Prince Charles Stuart and has been passed down through the generations." He flipped open the cover and showed me the list of names and birthdates. My heartbeat escalated when I saw the name *Augustus Stuart*, illegitimate son of Count Roehenstart.

Barnabas grinned wryly. "We're from a long line of bastards, ye ken."

I let out a laugh.

"Still breed some, too," he said sadly. "Broke my daughter's heart when we realized Edward had his own ideas about how things should be. Zealous. He changed his name to Roehenstart, wanting the world to recognize the line he comes from. Not that it's substantiated. Not officially anyway."

"So I'm guessing your grandson believes leading the SINS is his due?"

"Arrogant bastard—he has no idea what it means to be a leader. Malcolm was a good leader." He patted my arm even though I felt like I needed to be the one to comfort him.

"Campbell's not bad either," he added.

I smiled at his diplomacy, but there were more important matters to discuss. "Barnabas, do you have any idea where Edward could be?"

He shook his head. "I'm sorry, lass. I wish I knew more."

After saying goodbye to Barnabas, Nathan and I left. As we drove away from the farm, Nathan asked, "You trust him?"

"There's no guile in him," I said with assurance. "If he knew where Edward was, he'd have told us. He doesn't like his grandson any more than we do."

～

Our mission completed, we returned to the castle to pack up. I called Flynn to let him know how it went and that Nathan hadn't even had to pull out his gun.

Next, I called Don Archer. He didn't answer, and I left a message for him to call me immediately, no matter the time. I wanted this finished. I was tired of living with a cloud of fear over my head.

Before we left Dornoch to drive to Edinburgh, we stopped off to say hello to Glenna. She pushed three baby sweaters on me for Hawk and wouldn't take no for an answer. Much to Nathan's surprise, he got a sweater of his own.

"Those Highland sheep sure are warm," Nathan said, adjusting the collar of his new sweater.

"Aye, they are," Glenna said with a smile.

"And this was made in Dornoch?" he asked.

Glenna nodded. "But that particular sweater was made from the fleece of sheep in Lairg."

I frowned. Lairg. Something familiar about that town name…

We said goodbye to Glenna and settled in for our drive to Edinburgh. It wasn't until we were in Belfast that something clicked into place. When I'd spoken with Winters back when Hawk was missing, I'd met him just outside of Lairg. But we'd driven an hour or so away to a cabin in the Highlands. Though I didn't know the exact location, was it possible to narrow down where I had been taken? Google Maps were able to show street views, for crying out loud! What if Arlington was hiding out in Lairg or near Lairg? What if The Pretender was hiding there, too?

"You can take a deep breath now," I said to Flynn as I leaned over to kiss him hello. My mind was active with wanting to explore my intuition. But I pushed it away and picked up Hawk who'd been having a nap on Flynn's very comfortable chest.

"Nothing happened," I stated.

"I'm glad."

"No shootouts, no bad guys jumping out from behind any corners."

"Barrett," he sighed. "Be quiet and kiss me again."

I did as commanded, loving the shape of his mouth, the taste of his lips. I pulled back. "So, question."

He raised an eyebrow.

"How many times have you been shot?"

"I think six."

"Six?"

"This…" He gestured to his stomach. And then he pointed to his shoulder. "That was from the docks when we set up Marino."

I shook my head, marveling at the passage of time. I hadn't thought of Giovanni Marino in a while.

"What about the four other times?" I asked, not outright mentioning Dolinsky.

"I don't know if they count as being shot—bullet grazes, nothing more. All in all, I'm lucky."

I laughed. "Shot at six times, only one of which was nearly fatal. Yeah. Born under a lucky star, all right."

He chuckled. "We Campbells are pretty resilient."

I continued to rub Hawk's back. "Seriously."

∞

Everyone was suffering from cabin fever, so when Brandon suggested a night out at a local pub, everyone jumped at the idea. As soon as the sun went down, the house emptied except for Hawk, Flynn, and me. We had the place to ourselves. Not that we could make much use out of the sudden bout of privacy.

"Help me get up," Flynn said, moving the covers off him.

"Why?"

"Why?" he demanded. "Because I'm going crazy in this bed. Catheter has been removed, and it's been far too long since I've showered like a normal person." His eyes darkened. "And far too long since I've seen you naked."

"We can't do anything," I said. "You're not healed yet."

He grinned wicked. "Oh, love, we can still do plenty."

I kissed him, our tongues tangling in heat and passion. "Let me put Hawk down, and then I'll help you into the shower."

It had been so long since we'd connected sexually. So much of our intimacy was wrapped up in it, and I was glad that I was aware of it. I never wanted to forget how much I loved Flynn. No matter what was going on with SINS. No matter that our children would take a lot of time away from us as a couple.

After Hawk was down in his borrowed crib, his eyes drifting shut, I hurried back to Flynn. He'd managed to get himself up into a sitting position. His room didn't have a private bathroom, so we'd use the one in the room where I'd been sleeping. I helped him stand, but he tried not to give me too much of his weight.

"I can take a bit more," I promised, urging him to lean on me.

By the time we made it to the bathroom, Flynn was gray-faced and sweating. "Maybe this wasn't a good idea," I said, urging him to sit down on the closed toilet.

"It's a great idea," he said with a grimace. "But you might have to do most of the work."

I raised my eyebrows and he chuckled. "I meant washing my hair for me, love."

"Oh, sure, that's what you meant," I teased. I got the shower ready and then got Flynn out of his clothes. He was wearing a matching flannel pajama set, so it was relatively easy to get him naked.

I peeled away his dressing to reveal his injury. It was red but no longer swollen. The stitches were small and even. I cleaned and redressed it so it would stay dry.

I quickly shed my clothes. Flynn's eyes were on me, hot with lust. I started to laugh as I climbed into the tub.

"What?" he demanded.

"Whenever your sex drive is raring to go, I know you're fine."

He chuckled and then carefully stepped into the water. It was lukewarm, and I would've made it hotter, but I sensed Flynn needed the cooler temperatures or he might have passed out. I showered quickly while he braced his shoulder against the wall to keep himself propped up. He was tiring fast.

I gently washed his body but didn't linger like I wanted to. He leaned his head toward me, and I massaged his scalp with shampoo, glad we could at least be skin to skin.

"I won't make it back to my room," Flynn said as I eased him onto the edge of my bed, a towel wrapped around his waist.

"So stay here," I said with a smile. "Sleep next to me. The bed is plenty big enough for two."

"It would be nice to get out of that sick room," Flynn said.

"And sleep next to your hot wife."

He grinned. "And sleep next to my hot wife."

I dressed him in clean pajamas and then tucked him into bed. I kissed his brow and settled down next to him until his breathing evened out and he was asleep.

## Chapter 59

Jane Elliot returned to London. Ramsey's sunny mood deteriorated quickly and, soon Duncan and Flynn kicked him out, commanding him to leave Belfast and get his head on straight.

I told Flynn about my talk with Jane, and though his jaw had clenched, he ultimately agreed it was the best thing for her. Despite the fact that Ramsey was angry and heartbroken, it was better for him in the long run. Pain now would be nothing compared to a life built with Jane only to have her leave at a later time.

Ash and Duncan flew back to New York for some alone time together and took Daniel with them. Brandon was healed enough to want to get out of his parents' house and back to his life and so he left.

Over the next three weeks, Flynn recovered. He eventually moved from the bed to the couch. James made a considerable effort to forge a relationship with his nephew, and they spent hours talking and laughing, exchanging stories about Flynn's mother.

While Flynn healed, I took time to rest, too. When the weather turned, I took Hawk for walks outside.

One bright and warm early spring morning, I woke up

and looked down at my belly. It was no longer flat and had seemed to pop overnight. I glanced at Flynn who was asleep on his back. I poked him into waking up. He jolted and then smiled.

"Morning, love."

I lifted up my shirt. "Do I look bigger to you?"

"This is one of those moments I'm going to regret later, right?"

"I'm serious. I wasn't showing this early with Hawk."

"I'm sure you're fine, love."

I quickly did the math, realizing I was already twelve weeks along. I'd hardly noticed the passage of time, so consumed with other concerns.

Throwing back the covers, I climbed out of bed. "I'm going into Belfast."

"Now?" he asked in surprise. "Why?"

"It's time for another ultrasound."

He grinned. "Then I'm coming too."

We ate a quick breakfast while Moira called her doctor for me, pleading to squeeze me in. Because Moira had been a patient for years and the doctor had delivered all three of Moira's children, she did us a favor, promising to see us in the next hour before the office officially opened.

"That was nice of her," I said when Moira hung up.

"I'll drive you," Moira said. "It's close by, and I have to run some errands in town."

"Who's going to watch Hawk?" I asked.

James raised his eyebrows. "Do you think Moira took care of three children alone? I can watch Hawk."

I grinned. "No Irish whiskey shots."

Moira kissed James goodbye, and then we left the house. She climbed into the car, and I sat in the front passenger side, moving the seat forward so Flynn had enough room for his long legs. The doctor's office was fifteen minutes away, the parking lot relatively empty due to the early hour.

I opened the passenger door for Flynn, who was still moving slowly, but refused to ask for help. Moira came into the doctor's office with us, just to say hello to the gray-haired woman. Dr. Barrows and Moira chatted for a few minutes, exchanging chitchat about children and grandchildren before Moira waved goodbye.

"Thank you for seeing us this early," I said, climbing up onto the exam table. Flynn took a seat in one of the chairs along the wall.

"Not a problem." Dr. Barrows smiled and got the ultrasound equipment ready. "Moira said you're twelve weeks along?"

I nodded.

She gently lifted up my shirt and squirted my belly with gel. "How have you been feeling?" she asked, her eyes on me and not the monitor. It made me feel like a person instead of an incubator.

"Fine. The morning sickness has passed."

"That's good."

"This is my second pregnancy," I explained. "Is it normal to already have a baby belly at twelve weeks?"

"You've already had a child, so it's not unusual to show earlier the second time around."

I let out a breath and glanced at Flynn. He grinned. "Told you—you're fine."

"Fine, and the babies are perfectly healthy," Dr. Barrows said.

"Oh good, I'm glad—wait, did you say babies? As in more than one?" I demanded.

Dr. Barrows nodded. "Congratulations. You're having twins."

~

"Barrett," Flynn began, his shock apparently having worn off enough so he could finally speak.

"Don't talk to me," I snapped, sitting up.

Dr. Barrows slipped from the room without a word. Flynn watched her go, a look of resignation on his face. He glanced back at me.

"This is your fault," I continued. "You rotten, dirty—"

"Bastard?" he supplied, trying to be helpful.

"Husband," I finished with a glare. I dropped my head into my hands. "This is ridiculous."

"I'll get a vasectomy." He managed to stand up and come to me. Wrapping me in his arms, he pulled me close.

"We'll talk about it later," I muttered into his chest. "Three children. I'll be ready for the insane asylum."

Flynn stroked my back in an attempt to calm me down. It was working. He kissed my lips gently and cradled my face in his hands.

"We've survived crazier things, haven't we?" he asked with a calm smile.

I sighed. "We have."

"Let's celebrate," he said. "Because there are so many terrible things we could dwell on, but this is not one of them."

∽

I closed the door to the den so I could have some privacy as I answered a very important phone call.

"Barrett," Don Archer greeted. "Am I speaking to a real person or is this automated?"

I chuckled. "How are you?"

"Fine. Sorry it's taken so long to get back to you. What's going on?"

"I have some information that you need." I felt a twinge of guilt, having a conversation with Archer without telling Flynn.

"What's up?"

I gave him the brief watered-down version, eliminating any mention of Winters. I explained about Arlington funneling money and that Roehenstart was behind the House of Lords bombing.

It felt seedy and underhanded to get the FBI involved. I was going behind Flynn's back in order to protect him and those I loved from getting hurt. Duncan and Flynn were in no physical condition to challenge Roehenstart, and Ramsey wasn't groomed for leading the SINS.

Archer cursed. "You're not giving me a lot of time to pull this together."

"I have been trying to get in touch with you," I reminded him. "I didn't trust anyone else with this information."

He sighed. "Yeah. I know. I do appreciate it."

"I've done a little digging," I said slowly. "And I think I have an idea about where he might be hiding out." I gave him the location of the cabin an hour outside of Lairg.

"I'll have my guys check it out."

We hung up and I sat back in the leather chair, wondering if I'd just made a huge mistake.

There was a knock on the door, and a moment later, Flynn popped his head in. "What are you doing in here all alone?"

My pulse quickened. "Just thinking."

I wondered if he could smell the guilt coming off me.

"About the bairns?" he asked.

"No."

"About me?"

I smiled softly. "Maybe."

"Have you forgiven me yet?"

"Hmm."

"Was that a yes or a no?"

"I'm not sure yet," I teased.

He finally came into the room and dragged me out of the

chair and into his arms. He kissed me, driving away all thoughts of my betrayal.

"I think I know how to make it up to you," he whispered against my mouth.

"How?"

He said something dirty in my ear, and it made me shiver from my head down to my toes. I grabbed the front of his sweater. "Have you been keeping something from me?"

Flynn's hand caressed the back of my head as he said, "The doctor cleared me. Now, let's get upstairs. We have to make up for lost time."

## Chapter 60

"You're awake," Flynn said sleepily.

"I'm not used to our bed anymore. It's too soft."

"It's our first night back under our own roof. It will take some time to readjust."

Dornoch was home, but it would be a little while before we were in the swing of life.

"Come here, love," he said.

I scooted closer to him and pressed my head to his chest. I closed my eyes and breathed him in. After tomorrow, there was a good chance he wouldn't want to sleep next to me. Not when Flynn learned that I'd betrayed him and the SINS by speaking to Archer. But I didn't trust Roehenstart not to have something up his sleeve. The man had gone after my son.

"Are you worried about tomorrow?" he asked.

"A little, I guess," I admitted.

"Don't be."

"Easier said than done. You and Duncan are calling out The Pretender in front of the SINS."

He rolled me over and placed a kiss on my lips. "You trust me, aye?"

I nodded.

"Then trust that it's all going to work out."

I stroked my hands up and down his body; strength was in every muscle, strength he used to protect our family, even at the cost to himself. He was a true warrior, noble, loyal, fierce. He loved deeply. But so did I. And I protected those I loved.

"Do you still want to leave the SINS?" I asked, broaching the subject he had brought up when he was completely immobilized only a few weeks ago. Almost dying changed a person.

"I don't like what it's become," Flynn admitted. "Fighting The Pretender when we should be focused on our cause. I think I'll know if I want to leave based on how everyone reacts to Roehenstart's betrayal."

"When did it stop being about a free Scotland? When did it become a fight for power?" I asked rhetorically.

Men like Flynn would never do well taking orders from someone else. Even if Duncan became leader, Flynn would not adjust easily. He'd been autonomous in New York for so long and Malcolm had trusted him.

"You'd regret it, you know," I said. "Leaving the SINS. Maybe not at the moment or in the near future, but one day, you'll look back and regret it. You've been weaned on this cause, Flynn. That doesn't go away just because you decide you don't want to be involved anymore."

"Aye," Flynn agreed. "A blessing and a curse. Some days, I wish I never hungered for such things."

"But you do." I was quiet a moment. "Maybe it's not just a fight for the SINS. Maybe it's really about the fight you have with yourself." I lifted my head so I could look at him.

He smiled slightly. "I'm a lucky man. To have a wife such as you." His mouth met mine, hungry, devouring.

The time for talking was done.

∼

I rolled over and encountered a cold bed. Flynn was gone; no doubt he'd been tossing and turning until finally he'd gotten up so he wouldn't disturb me. Padding down the hallway to the nursery, I checked in on Hawk. He slept soundly. Maybe he was too young to remember being snatched from this room. Maybe it would never haunt him like it did me.

Flynn wasn't in his study, nor was he on the porch. I was just about to throw on a coat and boots to go look for him outside when I saw that his own outwear wasn't hanging on the hooks by the door. Frowning, I headed to the living room, wondering where he could be. Usually when he left the house, no matter if it was for a short walk, he woke me up to tell me. I headed back up to bed, hearing a faint buzzing sound.

My phone danced across the bedside table, and I wondered who could be calling me in the middle of the night.

"Ash," I said in greeting. "What is it?"

"Is Flynn home?" she asked, her voice desperate.

"No. He's not. I woke up and he was gone."

Ash let out a stream of curses. "Duncan's gone, too. I'm sitting here with Daniel who refuses to answer any of my questions. He says Duncan and Flynn are safe and not to worry—that they'll both be home before the SINS meeting tomorrow."

"That doesn't make any sense," I said. "Why would they go anywhere in the middle of the night?"

"I don't know. Did Flynn say anything to you? Anything weird?"

"Not that I can think of," I said truthfully. "Traipsing around in the middle of the night… Flynn's barely back on his feet. Where could they possibly—"

I cut myself off when I had a sudden thought. "Let me call you back."

"Fuck that," she stated. "I'm coming over. I'm not sleeping in this creepy old castle alone."

We hung up, and I held my cell phone for a minute in my hand before calling Flynn. It went to voicemail. I didn't expect him to answer. Leaving the bedroom, I walked down the long hallway to the other end of the house. I stopped outside of a guest bedroom and gently rapped on the door before pushing it open.

With the help of soft winter moonlight, I was able to see Nathan asleep on his back. I quietly walked to the chair where he'd set aside the decorative throw pillows. Picking one up, I crept toward him. Just as I was about to take aim and hit him, his voice stopped me.

"Whatever you're about to do, don't."

"How the hell—"

"Light sleeper," he explained. "Good in my line of work. Mind telling me what you're doing in my bedroom in the middle of the night?"

I tossed the pillow aside. "Mind telling me where my husband is?"

Nathan paused.

"You fucker," I seethed. "You know."

"I don't," he said quickly. "Honestly. He told me last night before going to bed that he would be gone in the middle of the night and to keep you safe, but I swear I don't know his location."

I growled in frustration. "Duncan is gone too. Ash just called me."

He nodded. "Not surprising."

"She's coming over," I stated.

Nathan threw back the covers and got out of bed. He reached for his discarded sweatshirt and threw it over his head.

"What are you doing?" I asked when he brushed past me to leave the room.

"I'll answer the door. You can never be too careful this time of night."

I refilled Ash's tea mug and then sat back down. Ash's bodyguard and Nathan were still in the living room, while Ash and I had made our way into the kitchen.

Ash stared at me a long moment and said finally, "You have an idea of where they are. Don't you?"

"I have a theory," I said slowly.

"Care to share?"

I sighed. "I did something. I called Don Archer and told him about Roehenstart and Arlington."

"What?" Ash breathed. "You didn't!"

I nodded. "I did. I also told him where I think Roehenstart was hiding out." I explained how I'd remembered Lairg and my meeting with Winters and Arlington.

"Why did you tell Archer?"

"Because," I said, suddenly frustrated. "Both Duncan and Flynn almost died because of Roehenstart. My son was kidnapped. Malcolm is dead. I was thinking that I wanted someone else to take down the dirty bastard."

"But you know how Flynn and Duncan feel about this stuff. This is SINS business. Do you think Duncan and Flynn went to…to take care of Roehenstart themselves?"

"I don't know. I mean, how would they know about his location? I didn't tell them."

"You didn't." She looked me in the eyes. "But maybe Archer did?"

## Chapter 61

*They moved liked shadows and became the darkness. Three brothers, bound by cause, bound by honor, bound by love, would not rest until The Pretender was dead.*

*After dispatching those that guarded the man while he rested, the three brothers crept forward. They skulked into the cabin, mindful that the wood planks were old and creaky.*

*They didn't speak—they had no need for words. They moved as one entity but fluid like water. Light came in the form of the dying fire. Only embers remained, glowing dull red as wood turned to ash. The Pretender slept peacefully, like a baby that knew no fear.*

*The younger Buchanan nearly snorted. A true warrior would not have been caught unaware. A true warrior would have known his life was in danger.*

*It was the older Buchanan who hauled The Pretender from his bed. The man was slight, almost fragile. Not a warrior, indeed.*

*The Pretender's eyes flipped open, his face registering fear. He clawed at the hands around his neck, spittle flying from gray lips. The older Buchanan dropped him, and the sound of a man's knees hitting wood echoed in the otherwise silent night.*

*"He thinks to lead the SINS?" the younger Buchanan asked in disgust. "He must be known for his words."*

"Aye," the Campbell agreed. "Get up. Face us like a man."

The Pretender struggled to his feet but finally stood. He kept his eyes downcast. His cowardice was maddening.

"Look at me," the older Buchanan commanded.

The Pretender reluctantly lifted his gaze. Even in the dying light, it was obvious that he was pale. How could such a small, spineless man have caused them all so much pain?

"Who backed you?" the older Buchanan asked.

"You know," The Pretender answered, his voice breathy.

"Say his name," the Campbell demanded. "I'll hear his name."

"Lord Henry Arlington." It was but a sickly whisper.

"And he financed The White Company," the older Buchanan stated.

The Pretender nodded.

The younger Buchanan was unusually quiet, his stare calm and steady. Though his anger simmered just below the surface of his placid facade, he was coiled, ready to strike.

"He financed the mercenaries that killed my father," the older Buchanan went on. "They almost got me, too."

"My son," the Campbell said. "Was taken from my home."

They continued to list The Pretender's transgressions, those that were personal and those that affected the SINS. In the end, the four of them knew the outcome of judgment.

The three brothers wanted blood. They weren't satisfied until The Pretender was dead at their feet, streams of red coating the old wood floor.

"It's done," the older Buchanan said.

"Not yet," the younger Buchanan stated, wiping his dirk on a white bed sheet, staining it crimson. He looked at the Campbell. "Your wife."

"I'll deal with Barrett," the Campbell said.

"If this happens again…" the older Buchanan trailed off, not having to finish the sentence. They all knew.

"Aye," the Campbell agreed. "But times must change."

"Some things will never change," the older Buchanan said as they all glanced down at the man who had betrayed them.

"What she did, she did out of love," the Campbell said. "Not out of some misguided notion. Not for power."

*The brothers fell silent. Before they left the cabin, they would make peace with what Barrett had done. They knew her mind, her heart. But she was an outsider, a foreigner, and her actions had only proven that.*

"*She is the mother of my child,*" *the Campbell stated.* "*I ask that she be spared.*"

*The older Buchanan looked at the man who was his brother in all ways except blood.* "*I will grant amnesty for this one transgression.*"

*This transgression and no others, the older Buchanan didn't say.*

"*On your honor,*" *the Campbell said.*

"*On my honor,*" *the older Buchanan repeated.*

## Chapter 62

I was still awake at dawn. Ash had long since fallen asleep, as had our two bodyguards. Hawk was conked out upstairs. I was alone in the quiet of the living room near the warmth of the fire.

Archer hadn't answered his phone or called me back.

Sitting on the couch, I waited. And waited. And waited. Finally, I heard the front door open and the sound of footsteps. I didn't get up or move.

"Barrett," Flynn said.

The way he said my name made me furious. It was commanding but soft. It was knowing and accusatory in its own right.

"Is Duncan with you?" I asked, refusing to look at him.

"No. He's back at home."

"His wife is here," I said. "She came over in the middle of the night when she realized Duncan was gone and there was no explanation."

Flynn moved to stand in front of me. He looked down, his arms crossed over his chest.

"Where were you?" I asked.

He paused. "Out."

"Out where?" I pushed.

"That doesn't concern you," he said slowly, his cobalt eyes dark and fierce.

"My how quickly things change," I stated, my lips quirking into an angry smile. "You used to confide in me."

"So did you," he stated. "When were you going to tell me that you'd called Archer to get him to handle Roehenstart?"

I rose slowly. "When Roehenstart was in English custody and we were safe."

Flynn shook his head and then looked to the celling. "You're in the wrong here, Barrett."

"Where. Were. You?"

His eyes came back to mine. "SINS business."

"Roehenstart?" I demanded. "Did you take care of him?"

A cell phone buzzing put our conversation on hold. Flynn answered it. "Aye, it's done. Thank you."

He hung up.

"Let me guess. Archer?"

Flynn's eyes were fierce. "Aye."

"When did you decide it was okay to go behind my back?" I demanded.

"Archer came to me, love."

My eyes widened. "Men. They dictate everything, and we womenfolk are just supposed to sit idly by while—"

"There are some things that will always have to be done the old way," he stated, cutting me off. "You took matters into your own hands when you spoke with Archer, giving him information you had no right to share."

"So he ran and tattled to you? Why am I not allowed to speak to Archer?" I demanded. "Because I'm a woman? Because I'm a foreigner?"

"Because you didn't talk with me about it first!" Flynn yelled, his temper finally unleashed.

"And what would you have said?" I shouted back, fury making me shake.

"I would've said no!"

I turned away in disgust. "So you and Duncan can make unilateral decisions without informing Ash and me?"

"No," he began. "You do not get to pull this shite. You started this when you went to Archer with classified information."

"I was trying to protect you—protect us all."

"You went behind my back," he growled. "You went behind the acting leader of the SINS's back. You compromised the cause."

I whirled. "Fuck the cause. It's brought me nothing but grief. You almost died. My son was kidnapped. And if I recall, you were ready to step down as leader. Guess that's changed."

He stalked toward me. "When did you stop confiding in me?"

"When did you stop confiding in me?" I demanded.

"If anyone else had gone to the FBI, they'd be dead."

I crossed my arms over my chest. "But because I'm your wife, I'm not dead?"

Flynn grasped me by the upper arms and hauled me close. "I haven't decided yet." His mouth swooped in to capture mine. We crashed together in lust and violence.

"God, you make me so fucking angry!" he growled against my lips.

I grasped him by his shirt. "The feeling is entirely mutual."

"Why? Why did you do it?" he demanded, his mouth breaking from mine. His hands reached up to cradle my cheeks. "Tell me, Barrett, because I swear to God—"

"I can't watch you die," I whispered.

His eyes softened. "Ah, love…"

"And you almost *did* die," I went on. "I thought I could do all this, but now there's Hawk, and the new bairns—"

Flynn pulled me to him. "Hush, love," he said into my

hair. His body was still hard, primed with anger, but he was melting.

"I'm sorry," I said. "I shouldn't have gone to Archer. Not without talking to you. That was wrong of me."

"I know why you did it," he answered.

"I betrayed you. I betrayed our family."

"No," he said, stopping me. "The SINS, they aren't your cause. I know that. You support it because you support me. But Hawk and I—we come first."

"And Ash," I said. "She's my family too."

"Aye. I understand. But my family is more than just us. It's the SINS, the men, women, and children—they are our clan."

"If you look at it that way," I began, "then I was protecting everyone."

"Some things will always have to be done the SINS way," he stated. "Duncan, Ramsey, and I dealt with Roehenstart. He won't be a problem anymore."

"But how—"

He smiled gently. "You didn't really think you could get away with going to Archer and I wouldn't know about it? You weren't acting like yourself, hen. I knew something was weighing on you. It didn't take a lot for me to piece it together. And then he called me."

"He did what—"

"I told him I'd gladly let the English have Arlington, but in exchange, we got to deal with Roehenstart ourselves. He agreed."

My eyes narrowed.

"He wanted something else, didn't he? Something bigger? What did you promise him?" I pressed.

He dropped his hands from my face and pulled me to him. "No more illegal guns into the States."

I gasped.

"Look at me," he said softly, but with a thread of steel in his voice.

I leaned back to stare up at him; his arms tightened around me. "You pull a stunt like this again, and we're going to have a serious problem. Hear me?"

Swallowing, I nodded.

"Say you hear me, love. I need you to admit that you made a wrong call. I was able to fix it. Outside the five of us, no one needs to know. It's been dealt with and handled. But you make this kind of mistake again, and I can't promise you there won't be backlash."

"I hear you," I whispered.

"I know you thought you were in the right," he went on. "I know you did it out of love and protection. Change is inevitable. But you can't change too much too fast. And if you go behind my back ever again, even in the name of protecting me, I'll—"

"Be very careful how you finish that sentence," I growled. "I was wrong, and I won't do it again."

"Good," he said softly though it was no less menacing.

"Forgive me?"

He made me look at him and smiled down at me. "I forgive you."

I leaned up and placed my lips on his. He kissed me back, gently, lovingly, without any anger.

"Let's go upstairs," I said.

"Aye."

The front door crashed open, startling me out of Flynn's arms. Duncan stormed into the living room, his face defiant.

"Where is she?"

I blinked. "Asleep upstairs."

"No phone call, no note. Nothing!" he yelled and then stalked from the room, cursing in Gaelic as he went.

"What's Gaelic for 'hypocrite'?" I asked Flynn.

The sound of slamming doors and yelling had me going toward the stairs. "Wait, love, I doubt it's a good idea to go up there. Let them have it out."

I looked at Flynn and grinned. "They can have it out all they want, but I know they're going to wake Hawk."

"Ah," he said, trailing after me.

By the time we made it to the upstairs hallway, Duncan and Ash were already facing off, glaring at each other.

"You're a rat bastard!" she shrieked like a violent harpy. "You're the one that snuck off in the middle of the night!"

"I was supposed to be back before you were even awake!" Duncan yelled back.

I made a face. "Wrong thing to say," I stated to Flynn.

"Aye," Flynn agreed.

Ash turned on us. "Can you not watch our fight? Please?"

"You're fighting in my house—in the hallway," I said with wide eyes. "And you're about to wake up my son."

As if on cue, Hawk's cry came through the doorway of the nursery. I looked at Ash. "See?"

"I'll go," Flynn said, heading in the direction of Hawk.

For some reason, Ash transferred all of her anger onto me. She crossed her arms and almost stamped her foot. "I thought you were still angry at them? For leaving in the middle of the night and not telling us that they were taking out Roehenstart?"

"Why don't you have this out with your husband," I suggested, turning away. "I've already made peace with mine."

## Epilogue

"Summer in the Highlands is gorgeous," Ash said, a glass of lemonade in her hand, Gucci sunglasses perched on her nose.

"Hmmm," I said, making a noise in the back of my throat.

"That was a decidedly Scottish sound."

"Thank you," I said with a teasing grin. "I'm currently two-thirds Scottish. I should be able to make the noises."

"How are you two-thirds Scottish?" Ash laughed.

I pointed to my belly. "Twins in there. Two of them. One of me. Do the math."

Ash laughed again.

The smell of heather surrounded us, and the sun was out in an unusual show. There were hardly any clouds in the sky. It made for a perfect day outside.

We sat in chairs on a grassy knoll that had a decent view of the surroundings. Booths of food and drinks were set up away from the competition fields. Men, women, and children of the SINS had gathered to share in a week-long celebration of family and Scottish tradition. Tonight there would be a ceremony that would make both Duncan and Flynn co-

# Birth of a Queen

leaders of the SINS. The members had voted weeks ago and refused to let either of them step down.

Flynn and Duncan strolled toward us, dressed in their different clan colors.

"Fuck, he's got nice legs," Ash breathed, a hand to her slightly rounded belly. Pregnancy looked good on her.

"You're talking about Flynn, right?" I asked, marveling at the sight of my husband's tan legs.

"Yeah," Ash said, and I knew by her tone she was rolling her eyes even though I couldn't see them.

"You're drooling," I quipped.

"So are you," she shot back.

"Hi, love," Flynn greeted leaning down to kiss my lips. I held out my hand to him, and he easily hoisted me up despite my bulk.

"That was a chaste greeting," I rebuked, tilting my head back, eager for something more. He obliged.

Cheers and applause went up around us. I pulled back, not even a little ashamed. Waving, I tried to bow but found it difficult. The laughter was friendly and good-natured.

"We came over here to inform you two ladies that we're about to start the caber toss competition," Duncan said, his arm around his wife, a look of adoration in his eyes.

"Then we should come watch, shouldn't we?" I said to Ash.

"Who has our son?" Flynn asked, an arm around my shoulders.

"Last I checked it was Barnabas."

"Barnabas?" Duncan said. "You trust that old goat with your son?"

"Sure," I said. "How many lambs has he birthed? I trust him with Hawk. Besides, it was his idea to look after him."

"You're kidding," Duncan said.

"Nope. He's been using Hawk to attract women. He's gonna score big tonight."

We all had a laugh. I'd made it my mission to find Barnabas a wife. He was lonely and his kids didn't live nearby. Over the past many weeks, I'd invited him over to dinner, hoping it would give him a new sense of family.

When we arrived at the small valley that had been cleared for the Highland Games, I was able to see a marvelous sight: Lacey, on the field with her camera, yelling out orders for the men in kilts to line up.

"What's she doing?" Ash asked.

No sooner had she asked did all the men turn around, hoist up their kilts, and show Lacey their backsides. She snapped her camera furiously, still yelling orders, making them pose.

Raucous laughter assaulted my ears. I glanced at Flynn. "Are you sure it's a good idea for the men to be throwing cabers? They've had enough ale to—"

"Aye, they're fine," Flynn said with a twinkle in his eye. He leaned down to kiss me again. "What will you give me if I win the caber toss?"

I whispered something dirty into his ear, causing him to throw his head back and laugh.

"That's an incentive if I've ever heard one," he said, his eyes bright in the sun.

I looked around and frowned.

"What is it, hen?" he asked.

"Where's Ramsey? Shouldn't he be here?"

"Ah," Duncan said with a wry grin. "He decided he couldn't wait anymore—he went to London."

"London?" I chirped. "I thought he was over Jane."

"No, not even a little bit. He's gone to London to win her over." Duncan grinned, obviously proud that his younger brother knew what he wanted and was going after it.

"Well, at least it'll be safe for him," I muttered. Lord Henry Arlington was currently in the custody of the English and awaiting trial. No one would be gunning for Ramsey's blood. Hopefully.

"Come on," Flynn said to Duncan. "I promise not to beat you too badly."

Duncan shoved Flynn's shoulder as they walked toward the giant tapered poles. A gaggle of children ran past us and stopped. Their eyes widened as they watched grown men showing off their brawn.

"What're they doing?" a little girl with a mop of blond ringlets asked.

A boy a few years older than her with the same hair color answered, "It's a caper toss."

Ash snorted and I hid my laughter behind a cough. The children peered at us in confusion but then turned back to the sight.

"Why do they do it?" the little girl asked, sticking her thumb into her mouth.

"I dunno," her brother answered. He looked at me. "Why do they do it?"

"Well," I began. "Back in olden times, it was a way for Scottish lairds to find their best warriors."

"But we don't have lairds anymore," the boy retorted loftily.

"No, we don't," I said.

"So why do we do it now?" he wondered.

"Hmm, I'm getting a snapshot into my future with kids," Ash muttered. I ignored her and kept my focus on the group of children hanging on my words.

"We do it now because we want to remember our past, even though things change. Scotland has a rich history and it would be a shame to forget it."

The children were quiet for another minute and then they ran off, no doubt in pursuit of food, their parents, or something far more entertaining than my history lesson.

"Good speech," Ash said.

"Thank you."

"Totally wasted on the youth."

I laughed. "Totally."

∼

Sounds of an early morning thunderstorm woke me. Flynn continued to sleep soundly. With a soft kiss to his head, I left our bedroom. I checked on Hawk who also showed no signs of stirring—just like his father, I thought with a smile.

I headed downstairs to the kitchen. I stood in front of the large windows that gave me an unencumbered view of Dornoch Firth. Violent waves crashed against the craggy outcrop, water beating mercilessly at gray stone. Feeble sunlight attempted to make its way through black shadowy clouds as light and dark warred with one another. I wondered which would win.

"Love," Flynn said softly behind me. He came and wrapped his large body around mine, placing his hands on my rapidly expanding middle. "Are you okay?"

I settled my hand over his. "Fine. Just wanted to watch the storm."

He kissed the top of my head. "What are you thinking about?"

"Lots of things."

"Your nightmares?"

"No, actually. I haven't had one of those in a while." I paused. "Do you think Hawk will ever lead the SINS?" I asked.

He thought but a moment before answering, "I hope Scotland is free long before Hawk ever has to think about that."

"What happens to the SINS when Scotland does gain its independence?"

"Change," he said automatically. "Into something else."

"But not disbanded."

"Never."

I nodded. Things, people, had a way of evolving and becoming something new.

Flynn and I were silent as we watched sunlight continue to battle its way through the inky clouds. Finally, the day won, pushing back the storm.

I looked up at Flynn and smiled. "Let's check in on Hawk."

Flynn took my hand and brought it to his lips. "Aye. Let's go see our son."

# Additional Works

**Writing as Emma Slate**

SINS Series:
*Sins of a King (Book 1)*
*Birth of a Queen (Book 2)*
*Rise of a Dynasty (Book 3)*
*Dawn of an Empire (Book 4)*
*Ember (Book 5)*
*Burn (Book 6)*
*Ashes (Book 7)*

*The Spider Queen*

**Writing as Samantha Garman**

The Sibby Series:
*Queen of Klutz (Book 1)*
*Sibby Slicker (Book 2)*
*Mother Shucker (Book 3)*

*From Stardust to Stardust*

## About the Author

Emma Slate writes on the run. The dangerous alpha men she writes about aren't thrilled that she's sharing their stories for your enjoyment. So far, she's been able to evade them by jet setting around the world. She wears only black leather because it's bad ass…and hides blood.